WEAPON OF VENGEANCE

BY
CHRIS A. JACKSON

ILLUSTRATIONS BY
NOAH STACEY

This book is dedicated to all the people who have written a review, sent me a message, posted a response, or walked up to me at a convention just to say thank you.

You motivate me…

Thanks again to Noah Stacey for excellent cover art, and to my ever-tolerant wife Anne for her editorial input, and for not bonking me on the head and rolling me into the ocean for perfectly valid reasons.

WEAPON OF VENGEANCE

WEAPON OF FLESH TRILOGY
BOOK 3

 BY

CHRIS A JACKSON

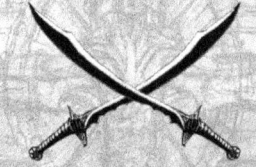

ISBN-13 978-1-939837-08-0

JAXBOOKS.COM

PRELUDE

Hoseph waited in darkness, as patient as death itself. *Death.* Though most feared it, Hoseph did not. He knew death, and even embraced it as a tenet of his faith. Death was his constant companion.

The Right Hand of Death.

He smiled at his little conceit, but there was no denying its aptness in describing his dual roles. In his devotion to Demia, Keeper of the Slain, Hoseph ushered troubled souls from life to their duly earned hereafter. In return, Demia conferred upon him her divine gifts. She had given him much, and he reveled in her cold grace. His fingers caressed the smooth curves of the small silver skull—her talisman—hidden within the sleeve of his robe, and felt the cool energy awaiting his command.

Hoseph liked to think that his goddess was pleased with his second calling as well. As the right hand of the Grandmaster of the Assassins Guild, he ushered many souls into Demia's keeping. Not personally, as a general rule, but in the performance of his duties: advising, strategizing, and passing on the Grandmaster's orders. His role also maintained the guild's most carefully coveted secret. Few knew that the Grandmaster of the Assassins Guild and Emperor Tynean Tsing II were the same man.

A latch clicked, and lamplight scythed through the room as the door swung open. An elegantly dressed man bearing a lamp entered and closed the door behind him.

Hoseph's wait was over.

1

"Good evening Baron."

Baron Eusteus Patino started only slightly, not because he didn't fear death, but because he was ignorant that he stood in its presence. Patino knew nothing of the Assassins Guild. He thought his visitor merely the emperor's messenger, and was used to Hoseph's unannounced arrivals. The baron turned toward the shadowed corner where the priest sat, and inclined his head in greeting.

"Good evening, Hoseph." Patino placed the lamp on the sideboard. The golden light gleamed off the highly polished wood and scattered though the crystal decanters. "I was about to pour myself a brandy. I'd offer you one, but I recall that you don't partake."

"Your memory is accurate, Baron." Hoseph stood, the hem of his robes brushing the priceless silk rug beneath his feet. Baron Patino loved his luxuries and had the means to support his penchant. But what he loved more was prestige, the honor and esteem that came from a noble title. And though being a baron was good, being a count would be better. That yearning for advancement had made it simple for Hoseph to recruit him. *That, and his misguided sense of intrigue.* "I received your summons. Please tell me that the news is good."

"The news is excellent." The lip of the decanter struck a musical note on the edge of the snifter as the baron poured. He swirled the liquor in the glass, poised his nose above the rim, and inhaled deeply. Sighing with pleasure, he sipped before continuing. "I received an interim report from Master Hensen." He withdrew a folded letter from the inside pocket of his smoking jacket and handed it over. "The two people he was contracted to protect are alive and well, and he believes that the most prominent threat to their lives is ended."

"That *is* excellent news. The emperor will be pleased." Hoseph scanned the letter.

Though relieved that Mya and her bodyguard were still alive—he had worried that the unanticipated contact meant bad

2

news—he wondered what had precipitated the early report. Unfortunately, the letter did not elaborate. Hoseph longed for details. What had happened to end the threat? Patino knew nothing, of course. The baron was nothing but a go-between. Hoseph needed to go to the source.

He tucked the letter away and bowed to the baron. "You've performed admirably, Baron. Your service to the empire is noted."

"Just doing my duty. Please give His Majesty my warmest regards." Patino smiled and raised his glass in toast.

"Of course." Hoseph nodded politely; he would certainly give the emperor Patino's regards. The baron was a perfect operative: loyal, competent, ignorant, and easy to manipulate with a few words of gratitude from on high.

Retrieving the silver skull from his sleeve, he murmured the invocation that called on Demia's power. Tendrils of her divine essence flowed from the talisman, as dark and cold as death itself, to embraced and consumed him. The baron, the study, the very world faded around him.

Hoseph blinked and opened his eyes onto an ethereal realm of lost souls, banished demons, and vanquished godlings. This was not a world, plane of existence, or even a place, really. Wizards, priests, and metaphysicists had hypothesized that it might be the fabric that bound the universe together, and had coined the name "sphere of shadows," which Hoseph though a misnomer. There were no shadows, for there was no light. Hoseph perceived his immediate surroundings as veils of vaporous essence, black and gray wisps swirling as if blown by unfelt winds. There were no sounds, no odors, or even air to breathe. Only Demia's grace allowed him to survive here, and to use the sphere as a conduit between points on his own world.

Picturing in his mind the destination he desired, the priest once again invoked his goddess' power. The sphere of shadow faded, and Hoseph materialized in a bedroom. Small and stark, only a few signs of femininity indicated that it was a lady's room, though nothing hinted at the owner's true nature. He quirked a thin smile; this was exactly where he wished to be.

Unfortunately, Kiesha wasn't there.

Patience...

Hoseph moved the only available chair to the corner out of view of the door, sat, and let his mind sort through the details he needed from her.

In time he heard voices outside bidding one another good night. The door opened and Kiesha walked in with a rustle of silk brocade, lace, and ruffles. Unaware of him, she closed the door and leaned back against it, her knuckles white on the latch. With a quick, sharp breath and a shake of her head, she took three quick steps to the clothespress, wrenching at the laces of her dress.

"Before you disrobe, I would like to speak with you."

Kiesha froze at the sound of his voice, but didn't turn. Unlike the baron, she knew he was the emissary of the Grandmaster of Assassins. She had no idea that Hoseph's master was also the Emperor of Tsing, of course, and never would.

After a brief hesitation, she resumed working on the laces, her tone impatient. "Speak quickly then. I've been in a corset for twelve hours, and I intend to remove it."

Hoseph regarded Kiesha as she loosened the laces, shrugged the gown off her shoulders, and pushed the voluminous garment down over her hips. The dress landed in a frothy pile. She stepped out of it and started on the laces of her corset. Long ago, Hoseph might have been moved by such a brazen display, but years of devotion to Demia had stripped away such distracting desires.

"You can't embarrass me, child. I came here for information on the report sent to Baron Patino, and I will have it."

"The report?" She turned to face him, her eyes wide with surprise. "Hensen only sent it this morning. Patino contacted you already?"

4

"Obviously. I know that Mya and her bodyguard are alive, but I need details. Exactly *how* was the threat to their lives ended?"

"You want details?" Kiesha squirmed out of her corset and heaved a breath as if it was the first she'd taken that day. A disdainful kick sent the garment skittering across the floor in the general direction of the dresser. Grabbing a robe from the clothespress, she pulled it on and turned toward him, her blue eyes blazing. "Fine. The four other masters are dead. How's *that* for a detail?"

Hoseph frowned. *Defiance?* Kiesha's reports were usually calm, succinct, and to the point, so her vitriolic response came as a shock. She was an invaluable operative, perfectly positioned to glean information from the Assassins Guild's principal rivals. It would be a pity if she developed a dangerous attitude.

"Explain how that occurred, please," he ordered. "From the beginning."

She sighed and sat on the corner of the bed, undoing her coif as she spoke. "I convinced Hensen to assign me to watch over Mya and her bodyguard, as you suggested, and learned that the masters had banded together against her."

"Did they discover that she was having a new guildmaster ring crafted?"

"No." Kiesha looked annoyed at the interruption. "They *discovered* that she never destroyed the previous ring."

"She what?"

"The masters thought she wore it. That it was protecting her against their assassination attempts. So they took another route and tried to kill her bodyguard. I thwarted that attempt."

"How?"

"I killed the assassin they sent after him." She said it matter-of-factly. "It was close, but he didn't see me."

"Good."

She glared at him. "I thought so too, until the masters decided to turn him against Mya."

5

"And how did they do that? He's under her control."

"If you let me *explain*..." Kiesha pursed her lips and tossed her hairpins onto her night table.

"Please do." *So acerbic.* She was definitely in a mood. What had provoked her?

"The masters learned that he can disobey her. They wanted him to kill Mya, since he's signed no blood contract and the ring wouldn't stop him, but apparently his inherent magic prevented him from killing her outright."

Hoseph huffed a wry laugh. "Yes, Saliez had a restraint worked into the weapon's magic to prevent it from turning against its master."

Kiesha's eyes narrowed. "The weapon's *name* is Lad. The masters kidnapped his daughter and offered to exchange her for Mya. Unfortunately for them, the plan blew up in their faces."

Hoseph gaped at her. "His *daughter*? Saliez's weapon has a daughter?"

"A family." Her piercing blue eyes smoldered. "If I had a way to *contact* you, I'd have been able to tell you."

Hoseph ignored her snide comment. He was having enough difficulty accepting the notion of a weapon of magic and flesh having a family. The animal instinct to procreate, perhaps?

"How can that be?"

"Lad's apparently...more than we believed him to be." She looked away, her voice faltering.

Ahhh, Kiesha, is that the crux of your anxiety? Have you developed empathy for this...Lad? "So, did he deliver Mya to them?"

"Yes." Kiesha shrugged and met his eyes again. "But it was a ruse. Her bonds were false. When the masters tried to double cross him, Lad and Mya attacked. The fight was..." Kiesha swallowed. "I've never seen anyone move like that. I did what I could to protect them. When it was over, the four masters were dead and their surviving guards had fled."

6

Hoseph considered the ramifications. Not entirely bad, actually. It meant that Mya could start with a clean slate, appointing her own faction masters, and not have to deal with hostile subordinates who would fight her every initiative.

Hoseph chuckled. "So, Mya wore the guildmaster's ring and couldn't be harmed."

"She *didn't* wear it."

"What? How did she survive?"

"She survived because you told me to keep her alive." Kiesha's eyes blazed with indignation for a moment. "I killed anyone who got close to her. Lad's *wife* wore the ring. She came to the exchange with Lad. It was part of the ruse. She used its protection to get their child away from the fighting."

Hoseph frowned again. "So, the wife wears the guildmaster's ring?"

"She *wore* it, I said." Kiesha's lips pressed into a line. "You made it clear that the Grandmaster wanted Mya to be guildmaster, so I...killed Lad's wife."

"You..." Hoseph stared at Kiesha, and a slow smile spread across his face. "That was very quick thinking. So, with the ring freed—"

"I *murdered* Lad's wife right in front of him!" Kiesha's anguish spoke volumes.

Curiously, her pain eased Hoseph's mind. She wasn't rebelling, she was just suffering from guilt. The mystery of her foul mood was solved.

"He's seeking her killer, set on vengeance."

"Does he know that it was you?"

"No." Kiesha shook her head. "I ran for my life afterward. He couldn't know, but my contacts tell me that he's determined to find out."

"Relax, child. I'm sure Mya won't let him go careening off on a hunt for his wife's killer. Now that she's guildmaster—"

"Why do you keep assuming that?" Kiesha's question was half incredulous, half scornful. "*Lad* put on the guildmaster's ring! He's got the entire guild out searching for clues to his wife's murder."

Hoseph's thoughts wavered. That could be a problem. "Did he see you?"

"He couldn't have. I *told* you, I ran as soon as..." Kiesha took a shuddering breath and let it out slowly. "There are all sorts of rumors flying around, but they all have one thing in common—Lad is in charge, not Mya. He's already appointed four new masters and made changes in the guild's business practices."

Hoseph listened to Kiesha's summary of those changes with only half his mind. With the other half, he considered the situation. Mya was not guildmaster as he had planned, but still, the situation had promise. The weapon was under control. He had much to consider before reporting to the Grandmaster.

The first priority, however, was to allay Kiesha's fears. "You've done well, Kiesha." He pulled a small satin pouch from a pocket and offered it to her. With seeming reluctance, the thief reached out, grasped it, and tossed it onto the bed. The contents rattled like dice, though their facets were valued in carats, not numbers.

"I need protection," Kiesha insisted. "If they get too close, I may need to disappear. If I had a way to contact you..."

Hoseph shook his head. "In due time, child. Don't worry, and don't do anything rash. The Grandmaster will deal with this. There's still work to be done. First, find out where this new guildmaster lives. Any more information on changes he's instituting would be helpful. I'll check back with you in a few days. If you need to disappear, I'll arrange a secure location."

"All right." She sounded calmer. Not happy, but resigned.

Hoseph flicked the silver skull into his hand and invoked the power of his beloved goddess. As Demia's cold grace consumed him, he caught one last glimpse of Kiesha's eyes, bright with the fear of death. That was enough, for now, to keep her under his control.

CHAPTER I

Lad slapped open the door to the butcher shop so hard that it cracked against the wall. He propelled his charge through the door, reigning in his boiling blood to keep from hurting the man. The fellow had been through enough already.

"Hey!" The proprietor looked up with a glare, then swallowed his reproof and lowered his gaze back to his work. He knew better than to interfere with people who came into his shop bearing the marks of recent violence.

Lad ignored the butcher's mutters and propelled his battered charge around the long counter and down a hall. A man with a cleaver at his hip stood before the door at the hall's end, huge arms crossed over a barrel chest, biceps straining the fabric of his shirt. A typical Enforcer. The thug grinned as they approached, eying Lad as if deciding how many pieces to tear him into.

The misconception was common. With a lithe, wiry build, nondescript clothing, and no weapons, Lad knew that many underestimated him. Generally he took pains to avoid conflict, but right now he wasn't in the mood for explanations. He nodded toward the door. "Open it."

"I don't know who you are, bucko, but you don't just come into this shop and—"

Lad thrust his fist out faster than the Enforcer could even reach for his cleaver. With exquisite precision, he stopped the blow an inch from the man's nose. The ring on Lad's finger—

obsidian woven with gold—widened the thug's eyes and closed his mouth. Lad bridled his urge for violence. The man was just doing his job. It wasn't his fault that he didn't yet recognize the new master of the Twailin Assassins Guild.

"Now you know who I am." Lad lowered his hand and nodded again at the door. "Open it."

"Yes, Master." The thug opened the door and stepped aside.

The room wasn't what one would expect in the back of a butcher shop. One side was furnished for pleasure, a well-appointed sitting area with a luxurious rug, a plush divan and low table adjacent to a mahogany bar crowded with decanters, bottles, and an array of cut-crystal glasses. The other side of the room was all business, with a broad desk of dark oak littered with papers faced by two leather-upholstered chairs.

Behind the desk sat a man who obviously believed in mixing business and pleasure. Dressed in a sharp, brushed-wool jacket and waistcoat with gold buttons, he appeared the epitome of a successful businessman. The provocatively dressed girl on his lap spoiled that image. The perturbation on his face at the unexpected visitors transformed to shock, and he surged to his feet, spilling the girl to the floor and her drink into his lap.

"Master!" Tiny silver rods chimed at his wrist as Jingles brushed the liquid from his trousers and hauled the girl to her feet. "Sorry about that. Just havin' a little bit of fun, you know." He patted the girl on the rump as he nudged her toward the room's other door. "Off with you now, Celia. We'll talk later. Ah…keep up the good work."

Lad watched the girl go. She couldn't have been more than sixteen years old, but the seductive smile she tossed his way suggested that she was already well-versed in her profession. Undoubtedly a portion of her earnings found their way into Assassin Guild coffers, though it looked as if Jingles might be taking his share in trade. What his Master Enforcer did for fun didn't concern Lad. He had a more important matter on his mind.

10

"Do you know this man?" Lad released his charge's collar. The man stumbled, looking as if he wished he were anywhere but here. He squinted out of his one good eye—the other was purple and swollen shut—and dabbed at his bloody split lip with a sodden handkerchief. One whole side of his face was a massive contusion.

"Can't say as I do offhand, but..." Jingles rounded the desk, still brushing at his damp crotch as he examined the fellow's face. "Look the other way so I can see you without that bruise."

The man complied.

"Come to think of it, yes, I think I do know him. Runs a bookstore off Briar Rose Avenue."

"A st-stationers," the man corrected. "Th-the Binder's Bin Stationers."

"Right! Quebeck's his name!" Jingles grinned as if he'd just solved a puzzle, but sobered when he saw Lad's grim expression. "What happened to him?"

"He was beaten and threatened, and his shop was tossed." Lad's anger rose again. "I ordered an *end* to this violence! Tell me, Jingles, did you order this?"

"I did *not*, Master." Jingles looked suddenly frightened. "I've followed your orders to the letter, I swear on my life!"

"An appropriate oath. Your life is *exactly* what it'll cost you if I find out you're lying." Lad turned to the trembling shopkeeper. "Did you know the ones who beat you?"

"I n-never saw them before today, sir. They weren't the ones who usually came by...before." He swallowed and wrung the handkerchief in his hands. A drop of blood fell to the expensive rug. "Please, sirs, they told me to be quiet about it. I don't want any trouble. They...they said they'd burn..."

"Nobody's going to hurt you, Master Quebeck, but we need answers to make sure that whoever did this won't come back." Lad clenched his jaw. The poor man was terrified. Lad had come upon him sweeping up glass from the shop's broken front window, in tears as he plucked pieces of fine parchment from the

11

muddy gutter. He hadn't wanted to accompany Lad, but the guildmaster had insisted. This was Jingles' territory, so the Master Enforcer would have to answer for it. Lad hoped the violence was the Thieves Guild moving in on their territory, though he dreaded that it wasn't. Jingles' denial seemed sincere, but Lad was determined to get to the bottom of the matter. "This is Master Jarred. He's going to ask you some questions."

"I'll answer as best I can, sir." The shopkeeper's voice still trembled, despite Lad's assurances.

Jingles eyed Quebeck critically. "Can you describe who beat you? How many, what they wore. Did they use names?"

"No names, sir. "Th-there were two of them. A man and a woman, though she was as tall and big as he." Quebeck glanced at Lad, then back to Jingles. "She had red hair tied back in a long braid, and a scar on the bridge of her nose. The man was a Morrgrey. Dark, of course, and wore a green felt hat with a cock's feather."

Lad saw the answer in Jingle's face even before he asked, "Do you know these two?"

"I do, Master." The Master Enforcer's hand twitched and the silver bars jingled. "The man's named Korlak, and the woman's Gerti Yance. They're ours."

"Ours..." Lad's knuckles popped as he clenched his fists. Forcing himself to take a deep, calming breath, he turned back to Quebeck. "How much damage was done to your shop?"

"Um, maybe twenty crowns worth, including lost inventory, and it'll be a couple of days 'til I can open back up."

"And how much cash did they take from you?"

"Just what was in the cash box. Maybe fifteen crowns."

Lad told Jingles, "Give him fifty crowns."

The Master Enforcer didn't even quibble. He went right to his desk, opened a drawer, and counted out the sum. Dropping it into a leather pouch, he handed it over to the man with the assurance, "I'll make sure this doesn't happen again."

Lad even believed him.

"You can go now, Master Quebeck." Lad nudged him toward the door. "Thank you." When the door had closed, he fixed Jingles with an even stare and said, "Who are Korlak and Yance?"

"Enforcers, sir, assigned to Molsen's area, near Eastgate."

"Take me to them."

"Now, Master?"

"Now."

"Yes, sir." Jingles went to his desk, pulled two daggers from a drawer, and put them in boot sheaths. He snatched up a walking stick and drew forth the gleaming sword that was attached to the polished gold handle. Snapping it back into place, he turned to Lad and nodded. "Ready, Master."

"Good." Lad noted Jingles' fine clothes, and considered his own simple shirt and pants. His shoes bore no shine, and he wore no weapons. Anyone looking at the two of them would think Jingles a moneyed gentleman and Lad his servant. That suited Lad just fine. "Where are we going?"

"Molsen's got them watching over a gambling house called *Lucky Bones.*"

"I know it." There weren't many places in Twailin that Lad didn't know.

"Business usually starts to pick up this time of day, so they should both be there."

"Let's go, then."

Jingles seemed to consider his next words before speaking. "If you tell me what you want done, Master, I'll see to it. There's no reason you need to—"

"There *is* a reason I need to see to this, Jingles. I want to know why it happened, and make sure it doesn't happen again!"

"As you say, Master. I'll tan Molsen's hide if I find out he knew anything about this, but these two might just be poachers, not acting on orders. It's your call, of course."

"Yes, it *is* my call."

13

Lad followed Jingles out the back door and around to the street, stopping abruptly as the Master Enforcer hailed a passing hackney. He generally walked wherever he went, but one look at Jingles' shiny, hard-soled boots told him that there was no way the man could walk to Eastgate. Lad didn't like coaches, but after a week as guildmaster, he had discovered a lot of things he didn't like that he was having to get used to. Going to bed every night without Wiggen at his side was the hardest.

As the coach pulled up, a woman in a simple dress hurried past and, for an instant, he saw Wiggen: her walk, her hair, her scent... He blinked, and the vision was gone.

Gone... She's gone... Lad followed Jingles into the coach and took a seat.

Clenching his hands at his sides, he forced down the urge to lash out, to vent the rage and frustration that continually threatened to overwhelm him. One by one, he flexed and relaxed each muscle in his body, an exercise he had been taught long ago to imbue calm. It didn't work, just as his morning exercises and meditation no longer brought the peace of mind they once had. Nothing helped. Everywhere he looked he saw her. Every scent and sight reminded him of the life they'd shared at the *Tap and Kettle*. He looked out the window at the passing city, searching for something, anything to keep his mind active, busy, away from dwelling on his empty bed, the smell of Wiggen's hair as he lay down beside her, one arm over her, the warmth of her body against him...

Wiggen...

"Here we are!"

Jingles' announcement snapped Lad from his reverie, and the guildmaster's blood chilled. He recognized Eastgate Street outside, but remembered nothing of the trip. *How long?* He considered the distance; fifteen or twenty minutes, at least.

Not again! Lad kept his face composed despite his mounting apprehension. He'd been trained from birth to be attentive to his surroundings at every waking moment, and it had saved his life many times. Since Wiggen's death, lapses like this, transient periods lost in thought, were becoming frequent.

Jingles opened the coach door and stepped out. Lad forced himself to focus on the here and now as he followed. They stood in front of the *Lucky Bones* public house. A broad sign—a pair of dice coming up double eights—pointed the way down the stairs to the drinking and gambling establishment tucked into the basement of a shoe factory.

"The manager's name's Lyghter. She's a hard case, but runs a good business. She's been one of our...clients for a long time now." Jingles flipped a half-crown to the coachman, and turned to Lad, jingling his bracelet nervously. "Master, if Korlak and Yance *are* poachers, they might try to bolt. A visit from me wouldn't startle them, but if I'm with someone, it might. Maybe I should go first?"

Lad nodded. "I don't want to disrupt business. Go ahead."

Jingles looked relieved. Descending the stairs, he pushed aside the heavy iron-bound door and entered. Smoke wafted out, along with the sound of clattering dice and amused chatter.

Lad looked up at the empty windows of the shoe factory. It was nearing the dinner hour, and work had ceased for the day. Foot traffic was brisk, and two others entered the pub. Lad followed them in. His eyes instantly pierced the dark, smoky atmosphere, and he scanned the room. It was still early, so the place wasn't very busy yet. About a score of patrons played cards, threw dice, or drank at the bar. Lad drew no attention, looking more like a cobbler than a killer.

Jingles was sauntering toward the bar, jauntily swinging his walking stick. The two Enforcers, Korlak and Yance, were watching Jingles, but didn't look upset. Lad moved to a table near the door where patrons were throwing dice, watching the pair as he listened to Jingles hail the one-eyed matron behind the bar. Lad focused, and had no trouble picking out their words over the noise.

"Evening, Lyghter!"

"Trouble, Jingles?"

"No, just need to speak to my people. Some privacy would be appreciated."

"Fine." She tossed him a key. "Last door down the hall."

"Thank you. This won't take long." Jingles strolled over to his two Enforcers. "I've got a change in your work assignment. Come with me."

Though Korlak and Yance exchanged wary glances, Jingles' casual manner seemed to put them at ease, and they followed him down the hall to the last door. When the door closed behind them, Lad moved. He was down the hall and through the door in a moment. As the latch clicked behind him, the two Enforcers turned at the intrusion.

"What the hell?" Korlak's hand dropped to the big knife at his belt.

"Shut your mouths and listen up!" Jingles snapped. The tip of his walking stick flicked out as quick as a striking snake, hovering an inch from the Morrgrey's nose. "This is your new guildmaster. Show some respect!"

Lad saw fearful recognition in their eyes; they had obviously heard about him. They both took a step back, and Korlak's hand moved away from his weapon. Not that it would have done him any good if he had tried use it. Their blood contracts prevented them from even attempting to harm either Lad or Jingles.

"What's this about?" Yance's wary expression suggested that she already had a good idea.

"This is about a broken window, a beaten shopkeeper, a threat of arson, treason, and fifteen gold crowns." Lad stepped up and examined them carefully, though he had to crane his neck to look them in the eye. As Quebeck said, Yance stood as tall as Korlak, and the Morrgrey was not a small man.

Lad read their guilt in the pulses pounding at their throats and the sweat beading on their brows. He could smell the rank odors of rage and fear, see the desperation in their darting eyes as they searched for an escape.

16

"Did Molsen order you to toss that shop, threaten and beat Quebeck?"

"No," Korlak said, and Yance shot him a glare.

"Good, the truth." The next answer, Lad knew, would not come so easily. "I'm going to ask you some questions, and you're going to keep telling me the truth."

"Why?" The defiance in Yance's voice surprised Lad as much as the puzzling question.

"Why am I going to ask you questions, or why are you going to tell me the truth?"

"Both!"

Lad fought to keep his instinctive reaction under control. The urge for violence, vengeance for their transgression, welled up in him, but five years as Mya's shadow had taught him that punishment should not be administered without explanation. The Grandfather had killed on a whim, and Lad had vowed to never become like the monster he had destroyed. He took a breath and let it out slowly, fighting for calm.

"I'm going to ask questions about why this incident happened so I can prevent it from happening again. You're going to tell me the truth because your lives are mine to spend. Whether or not I choose to spend your lives will depend on your answers. But if you don't answer, I promise you that your lives will be spent right here and now. Do you understand?"

They just stared at him.

"Answer him!" Jingles' command shook them out of their silence.

"I understand, Master," Korlak said reluctantly. He dropped his gaze to the floor rather than meet Lad's eyes, though the muscles bunching at his jaw revealed his frustration. He was a big man, strong and capable. He'd undoubtedly beaten and killed many people in his lifetime, probably even before he was in the guild. His attitude was that of a life-long bully, used to using force to get what he wanted. He wasn't accustomed to being frightened of someone half his size.

17

"Well, I don't!" Yance's face flushed, her hands clenching in impotent rage. She looked to Jingles. "This upstart orders us to be all nice and friendly to a bunch of lack-wit shopkeepers! No more protection rackets, no more beatings, and we're supposed to roll over like dogs? Just because he put that ring on, doesn't make him an assassin!"

Jingles stepped forward, but Lad raised a forestalling hand, his left hand. Upon it glinted the lustrous guildmaster's ring—the ring he had taken from Wiggen's dead finger. *Wiggen...* "You're right, Yance. Putting on this ring doesn't make me an assassin. What *does* make me an assassin...you wouldn't believe if I told you. What this ring does make me is your *master*. You'll *answer* my *questions!*"

"Fine. Ask."

"Why did you extort Quebeck?"

The two Enforcers exchanged a look.

"We...didn't like the changes," Korlak answered. Yance just pressed her lips in a thin line. "They seem foolish. We've taken protection money as long as I've been with the guild."

"So you broke your oath and went against my orders. Why? You're being paid the exact same amount you were earning before the changes."

"It's not about the money, you little—"

Steel flashed to Yance's throat, stopping just short of parting flesh. "One more word and it'll be your last!" Jingles hissed. His wrist twitched, and the tip of the sword from his walking stick pricked her chin. "This is your guildmaster! Watch your tongue, or I'll cut it out."

Waving Jingles back, Lad cocked his head, curious. "If it's not about the money, Yance, what *is* it about?"

"It's about *respect!*" Her eyes spit knives at him as Jingles sheathed his blade. "If we don't show these mealy-mouthed peasants who's boss around here, they'll think we're weak!"

"Respect?" Lad was taken aback. "You think a shopkeeper will *respect* you if you beat him up?"

18

"He'll bloody well respect my fist! And next time he'll cough up the money without me havin' to knock a lick of common sense into his thick skull!"

Lad stared at the Enforcer, utterly dumbfounded. "That's not respect, Yance. That's fear."

"What's the difference? Fear *is* respect!"

Suddenly Lad realized what her real reason was—she enjoyed meting out pain and fear. With that realization came the memory of the invasion of the *Tap and Kettle* by a team of Enforcers. They had taken pleasure in their work, far too much pleasure, delighting in the fear and anguish they evoked. Still blind to human emotion at that period of his life, Lad had not understood. Now he knew that there were people who enjoyed giving pain. Yance, apparently, was one of them.

Lad narrowed his eyes at her. "Did you ever meet the Grandfather, Yance, your previous guildmaster?"

Her throat flexed as she swallowed hard. "No. But I heard about him."

"The Grandfather killed on a whim and tortured for recreation. Did you respect him?"

"I didn't know him," she admitted.

"But he was strong, fearsome, and pitiless. You would have feared him, and been right to do so. I imagine that means that you respected him."

"I suppose...yes, then. I did respect him."

"Do you fear me, knowing that I can kill you and you can't do anything to stop me?"

She swallowed hard. "Yes."

"So, you admit that you fear me, but your contempt for my rules, and for me personally, clearly show that you don't respect me. You've made my point. Fear does not equal respect."

"You're *wrong!*" The muscles of her neck bunched and writhed with those two words. Lad recognized the tension in her body; it was exactly how he had felt when he wanted to kill the Grandfather...and couldn't.

"Explain how I'm wrong."

"I don't respect you because you didn't *earn* that ring!" Her face flushed scarlet. "You don't understand the guild. You don't understand what we are. People respect us because we're strong. If they don't respect us, we knock some sense into them!"

A murderous rage boiled the blood in Lad's veins. His mind's eye stared once more at Wiggen's terrified expression as a knife pressed to her throat. *People should not have to live in fear because they can't fight back*! That was the reason for his new rules, the truth he wanted to shout in Yance's face, but she would never accept that. The guild would never accept that. He bit back his anger and focused on the one truth that the guild might accept.

"It's you who doesn't understand, Yance. Fear doesn't earn respect, it earns hatred. The shopkeepers you beat into paying blood money don't respect you, they hate you! They fear you, and hate you, and if *ever* an opportunity arises to harm you, they'll take it! *That* is the position you've put the guild in with your actions. *That*, even more than your treason, is why I must now spend your life."

Before Yance could even draw another breath, Lad struck.

His kick smashed her ribs with such force that her lungs ruptured and her heart was pulped against her spine. Blood jetted from her mouth as she slammed back against the wall, landing in a broken heap of twitching arms and legs.

Korlak's boots scuffed the floor as he backed away. Even over the scent of blood, Lad could smell the man's fear.

Welcome to the world of the average shopkeeper, Korlak, he thought sourly.

The blinding rage and urge to kill ebbed, replaced by a flood of self-disgust. *What would Wiggen have said?* Yance would never have changed her ways, and lenience would only have led to more disobedience. He knew he was right. He also knew he was a murderer. Self-loathing welled up in him, palpable and nauseating. He turned toward the door.

"The other one, Master?" Jingles asked.

Lad looked over his shoulder at Korlak. He had known the moment he entered the room which of the two had instigated the assault on Quebeck. Korlak would fall in line, and even more important, he would spread the word of what Lad had said and done. But that didn't mean he didn't deserve punishment for his treason.

"Beat him exactly as you saw Master Quebeck was beaten." He turned to Jingles. "Do it yourself."

"Yes, Master."

Lad cast one more glance at Yance's body. Her bulging eyes stared blankly back. She'd been helpless, and he killed her. *She killed herself the moment she decided to betray the guild.* Lad wondered if the Grandfather told himself the same thing the first time he murdered a helpless underling.

Lad looked back to Jingles, refusing to let his disgust show. "When you're done, call in a crew to clean up the mess, pay Lyghter whatever you think is fair, and get back to work."

"Yes, Master."

Lad was out the door and halfway down the hall before he heard the first wet crunch of Jingles' fist striking flesh.

CHAPTER II

Captain Norwood rubbed his burning eyes and resumed pacing in front of the large diagram tacked to his office wall. He'd been staring at the damned thing for three days now, and knew it line by line.

"Fat lot of good it's done me."

He stopped pacing and stared some more. The diagram depicted the battle site near Fiveway Fountain. Quite detailed, it showed every bush, tree, lamppost, and bench. Stick figures represented the corpses, twenty-eight in all. Fewer than a dozen were stuck with yellow pins bearing tiny cards printed with personal information: name, title or profession, and next of kin. But it was the five black pins that drew his attention, each representing a corpse killed by a poisoned black dart. The same type of dart and the same poison they'd found on a dead woman in an alley not two weeks ago. Like the first dart, all these had lodged in the victims' throats at a steep angle, indicating that the killer had shot from a height.

The same assassin? If so, how are these two incidents related?

He glanced to the vial-encased darts on his desk. He still had no information on their origin. The duke had insisted that they first concentrate their investigation on identifying the victims, since at least three had been prominent citizens. Only in the last couple of days had Sergeant Tamir been investigating the darts. The poison, white scorpion venom, was common enough to be readily available, and therefore difficult to trace. The tiny spring-loaded missiles, however, seemed to have been custom-made. Finding the crafter of those darts had a high likelihood of leading them to the assassin, but so far they had nothing.

The knock on his door came as a welcome interruption.

"Come in!"

Tamir strode in, igniting a spark of hope in Norwood's heart. "Did you get anything?"

"Oh, plenty!" Tamir's smile oozed sarcasm. Reaching into his jacket pocket, he withdrew several items. "I got a solid gold pocket watch for only two crowns that stopped working fifteen minutes after I left the shop." He dropped the watch onto Norwood's desk. "I got a garlic peeler that's guaranteed never to need cleaning, though I haven't tried it out yet." The reeking device thumped down beside the watch. "And I got this here pen knife that has a cork screw, a pair of scissors, a toothpick, a nail file, a fish scaler, and a little thingy that'll trim your nose hairs!" He peered at the confusing contraption uncertainly. "No blade though, and I'm not quite sure which little thingy is which."

Norwood looked at his sergeant with an utter lack of amusement. "So, nothing on the dart."

"Not a thing." Tamir retrieved a glass vial from another pocket and shook it, rattling the little black dart inside. "Nobody's ever seen such a thing before, let alone made one. The closest thing to real information was a tidbit from that fellow who makes cuckoo clocks in a shop down on Mullet Avenue. He said he'd heard of something kinda similar, something that injected poison, I mean, from a man who used to hunt big game."

"Someone hunted big game with poisoned darts?" Norwood looked dubious. "Sounds like a good way to poison whoever eats the meat."

"No, no. He used poppy extract. Just put 'em to sleep. He'd hunt weird critters for the Imperial Zoo in Tsing. Used a crossbow, though; the bolts had a spring and plunger. Apparently the guy dropped a pachyderm with one shot, loaded it on a wagon, and brought it back for the crown prince's tenth birthday celebration."

Norwood sighed. "The crown prince is over forty now, so this hunter has got to be older than me. I can't see him running across roofs to shoot darts down at people. The hunter's name?"

Tamir consulted his notebook. "Wembly, but he moved to a village north of Tsing years ago. It'd take months to track him down to ask him questions."

"The clockmaker didn't know who made those bolts?"

"No."

"Anyplace you haven't looked yet?"

"I've not done much in The Sprawls yet." Tamir rattled the dart vial again and put it back in his pocket. "Nothing much down there but tinkers and pot makers. I figure whoever makes these things probably charges a few crowns apiece, and can afford to have a nice place in a better part of town."

"Well, we can't take anything for granted, so you can start slumming this afternoon. On the way, stop at our temporary office down by the docks and pick up Sergeant Maekin's report on the Bargeman's Guild." Norwood returned to his diagram and tapped one of the pins with a note attached. "Youtrin...a damned guildmaster. There's got to be something deeper going on here. Smuggling, maybe. Who knows?"

Guild war... Was this the culmination of the Assassins Guild "squabbles" that his late night intruder had told him of? Norwood wondered if the man he'd spoken with had been reduced to a stick figure on the diagram. So far, they'd been unable to connect any of the known dead to organized crime. If these people were members of the Assassins Guild, they'd hidden their illicit activities well. Tamir's voice intruded on his thoughts.

"We've been going through Youtrin's warehouses for a week, sir. He might be involved in some tithe dodging, but we've found nothing more illegal than that."

"So far, Maekin's only looking into his Bargeman's Guild connections. Tell him to cast a wider net. I want to know who owed Youtrin money, who he was sleeping with, who he paid rent to, and who paid rent to him. Everything. Do the same with the fencing master and the madam, and we'll see what connections we can make."

"Yes, sir." Tamir picked up the trinkets he'd bought. "You want the watch? It's solid gold!" He grinned at his scowling commander and pocketed the worthless piece of junk. "I know, I know. Get to work."

"You should open up a stall on Stargazer Street, Tam, because you just read my mind."

Tamir snorted a laugh and left. Norwood turned back to his diagram.

The three prominent Twailin citizens they'd identified among the dead were the only leads they had in this case, besides the darts, and all were turning up blank. His mind automatically veered back to that now-familiar train of thought.

What in the Nine Hells would a guildmaster in the Bargeman's Guild, a West Crescent madam, and a fencing master be doing with the Assassins Guild?

Gleaming steel flashed toward Sereth's gut. The Master Blade parried the lunge easily. His riposte rang off the quillons of his opponent's weapon, and he intercepted the counterthrust. Steel sang on steel, and the soles of his boots whisked softly as he danced away from his opponent.

By the gods, this is boring.

He stepped back to disengage and assess his student's stance. Though barely fifteen years old, the boy was a fair

25

fencer in a rote sort of way. He knew the basic forms, but performed them without imagination, no earnest threat, and entirely too much predictability.

In the neighborhood where Sereth grew up, this pretty boy wouldn't have lasted five minutes. By his age, Sereth had already mastered the art of fighting with dagger and short sword, and signed his name in blood on a piece of rune-inscribed vellum, dedicating his life to the Assassins Guild.

Never thought it would lead to begging nobles to let me babysit their whelps, playing patty-cake with blunted blades.

Despite the irony, Sereth was secretly pleased that his fencing studio had finally attracted its first noble-born student, the young Lord Leonard Barrrington. The rent in Barleycorn Heights was outrageous, but he needed to project the right image to attract customers, and money wasn't a problem. More students would follow, he knew, but he had to offer something that other instructors didn't. He had to stand out, and as yet he didn't know how to accomplish that. Unlike his former master, Horice, he couldn't rely on witty banter and high-class connections to bring in eager young nobles wanting to learn how to duel. After only two lessons with the young Lord Barrington, however, Sereth was less than enchanted.

The boy stamped his foot in a poor feint and lunged.

Time for a real lesson, boy.

Sereth stepped into the lunge with a twisting parry that denied a stop-thrust, locked his quillons to his student's, and pushed. Barrington strained to push him back, but Sereth's rear foot was well planted, and he outweighed his student by at least two stone. For a moment they stood, neither with an advantage, both knowing the first to break the clinch would be at a disadvantage. Then Sereth drew a stiletto from the back of his sparring jacket and poked the tip carefully into his student's belly, dimpling the boy's padded plastron by two inches.

"You're dead, young lord."

"What?" The surprise in the boy's voice was ridiculously satisfying. The strength left his stance and he stepped back, ripping off his protective wire mask to glare down at the blade in Sereth's off hand. "That's not fair!"

"No, it's not." Sereth removed his own mask and leveled a cold smile at his student. *This is what he needs*, Sereth realized. *This is what will set me apart from the other dueling masters.* "Life isn't fair. Fights *certainly* aren't fair. If you think otherwise, then your first *real* fight will be your last, young lord." He raised the stiletto in a mocking left-handed salute and tucked it away. "This is not a game."

"But, to strike with a hidden blade... It's..."

"Dishonorable?"

"Meaning no disrespect, sir, but *yes*."

"Your father's not paying me to teach you honor. He's paying me to teach you the art of dueling." Sereth racked his practice sword and waved his apprentice over. "Not all lessons are learned with the sword. Enough sparring for today, Lord Barrington."

Sereth's assistant, an eager young apprentice named Lem, dutifully took his master's mask, then assisted him in removing the padded plastron, leather gorget, sword-hand glove, and underlying jacket with its buckles in the back.

"But in a duel, you must fight according to rules," argued Barrington as he racked his own sword.

"And an honorable man will follow those rules. But what happens when you're challenged by a man who has no honor?" Sereth stripped off his sweat-sodden shirt and accepted a towel from Lem. "I've learned to expect less-than-honorable behavior when life and blood are on the line."

The boy gazed wide-eyed at the scars that crisscrossed Sereth's torso before continuing his argument. "But if an opponent resorted to a hidden weapon to win, my seconds would avenge me."

"If you choose your seconds well, yes, but being avenged doesn't make you any less dead, does it?" Sereth grinned, but there was no humor in it. Scrubbing himself dry with the towel, he caught the look of horror on the boy's face and laughed. "Do you think every man who calls you out for kissing his sister will be *honorable*?"

"Well, no, but... I mean..."

"And what if you're set upon by thugs? Do you think outlaws will fight honorably?"

"Well, I *know* Twailin isn't exactly *safe*!" The boy waved the notion aside. "I mean, there was a horrible slaughter in West Crescent just last week, but nothing like that could ever happen to one of *us*!"

The reminder of that night drained all of Sereth's mirth. In a flash of memory, he once again watched Lad slice Horice in two with the Master Blade's own enchanted sword. Watched...and did nothing.

I couldn't have prevented his death!

That truth comforted Sereth during sleepless nights. Though he had detested Horice, he would have fought to the death to protect him if there had been a chance. Against Lad, there was no chance. Sereth could never forget that if he wanted to survive the new guildmaster's reign. Snapping back to the present, he noted a dangerous look in his student's eyes; the notion that his noble birth kept him safe. In this city, that was a deadly assumption.

"I suggest you look back in history about five years, young Lord Barrington. Ask your father how many of his noble friends were slaughtered in their beds by dishonorable men." Sereth shivered with the thought that the one who had committed those murders was now his master. He covered the involuntary reaction by slipping a clean shirt over his head. The smooth, rich fabric caressed his skin like his old clothing never had, a perquisite of his new position. "I'll see you day after tomorrow."

28

"Will you teach me how to fight with both a dagger and rapier?" The enthusiasm in the boy's eyes was nauseating.

How eager they are to play at killing.

"Teach you how to fight dishonorably? I will *not!*" The affront on the boy's face was laughable, but it gave Sereth the opportunity to make his pitch. By giving Barrington something to tell his friends, some secret others couldn't offer, Sereth would gain students. And with a bevy of nobles sparring in his studio, who knew what gems of information might inadvertently drop. Raising an eyebrow in consideration, he eyed his student dubiously. "However, I *will* teach you to defend against it. Honorable men must, after all, be prepared to deal with scoundrels."

"Yes, Master Sereth!" Leonard's eyes lit with fervor. "Thank you!"

"Thank me by mixing up your attacks and remembering that a sword has only one purpose in this world, to end a life. Death is permanent, Lord Barrington, and not all those we fight will fight with honor."

"Yes, sir!"

Sereth waited until the door closed behind his student before secreting his various blades in their covert sheaths. He preferred daggers and stealth to the rapier he was forced to wear. Noting the smile on his assistant's face, he scowled. "And you, Lem, will not tell a soul what I'm teaching these young dandies. Is that clear?"

"Yes, Master." The smile dropped. "Perfectly clear."

"Good. Lock up before you leave."

The young man nodded and got to work cleaning up the studio. Relatively new to the Assassins Guild, Lem showed promise. Already expert with a dagger, he was a quick learner, and Sereth was training him to fence.

As Horice trained me…

Sereth let himself out into the twilight and headed down the street. Though his mind raced with the myriad details he had to attend to as Master Blade, he couldn't help but compare the sweetly scented air of Barleycorn Heights to the musky atmosphere of his own neighborhood. He'd leased a house near his business to keep up appearances, but he still called his tiny flat in the Docks District home.

Home... For the past two years, his home had seemed empty without Jinny, but he couldn't make himself leave the only place he'd ever been happy.

"Up for a little evening fun, milord?" A slim blonde woman sidled up to him and pinched his ass. "A knee trembler to whet your appetite for dinner, or perhaps for the missus?"

Sereth sighed at the reminder of his enforced celibacy. He had thought that streetwalkers would be discouraged in the city's finer neighborhoods, but it seemed that even the proprieties of upper class couldn't stem the laws of supply and demand. Each evening, young men and women plied their trade, seeking those with the desire for company and the means to pay. Sereth qualified on both counts, but he had no desire for the company of a prostitute.

"No, thank you." He made to push her away, but she grasped his hand with surprising strength.

"Come on, love. I'll give you a little discount." She leaned in, her chin on his shoulder, her voice a sultry whisper. "We need to talk, Sereth."

He glared at Kiesha in sudden recognition. That he hadn't penetrated her disguise right off perturbed him; his mind had been elsewhere. *Maybe I should take on one of my Blades as a bodyguard*, he considered, but quickly quashed the idea. If someone discovered his covert meetings with a Thieves Guild operative, his life wouldn't be worth spit, even if he was Master Blade.

Master Blade... Sereth's mind spun with the possibilities his new position might provide. Narrowing his eyes, he nodded to the narrow gap between two tall brick buildings. "There, in the close."

"Perfect!" Kiesha giggled girlishly and pulled him into the shadowed passage.

Though flames already flickered in the street lamps, their light didn't penetrate this niche where even sunlight rarely ventured. The walls loomed so close that Sereth could reach out and touch them both without extending his arms fully. In fashionable Barleycorn Heights, respectable folks didn't frequent such narrow alleys.

All the better. Neither of us is respectable.

Ten strides in, he wrenched Kiesha to a stop, grabbed her shoulders, and pinned her against the rough brick wall. "What do you want?" He hadn't seen her in a week, and had been torn between relief at being left alone, and worry for Jinny.

"Careful there, milord." The thief grasped his jacket and pulled him close. "Whispers only." Then, in a normal tone, "What'll it be, love? A little of this?" She groped his crotch, and he slapped her hand away.

"Stop it!" He wasn't about to play her lurid games. Her previous failed attempt to seduce him should have told her that.

"Now, Sereth, is that any way to treat an old friend?" Kiesha arched her back until her breasts strained against the thin fabric of her bodice, and lifted one long leg, planting her foot against the opposite wall. With a smile, she rubbed her inner thigh against his hip. "I congratulate you on your promotion, Master Blade. I'm impressed."

"How did you find out about that?"

"Aside from your new jewelry, you mean?" She laughed and writhed against him. "I have eyes everywhere, love."

Sereth wasn't sure what to make of that statement. Was she lying? Lots of people wore rings, and the master's ring was nothing unusual, just a black band. It discomforted him to think she was spying on him that closely.

Kiesha wasn't done. She hitched up her skirts and pulled him even closer. "You need to play the game, love, and I need to know what's been happening inside your new circle of friends." She pouted at his scowl, and ground herself against him. "You need to relax a little, Sereth. Why can't we both get what we want?"

He pushed her away, at least far enough that he couldn't feel her rubbing up against him. "What I *want* is my wife," he said between clenched teeth.

"Oh, your dear wife is just fine, but you've got to play this game properly, or bad things might start to happen to her." She fumbled with his belt buckle. "I *know* you know how to play. Your wife's very lonely, you see, and we talk a *lot* about you."

"Don't lie to me. Stop that!" His hands closed on her wrists hard enough to bruise. "I'm not doing this anymore, Kiesha, and I want Jinny back."

"Don't be *ridiculous*." All amusement vanished from Kiesha's voice, but she still kept up her pretense, writhing against him in mock passion. "Your new jewelry doesn't negate our arrangement. Now, tell me how things are progressing under your new guildmaster."

Sereth thought he detected a hint of desperation in her voice, but it might just have been his own fury building. "No. I told you: I'm not doing this anymore, and I want my wife back!"

"Maybe when all Nine Hells get snow!" Kiesha laughed and thrust herself against him again. "Hensen's not about to give up his best source of information, especially now that you're climbing the ranks!"

Sereth's vision blurred for a moment as his temper flared. Releasing her, he flicked his wrist and filled his hand with steel. The slim blade fairly glowed against her throat. "Let me ask you this, then: how would Hensen like it if I sent his pretty assistant back to him in pieces?"

"He wouldn't." Kiesha glanced down at the dagger and shrugged, apparently undaunted by his threat. "In fact, he'd probably return your dear Jinny to you in the same condition."

Sereth longed to slit her throat, but he knew she was telling him the truth. Never could he risk harm to his precious Jinny.

Neither, however, could he back down this time. "You tell Hensen I want her back. Now! I'm not playing this game anymore! I'm done!"

"And if he says no?" Her eyebrow arched and her lips pouted sardonically as she moved her hips against him. "What are you going to do? Stick me with your sword?"

"You just don't get it, do you?" Sereth knocked her leg down with a backhanded slap and sheathed his dagger. "I don't *care* anymore, Kiesha. I get my wife back immediately or I send my Blades for her, and everybody in that house dies!"

"And you think Lad won't find out?"

"I said, I *don't care!*"

"He'd *kill* you." Uncertainty tinged Kiesha's voice that Sereth had never heard before.

Good! He smiled grimly at her. "You're right, Kiesha. Lad would kill me. But not before I tell him who kidnapped my wife to pressure me into spying. And trust me, even if you escape my Blades, you won't escape Lad."

Sereth turned and walked away, out of the alley and down the street. He half hoped Kiesha would come after him, but she didn't. Night fell as he strode out of Barleycorn Heights toward the seedier parts of the city, all the while wondering if his threat had been idle.

No, he finally convinced himself, *it wasn't.* He'd had enough of this game.

CHAPTER III

For a woman who had once willingly submitted to torture under the Grandfather's hands, walking the streets of Twailin without a bodyguard should have been a simple thing. Mya was in no real danger, of course. The magic of her runes hummed under her skin, her constant companion, her only companion.

They keep me safe, she reminded herself, clenching her fists to keep from scratching. She wasn't sure if the sensation was real or imagined, but it never let her forget that she was a monster, a monster of her own making.

Mya couldn't shake the notion that everyone knew, that every eye on the street peered at her tattoos through her soft silk shirt, linen pants, and dark wrappings. Ridiculous, of course. The common people of Twailin had no reason to suspect that a monster walked among them. The rumors about her, she hoped, were confined to the Assassins Guild, and no one but Lad knew about her enchanted tattoos.

Lad...

Mya had walked these neighborhoods with him for five years. Without his reassuring presence at her side, she felt conspicuous, naked, and vulnerable. She hated it.

"Evening, Miss Mya. Got a table for you, and Pica's got a nice leg of lamb on the spit." The hawker outside an eatery she favored smiled and tipped his cap, waving a hand toward the street-side tables.

Glancing wistfully at the diners sitting there enjoying an early evening meal, conversation, or just a peaceful glass of wine, she shook her head. "No thanks, Dondy. Still working. Maybe later."

"Very good, Miss Mya."

Dondy knew what she was. Not that she was a monster, of course, but that she was a master in the Assassins Guild. And still he smiled at her. Most of the folks in her territory sported smiles these days. The tension in the atmosphere had eased, as if the last of the torrential spring rains had washed away all the fear and foreboding. The war among the guild factions was over. The unwonted violence had ended, and people could conduct their business without looking over their shoulders.

Of all the guild's territories, hers was the least affected by Lad's recent changes. Mya had done away with her protection rackets years ago at Lad's request. So now, while the other guild masters were frantically trying to adjust, her operation hummed along with few changes. Her Hunters did their jobs, fulfilled their contracts, and went about guild business like well-oiled clockwork.

Which reminds me…

She quickened her pace. The shop she planned to visit closed precisely at the top of the hour. This would be her last stop for the day, and so far nobody had been able to tell her anything about the poisoned dart that killed Wiggen. Her fingers caressed the smooth glass vial in her pocket, and she wondered how Lad would take the bad news. She wondered about Lad a lot lately.

He'd been her friend once, or at least the closest thing she had to a friend. She had hoped for a more intimate relationship, but he had made it quite clear that they would never be more than friends. Now, they were much less than friends. The Lad she loved was dead. This new Lad terrified her.

Wiggen's death had bent him far past the breaking point. He was colder, quieter, more withdrawn than ever she had seen him.

She sometimes overheard her people whispering about their new guildmaster as an emotionless weapon. Mya knew better; she'd watched him suppress outward displays of emotion for years. Now, she could feel his pain radiating through that armor, see his anger roiling beneath the surface, ready to explode. She hoped she wasn't around when he finally erupted because there was nothing she could do to save herself if he decided to end her life. She couldn't lift a finger against him.

If only he hadn't put on that damned ring.

She wondered for the millionth time since that dreadful night what would have happened if he hadn't put it on. Would she have taken up the ring and donned it herself, as the grandmaster had bid her to? Or would she have faded into the background and let the Twailin guild destroy itself as assassin fought assassin for mastery? Mya shook her head. The questions were moot; Lad *had* put on the ring, and he now wielded the guild. Not everyone liked the way he was doing things, but they feared him enough to forestall open rebellion…for now.

Mya turned onto Mullet Avenue and hurried along the riverfront, squinting as the late afternoon sun reflected off the water into her eyes. She almost wished for a gray, rainy day to match her mood.

The man you loved is dead, so just get over it. Your mother is dead. The Grandfather is dead. The other masters are all dead! You have no one to fear but Lad, and if you do your job and forget that you loved the man he used to be, you might survive.

She clenched her fists in her pockets, and once again felt the glass vial. A sudden thought struck her. That Lad trusted her with the dart—the only evidence they had to aid their search for Wiggen's killer—demonstrated a certain degree of confidence that she hadn't expected, given their recent estrangement. Maybe he wasn't totally lost to her. They would never be lovers, but perhaps they could be friends again.

36

If he would just let me help him... Against her better judgment, Mya's heart rose. *Lad's not dead, he's just in pain. Like an injured dog, he snaps even at a helping hand. He needs me and he knows it.* But how could she get beyond the gnashing teeth to help him?

An off-key twitter from a bedraggled clockwork canary overhead told Mya two things: it was the top of the hour, and she had reached her destination. She pushed open the shop's door to find the old dwarf shopkeeper reaching with a key to lock it for the night.

"Good evening, Crumly."

"Miss Mya!" The craggy old face scrunched as he squinted up at her through his spectacles. Crumly—Crumulus was his real name, but he'd gone by Crumly for longer than Mya had drawn breath—was nearly blind, and his once-strong shoulders were hunched with rheumatism, but he still made fine clocks, and knew more about mechanical devices than most people had forgotten. "I was just lockin' up!"

"I won't take two seconds of your time." Stepping into the shop, she held the glass vial close to his eyes. "Have you ever seen anything like this before?"

Crumly squinted into the vial for less time than Mya expected he would need before saying, "Oh, aye. I seen one just like it only yesterday!"

"You did?" Her heart skipped a beat. "Where?"

"Right in this very shop. Fellow by the name of Tamir showed me one and asked the very same question you just did."

"Really?" That was interesting. Who else had acquired one of the darts, and from where? And why were they interested in finding the owner? Mya pocketed the vial and smiled down at him. "And what, may I ask, did this Tamir look like?"

"Aside from wearin' the duke's own crest on his shoulder and sergeant's bars on his collar, you mean?" He emitted a snort that did his prodigious nose credit. "You tall folk all look alike to me, I'm afraid."

37

"A royal guardsman, eh?" That was interesting indeed. Her plans for the evening flew out the window in an instant, not that sitting in the *Golden Cockerel* eating a solo dinner while going over her correspondence held much allure in the first place. She might not have found the dart's maker, but she'd found something she could bring to Lad. Crumly was notoriously stingy with information, but she knew his weakness.

"I tell you what, Crumly, I just passed the *Prancing Pig*, and Dondy told me that they've got lamb on the spit. How about I buy you dinner and a cup of wine, and we have a little chat about this Tamir."

"Well, I was headed home to the missus..." The dwarf frowned and fingered his whiskers.

"Two cups of wine, and whatever they've got for sweets after."

"Done!" The dwarf grinned and held up his key. "The wife's a miserable cook anyway. Just let me lock up."

"It feels good to get out of the house, doesn't it, my dear?"

"Yes, sir." Kiesha lied well, and long practice had taught her not to be contrary when her father wanted her to simply smile and agree.

Hensen wore her like a corsage, an adornment to his own splendor. He wanted her to accompany him to dinner, so she went, though she despised associating with him in public.

Matching her stride to his, she maintained a pleasant expression as they strolled along the upscale avenues of the Hightown District. The truth was, she'd been out all day, hurrying throughout the city in an endless quest for information, and her feet hurt. She wondered if he knew...or cared. Had he chosen to walk as some type of subtle punishment? Of course, that she had been on her feet all day wouldn't matter to him;

other people's comfort didn't enter into his decision-making process. Hensen only cared about Hensen.

"It's a beautiful evening."

"Yes, the spring rains have finally ceased." He sighed and strolled on. "Now we only have the sweltering heat of summer, the dreary fog of autumn, and the chill drizzle of winter to endure before next year's deluge. I sometimes think that the gods torture us intentionally."

"I often think that very thing as well, sir." Why else would they give her a father like him?

"Well, I suppose we should be thankful for what we have."

They turned onto View Street, a promenade along the edge of the bluff overlooking the sprawling city south of the river's fork. Others of Twailin's upper crust strolled along, displaying their elegant clothing and elaborate coifs, pausing here and there to admire each other even more than the splendid view. Their numbers had increased the last few days as people started to feel safer. Even though the years of escalating violence had never really spilled into Hightown, the nobles and wealthy who lived there felt the pressure. The subsequent week of peace, not to mention the beautiful weather, had brought people out in droves.

Kiesha casually analyzed the passersby as she'd been trained to do. Despite their carefree airs, the strollers were not leaving their security to chance. At least one and often two bodyguards trailed discreetly behind each couple or group.

I wonder how many of their hired guards are Assassins Guild? Quite a few bore that distinct look of professionalism with a hint of underlying violence. One bit of information she had picked up today was that Sereth had begun hiring out his Blades to the very people whose businesses they'd been fleecing for decades. Perhaps he was hiring his people to nobles and gentry as well. She found the strategy brilliantly ironic; the Assassins Guild was profiting by protecting against the violence they had originally incited. *Sereth's a genius…*

Sereth!

His refusal to cooperate exasperated her. The information he gave her was worth more than all the myriad scraps the rest of her operatives scavenged from the periphery. Moirin had been the best of these, insinuating herself deep into the Hunters' headquarters, but she was gone. Truth be told, Sereth's ultimatum frightened her. If he brought the Thieves Guild's involvement to Lad's attention…

"Things could be worse for us, you know." Hensen's voice snapped her back to the moment. He swept a hand in an arc to indicate the view. "We should take what enjoyment we can, don't you think?"

"I do, sir." Kiesha gazed out at the scarlet sunset fading into a star-studded, deep-blue veil overhead. Street lamps flickered below, a terrestrial starscape outlining the dark, sinuous track of the river. Thousands lived their entire lives down there, never even visiting the vaunted heights of the upper city. She knew that this was what Hensen meant by his comment. A laugh drew her attention back to the strutting nobles, the pretentious prigs with whom Hensen endeavored to socialize. Kiesha smiled sweetly through her disgust. If they ever learned what her father really did for money, they'd run him out of town tarred and tied to a burning lodge pole.

So many lies…

Her entire life was nothing but a tangled web of interconnected falsehoods. Her clothes, her manners, her training, even her obedience to the man who had sired her. Every day, she continued to live that lie. How could she not? It was all she had ever known; a father who would not even acknowledge their tie of blood. Was it any wonder that she accepted Hoseph's offer to spy? Suddenly spiteful, Kiesha secretly hoped that Hensen would one day discover her betrayal. Even if he killed her for a traitor, it would be worth it just to see the shock on his face.

"Do you, my dear?"

"I'm sorry, sir?" Hensen's question caught her off guard.

"Do you take enjoyment?"

"In what, sir?"

He looked at her with a furrowed brow. "In *anything*, my dear."

What the hell is he talking about? Her face must have shown her confusion.

He squeezed her arm and shook his head. "Never mind." He tugged her toward the restaurant. "Shall we eat?"

"Of course, sir."

Their destination shone with a riot of colors, trellised in an array of flowers lit by cunningly mounted lamps, as resplendent as the gaudily clad customers. The upper floors sported glorious balconies where diners could take in the view. Luscious aromas wafted forth and, despite her foul mood, Kiesha's mouth started to water.

"Welcome to *The Overlook*, Master Hensen. It's been too long since we enjoyed the pleasure of your company." The hostess beamed at him, stunningly encased in a black sheath evening gown so low-cut that her toes might be visible in the cleft between her breasts if she bent over at the proper angle. She summoned a waiter with a snap of her fingers. "Sergei, take over here while I *personally* show Master Hensen to his table."

Nice of you to notice me, bitch... Kiesha bridled her spite and followed.

The hostess batted her eyes and gently touched Hensen's arm as she guided them to an ingenious device that lifted them up two floors without them having to climb a single step. Hensen flirted back, of course. Kiesha would have summoned a physician to check him for brain fever if he hadn't. Once seated at a prominent balcony table, Hensen produced a gold-embossed card from his waistcoat pocket and handed it to the woman.

"I wonder if you might call on me at your convenience." He smiled like a crocodile. "I'm planning a private function, and I think it would benefit from a lady's touch."

41

"It would be my pleasure, Master Hensen." Tucking the card into her voluminous cleavage, the hostess placed Hensen's napkin in his lap with a practiced flourish and, if her father's spreading smile was any indication, a subtle caress.

"Delightful. Thank you, my dear." He watched her walk away, entranced by the swing of her hips. Finally, after his conquest passed out of view, the Master Thief returned his attention to Kiesha. "Well, that was invigorating, wasn't it?"

"If you say so, sir." Hensen's dalliances disgusted her. His paramours came and went more often than the seasons. Occasionally they would stay for months, but more often they lasted only weeks. In fact, Jeremy, his most recent, left only yesterday in a huff. Twenty-four hours was about right, as far as her father's usual period of mourning went.

"I *do* say so, my dear, and that's exactly what I mean by enjoyment. You need to smile occasionally, or this business will make a bitter old shrew of you." He sipped iced water with lemon and perused the menu. "And we can't have that."

"No, sir." Kiesha looked at the menu, recalling her recent similar suggestion to Sereth. He had accused her of playing manipulative games, but Kiesha had been sincere, both in her philosophy and her attempt to seduce him. It wasn't love, of course. Sereth was in pain, and Kiesha felt her life was killing her. Mightn't they ease each other's woes with simple physical pleasure? Her failure made it hurt all the more. She found Hensen's sudden interest in her enjoyment astonishing, since he usually only concerned himself with her obedience.

"I need your honest assessment, my dear. I'd like to know what you think."

"I think she's very beautiful, sir, but anyone who wears a dress like that has probably seen more naked men than the scrub girls at Kovi's Bathhouse."

"Kiesha!" He shot a glare over the rim of his menu.

"I'm sorry, sir. Was there something *else* you wanted my opinion on?" She knew perfectly well that wasn't what Hensen

42

was getting at, but she couldn't resist the dig. To mollify him, she risked a tentative smile. "You *did* tell me to find some enjoyment, didn't you?"

"Ah, so I did. Well played." He winked and went back to his menu. "No, I need your assessment of the city's mood. Our opposition seems to have hit on something with this new business strategy, and if we don't adjust our own in some way, we're going to find ourselves in dire straits."

"My assessment?" His request took her aback. Hensen rarely asked her opinion. She provided information, and he made the decisions. This was something new. *Maybe he does care what I think.* The idea buoyed her mood as she considered what she'd seen during the last week. "I think it's too early to tell how things are going to develop. Our opposition isn't as weakened by the recent...infighting as we'd hoped. Their change in business strategy could cause us serious problems where our interests overlap, but the affected operations bring in only a small percentage of our total earnings. The public's opinion of our opposition has improved, but again, this only works to our disadvantage where we overlap. We provide many services that our opposition doesn't. In these, we should be unaffected."

"So, we hold the fort and wait."

"And watch, sir. We mustn't forget that."

"Of course." His eyes flicked up, then back to the menu. "And the investigation into their guildmaster's recent loss? Has it borne any fruit?"

"Not yet, sir. I'm watching that as well." Kiesha focused on her menu, hoping Hensen wouldn't probe. She hadn't told him about Sereth's ultimatum. Her failure there would only earn her punishment, and she still had the upper hand—Sereth wouldn't dare do anything that might result in harm to his precious wife. She was sure she could convince the Master Blade to be reasonable and cooperate again. Thankfully, the arrival of their waiter precluded further questions.

"It's about time." Hensen glanced at the waiter and squinted.

Kiesha knew that look, and cringed. The fellow's suit was wrinkled, his chin sported the shadow of whiskers, and an errant curl had escaped from his otherwise neatly clubbed hair. She found him cute, in a frazzled sort of way.

"Have you made a decision yet, sir?"

"Yes…" Hensen closed his menu and dropped it on the table as if offended. "I'll have the crayfish and mussels in garlic cream sauce."

"And you, ma'am?" He picked up the dropped menu and turned to Kiesha.

"The pork medallions in port wine sauce, please." Kiesha handed over her menu.

"Very good." The waiter started to leave, but Hensen cleared his throat.

"We would like *wine*, dear boy. Please have the steward pick out something nice to accompany each of our meals. And there is one more thing."

"Yes, sir?"

"You are rude and incompetent. Proper decorum requires that you take the lady's order *first*. Your manners are abysmal, your personal grooming abysmal, and your clothing disheveled." The volume of Hensen's voice drew glances from several nearby tables. Nobles sneered, and one young lady giggled behind her hand. "Please have the proprietor see to your appearance. Your slovenly attire and unkempt appearance have nearly ruined my appetite."

Kiesha's face burned with embarrassment for the poor man.

"I…uh…" The young man's face flushed red.

"Rest assured, I'll be speaking to the proprietor when I leave."

The waiter stood up straighter and tugged his jacket, the muscles of his jaw twitching. "Yes, *sir*." He turned on his heel and fled.

44

Kiesha kept her eyes down. She'd been the focus of her father's public ridicule far too many times to find the exchange amusing. Hensen sipped his water as if nothing had occurred. He probably felt it his civic duty to humiliate the man. Kiesha thought it abhorrent. She wondered if he'd done it to punish her for her comment about the hostess.

It would be just like him…

Kiesha often wondered if she loved her father or hated him. Once more, he had lifted her hopes with his barest encouragement, only to crush them into despair. Hensen acted as if the entire world was fashioned for his entertainment. He could be sweet when it served his purposes, but those times were rare.

The problem, she realized, *is that I both love* and *hate him.*

"Any other impressions, my dear?" Hensen seemed oblivious to her sudden shift in mood.

With a surge of hatred overwhelming her dwindling love for him, she decided to play the one card she knew he feared above all others. It might earn her punishment, but frankly, right now she didn't care.

"Yes, I do have something you need to hear. It's about our friend who works for the opposition."

"Yes?"

"I met with him yesterday, and he was more than a little upset."

"That sounds perfectly normal. What news did he have?"

"None. He refused to give me anything at all."

"What?" Hensen's eyes widened, then narrowed. "Why didn't you tell me about this yesterday?"

"I was hoping to resolve the situation today, but it didn't work out." The lie came as easily as breathing. "He's still stonewalling."

"That's not very smart of him. Doesn't he know there will be consequences to his actions?"

45

"I made that clear to him, sir, but he said he doesn't care anymore. He told me that if we don't give him back what we took," she fixed her eyes on his, "*everybody* concerned would share the same consequences."

"Did he now?" Incredulity arched Hensen's brow, creasing the powder on his skin into fine lines.

"Yes, sir. And I think he's serious." She sipped her water, her throat suddenly dry. Now for the final thrust. "He said he didn't care if his supervisor discovered our...partnership."

"And do you believe him?" Lines of worry appeared between his knitted brows.

Fear... There were few things that Hensen truly feared, but Lad was definitely on that list.

"I don't know, sir. He's in a very dangerous state of mind. He might—" Kiesha stopped short as a man in an impeccable suit approached the table, the owner of *The Overlook* himself.

"Well, well!" Hensen smiled at the approaching restaurateur.

"Master Hensen, let me apologize for your unpleasant experience with our waitstaff. The fellow was new, but will not have another chance to displease *anyone* in my restaurant. Let me make amends." A flick of a finger summoned the wine steward, two bottles cradled in his arms. Bowing, the steward presented them for approval. "Allow me to offer you these fine vintages free of charge."

"What a lovely sentiment." Hensen examined the bottles and arched his plucked eyebrows. "A very lovely sentiment indeed. Thank you."

"It's my pleasure, Master Hensen." The restaurateur left. The steward drew the corks and poured their wine with all due ceremony, then departed.

"To the fruits of our labors, my dear." Hensen raised his glass to Kiesha, admiring the vintage's light auburn hue in the candlelight before taking an appreciative sip.

Kiesha raised her own glass a scant inch and sipped the blood-red wine. It was delicious, of course. And all it had cost was one young waiter's job. She wondered if her father realized how often his belligerent actions made him new enemies, or if he simply didn't care.

"About our…friend?"

"We may have to deal with that soon, dear Kiesha, but I think he's just upset. He'll settle down soon enough. He always does. Then we'll continue where we left off."

"And if he's not bluffing?"

"Then we'll have a serious problem on our hands." Hensen swirled the wine in his glass and sniffed the bouquet. He sipped the wine, swished it, and swallowed, then looked vaguely disappointed. Perhaps the fruits of his labors weren't so sweet after all. "Yes, a very serious problem indeed."

Chapter IV

T *wenty thousand souls...*

Gazing out at a sea of tiny yellow spheres flickering in the pre-dawn mists, Lad wondered if there were as many lamps in Twailin as there were people. He used to love this sight. Many a night he had perched high atop the bluff to enjoy the view of the flame-bejeweled city. But as much as he loved the city, he loved its people even more. Twenty thousand souls living and working, sleeping and dying, loving... Now the view only reminded him of one soul, the one soul that called to his, the one soul absent from this sprawling mass of humanity. His city...each and every street, lane, and alley as familiar as his wife's face.

"Wiggen."

This would have been the tenth morning he woke without her...if he had slept. Before Wiggen, sleep had been just a necessity, an antidote to fatigue. But sleeping with Wiggen had been his greatest delight. Beyond the lovemaking, the mere act of lying with her—skin to skin, her familiar scent, the beat of her heart against his chest—had lulled him into peaceful rest each night. Lad no longer enjoyed sleeping. The insomnia, nightmares, and loneliness offered nothing but torment. He had no one to lie beside, no one to whisper to, no one to share his life with...no Wiggen.

Lad shivered, but it wasn't the morning chill that snaked coolly up his spine. Insomnia had sent him out prowling the night before, which wasn't unusual. He usually found solace in prowling. Last night, however, he'd had a lapse. Suddenly, he found himself by the riverside with no memory of getting there. The shock of realizing he'd been walking insensate through the streets shook him badly. He wondered what would happen if some petty thug or cutthroat attacked him during one of these lapses. Would he simply stand there as a knife sliced across his throat? Would he die? Would death stop the pain?

Would *anything* stop the pain and bring him peace?

One thing might...

Amongst those twenty thousand souls walked the one who had killed Wiggen.

Vengeance... Vengeance will bring me peace.

The street lamps faded as the sky brightened, and Lad swept his keen gaze toward the Eastmarket district with its tidy shops and inns. His eye sought out a distinctive peaked roof with four chimneys; the *Tap and Kettle*, his home for so long. Maybe his vengeance would bring peace there, too, to those who had lost a daughter, an aunt, a mother...

Lissa...

Lad's arms ached to hold her, touch her silky hair, feel her cheek so soft beneath his lips. He dared not go back, even to catch a glimpse of her. Leaving her had felt like Wiggen dying in his arms all over again. If he ever went back, he didn't know if he could ever summon the strength to leave her again. He couldn't risk her life to satisfy his own longings.

Lad gripped the balcony rail in frustration. *Assassins don't have families...* He squeezed the cool stone balustrade until his fingers ached.

Dawn's light burst from behind the distant mountains, and the city came to life below him. Footsteps mounted the stairs of his townhouse to the third floor, then scuffed across the hall carpet outside Lad's room. That would be Dee with breakfast.

Punctual, as always.

Much to Mya's chagrin, Lad had commandeered her assistant. By Lad's own admission, he knew nothing about the

49

bureaucracy of the guild, and little of the duties of a guildmaster. He needed someone knowledgeable, efficient, and savvy in the ways of the guild.

Too savvy by far, Lad thought as he glanced over his shoulder at the opulent suite. He would have been perfectly content with a room in an anonymous inn somewhere, like Mya had in the *Golden Cockerel*, but Dee had shown unexpected fortitude in his protests.

"A guildmaster doesn't live in a hovel, Master. If you want to be treated with the respect, you have to fulfill certain expectations. To *be* successful, you must *look* successful."

Shortly after Lad's reluctant agreement, Dee acquired this three-story townhouse in Barleycorn Heights, complete with cook and maids, though Lad had balked at submitting himself to the ministrations of a valet. His only mandate had been a view of the city—of Eastmarket in particular—and minimal interference by the house staff. He might have to play the gentleman in this farce, but he would not tolerate anyone fussing over him.

The door opened and closed, and he listened to Dee setting out breakfast. The scents of blackbrew, bread, bacon, and spiced porridge wafted onto the balcony in an aromatic tide. Lad's mouth watered despite his lack of appetite. His body knew it needed food, even if he forgot. Loitering another minute on the balcony, he watched the mists recede from the rooftops below and listened to the cocks crow in the new day.

Another day without Wiggen.

"Breakfast, Master."

"Yes, Dee."

Lad turned away from the beauty of the sunrise and strode to the table, scowling at the white linen, silver flatware, and porcelain dishes filigreed with gold. He was a simple man with simple tastes; this luxury rubbed him the wrong way. Dee steadfastly remained standing—"It's only proper for me to wait until you're seated, Guildmaster," had been his excuse—until

Lad dropped into his chair. As Dee took a chair across the table, Lad picked up the cup of blackbrew perfectly lightened with cream and sipped.

"What letters today?" He nodded to the short pile at Dee's elbow as he slathered a slice of warm bread with strawberry preserves. He ate mechanically, ignoring the flavors and aromas. They only reminded him of home, though the bread wasn't nearly as good as Forbish's.

"Yesterday's progress reports from the masters," Dee pushed several sheets of parchment across the table, "a note from the moneylender we set up your accounts with," he added a formal letter that bore the embossed crest of Lad's bank, "and this." He held up an envelope, a quizzical expression on his face. "A private letter. It's sealed, so you'll have to open it yourself."

"Who would be sending me a private letter?" Lad stuffed the rest of the bread into his mouth and chased it with a swallow of blackbrew before snatching the envelope and reading the front. His newly assumed name and address gleamed black against the expensive white vellum. "Is this from one of the masters? I've only had this name and address for three days. Who else would know it?"

"No, sir, it's not from any of the masters. It's possible that a local social organization obtained your new name from the lease of the house and sent you an invitation, but..." Dee looked dubious as his voice trailed off, and he motioned for Lad to flip it over. The envelope was sealed with black wax, conspicuously smooth. "Social clubs generally don't use magic to seal their missives."

"No imprint?" Although Lad had received few letters in his life, he had seen enough to know that a person's seal was their calling card, a little bit of ego impressed in wax. "Could it be a trap?"

"It's possible, Master. Pressing your ring against the seal will tell you if there's any dangerous magic."

51

Thankful for the reminder, Lad pressed the guildmaster's ring to the black wax. The mild tingle told him that the letter was merely sealed to prevent someone other than the recipient from opening it. An electric jolt would have indicated a malicious spell. He was relieved, but knew that there were other threats that his ring would not detect. Holding the envelope to his nose, he inhaled, but detected no odors that would indicate poison. Still, he felt apprehensive.

"We *can* find out what's written inside without opening the envelope, can't we?"

Dee stiffened, and his gaze dropped. "Yes, sir. I hadn't thought of that." He rose and walked to the ornate credenza that dominated one wall of the suite's salon. After retrieving an object from a hidden compartment in the center drawer, he returned and handed it over.

Lad took the small magical magnifying glass. *No wonder Dee hadn't thought of it.* He probably didn't like to remember Moirin, the barmaid who had seduced him in order to spy on Mya. Not only had his affair with the woman allowed her access to Mya's business and personal documents; when he caught her, she had taken poison to evade capture. She'd died in Dee's arms. Lad knew what that felt like.

Mya had given the glass to Lad with the simple explanation, "You need it more than I do." He'd been shocked to discover the rarity and intrinsic value of such devices. If he sold it, Lad could afford to buy his townhouse outright, rather than lease. But it was too useful to sell.

Lad passed the magnifying glass over the sealed envelope, and precise script swam up through the fine parchment. Squinting through the confused overlap due to the fold, he was able to decipher enough to make him catch his breath. Dropping the glass, he broke the seal, slipped the letter out, and read. The message was brief, to the point, and utterly impossible.

Guildmaster Lad

Twailin Assassins Guild

It has come to my attention that you have assumed the position of Twailin Guildmaster. Although you were not my first choice, I am not particularly displeased with the outcome.

Congratulations.

Allow me to lay down the rules. Your unprecedented ascension to the guildmaster position will not excuse any delay in payments to the guild. My collectors will continue to inspect your finances at quarter-year intervals.

You will travel to the city of Tsing within two months of your receipt of this letter so that we may personally discuss the particulars of your new position. Notify me through the usual communications channels of your anticipated date of arrival in the city. You will travel under your assumed identity, and engage a room at the *Drake and Lion* inn in Tsing. Dress appropriate to your station, and formally for our meeting. My representative will meet you at the *Drake and Lion* to provide you with the details of our meeting. Master Hunter Mya Ewlet will accompany you to this meeting. She will travel in the guise of your wife to avoid unwanted attention.

Sincerely,
Grandmaster

Lad read the letter a second time, shaking his head in disbelief as he handed it to Dee. "This can't be real, can it? Doesn't the Grandmaster live in Tsing?"

"He does, sir."

"It would have taken a letter at least a week to reach Twailin by the fastest messenger. I didn't even have my new identity or this house a week ago. How could this happen?"

"I...don't know, sir." Dee took the letter to the balcony and held it up to the morning light. "This *is* the Grandmaster's crest." Turning, he jumped to find his master right behind him.

Lad stepped back. He didn't try to move silently, he just did. At least Dee had stopped yelping when startled by Lad's inadvertent stealth. Lad snatched the letter back. "How can this be? Are there magical means of delivering a letter?"

Dee shrugged. "None that I know of. Perhaps it's a forgery. If you press your ring to the crest, it should verify its authenticity."

Lad did as Dee suggested, and the now-familiar tingle ran up his arm. "It's genuine."

Dee bit his lip. "It could be that the letter didn't come from Tsing at all, but from someplace closer. That would mean..."

Lad tensed as he finished Dee's sentence. "That the Grandmaster's here in Twailin."

Dee shifted, obviously discomforted by the conclusion. "Yes, sir."

"How could he be here? I thought he never left Tsing!"

"That's what everyone *says*, sir. When the Grandfather was killed, he just sent intermediaries. But no one in Twailin knows who the Grandmaster is or what he looks like. Only the guildmasters ever meet him in person."

"But why would he come here? The Grandmaster wouldn't ride for two weeks in a carriage just to deliver a letter!"

"I...I don't know, sir." Dee bit his lip again and took a step back, fear clear on his face.

Lad sighed in exasperation and forced his temper down. He couldn't have Dee too frightened of him to speak his mind. "I'm not going to kill you because you don't know everything, Dee. Relax and finish your blackbrew."

"Yes, sir." Dee returned to the table and refilled their cups, though his hand trembled slightly as he poured the cream. "Do you wish to send a reply?"

"I suppose I have to at least confirm that I got his *invitation*." Lad reached for more bread and preserves, his mind working over his concerns as he chewed and swallowed.

Two months... The standard coach to Tsing took almost two weeks, leaving him only six weeks to find Wiggen's killer before he had to leave for his meeting with the Grandmaster. He would not—*could* not—leave Twailin before he avenged his wife.

"Draft a letter thanking him for his understanding of the situation, and say that I'll make every effort to be there within the allotted time. Make it cordial, but don't make me sound like..." *Like what?* "...his slave."

"Yes, sir." Dee jotted a note in the tiny book he kept in his pocket. "You'll...um...need some new clothes for the trip, sir."

"Clothes?" The mundane issue irritated Lad to no end. It seemed like just another distraction from working to find Wiggen's killer. "You just bought me a whole closetful of clothes. What's wrong with them?"

"Nothing, sir, but you'll need travelling clothes, as well as something suitable for Tsing. It's the capital of the empire, after all. And, of course, something formal for your meeting with the Grandmaster." Dee sipped blackbrew, furrowing his brow as he considered his master. "He did stipulate formal attire, sir. If you insult him, you'll not live to regret it."

"Fine!" Lad tossed back the last of his blackbrew and stood. "Buy me some new clothes."

"You'll want a tailor to—"

"Then hire a tailor! Hire whoever you want! Buy a whole *house* full of shit I don't need!" He threw down his napkin and started for the door. "I'm going out! I'll read the rest of the letters later. Tell the masters to be here tonight at sunset. I want to hear their reports from their own mouths."

Lad was out the door and halfway down the stairs to the street before he heard Dee's tentative, "As you wish, Master."

The urgent knock snapped Norwood's train of thought. He threw his pen down and glared at the door as it opened partway. "I *told* you—"

"Sir!" The desk sergeant peered around the door, his face a mask of worry. "There's a Lord Barrington here to see you. He requests—"

The door burst all the way open before the sergeant could finish, and a tall man pushed his way into the captain's office. The man's brilliant green velvet jacket, gold waistcoat, and ornate rapier screamed wealth, and the small coat of arms on his breast pocket stated as clearly as a herald's cry that blood as blue as a summer sky pulsed through his veins.

"Lords of the realm do not *request* anything from the Royal Guard, Sergeant. Your *purpose* is to serve and protect us."

"Your pardon, milord." The sergeant stepped around the lord, his face flushed as he saluted stiffly. "Lord Barrington would like a word with you, sir."

"Thank you, sergeant." Norwood shifted his expression from annoyance to pleasant neutrality as he stood to greet the intruder.

Norwood disliked dealing with sanctimonious nobles, but Lord Barrington was essentially correct. Some nobles pushed the bounds granted by title, influence, and money. Lord Barrington obviously possessed all three entitlements, and expected his due deference. The captain had learned long ago that a little servility—ass-kissing, as Tamir put it—was the most effective means of dealing with this breed.

"What can the Royal Guard do for you today, milord?" He executed a precise military bow.

56

"The reason for this visit is not what you can do for us, Captain Norwood, but what we can do for you."

"We, milord?" Though of noble blood, a mere lord was not due the royal 'We'.

Barrington suddenly realized that he stood alone and called sharply over his shoulder, "Leonard!"

"Sorry, father." A bright-eyed boy hurried in and shut the door. "I was just looking at the map they had out there. It's fascinating!"

"Captain Norwood, this is my son Leonard. He has made a discovery."

"Discovery, milord?" Norwood shifted his attention from the man to the boy. "What discovery?"

"Tell the captain what you told me, Leonard."

"Yes, sir." The youth turned to Norwood with the exuberance of a pup with a stick. "Well, sir, it's about my arms training. My father though it would be best if I took dueling lessons, and we decided to hire someone different. Not the usual fencing master, you know." He paused as if expecting a response or affirmation.

Norwood smiled patiently, stifling his desire to wring the words out of the boy so he could get back to work. "No, I'm afraid I don't know."

"Father says most of Twailin's arms trainers have become staid in their techniques. He thought someone new might…give me an edge, so to say. So, he sent me to this new fellow, Sereth VonBruce. He's got a place on Copper Street, just south of the bridge." He paused again.

"All right." Norwood knew the street and the neighborhood, but not the specific trainer.

"To the point, Leonard," Lord Barrington prompted.

"Yes, sir. Well, I was coming from my lesson the other day, and met my friend Torrie Atchinson outside, coming from his flute lesson. When I pointed VonBruce out to him, he said that I was being cheated, that VonBruce was nothing but a pretender, not a real arms master at all." The young man puffed out his skinny chest and snorted in derision. "Well, I told him I'd be *happy* to show him a trick or two—Master VonBruce is teaching me how to deal with dishonorable attacks—but Torrie said that VonBruce was nothing but a bodyguard. Said he'd seen him trailing after Master DeVough, the fencing master Torrie used to train with. Of course, DeVough is dead now. He was killed in that massacre last week, you know, and the duke even confiscated his holdings!"

"Wait! Horice DeVough?"

"Yes, sir."

That name Norwood knew very well. He had to force himself not to glance at his diagram of the Fiveway Fountain massacre. Horice DeVough had warranted two pins—one for each half of his body. Unfortunately, by the time they had identified the body, his fencing salon had been abandoned, and most of his employees and associates had vanished. Only a few servants remained at DeVough's home, and they—if they were to be believed—knew nothing about their master's business. There had been no mention of a bodyguard.

"You see? When I found that out, I told father, and he suggested that we come to you!"

"That was wise of you, Lord Barrington. Thank you." Norwood plucked a notebook from the clutter of his desk. "What's the name of VonBruce's training academy, please?"

"It's called *The Dangerous End*," Leonard said. "Do you think Master VonBruce was involved in the killings?"

"Oh, I doubt it," Norwood assured the lad with a casual smile. He didn't want rumors to start spreading. "More likely his old boss just got tangled up with the wrong sort. Rest assured, we'll look into it."

"Captain," Lord Barrington leaned closer, his brow wrinkled with concern, "do you think it's dangerous for my son to continue training there?"

"Oh, I don't think so, but I certainly wouldn't go boasting about it." Norwood leveled a serious stare at Leonard. "In fact, I'd much rather you didn't cancel your contract with VonBruce. At least not yet. I'll be sending someone down there to ask some questions, and it would be best if the fellow didn't find out who tipped us off. Even if this is nothing, there might be hard feelings."

"And if this VonBruce was involved in the recent violence, my son's life is at risk." Barrington's eyes flicked to his son, then back to Norwood.

"Oh, *father!*"

"I won't have you used as bait in some plot to—"

Norwood held up a hand. "Please, milord, let me explain my request." He nodded to the boy. "Consider for a moment what VonBruce might think if, after my officer shows up to ask questions, he looks over his appointment book and sees that young Lord Barrington's contract has recently been cancelled."

The elder lord pursed his lips. "I see."

"At present, there's no reason to suspect that this VonBruce is anything more than a well-trained swordsman trying to earn a living in a career more peaceful than that of a mercenary, and more lucrative than that of a guardsman. It seems natural to me that he would gravitate toward his former master's vocation. We'll know more once we ask some questions, but until we do, it would be more dangerous for your son to quit his lessons than to continue."

"So you suggest we simply carry on as before?"

"Exactly as before, yes. It would be wise not to let on that you know of VonBruce's association with DeVough."

"Oh, that's no problem!" The boy grinned like he'd been given a secret assignment by Duke Mir himself. "All he ever talks to me about is where to put my feet, anyway!"

"Good." Norwood bowed to his visitors. "Thank you for bringing this to my attention."

"I'm trying to teach my son that being a lord is more than simply holding a title." Barrington fixed the boy with a meaningful stare. "It's about putting the needs of the empire above your own. As nobles, we have a duty to uphold."

"He's got a fine teacher, then, milord." Norwood bowed again, more to hide his smirk than as a sign of respect. *Duty!* Barrington had never served in the military, and had certainly never put the good of the empire over his own political and financial ends. He had earned nothing on his own, inheriting his title and fortune from his father, who had, in turn, inherited it from his. "Now, I must do my duty as well."

Once the door had closed behind their noble backs, Norwood sat down at his desk and referred to his notes. Tamir was probably sick of canvasing tinkers' shops for the maker of the black darts, and might welcome an opportunity to do a little interrogation. He just hoped his sergeant wasn't too hard on the new fencing master.

Chapter V

Mya glanced up at the street sign. *Greensleeves Way.* *Almost there.* Stopping, she turned to look back down at the stunning view of the lower city. The morning sun glinted off the river in a breathtaking display, beauty reserved for the affluent living on the hill.

"Pardon, milady."

Mya stepped back to avoid the dust of a street sweeper as he worked his heavy broom along the gutter. She hurried along, trying to remember if she'd ever seen anyone sweeping in Westmarket. Generally, the poorer classes just hoped for rain to wash the offal and dirt down to the river. Mya didn't visit Barleycorn Heights often, but she was getting to know the neighborhood better. Lad's new home stood less than a block ahead, one of a row of stately graystone townhouses. As she approached, three carriages pulled up in front of the house, right on time.

A wry smile tugged at the corner of her mouth as she guessed which carriage belonged to which Assassins Guild master. The gaudy gold filigree had to be Bemrin, the new Master Inquisitor. The flashy bastard dressed like a court dandy and strutted like a cock of the walk. The plain black carriage with polished brass lanterns could only be Master Alchemist Enola. For some unfathomable reason, Enola had begun wearing all black.

Could she actually be mourning Neera? Mya shuddered with the memory of the bestial form Neera had assumed during their final battle. At least Enola seemed to be saner than her predecessor.

The last of the three, a common hackney that wouldn't have drawn a second glance anywhere in the city, would be Jingles. He, at least, knew the value of discretion. Fortunately, carriages of all types rattled around the streets here, so none drew more than a passing glance.

Deathtraps. Mya chose to walk, despite the dress and uncomfortable shoes she wore to blend in with the gentry. Her gifts blocked fatigue and pain, and Lad had taught her to shun carriages. Old habits died hard.

Movement drew her eye—Sereth, striding out of the nearby side street. He, too, had chosen to walk. Spotting her, he nodded in recognition and altered course.

Mya analyzed him as he approached. Like most successful assassins, Sereth wouldn't stand out in a crowd. Of average height and build, his jet-black hair and olive skin indicated Morrgrey ancestry, which was common enough in Twailin. He wore nondescript clothing, neat and well-made. A rapier hung from his hip with professional ease, as befitted an up-and-coming fencing master. A passerby would never detect the daggers secreted in his boots and sleeves, though Mya had no problem. She, too, carried blades ingeniously secreted in her clothing.

"No bodyguard?" she asked as they fell into step. "After working so long for Horice, I thought you'd want someone watching your back."

"I don't have any enemies."

Was that irony or a joke? Sereth wasn't naïve enough to think they didn't all have enemies aplenty. She noticed that he didn't ask why she didn't have protection of her own. Of course, he'd seen her rise from a death-stroke and join Lad in the slaughter near Fiveway Fountain. That he walked beside her now without flinching either spoke well of his courage or branded him a fool.

She tilted her head toward the other masters mounting the townhouse steps, each accompanied by a bodyguard. "Evidently, you and I are the only ones who don't."

"Evidently." Sereth nodded absently. "Any progress?"

"Some." She fingered the vial in her pocket and considered what Crumly had told her.

"Did you get Jingles' note?"

"Yes." The news of Lad's execution of Yance had struck Mya like a blow. The Lad she knew would never have murdered someone like that. But then, this wasn't the Lad she knew. "Lad's...in a dangerous state of mind."

Sereth's harsh bark of laughter caught her off guard. She glanced at him, but he just shook his head. "You have a gift for understatement."

"Nice of you to notice."

"Right."

When they reached the steps, Sereth gestured for Mya to precede him.

Gallant or paranoid? she wondered. Regardless, she climbed the steps without a backward glance. She had nothing to fear from Sereth. She could kill him before his dagger even cleared its sheath.

Dee met them at the door, looking dapper in a tailored jacket and cravat, the perfect image of a wealthy gentleman's assistant. He had good taste, and had always been after her to upgrade her own quarters and wardrobe, to no avail. It seemed he had finally found a situation where he could exercise his talent for elegance.

"Hello, Dee. You're looking well."

"Miss Mya. I'm doing well, thank you. The guildmaster keeps me busy." He smiled, but the dark circles under his eyes suggested that his new position wasn't all silk sheets and roses.

He waved them into a broad, dark-paneled hall that ran the length of the house. To the left, beside a wide staircase to the second floor, sliding doors opened into a parlor. To the right, similar doors opened into the dining room. Hardwood floors gleamed underfoot, and silver vases of fresh flowers adorned every tabletop. The other masters also looked around curiously.

"You've done well with the house." Bemrin scrutinized the elegant décor with an appraising eye. "Masculine with a hint of nouveau riche. The guildmaster will have beautiful young gold diggers beating down his door in no time."

Mya glared at the tasteless remark; Lad's wife had been killed only weeks ago. Dee's appalled expression surprised her, however. He had never shown any particular liking for Lad. *Why now*? Then she remembered Moirin. The woman had been a spy, but she'd also been Dee's lover. Her death had apparently affected him deeply enough for him to empathize with Lad.

"This way if you please, masters." Dee resumed his expression of blank attentiveness and led them down the hall. He opened a door at the end into an airy library. The room boasted bookshelves on two walls, portraits on a third, and windows that looked out onto the landscaped garden behind the house. Blooming shrubs colored the view, and ivy climbed the high brick walls that ensured privacy.

Lad stood before the windows, gazing outside. Unmoving, he seemed to be either lost in thought or intentionally ignoring his guests. He was the only man Mya knew who could look graceful standing still. She felt a faint flutter in her chest. Every time she saw him, she felt the same conflict—her heart hadn't caught up with her head yet. She hid her consternation by inspecting the room.

The bookshelves were filled with leather-bound classics. The portraits were of stern-faced men and genteel women who bore a vague resemblance to Lad. Dee had done well, indeed. A visitor would assume they were the young gentleman's ancestors. Lad, of course, had no living forebears that he knew of.

Something we've got in common, Mya thought, *though for different reasons.*

The chime of Jingles' ridiculous bracelet caught Mya's ear, and she glanced at the Enforcer. He was nervous, but that was no surprise. They all had good reason to be nervous. None of them knew why Lad had called this meeting.

"The masters are here, sir," Dee announced, his voice oddly loud for the enclosed space.

Lad stirred, his shoulders stiffening slightly. "Good." Turning, his eyes flicked over each in turn.

Mya tried not to fidget under his scrutiny. She knew he saw more than most. *What does he see in me?* Could he see her fear? Could he smell it, as she smelled the fear from Enola and Jingles? How did he feel about being the cause of that fear?

"Sit down." Lad nodded to the plushly upholstered chairs circling a low table, but didn't take one himself. He looked oddly uncomfortable, as if his clothes didn't fit properly. Mya suddenly realized why. Everything—Lad's clothes, the room, the entire house—was perfect; it was Lad that didn't fit.

The masters all took seats. Enola descended stiffly into the nearest chair, sitting like a puppet with over-taut strings, her dark cloak drawn around her like armor. Bemrin flounced onto the divan with no small measure of grace, crossing his legs and looking to his master with an open expression, fearless in his ignorance. Jingles sat at rigid attention, twitching his wrist just enough to make his bracelet jingle. Sereth was the enigma. Mya had never seen him show fear, even the moment after Lad had killed his former master, but the Blade was neither cocky nor stupid. He seemed to face every situation with the practiced poise of a veteran warrior going into battle, ready to face death at any moment. He took his seat, perfectly at ease, focused, and calm.

Did he learn that from serving the Grandfather? Mya sat beside Bemrin on the divan.

Dee sat at a small desk, took up a leather-bound ledger, and started scratching notes.

Lad stood like a statue, surveying them with eyes like chips of mica. "I want to know how things have been progressing in both business and the investigation. I've read your reports, but I want to hear it from you. Jingles, you first."

With a quick jingle of his bracelet, the Master Enforcer began. "Things have quieted down since our little discipline problem. The message you sent has been understood and accepted. The City Guard is still crying and moaning about us cutting off their bribes, but we're telling them to piss off. As long as we keep the really illegal stuff out of sight, we'll be fine. There's some squabbling on the fringes of the Docks District—a couple of The Sprawls gangs trying to horn in on our territory." He shrugged as if the young thugs were of no consequence. "We're telling them to bugger off as politely as possible."

"Have you considered trying to recruit them? Having eyes in The Sprawls might help us find Wiggen's killer."

"Yes, Master, but they're an independent lot." Jingles glanced to Sereth and jerked his left hand in a practiced flip. *Jingle jingle.* They all knew the Master Blade's origin, and that he didn't like to be reminded of his youth. "In fact, more than one has told *us* to bugger off. It probably wouldn't be worth the trouble. Our operations in the South Docks District are going well. As to the investigation, I've got every cutthroat and loan shark south of the market districts chasing rumors. So far, nothing."

"Keep working on the gangs. Tell whoever will listen that we'll pay for information about anyone who had contact with the former masters, or anything concerning me or my family. And keep chasing rumors." Lad's eyes flicked to Jingles' left. "Enola?"

"Business is virtually unchanged, Master." Her voice barely reached the corners of the room, and her eyes remained fixed on her lap. "The poison from the dart is nothing special. White scorpion venom. You can get it in any one of a dozen shops, including mine. The dart itself is quite a piece of work: spring loaded. It delivers a huge dose of the venom."

"Then whoever used it must have purchased a lot of the venom. Find out who bought large quantities of that poison." He looked to the Master Inquisitor next. "Bemrin?"

"Business is booming, Master." He grinned broadly, one bejeweled hand sweeping in a foppish gesture worthy of the duke's court. "I've got my girls and boys busy in every parlor, bedroom, backroom, and alley both north and south of the river. Gossip and gold are flowing like wine. You have my report on the financial aspects, of course. As far as rumors go, everyone seems to think the disreputable elements of Twailin killed each other off in one big, bloody battle, and everyone's safe now."

"Are any of those rumors helping our investigation?"

"Not directly, Master, but there is plenty of chatter."

"Stop chasing gold and start chasing rumors. You're supposed to be an *Inquisitor*. Start asking questions!"

Bemrin's were the only shoulders that didn't tense at the frustration in Lad's voice. "Rumors it is, Master!"

Is he really that oblivious? Mya wondered.

"Sereth?"

"My new fencing salon is progressing about as well as expected, for the short time I've been at it. Clients are enrolling slowly but surely. As you know, I'm also running a security business. Vetted security personnel is the idea. Aside from the income, they're well placed to hear rumors, or spread them for that matter. Other than a few outside contracts for muscle, intimidation, or outright assassination, business is more legal than illegal, so we're not drawing much attention. As to the investigation, I've little to report. Blades simply aren't trained for ferreting out secrets. It's not our bailiwick. I've got those working as bodyguards listening and asking questions, but I don't want to provoke suspicion. It's been *suggested*"—he glanced sharply at Bemrin—"that I bring an Inquisitor into the fencing salon to ply the young lordlings for information, but I'd rather not risk my public identity."

"I agree. Any discipline problems?"

"None whatsoever, sir."

Mya noted the faintest relaxation of Lad's posture, a lessening of the wrinkles that seemed to perpetually crease the corners of his eyes nowadays. She suspected that Yance's execution had taken a toll on him, and that he was relieved to not have to repeat the lesson. With the rumors that must be flying around the guild about him after the Fiveway Fountain massacre, she was surprised anyone had been stupid enough to flout his authority in the first place.

"Good." Lad turned to the Master Hunter. "Mya?"

"Business is virtually unchanged, since we instigated these practices years ago. And my people know you, so there's no problem with sedition." Mya pulled the vial holding the dart from her pocket. "I did find out something about this, however."

"The crafter?" Lad's face lit up with eagerness.

"No, Master." She hated to dash that glimmer of hope, but she'd been convinced that Crumly didn't know who had made the darts. "Nobody I talked to had ever seen anything like this. But one old clockmaker told me that the Royal Guard has been asking the same questions I have. They evidently recovered an identical dart from somewhere, and they're looking for whoever made it."

Lad's eyes narrowed. "And have *they* made any progress?"

"I have no way to know, Master." She looked toward Bemrin. "We might be able to find something out between the sheets, if you want to go there."

"Bemrin?"

"I'd be happy to try, sir."

"Do it. Find out where they got that dart and if they've found its maker." Lad's eyes snapped back to Mya, a pair of needles that pierced her to the core. "Who was asking the questions?"

"A sergeant named Tamir. He's Norwood's number one."

"Norwood..."

For a moment Lad's eyes took on a faraway look, and Mya's heart sunk. *Gods, not again!* Lad's first visit to the Royal Guard captain had seemed foolhardy; repeating the stunt would border on insanity. She opened her mouth to warn him, but then clapped it shut. Lad didn't know that she had discovered his nocturnal visit to Norwood; telling him now would earn her no favors. Thankfully, Lad's gaze had drifted to a spot on the rug. He hadn't noticed her expression of concern.

Everyone sat perfectly still, waiting for their master to resume the conversation, but he didn't. Lad seemed utterly lost in thought, but no one dared interrupt. Bemrin shifted in his chair, and Jingles and Sereth exchanged glances. Even Enola looked up to see what she might have missed, before dropping her eyes once again to her lap. The silence dragged on, broken only by the mantel clock chiming the quarter hour, and still Lad remained focused, oblivious to their growing discomfort.

This isn't like him at all. Lad was the most attentive human being Mya had ever met. When they walked the streets of Twailin together, he would react to the drop of a coin a block away.

Dee cleared his throat loudly, and Lad's head snapped up like a bird dog attending a flushed pheasant. He blinked and looked around, almost as if he'd woken from a dream.

What the hell...

"Yes... Yes, do that. Mya, you work with Bemrin. Start with someone who works under this Sergeant Tamir."

"Yes, Master."

"Business is going well, so no changes there, but I find that I'm pressed for time." Lad began to pace, his words clipped.

"The investigation has to be concluded quickly. I expect you all to push forward on this. Money, pressure, use whatever means are necessary to follow a lead. If it comes to violence, clear it with me personally first."

"Yes, Master."

"Good. Mya, I need to talk to you. The rest of you can go."

What the… Fear gripped Mya. She watched helplessly as the others stood and left. Dee shot her a sympathetic glance as he closed the door on his way out. She stood and clenched her hands behind her back, facing her master, but kept her eyes fixed on the top button of his shirt. She didn't dare look into his eyes.

Lad held out a hand. "Give me the dart."

Fishing the vial out of her pocket, she put it in his hand without a word. Her fear eased a trifle. *Of course, he needs it to take to Norwood.*

"I received a letter that concerns you." He pocketed the vial as he strode to the desk. When he returned, he held out an envelope. "Read it."

The familiar press of black wax sent a shiver down Mya's spine. Her heart sank when she recognized the embossed crest and scrawled signature on the letter.

I warned him that there would be repercussions…

Then she read, "Master Hunter Mya Ewlet will accompany you to this meeting," and her mouth went dry. *Oh, gods…* Memory flashed, and Mya saw the Grandmaster's letter burning in her hearth, crumbling to ash. She had literally thrown his offer in the fire, refused to accept the guildmaster position. Now she would pay for her fear-driven actions.

Mya's mind buzzed with possibilities, potential actions, and consequences as it always did when she faced mortal peril. She couldn't fight, couldn't flee, and knew perfectly well what a meeting with the Grandmaster could mean. Her death loomed large before her eyes.

"How could he know so fast?"

"What?" The question caught her off guard. "Know what?"

"I received that letter this morning, one *week* after I sent him a letter announcing my assumption of the guildmaster position." Irritation edged his voice, and his hands clenched and unclenched at his sides. "My letter should only be arriving in Tsing right now, and yet we already have his reply." He flicked the envelope in her hand. "He addressed it to my *assumed* name, which I've only had for three days. And before you ask, the answer is yes, the seal is genuine."

"I understand." Mya handed the letter back, chagrined that she'd been distracted by her own plight, blinded to the apparent enigma of the letter itself.

"Then explain how the Grandmaster managed to send me this letter."

She shrugged. "He must have a means to send documents quickly, perhaps magic, perhaps mundane. The Grandfather used birds to carry messages."

"Birds?" He waved the perfectly creased and unmarred letter in front of her. "You think a *bird* carried this from Tsing?"

"No, Master. It doesn't appear so." She swallowed. What did he want from her? "It must have been sent magically. I don't know how. I can try to find out if a wizard can be contracted to send a letter quickly."

"Think like an assassin, Mya!" Lad flung the letter onto the desk. "What *else* does this mean?"

"What else?" Mya bristled at having her own words thrown back at her. She always thought like an assassin. Why was he so angry with her about this? She had nothing to do with the damned letter. Forcing down her ire, she cleared her mind and thought for a moment. An answer snapped to the fore. "It means he has someone watching you, and they have methods of communication way beyond anything I've ever heard of. It also means he *wants* you to know he's watching you, or doesn't care if you know. A reminder of his power over you, I suppose. I don't know what else you want me to tell you."

"I want you to tell me who's spying on me, Mya! And I want you to tell me who killed Wiggen before I have to sit in a gods-damned carriage for a *month* on my way to and from Tsing, just to meet a man who will probably tell me to drop our investigation and concentrate on making money for the guild!"

The desperation in Lad's eyes belied his angry tone. She looked down, cursing herself for meeting his gaze, knowing it would tear at her heart. He didn't want pity from her; he wanted answers. Unfortunately, she had none.

"I'll do whatever I can to help, Lad." She bit her lip at her slip of the tongue—she hadn't called him Lad since the night he put the guildmaster's ring on his finger—but he didn't seem to notice her lapse, so she forged ahead. "The spies could be anyone, anywhere. In an organization of our size, it would be virtually impossible to find them. Consider Moirin. If Dee hadn't inadvertently caught her in the act, she would have continued reading my correspondence and reporting to who knows who. We could try leaking misinformation to specific people and wait to see if any of it comes back through the Grandmaster, but that would probably take too long to be useful. It'd be easier to just take strict precautions, restricting vital information to only those you trust."

Lad arched an eyebrow. "Which leads to the question: who can I trust? 'There is no one in the world who wouldn't betray someone with the right incentive.' Those were your exact words to me not too long ago."

"In general that's true. But what I've learned over the last five years of running the Hunters is that you've got to trust *someone* or nothing will get done." She swallowed hard and fixed her eyes to his again. "Master, you can trust *me*." There it was. He could take it or not.

Lad stared at her, but did not respond.

Discomforted, she looked away and continued. "As far as the trip goes, I don't see any way to avoid it. Disregarding the

Grandmaster's summons would only bring you grief…or worse. We'll just have to find Wiggen's murderer before you leave."

"Before *we* leave, you mean."

"Yes, of course. *We*." It had been an honest mistake. Mya didn't want Lad to think she was trying to weasel out of the trip.

"Why do you think he wants to meet you?"

"I imagine he wants to know why I'm not wearing that ring on your finger." The answer came out more acerbic than she had intended. "If he knows I threw his letter into the fire, I'm dead. I only told you about it, but Moirin was reading my mail, so…"

"I won't tell him you burnt his letter if you don't tell him I lied about destroying the ring in the first place."

"I'm afraid he might already know both those things." At least Lad wasn't raving any longer. Her willingness to help seemed to have calmed him. Mya laughed without humor. "It could be worse. He could just have us both killed."

"I'd almost prefer an assassination attempt to a month in a carriage wearing a neck cloth and jacket." He flipped his lapel with distaste. "Dee told me I needed new clothes for the trip. And if I have to dress like a gentleman, *you* have to dress like a lady."

Spies, poison darts, and a summons by the Grandmaster, and he's worried about clothes? She tried not to think of the trip to Tsing. Though a corset wasn't comfortable, it beat a dagger in the heart. It would be a sore trial if she endured the former only to suffer the latter.

The chime sounded, and Lem hurried to answer the door.

Sereth kept his attention on his opponent, though his curiosity was piqued. *Another new student, maybe. More skilled than this one, I hope.* He side-stepped a sword thrust, tapped his foot in a feint, and parried the expected stop-thrust. His riposte was deflected, and the exchanged continued with a quick rattle of steel on steel.

Lem's voice rose in protest, then quieted. *Not a student, then.* Heavy footsteps clomped across the wooden floor, and Sereth's student turned his head toward the interloper. Sereth took the opportunity, lunging full extension to thrust the tip of his sword hard into his opponent's chest.

"You're dead, young lord!"

"Damn it!" The boy pressed a hand to the spot, but dutifully lowered his rapier and stepped back, breathing hard beneath his wire mask.

"Never, *ever* let yourself be distracted while in combat. That's a quick way to die."

"Or get your nuts cut off!"

Sereth bristled at the crude comment and yanked off his mask. A burly man wearing the livery of the Royal Guard and a friendly smile stood just off the practice area. Sereth ignored the smile, stifled his response, and turned back to his student.

"That's all for today, Lord Westin. I think we're doing well here. You have the basics, but you need to break up your patterns. Mix things up. Fighting isn't ballroom dancing; if you lead your partner, you'll get a blade in your gut. And remember: concentration is key to survival."

"I'll remember, Master VonBruce. Thank you." The young noble racked his weapon and accepted Lem's help with the buckles of his fencing gear.

Sereth racked his practice sword and hung up his wire mask before he turned to face his visitor. "To what do I owe the pleasure of a visit by the Royal Guard?" He noted the stripes on the guardsman's collar. "Sergeant…"

"Tamir." The sergeant extended a hand.

Sereth removed his fencing gauntlet to shake it, and found himself automatically assessing the man. The handshake was firm, but without the undue pressure of intimidation. Scars of experience on the man's fingers and hand indicated that he was a swordsman, though a cauliflower ear suggested that he wasn't a stranger to fisticuffs. And despite being shorter than Sereth by several inches, the guardsman outweighed him by at least two stone. But what caught Sereth's attention was the name—*Tamir*. This was Norwood's first sergeant, who, according to Mya, was pursuing the black darts. *What in the Nine Hells is he doing here?*

"Sereth VonBruce at your service, Sergeant." He loosened the clips of his plastron, and draped it over the rack. "What can I help you with?"

"I have a few questions, Master VonBruce." He looked around as if thinking of buying the place. "You just opened this little training school, didn't you?"

"Yes, I did."

The door chime jingled again as the young noble departed. Lem began tending to the fencing gear. Sereth took no overt notice, but realized that the move put the guardsman between them. Lem was prepared for trouble, and inexperienced enough to precipitate it. The last thing Sereth needed was a dead guardsman on his hands. Not only would he have to abandon the salon, he'd need an entirely new identity.

"Lem, help me out of my gear while I speak with the sergeant here."

"Yes, sir." Disappointment flashed across Lem's face, but he dutifully did as his master requested.

Sereth turned back to Tamir with a smile. "To answer your question more precisely, Sergeant, I opened the salon just over week ago. Does the Royal Guard now investigate all new businesses?"

"Not all of them. So, you're new to teaching, eh?"

"No. I sometimes helped train the novice students for my former master."

"Horice DeVough."

"Yes." *So that's it. Someone must have identified me as Horice's bodyguard.* Sereth turned so Lem could unbuckle his practice jacket.

"And Master DeVough died recently, didn't he?"

"Yes, he did." Sereth wasn't worried. He had prepared for this possibility, and his answers came easily. The Master Blade shook his head ruefully. "I also worked as his bodyguard, so you can imagine how I felt."

"Yeah, having a bodyguard didn't seem to help him much. I take it you weren't there when it happened?"

"No. I didn't even know he'd gone out that night."

"So how did you find out he was dead?"

"When I showed up for work the next day, the household staff told me Horice had gone out and not come back. The following day it was all over the city that he was one of those killed in West Crescent, so I assumed I was out of a job."

Tamir narrowed his eyes. "Why didn't the household staff mention a bodyguard?"

Sereth shrugged. "I don't know, Sergeant. I guess you'll have to ask them."

Sereth was, in fact, telling the truth. He had arrived at Horice's the day after the battle to establish an alibi, but hadn't been back since. It was curious, though; if the staff hadn't told the Royal Guard about him, who had?

"I will. So, let me get this straight. He employed you as his personal bodyguard, then didn't take you along on the night he was killed?" Tamir's snort of laughter might have been either derision or disbelief. "That was stupid of him, wasn't it?"

"Yes, it was."

"Did Master DeVough often go out without you?"

"How would I know if he did?"

"I don't know. That's why I'm asking."

"Not to my knowledge."

"And you went with him everywhere else?"

"I have no way to know that, either." Sereth shrugged out of the stifling jacket and wiped the sweat from his face with a towel. "I accompanied Master DeVough a great many places. At least once, I wasn't there to protect him."

"And where exactly were you when your master was killed?"

"Home."

"Alone?"

"Yes."

"So, you don't know who he went out to meet?"

"Sergeant, if I didn't know he'd gone without me, how would I know who he went to meet?" Sereth frowned at the guardsman. The tactic was old and simple; Tamir was trying to trip him up. But Sereth was neither stupid nor unprepared for this line of questioning. "Do *you* know who killed him?"

"Not yet, but we expect to find out soon. Do you know if DeVough had any business with the master of the Bargeman's Guild? A Youtrin Dorfino?"

"No."

"What about a West Crescent madam by the name of Patrice DeLaCourse?"

"Horice did go to West Crescent on occasion. I don't know that name, but he had a number of...lady friends."

"Anyone in particular stand out?"

"Not really, Sergeant. They were pretty much all birds of a feather, if you know what I mean."

"He didn't tell you about any of these ladies?"

Sereth sighed in feigned exasperation. "I wasn't his *friend*, Sergeant Tamir, I was his employee. It wasn't my job to pay attention to the women he...slept with. It was my job to keep him alive."

"And you failed, didn't you?"

"That's right, because my master was an idiot."

"That's not a very kind thing to say."

"You didn't know him, Sergeant. Horice wasn't a very kind person."

"You apparently didn't know him very well either if you didn't know who he was doing business with."

Sereth barked a laugh. The sergeant was no fool. "You're right there."

"And now you've got your own training school." Tamir looked around again. "Must have put you in debt to set this up. Is it paying off?"

"Not yet, of course, but I've got other irons in the fire."

"Oh? And those are…"

"I provide personal security for people who can afford it. You may know some of my clients. Most of them live north of the river."

"Personal security. Is that a fancy way of saying that you hire out bodyguards?"

"Yes. If you'd like a list of my clients, I'd be happy to provide it."

"Do many of them know that your former master died because you weren't there to protect him?"

"I wasn't there to protect him because he didn't want me there, Sergeant Tamir."

"And do you know why he didn't want you there?"

Sereth rolled his eyes. "No, Sergeant, Horice didn't tell me he was going out late at night without my protection, why he was going out, or who he was going to meet. If I knew the answers to any of those questions, I'd tell you. I didn't like Horice much, but I didn't want him dead."

"But, because he's dead, you've got this nice business." One of the sergeant's thick eyebrows rose.

Sereth narrowed his eyes. "I resent your implication, Sergeant."

"Was I implying something?" Tamir's look of surprise was so utterly false that it would have gotten him a round of laughter had he been on stage.

78

Sereth didn't laugh. "I gained nothing from Horice's death except the impetus to strike out on my own. I now earn less, work harder, and am obliged to rely on my reputation with the young gentlemen who are my students, a reputation that you probably just damaged by barging into my school in the middle of a session."

"Don't take offense, Master VonBruce. I'm only trying to solve a murder here. Several, in fact."

"I wish I could help you, Sergeant." Sereth put everything he had into the lie. Fortunately, years as a spy within his own guild had prepared him well.

"Very well then, Master VonBruce." Tamir sketched a short bow just a shade away from mockery. "Good luck with your new business. I hope the personal security you hire out are better at keeping their charges alive than you were."

Sereth was too experienced to fall for Tamir's provocative taunt. "Lem, show the good sergeant out. We're done here."

Tamir smiled, nodded once, and left.

As the ring of the door chime faded away, Sereth heaved a sigh, pleased with the way the interview had gone. There was no way he could be connected with Horice's death.

"Clean up here, Lem. I'm going home."

"Yes, Master."

Sereth changed his shirt and donned his jacket and weapons, all the while deep in thought. He found it interesting that Tamir was investigating both the Fiveway Fountain killings and a black dart that apparently matched the one that that had killed Lad's wife. Of course, that was where she was killed. Had more darts been fired that night? Regardless, Lad would want to know about Tamir's visit.

As Sereth left the studio, he considered Lad. At their meeting yesterday, the guildmaster had appeared distracted, though no less committed to finding Wiggen's killer. Even desperate.

I can't blame him. Sereth's mood plummeted as he considered his own plight, and his pace quickened. *At least Jinny's alive.* But for how long, if she remained hostage to Hensen's growing demands?

Two days, and still no word from Kiesha... They weren't taking his ultimatum seriously. They'd called his bluff, but they didn't know that Sereth wasn't bluffing. Come hell or high water, he was going to get his wife back. And if Hensen wouldn't give her back, Sereth would just have to take her.

Chapter VI

Kiesha lurched out of a fitful sleep, the screams from her nightmare fading into the chiming of a bell. It was the smallest of the three bells beside her bed, high-pitched and harsh, announcing a visitor at the door. A glance at the clock on her dresser told her that this wasn't a social call. It wouldn't be the first time one of her spies arrived late with urgent news. Blinking away sleep, she pulled on a robe as she trundled downstairs.

At the bottom step, she jolted to a stop. "Sereth!"

The assassin squared off with Jamesly, the night butler, his arms crossed, a determined look on his face...and all his weapons in place. Jamesly looked equally determined, and well he might. He had orders that Sereth wasn't allowed one step further into the house without disarming. Neither man appeared ready to relent.

At least he's alone, Kiesha thought as she noted the bolted front door. Even if a dozen Blades lurked outside waiting for Sereth's signal to storm the house, they would find no easy access. Every door and window was secured with deadly traps, and Jamesly was much more than a butler, capable and deadly, and within arm's reach of the bell pull that would summon the house guards. The master of the Thieves Guild didn't sleep unprotected.

Cinching the belt of her robe tighter, she stepped forward, but stopped well out of the assassin's reach.

"Good evening, Sereth."

"It will be if I leave here with my wife. Now, get Hensen."
He issued his command without taking his eyes off Jamesly.

So, it's to be another bout of impotent insistence. Hensen
had been right; Sereth was upset, but not suicidal. She could
deal with this. "I'm sorry, Sereth, but Master Hensen isn't
available right now. If you want to talk, just hand your weapons
over to Jamesly, and we'll talk."

"I'm through talking to you, Kiesha. It gets me nowhere."
He stepped toward her, but Jamesly moved between them.

"Sir, I really must insist—" The butler's hand shifted toward
the back of his jacket.

A dagger appeared at Jamesly's throat. Sereth had drawn it
so fast that the steel seemed to have materialized in his hand.
The assassin scraped the edge of the blade along Jamesly's neck
until it rested under his jaw.

Sereth's lips pulled back from his teeth in a sneer. "Go
ahead. Insist."

"Sereth, please!" Throwing caution to the wind, Kiesha
stepped forward, her hands open and unthreatening. "Just relax.
I'll get Hensen for you, but you barging in here with steel in your
hand isn't going to get you what you want."

"Oh? And how do you know that?" Without moving his
blade from Jamesly's throat, he reached around and confiscated
the dagger sheathed beneath the butler's jacket. Flipping it in his
hand, he aimed it at Kiesha. "Maybe I don't want what you think
I want."

Kiesha froze. She had little doubt that he could bury the
blade in her throat with a flick of his wrist. Was he really so
desperate that he would kill her? He had to know what would
happen to his wife if he did. She took a deep breath and girded
her nerve.

"Killing Master Hensen's *butler*, or even *me* for that matter,
is not going to get you Jinny back, Sereth! If you want to talk to
Hensen, you're going to have to give up your weapons. He
won't speak to you if you're armed."

82

"Wanna bet on that?"

"I don't—"

Sereth moved.

Before Kiesha could gasp, he snatched her wrist and jerked her into a hard embrace, a blade resting against her neck. His other dagger stood out from Jamesly's right shoulder, buried hilt-deep. The butler staggered back with a grunt.

"I think he'll talk to me now."

"Sereth!" She grasped his wrist with her free hand, but couldn't pull the knife from her throat. Cold steel scored her flesh when she swallowed. Her other hand throbbed, clutched so tightly in his grasp that she thought her bones might snap.

Jamesly drew a second dagger from beneath his coat. He ignored the blade in his shoulder, though his right arm hung limp. "Let her go!"

"Go piss up a rope, Jamesly." Sereth's grip and stance remained firm. "One step and I cut her throat, then I draw this pig sticker at my hip and put it in your eye."

"Jamesly, don't!" Kiesha swallowed her fear. She had never thought that Sereth would go this far to get Jinny back. Even though he hadn't slit Jamesly's throat when he easily could have, he'd already crossed the line. He was desperate enough to risk his life, and probably wouldn't balk at taking hers. But she wasn't about to give up yet. "Just pull the bell rope for Hensen, and—"

"I give the orders here, Kiesha, not you." Sereth's grip on her wrist tightened even more, pain lancing up her arm as the bones ground together. "Touch a rope, Jamesly, and it'll be the last thing you ever touch. Drop the blade and get face down on the floor. Now!"

"Do it!" Kiesha ordered. She didn't want Jamesly to die on her behalf.

"I can't lay flat with your knife in my shoulder," Jamesly complained.

"Pull it out then, but drop the other first."

Steel thumped to the carpet. Jamesly hissed in pain as he pulled the knife from his shoulder and dropped the blade. A dark red stain began to soak through his immaculate white jacket. Ripping a pocket off his shirt, he pressed it into the wound to staunch the bleeding.

"On the floor!"

Jamesly knelt, then lay flat.

"Good. Now, hands behind your back."

Sereth snaked a leg around Kiesha's and flipped her down onto the floor next to the hapless butler, twisting her arm and pinning her wrist between her shoulder blades with his knee. She could barely breathe, and thought her shoulder might pop out of the socket. A bloody dagger lay only inches from her face, but she knew she'd die if she tried to reach it. Jamesly grunted, and she heard cloth ripping, but couldn't turn her head to see. Finally, the pressure on her back eased, and Sereth jerked her to her feet, his knife back at her throat. Jamesly lay with his forearms tied together behind his back, a jacket sleeve serving as a gag.

"Sereth, please." Kiesha gasped in pain as he pulled her arm back behind her, locked in his iron grip. She grasped his other wrist with her free hand, trying to keep the knife from her neck, but she couldn't budge him. *Gods, he's strong*! "This isn't the way!"

"What *is* the way, then, Kiesha? I've tried talking. I've tried *begging*!" He frogmarched her to the stairs. "Now I'm going to try a simple trade: you for my wife. Either I get Jinny tonight, or you die, and I see how many pieces of your boss I have to cut off before he sees things my way. Now, where is he?"

"He's in bed." *Alone, I hope.* The hostess from *The Overlook* had attended a small dinner party that evening. Kiesha didn't know if she had stayed. "Third floor, to the left."

"Let's go wake him." He pushed her up the stairs without releasing his hold. She had to climb or fall, so she climbed. "Feel free to scream…once."

"I won't scream, Sereth, but I tell you, this won't work! Hensen won't trade your wife for me."

"Then your future's not looking very bright, is it? Move!"

They reached the third floor without incident or any more conversation. Kiesha, however, was anything but idle in thought. Sereth was a professional killer, with the strength and skill of a lifetime of training. If she provoked him, he'd slash her throat without a second thought. To survive this, she had to distract him and break free, divest him of the knife, or incapacitate him…before he could cut her throat.

None of those seemed likely to succeed.

At the third floor, Sereth pushed her toward the double doors at the end of the hall. Twisting Kiesha to one side, he smashed the latch with his boot heel. As splinters flew from the dead bolt, he thrust her to the fore and strode into Hensen's bedroom.

The woman's scream was truly spectacular.

By the time Kiesha's ears stopped ringing, Hensen had lifted his hysterical paramour from his lap and flung her aside. Fortunately for her, the bed was wide enough for six, and she landed in a rumple of silk sheets and pillows. Hensen rolled off the far side of the bed and leapt up with a short dueling sword in his hand. Considering his nudity and state of arousal, the blade seemed the lesser of two weapons.

"Sereth! What a surprise!"

To Kiesha's consternation, Hensen dropped the sword onto the bed and casually tugged his robe off the wall hook. His smile looked genuine, and he seemed unperturbed to have his lovemaking interrupted by an assassin holding his assistant hostage. He turned to his lover where she cowered against the headboard, clutching the sheets to her breast.

"Relax my dear. This won't take a moment, and then we'll get back to where we were." With the robe secured about his waist, he retrieved the sword and addressed the interloper. "Now, Sereth, I assume you barged in here for a *reason*. Did you want something specific? Did you bring my assistant along in hopes that we could have a foursome?"

"Shut your filthy mouth and bring me my wife!" Sereth pushed Kiesha forward, sidestepping to put the wall at his back.

"Your dear Jinny is no longer here, Sereth." Hensen used the tip of his sword to clean a fingernail.

Kiesha gaped at his blithe lie, but remained perfectly still in Sereth's grasp.

"You really should learn not to betray your intentions with impotent threats. The moment Kiesha told me you planned to tell your master of our arrangement, I had your wife moved to a new, albeit slightly less comfortable, location. I'm afraid you're barking up the wrong tree, my boy."

"Then you better bring her here, or I'll stain your pretty carpet with this whore's blood!"

Hensen's benign smile fell and his eyes narrowed, belying his casual tone. "Let me explain exactly what will happen if you murder my assistant, Sereth. Even if you manage to kill me, which would be truly foolish of you, since I *alone* can free your wife from her captivity, the nice men holding Jinny will receive notice. They will then open a sealed envelope that contains explicit instructions as to just how your dear wife is to be brutalized. If she survives, they'll then sell her to a slave merchant who makes regular deliveries to the ogre tribes inhabiting the Forendell Pass region. You *do* know that the emperor signed a treaty with their chieftain that ensures peace between our peoples as long as a certain number of slaves are delivered every month, don't you? It seems they use them up rather quickly."

Kiesha marveled at the ease with which her father lied. She would have believed him herself if she didn't know that Jinny was actually only a hundred feet from where they stood, probably fast asleep in her plush feather bed. Even Hensen's lover's scream wouldn't have disturbed her, since her father had contracted a wizard to place a simple spell of silence upon the

86

room. Jinny could no more hear noise from outside, than the neighbors could hear her cries for freedom.

"You think you can take me, old man?"

"I might surprise you." Hensen flourished his sword with a leer toward the terrified woman in his bed. "Many are surprised at my...prowess."

The double-entendre passed by the hapless woman without recognition. *Too scared or too stupid,* Kiesha wondered.

"Regardless of whether *I* can take you, I'm sure my house guards can." As if on cue, the rumble of boots on the stairs reached them. "So you see, Sereth, despite the hostage you hold, you wield no real power here. I can get a new assistant in a week, a new carpet in less, and nothing you can do will save your sweet wife."

Kiesha felt a familiar wrench of pain in her heart. *Does he really care so little for my life? His own daughter?*

The house guards arrived with a clatter of steel. Four wielded swords, and two raised crossbows, all of them aimed at Sereth. Kiesha felt her captor shift his stance—just the distraction she needed. She dropped her hand away from Sereth's wrist, let her head loll forward in the semblance of a faint, and folded her knees. If he didn't cut her throat out of hand, this might work.

Sereth staggered with her weight, and pulled the dagger slightly away from her neck.

Now!

Kiesha reached back to Sereth's crotch, grasped the soft bulge of his testicles, and pulled down hard. At the same moment, she flung her head sharply back into the bridge of his nose.

The blade scored her neck before falling from his limp fingers to the carpet. Sereth collapsed to his knees. A wheezing moan escaped his bloody lips as he toppled over, both hands clutching his crotch. The guards charged, blades raised, but Kiesha stood her ground.

"Stop! We need him alive!" The wound on her neck stung as she probed it with her fingers. Though bloody, it was only superficial. She breathed a sigh of relief.

"She's quite right. We do need him alive." Hensen sheathed his sword, and reached for a dark wine bottle nestled in a silver ice bucket beside the bed. As if nothing untoward had happened, he poured fizzing pale wine into a pair of crystal flutes and handed one to the woman in his bed. She took it with a shaking hand and downed it in one gulp. As Hensen sipped the wine, he glanced over and frowned at Kiesha. "You're bleeding on the rug, my dear."

Kiesha stared at him for a heartbeat before recovering her composure. "Sorry, sir." She pressed the collar of her robe to the gash as the guards disarmed the hapless assassin and lifted him to his feet. "What do you want done with Sereth?"

Hensen pursed his lips. "Disarm him and take him home. I think he's learned his lesson."

"Very good, sir." Kiesha nodded to the guards, and they dragged Sereth out of the room. She paused at the door. "Anything else, sir?"

"Mmm." Hensen downed his wine and loosened the tie to his robe, his attention returning his paramour. "Yes. Have Sereth's wife moved in the morning. Someplace secure, but comfortable." He shrugged out of the robe, utterly unconcerned by his daughter's presence, and evidently undiminished in his ardor. "Now, my dear, where were we?"

Kiesha closed the mutilated door behind her and descended to her own room. *I can get a new assistant in a week...* Her stomach knotted with cold loathing as she slammed her bedroom door and examined her wound in the mirror. It was just a scratch. A dab of ointment and a bandage, and it would heal without a scar. The emotional wound, however, ran deeper.

Her hands shook as she opened a drawer beside her bed and withdrew a small bottle of spiced rum she kept there for nights when she couldn't sleep. She wrenched the cork free and took a long pull of the sweet liquor. The burn dissolved the lump in her throat and justified the tears that leapt to her eyes. Breathing deep, she willed her heart to stop pounding.

"Would a simple 'Thank you' have been too much to ask, you bastard?"

"Insomnia, Captain Norwood?"

"What the—"

The captain of the Royal Guard reacted with a soldier's reflexes, reaching for the sword that stood beside his bed and jerking it from its scabbard. His eyes scanned the darkness and centered upon Lad. Shrouded in shadow in the farthest corner of the captain's bedroom, he should have been all but invisible. The faint glow of his eyes must have given him away, but that didn't matter. He was just glad Norwood had finally come up to bed. Two hours sitting in the light evening breeze that wafted through the open window had tested Lad's patience. Staying focused was so much harder than it used to be.

"Please, Captain. I only came to ask a few questions, as before, but if you don't put down that sword, I may be forced to hurt you taking it away."

"I don't know who the hell you think you are, but you can't just break into my home whenever you feel like asking me questions!"

"Why not?"

The frank question seemed to take the wind out of the captain's sails. The tip of the sword drooped, but he didn't put it down. Frankly, Lad didn't care if Norwood was upset. He only cared about the information he could provide.

"I'm willing to trade information with you as I have in the past, Captain. I don't want to hurt you, but that sword in your hand only makes this conversation more dangerous. Dangerous for you, not me."

"Cocky bastard!" Norwood propped the sword against his night table, then sat rigid on the edge of the bed.

"I never boast, Captain. Believe what I tell you, for your own good." Lad withdrew from his pocket the glass vial that contained the black dart and tossed it onto the bed beside the captain. "My first question is: where did you come by a dart like this one?"

"I'll have to strike a light."

"The lamp next to you will do, but keep it low." Lad pulled the hood of his cloak down to hide his face as Norwood struck a match and lit the lamp. The warm orange glow illuminated the captain, but didn't penetrate the shadows.

Norwood squinted at the vial in the lamplight, and his eyebrows arched. "We found five darts like this at the site of a mass killing in a courtyard east of Fiveway Fountain."

"Five?" Lad failed to stifle his surprise. "How—"

"My turn," Norwood insisted as he held up the vial. "Where did you find *this* dart?"

"The same courtyard. Where *specifically* did you find them?"

"Lodged in the necks of five corpses scattered around the courtyard. Were you there?"

Lad's mind whirled. Wiggen's murderer had also killed five assassins during the battle. Why?

"*Were you there?*"

Lad focused on Norwood again, and answered slowly. "Yes, I was there."

"Whoever fired them knew what he was doing. The poison was—"

"White scorpion venom," Lad finished.

Silence reigned for a long moment before Norwood asked, "What the hell happened in that courtyard?"

Lad saw no reason not to give Norwood the truth. "I told you before that the factions of the Assassins Guild were fighting amongst themselves."

"Yes."

"They fought it out in that courtyard. The matter has been resolved. I'm sure you've noticed that violence around the city has eased off."

"I've noticed." Norwood frowned and shrugged. "I guess I can't complain when assassins kill assassins. That explains the other dart, too."

Lad sat bolt upright. "What other dart?"

"We found the first one a couple of weeks ago, over in Westmarket. Same type of dart, same method of attack, a shot to the neck from above. Two constables found a dead woman in an alley. They thought it was just another prostitute until they tried to move the body. She had a poisoned ring on her finger, and one of them grabbed it accidentally. He died in seconds."

Norwood's recitation hit Lad like a thunderbolt. He pictured the ring, its grooved needle dark-stained with poison. The woman had been trying to kill him, but instead had died with a black dart in her neck. The memory ignited a startling realization. *The assassin who saved my life that night also killed Wiggen. That doesn't make sense!*

After his near brush with death, Lad and Mya hypothesized that the Grandmaster sent someone to protect Lad so that he could, in turn, protect Mya until she assumed the guildmaster position. That the same protector had killed assassins during the Fiveway Fountain battle fit well into that theory. But if that was so, why was Wiggen killed? She posed no threat to either him or Mya. She was only there to protect Lissa because she wore the—

Guildmaster's ring. Lad clenched his fist on the ring on his finger. *Could the Grandmaster have ordered Wiggen's death? Impossible! No one knew she wore the ring except me. I gave it to her to protect her. Would she still be alive if...* Guilt washed over Lad like a scalding tide.

"The poison on the ring was different from that in the darts." Norwood's voice startled Lad out of his musing. "It was very

91

unusual. Something from a tropical fish. We haven't been able to trace its purchase or even find any shop that carries it."

"A tropical fish?" Lad knew of several toxins from tropical fish. A rare toxin might help him discover who sent the woman to kill him, and might even lead to the identity of his savior, Wiggen's killer. He wasn't about to discount *any* potential lead. "Do you remember the name of it?"

"Stone-something, I think. Stone-step fish, maybe?"

"Two-step stonefish." *Deadly indeed…*

"Yes. You're familiar with it?" Norwood sounded surprised.

"I've heard of it. What about the darts? Have you discovered who crafted them?"

"How do you know we're looking?" Norwood's eyes narrowed in suspicion.

"Because I'm looking, too, and we happened to look in the same places." Norwood scowled, and Lad saw the skepticism there. "Don't worry, Captain. You're my only informant within the Royal Guard."

"I'm not your *informant*!" He flushed with anger, but finally answered. "No, we haven't discovered the crafter, but we will. The darts are unusual enough that they should lead us to the killer."

"My thoughts exactly." Lad stood, tilting his head to keep his face in shadow. "I'd like my dart back please."

Norwood threw it to him without a word.

"Thank you, Captain. Please put out the lamp."

"One more question first. Did you ever find out who killed that wizard, Vonlith?"

"Yes, Captain, I did."

"And would you mind telling me who it was, and why the man was killed?"

Lad wasn't about to give up Mya, but he could give the Captain something. "Vonlith died, as most wizards do, because he knew too much. Knowledge can be deadly, Captain, which is why I won't be telling you the name of the murderer."

"You mean that if you told me, you'd have to kill me?"

"No, I wouldn't kill you. If I told you, you'd go looking for the killer, and *that* would get you killed."

"Why don't you let me be the judge of the danger?"

"Because you have no notion of the danger I'm talking about, and no way to protect yourself from it." He nodded to the lamp. "The light, Captain."

Lad waited until the lamp was doused, then reached for the window frame.

"One last question!" Norwood seemed determined to get all he could out of his visitor, but Lad paused, balanced on the frame. "The battle near Fiveway Fountain, the one between the Assassins Guild factions: who won?"

"I did."

Lad was out the window and up the drain pipe to the roof before Captain Norwood's jaw dropped.

CHAPTER VII

Lad strode through the early morning streets of the Eastmarket District after another sleepless night. This one, however, hadn't been due solely to obsessive thoughts about Wiggen. Since his meeting with Captain Norwood two nights ago, his mind had roiled like pit of vipers: darts and rings, toxins and poisons, assassins killing assassins.

Who can I trust? The list had become very short.

Could the Grandfather have ordered Wiggen's death to free the guildmaster's ring for Mya? Try as he might, Lad didn't see how it was possible. The Grandmaster might be able to get a letter from Tsing to Twailin in days instead of weeks, but only minutes had elapsed between the discovery that Wiggen wore the ring and her death.

And she was shot in the back, he reminded himself. All the others were shot in the neck. Was that difference relevant? He didn't know. What he did know was that there was a possibility—slim but undeniable—that the Grandmaster might have played a role in her death. *The one person in the world I can't kill.*

Lad's first thought had been to tell Mya and the other masters so they could include his supposition in their investigations, but careful consideration had changed his mind. If he told them of his suspicion, he'd have a rebellion on his hands in seconds. And while they might not be able to attack Lad directly, they could certainly denounce him to the Grandmaster. The trick, he'd realized, was to enlist their help

94

without giving them the incriminating details. That task was what had brought him on this errand.

The shop that Enola had inherited from Neera came into sight, a large, three-story building on the corner. A mortar and pestle decorated the placard that jutted out above the door, *The Perfect Solution* written in broad gold letters beneath. Through the smoked glass windows he saw that they already had customers. He'd hoped to arrive before they were busy.

A thousand scents assaulted Lad as he pushed open the door. Herbs and oils, extracts and toxins, acids and caustics all vied for his olfactory attention. His eyes, however, had little trouble picking out what he was looking for.

The Master Alchemist bent over an elaborate calcinator, peering in at the smoldering contents. Glancing up, she noticed Lad, and her naturally pale face blanched even more. Her mouth shifted—Lad could almost see her forming the word "Master"—but a quick look around the busy shop stopped her. Enola blew out the alcohol burner under the calcinator and hurried up to the thick stone counter that separated the work area from the shelves of merchandise.

"May I help you, sir?" Her strained smile and tremulous voice confirmed the subtle scent of fear that rose above the alchemical mélange.

Her fear roiled his stomach like the odor of rotten meat. He needed his masters to work with him, not fear him. A certain amount of fear was to be expected when someone held your life in their hands, but it was a poor substitute for devotion.

"I hope so." Lad kept his face neutral. "I require your services. May we speak in private?"

"Of course." Enola gestured, and he followed her into a cluttered office. Closing the door behind him, she turned and curtsied. "May...may I can help you with something, Master?"

"Yes. I need to know if you've ever used two-step stonefish toxin."

"I..." Her face paled again. "Yes, I have."

"Did you buy it somewhere here in Twailin?"

"No, Master. I extracted it myself from stonefish Master Youtrin smuggled in from Southaven. It's a rather tricky process."

Lad might have guessed. Enola was a gifted alchemist. It was no surprise that such delicate jobs had been entrusted to her.

"Did you know that Neera used it to try to kill me?"

"I did, Master." There was still fear in her eyes, but no evasion.

Lad remembered just how close he had come to dying that night, and clenched his hands to keep them from around her neck. *She was only doing her job…*

"Why didn't you inform me of this?"

"Why…" Enola wrung hands prematurely wizened from years of damaging chemicals, clearly flustered by his question. "The attempt failed, Master. I didn't think it important to inform you. Did I do wrong?"

"As it turns out, the authorities recovered the poisoned ring and identified the toxin, so that makes it important."

"Yes. They came asking questions about stonefish toxin. I told them nothing. I swear it."

"I'm not here to find fault, but to make a point. It's not for *you* to decide what is and isn't important. That's my job. But I can't do my job if I don't have *all* the information. So I need to know everything you know about the attempts on my life, Mya's life, or the lives of my family. Is that clear?"

"Perfectly clear, Master." She ducked her head, her hands clutched so hard her knuckles shone white. "I know that we sold sand-wasp venom to Horice about a month ago for an attempt to kill Mya. The month before, Neera sent someone to the *Golden Cockerel* to slip deadly nightshade into Mya's food, but we found out that the old barkeep caught the girl and made her eat it herself. That's all I can think of off the top of my head."

So Paxal killed to protect Mya. Interesting. "There was a spy caught at the *Golden Cockerel.* She took poison rather than be interrogated. Was she one of Neera's, too?"

"No, sir." Enola looked up at him with honest curiosity. "But if the body's still around, I might be able to extract the poison and find out what she took. Maybe I could trace it."

"I think the body's long gone. Ask Mya."

"Yes, Master. I'll be more forthright from now on."

Her willingness to improve encouraged him. "It's not your fault, Enola. The factions have worked independently for so long that learning to cooperate again may come hard, but it's essential. All the masters need to be open and upfront, both with me and each other." The truth of that made him feel like a traitor for keeping his own secrets from them.

"Yes, sir. I'll review my notebook and talk to my people to see what they know."

"Do that. Now, do you have any stonefish toxin in stock?"

"Yes, Master. I have some in my private collection. I'll get it for you!"

Enola rushed from the room before Lad could stop her. He hadn't intended to take the poison with him, but only to tell her she might want to dispose of it, since the Royal Guard was looking for it. The sudden thought of using it on Wiggen's killer, however, struck him as apropos. *The perfect vengeance...*

In less than two minutes Enola was back, proffering a tiny vial. "It doesn't look like much, but this is enough to kill a dozen people. This needle"—she pointed to a sliver of metal within—"is affixed to the cap, and hollowed to hold a single dose. Simply take off the cap, run the tip of the needle over whatever you want envenomed—dagger, arrowhead, whatever—and you're ready to go. I designed it myself."

"Ingenious." Lad liked the invention, but liked the twitch across her lips and a slight squaring of her shoulders more. He plucked the vial from her fingers and tucked it into a pocket.

"Only one more thing: have you finished compiling that list of large purchases of white scorpion venom?"

Enola's face fell and she swallowed heavily. "Not yet, Master. I'm having trouble—"

"This is why we're a guild. Ask for help. Work with Jingles if you need muscle, Mya if you need someone found, and Bemrin if you need to get the truth out of a contact. Clear?"

"Perfectly clear, Master."

"Good. Then we're done." He followed her out to the front of the shop, where he thanked her for her assistance, and they exchanged pleasantries.

Outside, Lad gulped a breath of fresh air in an attempt to banish the stifling atmosphere of the shop. He hadn't learned anything new, but at least he'd alleviated some of Enola's fear, which seemed to motivate her.

What next? What am I missing? Think! If he could just keep his thoughts from wandering, he might have a chance to find Wiggen's killer before he had to go to Tsing.

"It's been a godsdamned week! Where the hell is Hoseph?"

Kiesha scanned the bustling crowds of the Westmarket bazaar, looking for faces she didn't want to see. With Royal Guards and the Assassins Guild scouring the town, asking questions about black darts, she was getting nervous. It was only a matter of time before the garrote tightened and she was found out. How ironic that the very weapon she'd used to take so many lives might lead to her own death. She never thought she'd rue her choice of weapon. She had wanted the best, the most lethal one-shot-kill weapon she could get. How foolish she'd been, in retrospect, to have such unique if admittedly effective projectiles crafted.

I have to get out of here! Hoseph had promised to be in touch, to help her flee, but he'd left her dangling like a corpse on a gibbet. She cursed him silently for not providing her with a means to contact him. *Patino has a way.* Well, if she had to go through Patino, so be it.

Kiesha touched the wide silk choker that concealed the wound from Sereth's knife. It matched her fashionable gown perfectly. For a little while, she would be just one of the many gentry who had traversed the river on this fine summer day to attend the bazaar. She could think of no better venue to approach her quarry.

Gaily colored tents filled the public square, each fronted by a merchant hawking fabrics, trinkets, spices, or jewelry. The bazaar was more of a social event than serious shopping for the rich from Hightown and The Bluff districts. Here, they could titter over their lace-gloved hands at the quaint merchandise.

Kiesha searched the crowds. She knew Patino's face and habits from her investigation for Hensen. Unfortunately, she had never actually met him. She would have to bluff an introduction, but she wasn't worried; it was just another lie.

There!

The baron strolled through the bazaar as if he owned it, smiling and nodding to his peers. He was alone, save for the hawk-faced bodyguard following discreetly a few paces behind.

Got to be quick, before the lout steps in.

Kiesha planned her approach to take advantage of Patino's reputation as a lady's man. She took a perverse pleasure in using the beautiful clothes that Hensen provided her for such a clandestine purpose. Painting on a brilliant smile, she set forth to intercept her prey.

"Baron Patino! How very lovely to see you!"

"My dear, you look stunning today!" As Patino leaned over her gloved hand to kiss it, she noticed his gaze lingering at the cleavage revealed by her fashionably low neckline.

"Oh, you flatterer!" She batted her eyelashes and slapped her hand playfully against his chest. The bodyguard stepped forward, but the baron waved him away.

"What brings you out on this beautiful sunny day, my dear?"

"How could I stay indoors in such weather? After so much rain, I feel as if I'm bursting forth like a flower in bloom." Kiesha flung her head back and her arms out, knowing exactly the effect it would have on the man. He responded as if following stage directions, stepping in close to offer his arm, which she gratefully accepted. "I must say, you look quite dashing in that hat. Is it new?"

"Why, thank you. Yes, it is." Though obviously delighted to be promenading with such a beautiful young woman, Baron Patino's eyes clouded with consternation. Leaning in close, he lowered his voice and said, "I must apologize, my dear, but I don't quite remember where we've met before."

"We haven't." Kiesha squeezed his arm and smiled at his furrowing brow. "We do have a mutual acquaintance, though."

"Oh?" A wisp of suspicion crossed his brow. "And who might that be?"

Maintaining her delighted façade, she lowered her voice even further, leaning in as if they were deep in a tête-à-tête. "Suffice it to say that we work for the same person, Baron."

"Work?" Patino chuckled, looking honestly surprised. "My dear, I'm of noble blood. I don't—"

"Oh, come now, Baron. Surely you remember our friend of the dreary crimson cloaks. He comes and goes like a breath of wind."

Patino stopped dead in his tracks, his eyes wide. "Who the hell—"

The bodyguard stopped also, his eyes narrow, his hand resting on the sword at his waist.

Kiesha laughed as if she had shared a shocking joke, patted Patino's arm, and tugged him back into step. "Now, now, Baron, we're on the same side here. I just need you to contact our friend for me."

"I don't know who you are or what you're talking about." His voice, though barely audible, shook with intensity.

Is he suspicious of me, or just nervous about talking here?
Kiesha wondered.

"I simply need to contact our mutual friend." She smiled at
him again and winked. "I know that you know who I mean, so
there's no point in continuing the charade."

"I am a noble of the Royal House. The only person in this
world I *work* for, my dear, is His Majesty, Tynean Tsing II!"
His eyes narrowed, though the rest of his face remained as blank
as a mummer's mask.

She couldn't fault the baron for not blurting out his
association with the Assassins Guild, but he was taking the
deception a bit too far. Breathing deeply to calm herself, she
forced a smile, squeezed the baron's arm, and stepped back.
"Your loyalty does you credit, Baron. I'll be sure to mention it
to our mutual friend when I next see him. And it's *essential* that
I see him soon. Please contact him and tell him that Kiesha
sends her regards, and that she must speak with him
immediately."

"I'll do nothing of the kind." He took her hand and kissed it,
then hardened his grip on her fingers. "I will, however, mention
your name when I next meet our friend. And I'll tell him that
you're woefully indiscrete. If you are what you claim, you *may*
only receive a reprimand."

"I would welcome a reprimand, Baron Patino." She smiled
broadly, curtsied, and left him. At least he finally admitted to
knowing Hoseph. She could only hope that he would contact
him, even if only to complain about her. She didn't care how
angry Hoseph might be, she wanted out of this mess. But until
she heard from him, what could she do but wait?

Kiesha fretted as she pretended to browse the bazaar, smiling
at the merchants while her mind whirled through her dilemma.
Nothing to do but wait... She had never been one to wait when
action might solve a problem more readily.

Who else could she turn to? Certainly not Hensen. *I can get
a new assistant in a week...* She wondered if she had unknown

brothers or sisters waiting in the wings to take over if she met her end.

No Hoseph, no Hensen, no hope. Kiesha had only herself to rely on. *It's time I started covering my tracks.*

"Who the hell is that?" Sereth watched Kiesha as she strolled through the bazaar in the company of an unknown nobleman. At least the man looked like a nobleman, though Sereth didn't recognize the coat of arms on his fancy jacket.

"Pardon me, miss." The pretty young girl arranging silk scarves in a stall's display turned to him with a smile. "Who's that fellow with the top hat there?"

"Oh, that's Baron Patino! Rumor is he's a lady's man, and the baroness don't even care. He's always got some fancy bit o' fluff on his arm. Bet you got a lady of your own who'd like a pretty scarf. You bargemen got a girl in every port, don'cha?"

Sereth smiled, passed her a silver half-crown and accepted the scarf she'd been showing him, all the while keeping an eye on Kiesha. Both of their disguises seemed to be working. While she blended in with the gentry, his canvas jacket and straw hat rendered him virtually invisible among the common folk. Bargemen were as common as cobbles in Twailin. No one gave them a second look.

He eased away from the stall as Kiesha left the baron and followed her through the bustling crowd. After some aimless frittering at the stalls, she left the bazaar and hurried down the street deeper into Westmarket. Sereth kept her just in sight. He'd been tailing her all day. At some point, he reasoned, she would lead him to Jinny.

Then it's payback time...

He winced as he rubbed his aching nose. The lingering pain, more to his pride than his face, reminded him that Kiesha was much more than just Hensen's assistant and go-between. He'd underestimated her. She'd gotten the drop on him and taken him down with uncanny skill. What other surprises did she have in store?

A few more blocks and Sereth knew where she was going. He'd tracked her from Hensen's home this morning to an undistinguished inn. She'd walked in wearing a simple day dress, and walked out looking like a countess. It made sense that she had someplace where she could store and change into her disguises; she could hardly come and go from Hensen's upper-class residence dressed like a streetwalker. As she entered the inn once again, he wondered who she would be next.

Sereth took a sidewalk seat at a blackbrew café two doors down and across the street, ordered a cup and a pastry, and watched. He had a perfect view of the inn's front and side doors, the only ways in or out, barring a window. He examined every woman who exited the inn: well-bred matrons, blushing maids, and servants sent out on errands. He spared barely a glance at the scullery maid in the nondescript gray dress stepping out of the inn's side door.

Not her style.

He was about to order another cup of blackbrew when the maid adjusted her headscarf. Her hand was pale and smooth, the fingernails clean and neatly manicured, not the red, calloused hand of a scullery maid.

Damn, she's good!

Sereth rose casually to his feet, dropped some coins onto the table, and started after her, lagging back a half block. Tailing Kiesha gave him a new appreciation for Hunters, and an admiration for the thief's skill. Her imitation of a work-weary scullery maid was flawless, and she made her occasional glance over her shoulder look casual. Even with so many people out and about, Sereth was hard-pressed to maintain his distance and also keep her in his sights. Scullery maids were as common as bargemen, and just as invisible.

Weapon of Vengeance

Kiesha trudged across the arched span of High Bridge, one among hundreds of people making their way from home after a hard day's work. On the other side of the river, she turned onto South Waters Avenue, following it for several blocks before turning into The Sprawls.

Sereth wrinkled his painful nose with distaste. The Sprawls wasn't where he had expected Kiesha to lead him. He knew the downtrodden district all too well, and the residents didn't care for strangers.

Nearly a third of Twailin's entire populace lived in The Sprawls...the bottom third. Most of them provided simple, unskilled labor to those who lived in the nicer districts: hauling cargo, delivering goods, cooking, cleaning, sweeping streets, grooming horses, and collecting waste. They lived here because they could afford no better. The environment fostered an "us versus them" attitude, and though most accepted their lot in life, there were others who fought to escape. Long ago, Sereth had been one of the latter, and he'd never looked back.

On these seedy streets, one more stooped and tired scullery maid heading home drew no notice. Few bargemen walked here, however, unless they were headed toward one of the seedier gambling dens, whorehouses, or taverns. Sereth ditched his straw hat and jacket in an alley, and dropped back farther. Kiesha glanced about whenever she turned a corner, but she hadn't spotted him yet.

Another corner, another glance, and Sereth ducked into a shadowed doorway, glad that he'd worn dark shirt and trousers beneath his disguise. Her gaze passed over his hiding spot without pause, and she moved on. Hurrying up to the corner, he peeked around the crumbling bricks. Dumpy little shops lined the block: pot makers, tinsmiths, and tinkers, if their faded signs were to be believed. Kiesha crossed the street and ducked into a tiny shop. Adopting the wary stride of a Sprawler—far too easily remembered for his comfort—Sereth walked past the shop, glancing sidelong at the grimy storefront. No placard

104

identified the shop, just a single character drawn on the black door in flaking gold paint. Sereth couldn't read the mark, but knew it was gnomish.

"What are you up to, Kiesha?" He swallowed hard as he imagined Jinny captive in this rat-infested section of town. Neither the Thieves Guild nor the Assassins Guild did much business down here, leaving the impoverished territory to the local street gangs.

Stopping at the corner, he leaned against a drainpipe in the twilight shadows and watched. The streets were still reasonably busy, but traffic declined as night fell. Honest folk didn't venture out after dark in this part of the city.

A gang of four street toughs rounded the far corner and strutted down the street. *They get younger every year*, Sereth thought. The oldest looked about fifteen. Each carried a stick with a long nail pounded through the end, identifying them as members of the Spikes gang, and Sereth was on their turf. Spying Sereth, they altered their course, grinning dangerously.

"You waitin' for a hackney, Norther?" the largest asked, flipping his spiked club in the air. The haft made a meaty pop when he caught it. Sprawls gangs referred to anyone who lived north of their own territory as Northers.

"Bugger off." Sereth drew two gleaming daggers from his sleeves. "I'm here on guild business, and it's not yours." He didn't say which guild. It wouldn't matter to the Spikes anyway.

"Your guild don't have no business down here, Norther, but I might take one of those shiny daggers from you for a souvenir." The others chuckled as they approached.

The last thing Sereth needed right now was a fight, but he'd have to deal with these toughs so he could resume his watching in peace. Even as he opened his mouth to warn them off, he noticed Kiesha emerging from the shop. *Damn!* The four Spikes stood between Sereth and his quarry, but he didn't want to draw her attention. She closed the door carefully, but then only glanced his way before hurrying in the opposite direction. If Sereth didn't conclude this soon, he would lose her.

"I don't have time to kill you right now, so why don't you just take one of my daggers and go." Sereth flipped his right-hand blade and threw it. The fine steel thunked into the leader's raised club. Sereth had another dagger out before the boy even realized what had happened. "Now bugger off, or each of you gets a souvenir in the eye."

The Spikes gaped. The stunt stopped them cold, just as Sereth intended, but they still stood between him and Kiesha. If he tried to force his way past them, he'd likely get a spike in the back of his head.

The leader wrenched the dagger from his club and examined the blade. Like all of Sereth's knives, it was perfectly balanced and razor sharp. The boy's eyes widened as he realized that it would sell for more than he made in a week, then narrowed and darted toward his friends. Sereth recognized the struggle between defiance and avarice. No Sprawls gang member could afford to appear weak among his fellows. Sereth had to give him a way out.

"I tell you what. Consider that a down payment. You may have heard that the guild is recruiting down here. We're serious about it. My name's Sereth, and I'm the guild's Master Blade. You come onboard with us, and every single Spike will be carrying a dagger like that. You can still be Spikes and keep your territory, but you can be Blades, too. Tell your boss about my offer, and ask for me at Donnovon's Chandlery on South Waters."

The defiance in the boy's eyes shifted to determination as he gazed again at the shiny dagger. He nodded. "We'll see what Dangley has to say about your offer."

"Good." Sereth hadn't known the Spikes had a new leader, but then, gang leaders didn't last long in The Sprawls. Tucking his daggers away, he nodded down the street. "Now, if you don't mind, I'm *working*."

"Oh, uh. Yeah. Sure." The leader nudged his mates and they moved along.

Kiesha had vanished. Sereth dashed to the corner and peered around, but she was nowhere to be seen.

"Damn!" The Blade hesitated. Should he hurry back to the inn where she changed clothes or... He looked over his shoulder at the tiny shop. Curiosity niggled the back of his mind. What was Kiesha doing here? He could always pick up her trail back at Hensen's house, but right now, he needed to know what was inside that shop.

Sereth strode back and turned the door handle. It didn't budge, and a glance confirmed that a shade had been pulled down inside the filthy window. Up and down the street, other shops remained open late to serve homeward-bound residents. Why was this shop locked up, not only early, but right after Kiesha left?

Only one way to find out.

Sereth fished a tiny packet of tools from his back pocket, glanced up and down the street to confirm that the few passersby were paying him no attention, and slipped two picks into the lock. A wiggle and careful pressure with one while he flicked the other over the tumblers yielded immediate results. The handle turned in his grasp, and the door swung open.

Sereth ducked under the low lintel and entered the dark shop, wary of the low ceiling within. The gnomish symbol and diminutive door warned him that the shop would be unaccommodating to someone over six feet tall. The shorter races built to their own dimensions. If humans and elves didn't deign to stoop, well, they needn't enter.

The darkness around him buzzed with the ticks and whirs of clockwork devices, but there was no greeting or warning from a proprietor. Closing the door, Sereth noted a metal-reinforced frame and heavy iron bar meant to secure the door from the inside. *So why wasn't the bar thrown when the door was locked?* He secured the bar now to ensure that no one else could enter, and waited while his eyes adjusted to the gloom.

As shapes resolved around him, Sereth was surprised to discover no clocks in the shop. Instead, the shelves were crowded with finely crafted clockwork toys. Windup dogs, cats, horses, people, and even pigs blinked and nodded at him. Sereth had seen similar toys in other shops, but closer inspection revealed a macabre theme to these creations.

A rocking horse bobbed up and down, its little rider swinging a thin wire lariat that garroted a fleeing man. Two goblins rode a seesaw, a human head sliding back and forth on a wire between them in a gruesome game of catch. A headsman wielded a bloody axe to lop off a woman's head, which tumbled into a little basket before popping up to be lopped off again. A zombie beat a teasing dog with its own severed leg...

Sereth marveled at the ingeniously grim toys—*Gnome humor?*—before recalling his real question. *Why did you come here, Kiesha?*

He moved through the shop, careful not to touch any of the toys. Gnomes also enjoyed crafting deadly little traps to dissuade would-be thieves. Beyond the shelves stood a knee-high counter, a veritable sea of clockwork fishes and frogs swimming beneath the clear glass. Behind the counter, a simple curtain blocked his view into the backroom. Sereth stepped silently around the counter and stood with his back to the wall beside the doorway. The tip of his longest knife teased the curtain aside. He was greeted by the dim glow of lamplight and the sickly sweet scent of blood.

Peering through the gap, he spied a diminutive corpse beside the workbench. He eased the curtain back and scanned the tiny back room; no one else was here.

Sereth slipped inside and squatted down, careful to avoid the congealing pool of blood around the gnome's oversized head. The little toymaker's eyes stared blankly at the ceiling, his expression shocked and pained. His throat had been efficiently cut, so recently that blood still oozed from the wound. Sereth laid a hand on the corpse's forehead; still warm.

Standing, the assassin surveyed the scene with a professional eye. Blood spotted the tools and partially finished devices atop the bench, and a trail of droplets decorated the wall behind it. The toymaker had apparently been killed at his bench, his throat cut from behind. *A clean job*, Sereth decided, *worthy of an assassin. Kiesha's just full of surprises...unless she had an accomplice.*

Sereth glanced around, but not even a gnome could hide amidst the benches and shelves of junk. The shop's back door was barred and padlocked. A quick inspection revealed dust on the lock. No one had gone out that way recently. Beside the door, a ladder led up to a hatch in the ceiling. The gnome probably lived up there, and if Kiesha did have an accomplice, they might be up there right now. Sereth listened carefully. No noise from above, but that might mean that someone was listening for him. Dagger at the ready, he put his foot on the lowest rung and lifted the trap door a finger-width.

Nothing.

Cautiously, he poked his head into the upper space. As suspected, it was a small apartment, boasting only a mattress on the floor, a tiny dresser, an undersized table, and single chair. No accomplice lurked in the shadows.

Sereth shook his head in wonder as he added assassination to Kiesha's list of accomplishments. He wouldn't underestimate her again. Staring down at the body, curiosity spun in his head like one of the gnome's macabre toys.

Why in all the Nine Hells and Seven Heavens would you kill a gnome toymaker, Kiesha?

Sereth meticulously searched the workshop, picking cautiously though the pervasive clutter, looking for answers. Tools, paints, and a thousand tiny clockwork parts filled boxes and shelves, but nothing that might interest a thief...or provoke a murder.

Drawers, cupboards, and the bench top finally completed, Sereth ran his dagger beneath the lip of the bench, stopping when the blade clicked against metal. Still wary of traps, he slowly applied pressure, and a hidden catch popped open. A slim drawer slid silently out from the shadowed recess on long, well-oiled hinges. Sereth caught his breath.

"Motherless son of a…"

A dozen black darts nestled in velvet-lined nooks, darts identical to the one that killed Wiggen. Not one assassin at the Fiveway Fountain battle had been able to lift a hand against her because she wore the guildmaster's ring. But the ring wouldn't have prevented a thief from killing her, a thief skilled at assassination. He glanced at the dead gnome at his feet.

Kiesha!

The darts were the method, and the dead gnome indicated that she had the skill. *Opportunity?* With a sinking heart, Sereth recalled Kiesha's attempted seduction. He had tried to expunge the memory, but now recalled how he had blurted out the location of the planned exchange of Mya for the guildmaster's baby daughter.

What about motive? What could possibly have provoked Kiesha to kill Lad's wife?

That, Sereth decided, *is for Lad to discover.*

He lifted a dart from the tray to present to his guildmaster as evidence, but before he slipped it into his pocket, another thought came to mind. The Royal Guard was also looking for whoever had made the darts. A decaying corpse would draw vermin and eventually the authorities, even in this neighborhood. He couldn't afford to have them make the same discovery. He emptied a small box of springs and gears onto the cluttered bench top, and put the entire contents of the hidden drawer—the dozen darts and loose components for several more—into it. He pressed the wooden lid snugly atop the box, and slid the drawer back into hiding.

Now to get the hell out of here without being seen.

110

Barred doors would delay the discovery of the corpse, so he needed another way out. Tucking the box with the darts under his arm, Sereth climbed the ladder and crawled into the dingy little loft. A window in the back wall opened into the narrow alley.

"Perfect."

Sereth grabbed a soiled blanket from the rumpled little bed and tied the box into a bundle he could sling over his shoulder. He peered out the window, wrinkling his nose at the stink of refuse. Night had fallen, and the alley was empty. The assassin wormed his way out of the window, and hung from the crumbling brick casement by one hand while he closed it behind. He dropped down to the ground. As he started down the alley, the evidence bouncing over his shoulder, yet another thought struck him.

Lad will ask how I discovered this. His steps faltered. The truth would bring out his association with Kiesha and his treason against the guild. *He'll kill me.* Sereth's deep-rooted sense of self-preservation rose, and for a moment he considered throwing the parcel into the heaps of trash that fouled the alley. Then he reconsidered.

Lad would give anything to find his wife's killer, and Sereth now knew who that killer was. The information was priceless, but was it worth enough to spare Sereth's life? Even enough to get Jinny out of Hensen's clutches?

It all depends on Lad.

The guildmaster knew what it felt like to have a loved one taken from him, to be pressured into betrayal. He had killed the other masters not out of hatred or retribution, but to save his daughter.

There was only one way to find out: tell the truth.

Sereth thought long and hard on his walk home. By the time he was out of The Sprawls, an alarming notion resolved in his mind. *Kiesha killed the gnome because she knows Lad is hunting her! She's covering her tracks.* That meant she was

111

running scared, perhaps intending to flee. If Sereth delayed, she might vanish, and his evidence would be worth nothing. Urgency now trumped caution.

"Tonight. It has to be tonight..."

CHAPTER VIII

By the time Kiesha reached home, evening had deepened into night, and her feet were long past aching. With the gnome dead, all she had to do was to get rid of her blowgun and darts, and there would be no physical evidence linking her to Wiggen's murder. Only two people knew for certain what she'd done, and neither her father nor Hoseph seemed likely to betray her. Sereth might suspect that she had been at the scene, but she had the threat of Jinny to manipulate him.

The backdoor lock clicked as she turned her key to the right, then clicked and clacked again as she turned it back to the left. She felt a tingle up her arm as the elaborate device disengaged. If she'd released the key or inserted the wrong one, the magically sealed portal would have reduced her to a smoldering corpse. *Only the best security for the Master of the Thieves Guild*, she thought sourly.

Slipping inside, Kiesha gently pushed the door shut, inserted her key and turned it again. The clatter of the mechanism relocking made her cringe. If anyone saw her, they'd immediately inform Hensen, who would insist that she come in to dinner and give a report of her activities.

The far louder clatter of pots and pans set her mind to rest. The staff was busy preparing the evening meal. Slipping past the kitchen and scullery without anyone spotting her was easy. Up the service stairs and down the hall, she thought of where best to dispose of her weapon and darts. *The river or the sewer*? The former was farther, but more likely to keep the evidence lost.

Easing into her room, Kiesha closed the door and breathed a sigh of relief.

"Good evening, Kiesha. I trust you're well."

Hoseph's greeting startled her at first, but then a flood of relief washed over her. He had gotten her message after all. Then she remembered why she'd gone to Patino in the first place, and the rest of her excruciating day, and anger supplanted all other emotions.

"No, I'm *not* well." She sat on the edge of her bed without even looking at him, and plucked at the laces of her shoes. "I've been dancing on a frying pan, and *you* were nowhere to be found! You *said* you'd be in touch!"

"Calm down, and don't bother taking off your shoes. We're leaving directly." He stood up from her dressing chair, his sanctimonious manner unaffected by her tirade.

"Leaving? I can't leave right now. I've got things to do."

"Don't be petulant, Kiesha. I told you I'd take you to a safe place. Your recent activities have made it too dangerous for you to stay in Twailin."

"My recent *activities*?" She gaped at his gall. "When you didn't show up for a *week*, I decided to take matters into my own hands."

"Yes. You contacted Baron Patino." His lips pursed into a disagreeable moue. "That was not wise."

"Well, at least it got your attention. If you'd given me some means to contact you myself, as I asked, I wouldn't have had to go to Patino. You said you'd be in touch, and left me hanging. What did you expect me to do? Anyway, I don't need rescuing anymore. I've been covering my tracks. I've a couple more things to do, then I should be safe."

"What you've done is ruin a perfectly good operative, draw attention to yourself, and put your master's interests in jeopardy." He stepped toward her and held out one hand while flipping that creepy little skull into his other. "Now come along."

Kiesha glared at him. He hadn't listened to a thing she'd said. It was just like her father all over again. Well, she wasn't going to kowtow any more, and there was no way in hell she was going to take his hand. When he said he'd take her to a safe place, she'd assumed it would be by carriage, not wafting through the cosmos like smoke on the breeze.

"No!" She leapt off the bed, reaching for the dagger she'd used to kill Ghulgen. Though she didn't draw it, the solid hilt felt reassuring in her hand. "I've got one more thing I need to do tonight. There's still evidence linking me to Wiggen's death. I've got to get rid of it!"

Hoseph's face darkened, and the muscles of his jaw bunched. "You've already done too much that you weren't told to do! Our master doesn't want *initiative* from you, only obedience. Now come here!"

He stepped forward, but she sidestepped again.

"If *your* master wanted a spy who didn't think for herself, then you recruited the wrong woman!" She slipped the knife from its sheath and held it steady in front of her. "You may as well leave. I'm not going with you, and one scream will bring the house guards."

The priest's eyes flicked between the knife and her face. "You will *not* scream, Kiesha." He looked more annoyed by her reaction than concerned about the dagger in her hand.

"Oh? What makes you think—"

With a single mumbled word, a chill flash of blackness burst forth from the little skull. Her mouth gaped to scream, but only a whimper escaped as despair crushed her heart. A lifetime of shame, guilt, and self-loathing sapped her anger, her strength, and her will to resist.

Hoseph stepped toward her, reaching out his hand, and she stumbled back, jerking her weapon out of reach. The dagger felt heavy, her grasp clumsy. He snatched her other wrist with a grip like a steel trap. Dark tendrils blossomed from the skull talisman, writhing to engulf him, snaking down his limbs and

115

stretching out toward Kiesha. Where the tendrils touched, flesh faded into mist.

"N….no!" A deathly chill shuddered through her as she watched her captive hand swallowed up.

With a strength born of terror, she clutched the dagger so tightly her knuckles whitened. Her very first knife-fighting lesson came back to her then. *Put the point into a vital spot, and you're done.*

Bending all her will, Kiesha thrust the blade into Hoseph's chest. Too late. The dagger pierced only the black mist. There was nothing left to stab. One last moment of panic, and the coldness of the grave pulled Kiesha into darkness.

"Master?"

Lad blinked. In front of him lay the list of names that Enola had provided. He remembered starting to review it, wondering if the owner of one of these names had killed Wiggen. Then, nothing…

How long this time? It had been early evening when he sat to read the list. Now it was full dark outside, and his back and neck ached from sitting at the desk. *Hours, at least.*

Looking up to Dee standing at the study door, he asked, "What is it?"

"Master Sereth is here, sir. He says it's urgent."

"What's the hour?" Lad stood and stretched, vertebrae popping with each twist.

"Near midnight, sir."

Four or five hours, then… He clenched his teeth so hard that his jaw ached. *This has to stop! I have to focus!* Forcing himself past the exhaustion, past the memories, he realized what Dee had said. *Sereth…urgent…near midnight…* "Bring him here."

116

"Yes, sir." Dee left, and a moment later returned with the Master Blade in tow.

At first glance, Lad could see that Sereth was upset. He was also sporting a recently broken nose. Usually the most stoic of the masters, the Blade's face was rigid with tension, his eyes wide with worry and fear. Curiously, one of Sereth's six daggers was missing. He also wasn't wearing his rapier, and he clutched a small wooden box protectively. Lad's senses heightened at the irregularities.

"Thank you for seeing me, Master." Sereth bowed, stiff and jerky, so unlike his customary fluid and precise movements that it screamed apprehension.

This is serious. "What is it?"

The Blade cast a glance at Dee. "Alone, if you please, Master."

The strange request put Lad even more on edge. He had come to trust Dee more than he trusted most of the masters. His assistant saw more sensitive guild business than Sereth ever would. Despite his unease, he could think of no reason to refuse. After all, Dee was not a bodyguard, and Sereth could no more hurt Lad than he could pluck out his own eyes.

"Very well. Dee, wait outside."

"As you wish, Master." Dee bowed and left the room, his face stiffly expressionless. Lad heard him take five steps down the hall and stop there, close enough to quickly answer a summons, but far enough to give them privacy.

Lad nodded to Sereth. "Now, what is it?"

"The contents of this box will explain much, Master." He held out the container.

Lad's suspicion flared. Could this be a trap? The master's ring prevented Sereth from raising a hand to harm him, but what about handing over a lethal gift? Maybe he was being paranoid, but Lad was no longer just Mya's bodyguard. As guildmaster, he was a target, and he wasn't going to risk his life to ignorance, especially with Sereth acting so strangely.

"Take the lid off yourself."

"Of course, Master."

Sereth flipped open the lid without hesitation or any hint of evasion, and again held out the box. Convinced there was no threat, and consumed by curiosity, Lad took it.

Inside, black darts gleamed in the lamplight, identical to the one that had killed Wiggen. Lad's mind spun, and his hands trembled so badly that the contents of the box rattled. Among the darts lay a number of springs, cylinders, pins, and tiny needles. Disassembled darts, apparently. *Or preassembled!* Hope surged. Sereth had discovered the crafter.

"Where did you get this?"

Sereth hesitated, still clearly uneasy. "A gnome's shop in The Sprawls. A toymaker. I found him with his throat slit."

"What?" Lad's hope plummeted. With the crafter dead, the trail to Wiggen's murderer was broken. "We have to find out who killed him! Pull in all the—"

"Master, please." Sereth held up trembling hands. He took a deep breath and exhaled slowly. "I know who killed the gnome, and I know who murdered your wife."

The box fell from Lad's hands.

Vengeance…

Darts and components skittered across the rug like deadly black spiders. A scalding wave of heat flooded through him, igniting a visceral urge to strike out, to kill. He clenched his hands at his sides and stepped toward Sereth. "Tell me! Now!"

"I will, Master." Sereth stood his ground. "I'll tell you everything, but first I must ask you a favor."

"A *favor*?" Lad's teeth ground together. "What the hell are you talking about? Tell me who killed Wiggen this instant!"

"I'll tell you, Master, though it may mean my life."

"Your life is *mine*, Sereth!" Lad burned with the urge to break the Blade in half.

118

"Yes, Master." Sereth's jaw clenched, but his voice remained firm. "I only ask that you remember what it felt like when your daughter was held hostage."

"*What?*" Lad fought the urge to strangle the truth out of the Blade. What did Lissa have to do with this? "I'll *never* forget how that felt, Sereth. Now explain yourself!"

"Yes, Master. I ask you to remember, because our situations are similar."

"Similar?" Frustration surged into anger. Lad's hand shot out and grasped the front of Sereth's shirt. He jerked the Blade forward until their noses were barely an inch apart. "Stop talking in riddles! What in the Nine Hells is going on?"

"My wife has been held hostage by the Thieves Guild for more than two years."

"Your..." Lad's fury quenched as if he had fallen into an ice-bound river. He hadn't even known Sereth had a wife. He opened his hand, and the Blade stumbled back a step. *Two years...* "Why would they keep—"

"I've been spying for them, Master." Sereth's words came in a rush now, as if he was afraid that Lad would kill him before he had told his story. "They took her, and blackmailed me into spying for them. When I refused to give them any more information, they threatened to...to do horrible things to her."

"What does this have to do with Wiggen's murderer?"

"I was following one of their spies, the woman who was my contact, in hopes that she'd lead me to my wife. Instead, she went to the gnome's shop. After she left, I investigated and found the gnome murdered. I didn't understand why she would kill a gnome toymaker, but then I discovered the darts." Sereth swallowed and the muscles of his jaw clenched briefly. He took a shuddering breath and continued. "I remembered that I'd told her where the masters were going to exchange your daughter for Mya. I didn't know then that she was a killer, but when I saw how professionally the gnome had been murdered, and then found the darts, it all made sense. She must have been the one who killed your wife."

"You…" A chill trickled down Lad's spine. "You told them where to find us…"

"Yes, Master."

Lad reached out faster than a striking viper, not to grasp Sereth's shirt again, but his throat. The Blade's life pulsed beneath his fingers. He thought of all the delicate bones that would shatter if he just closed his hand. Sereth stood there helpless, unable to fight, and from the look of resolve upon his dark features, ready to die.

"I should kill you."

"My life is yours, Master," Sereth rasped. "That's why I asked you to remember how it felt to have your daughter held captive. If anyone could understand why I betrayed the guild, it would be you."

"And you think that will keep me from killing you?"

"No, Master, but at least you'd know why. I had no idea they'd kill Wiggen."

Was that the truth? In the end, it didn't matter. Wiggen was dead. Killing Sereth wouldn't bring her back. It would only prevent Lad from ever exacting vengeance on the person responsible for her death.

"You'll tell me this woman's name and where to find her. *Then* I'll decide whether or not to break your neck."

Sereth's throat flexed under Lad's fingers. "Yes, Master. Her name is Kiesha. She works directly for the master of the Thieves Guild, a man named Hensen. They live in a townhouse on Four Bells Avenue, here in Barleycorn Heights, two blocks south of the river on the east side of the street. It's the largest house on the block. If you want to catch her, you should act quickly. She knows you're hunting Wiggen's killer, and she's running scared."

Sereth took as deep a breath as he could with Lad's hand around his throat, his eyes now resigned. "If you intend to spend my life, sir, I'd ask that you please find my wife and free her. Hensen knows where she's being kept."

"But if you're dead, they have no reason to keep her, do they?"

"No, sir, but she knows too much. They might kill her to keep her quiet."

Lad stared at the Master Blade. Now he recognized the look in Sereth's eyes. It wasn't fear for his life. It was fear for the life of a loved one. *His wife...* Knowing what that felt like opened Lad's hand. The Master Blade gasped a breath and staggered back. Lad hadn't ruled out killing Sereth yet, but he needed information first.

"Why did you tell me this? Why not bargain with the Thieves Guild, your silence for your wife? You spied for them when you worked for Horice, why not now?"

"I'm done living like that, Master. I spied on Horice because it didn't seem like I had any choice. He would have killed me without listening to a word, and Jinny would have paid the price. Now...I do have a choice. I'd rather trust you than them. So if you decide to spend my life, please, just see that Jinny is freed." Sereth closed his eyes. "She's innocent, just like your daughter was innocent. I was stupid to marry her. All I did was put her in danger."

Was I stupid to marry Wiggen? Lad considered the notion and rejected it outright. He couldn't conceive what his life would have been without her. There were many things he would have done differently if he had the chance, but loving Wiggen wasn't one of them.

"Love sometimes makes us stupid, Sereth, but without it, what are we?"

The Blade's eyes opened, and desperation vied with hope within them.

"I want answers, Sereth, not just revenge. You're coming with me to find this Kiesha, and we're going to find out what's really going on here."

"Yes, Master." Sereth took another deep breath and rubbed his throat. "I can't think of a motive for Kiesha to kill your wife. She's Hensen's personal assistant, so obviously the Thieves Guild is involved. You'll have to ask Kiesha or Hensen."

"We *will* ask. But before we do, I need to know exactly what you told them in the weeks before Wiggen's death."

Sereth answered directly, though he looked abashed. "They were interested in anything and everything to do with you and Mya."

That stopped Lad in his tracks. Realization slammed through his mind: if Kiesha killed Wiggen, she also saved Lad's life in that rain-soaked alley. He and Mya had surmised that the Grandmaster of the Assassins Guild might be protecting them, but how could the Thieves Guild be connected? None of this made sense, but there was only one way to find out.

Lad strode to the door and opened it. "Dee!"

"Yes, sir!"

"Bring my work clothes. Sereth and I are going out."

Chapter IX

No place is impregnable to a sufficiently skilled and determined assassin. Remember!

Lad assessed Hensen's home as he assessed anyplace he wanted to break into. A thin strip of well-manicured grass and a low wrought-iron fence buffered the property from its neighbors. The house was twice the size of Lad's, built of tremendous granite blocks set close and polished smooth. The windows gleamed and the latches looked freshly polished. The front door—as wide as Lad was tall, and half again as high—stood in a marble portico lit by a hanging lantern. At its center hung a gold-plated knocker wrought in the likeness of an eagle, its talons gripping a crystal-studded laurel wreath. The overwhelming impression was rich, solid, and secure.

Lad picked out several different paths to the third floor window that would normally have been his chosen point of entry. Unfortunately, this was the home of the most powerful thief in Twailin. And thieves were just as skilled at keeping people out as they were at breaking in. They had to assume every door, window, pane of glass, and air vent was trapped. Jimmying a latch to crawl through a window would likely be a quick way to die.

Lad preferred working alone, but he couldn't deny that he needed Sereth's help here. The Master Blade knew the layout firsthand, and only he could identify Hensen and Kiesha. And yet, though Lad had resigned himself to Sereth's plan of entry, just the thought of it raised the hairs on the back of his neck. When Sereth first proposed it, Lad thought he was crazy.

"You're seriously suggesting we just walk up and knock?"

"Why not?" Sereth had ticked the reasons off on his fingers. "Someone's stationed in the front hall around the clock. Hensen gets reports at all hours. And they know me."

Lad remembered Norwood recounting the murder of Vonlith. Despite innumerable spells and magical traps, the runemage had fallen prey to an acquaintance—Mya—who gained entry simply by knocking. If the straightforward approach worked for her, perhaps it would work for them also.

Back at his house, the idea seemed feasible. Now Lad was having doubts again. "You're sure someone will answer? It's well past midnight, and there are no lights."

"I'm sure, sir," Sereth assured him. "Remember, the butlers wear daggers under their jackets, but this late, there might be a regular guard on duty. Whoever it is, don't let them pull on a bell rope."

"I remember." Lad glared at the Blade. "And *you* remember: don't kill anyone unless it's absolutely necessary. I don't want to start a guild war if I can avoid it. We're here for information, not blood." The blood would come later, once he knew exactly who was responsible for Wiggen's death. Kiesha may indeed have fired the lethal dart, but under whose orders?

The distant click of metal on metal caught Lad's ear. He tapped Sereth's shoulder, and they edged further back into the shadows of the manicured hedge. A moment later, a squad of city guardsmen rounded the corner and strolled past. In this upscale district, patrols were frequent.

When they'd gone, Lad whispered, "Your people are in position?" Another of Sereth's suggestions; Blades had been assigned to watch all possible exits, with orders to capture anyone who tried to escape.

Sereth checked his pocket watch. "They're ready, Master."

"Good. Let's go."

124

Lad and Sereth crossed the street and approached the house from an oblique angle. Lad strolled casually, his senses on high alert. Though he detected no shifting shadows or subtle noises that might indicate Thieves Guild watchers, he couldn't detect their own people either. Walking in the open made his skin crawl. Lad left Sereth before he could be seen by anyone peering out through the front door viewing glass, and sidled up beside the door with his back against the wall.

Pressing an ear against the doorjamb, Lad listened; breathing, a single heartbeat, and the scuff of a boot on a rug. Someone paced inside, probably trying to stay awake and alert.

Sereth walked right up to the viewing glass and rapped the polished bronze clapper three times. Lad held up a single finger and pointed to the door. Sereth nodded minutely.

Another boot scuff from inside, just beyond the door now. The guard was undoubtedly examining the late-night visitor through the glass. Sereth held his hands up in a submissive gesture. He'd told Lad of his failed attempt to forcefully rescue Jinny. Hopefully, Hensen would be more eager to continue receiving intelligence from his spy than to ban Sereth from his house.

Four bolts clacked open, and a complex locking mechanism clattered before the heavy door opened. A length of a thick-linked brass chain stopped it from opening more than three inches. The voice from inside sounded tired and irritated.

"What is it, Sereth?"

"I need to talk to Kiesha."

"She's sleeping. Come back in the morning."

Lad tensed as the door started to close, but Sereth stomped his foot between the door and frame.

"Of *course* she's sleeping, Worton. The whole damned city's sleeping! *I'd* be sleeping if I had any choice in the matter, but your master made it quite clear that I do my job...or else." Sereth fingered his broken nose and huffed in annoyance. "If you don't let me see Kiesha, I guarantee that Hensen will have *your* balls in his egg cups for breakfast, not mine."

"Don't threaten me."

"Get Kiesha, and if you're too timid to wake her, go get Terrence or Jamesly and let them take the heat."

Worton paused for two heartbeats before relenting.

"All right, but don't think you can pull the same shit on me that you did on Jamesly. And you're damn *right* I'm gonna wake Terrence. Wait there while I ring him."

"Wait out in the street for another City Guard patrol to come by? Are you daft?" Sereth glanced up and down the street nervously. "I'll wait inside, or I'll come back midmorning, and *you* can explain to Hensen why he didn't get my report sooner!"

"Fine!" The man sounded irritated, but resigned. "Move your foot so I can let you in."

Sereth complied, and the door closed. The chain rattled, and the door began to open again.

Lad moved in a blur. This part of the plan they agreed on. Their first priority was silence. He thrust the door open with one hand and smacked the edge of the other into the guard's throat just below the larynx. The blow wasn't lethal, just enough to stun and silence any cry for aid.

Worton stumbled back and raised a crossbow. As his finger tightened on the trigger, Lad plucked out the bolt, flipped it, and poised the tip an inch from the startled guard's eye. The crack of the empty crossbow was no louder than the bronze door knocker.

"One word and you're dead!"

Ignoring the menace, the man dropped his crossbow and tried to bat the bolt away while reaching for his sword with his free hand. Sereth lunged to catch the crossbow before it could clatter to the floor. Lad thrust the bolt through the guard's sword hand, kicked him squarely in the crotch, clapped a hand over his mouth, and caught him before he fell to the floor. Sereth closed and bolted the door, then lay the crossbow aside.

They were in.

126

Lad kept watch as Sereth gagged and bound their captive. The guard's moan seemed loud to his hypersensitive ears, but he detected no disturbance in the farther reaches of the house. Glancing back, he watched Sereth finish the knot in Worton's gag, then stand and draw two daggers. The Blade nodded toward the stairs.

Lad silently led the way, Sereth's tread barely audible as he followed. The low light of ornate wall lamps illuminated their passage. Pausing at the second floor landing to listen, he heard nothing to indicate that an alarm had been sounded. They continued up. At the third floor, they stopped again. To the left, double doors at the end of the hall led into Hensen's bedroom. Ahead, along the front of the house, was Hensen's office. The two doors down the hall to the right were unknowns.

Never leave a potential threat behind you. Remember!

Lad pressed an ear to the office door and each of the unknowns in turn, but heard nothing. His heart sank a little; he'd hoped that Kiesha slept behind one of them.

Not that easy…

Lad turned to Hensen's door. Pressing an ear to the thick oak planking, he discerned two muffled heartbeats and light, regular breathing. He held up two fingers to Sereth and pantomimed sleep. The Blade nodded.

The ornate brass thumb latch above the handle depressed with a quiet click, but the door didn't yield to gentle pressure. Lad released the latch and withdrew a set of fine picks from a pocket. He didn't often practice lock picking, but he also didn't lose skills once they were learned. Lad remembered every lesson he'd ever been taught as if they had taken place yesterday.

The picks ticked against the double rows of tumblers, an intricate lock indeed, but hardly beyond his skill. When the last tumbler clicked into place, the deadbolt turned easily. Lad carefully rewrapped the picks and slid them back into his pocket. This time when he depressed the latch, the door swung silently in on its hinges, but stopped suddenly when a restraining chain came taut. The clatter of the chain wasn't loud, but the easy cadence of breathing inside the room changed. Either Hensen or his companion had awakened. Stealth had just been superseded by the need for haste.

Lad reached through the gap in the door, grasped the chain, and pulled.

Metal and wood screeched, but he was through the portal in a flash, taking in the entire room in one sweeping glance.

The woman sprawled on the near side of the huge bed was just waking, and posed only an inconvenience rather than a threat. Sereth would deal with her. On the far side of the bed an older man, presumably Hensen, stretched out a hand. Whether he was reaching for the sword propped against the nightstand or one of the three bell ropes that dangled beside the bedpost, Lad didn't know. All he knew was that he had to stop him.

Three steps and Lad leapt over the bed. His outstretched hand snatched Hensen's wrist, but too late. The master thief's fingers were already closing on the nearest of the three bell ropes. Lad's momentum not only jerked the man right out of the bed, but also wrenched the bell rope right out of the wall. Lad landed and flipped Hensen facedown onto the floor, pinned his arms behind his back, then lifted him to his feet.

Sereth had the startled woman's face pressed into a pillow to stifle her protests. "He pulled a bell rope?"

"Sereth?" Hensen peered across the bed toward the Blade's voice, squinting in the dim light. "Again? I already told you—"

"Quiet!" Lad twisted the thief's pinned arms, not enough to pop a shoulder out of the socket, but enough to elicit a gasp of pain.

"Guards will be here in about thirty seconds." Sereth whipped a short piece of rope around his captive's wrists, tied it tight, and let her go. "Don't scream, miss. You're boyfriend has already called in his goons."

"Bastards!" the woman spat as Sereth got up to close and lock the door. She rolled over and glared at each of them in turn, apparently unconcerned with her state of undress. "Don't people *ever* get tired of barging in on you, Henny?"

"I'm sorry, my dear, but—"

"I said quiet!" Lad twisted Hensen's arms again. "Both of you."

If the woman's eyes had been daggers, Lad would have had his hands full dodging them.

"You shut up or you get gagged. Your choice." Sereth withdrew another length of cord from a pocket.

She glared at him, but remained silent.

"Thought so." The Blade drew the blanket up to cover her, and turned to Lad. "The other night there were six guards: two crossbows, four swords." Picking up the daggers he had dropped to tackle the woman, he flipped one for throwing. "Dead or alive?"

"Your choice, Hensen." Lad spun the master thief around to face him. A chill gripped his gut as he recognized the man's face. He'd seen it in the *Tap and Kettle* late one night not long ago, had even served the man a glass of wine.

They were spying on me, even then. The chill wrenched him hard at his next thought. *He knows where my family lives! Lissa!*

Hensen must have seen the pending violence in Lad's eyes, for his pupils dilated, his face flushed, and his heart raced. His outward countenance, however, remained calm and composed. Master Hensen, it seemed, was a very cool-headed thief.

The pounding of boots on the steps snapped Lad back to task. Hensen's guards would be there in seconds. "Do we kill your guards or not?"

"I'd prefer that you didn't, of course. Good help is *so* hard to find." He rubbed his shoulder and gestured to the silk robe hanging on a hook beside the nightstand. "Might I put on a robe?"

Cautious of hidden surprises, Lad reached over and lifted the robe off the hook. After a quick search, he handed it over. "If you try anything, I'll break your leg."

"I would *not* be so foolish, Lad." Hensen donned the garment with exaggerated care. "May I call you Lad, or do you prefer Guildmaster?"

"Call me what you like."

The pounding of boots halted just outside the door, and the doorknob rattled. A knock accompanied an urgent, "Are you all right, sir? You rang the bell!"

"Invite them in, and tell them to put their weapons on the floor," Lad instructed. "If they don't do as you say, I'll kill them."

"Very well." Hensen cleared his throat. "Basil, I have guests who are very upset. You and your people will come in and place your weapons on the floor. Do you understand?"

"Yes, sir."

Lad nodded to Sereth, who flicked the dead bolt and backed away, daggers poised. The latch clicked, and the door swung open. Five guards entered, four men and one woman, two with loaded crossbows.

"Where's the sixth?" Lad demanded.

"You tell me. Worton was assigned the front door."

Lad ignored Hensen's snide manner, his gaze fixed on the guards. The leader returned the scrutiny, his eyes narrowing as they roved over Lad, undoubtedly noting his lack of weapons. The corner of his mouth twitched and his knuckles whitened on his crossbow, and Lad knew he was contemplating violence.

So was Lad.

"Put your weapons down this instant!" Hensen ordered, his voice suddenly hard.

"Listen to your master," Sereth warned from behind them, his daggers poised to throw.

The guards slowly lowered their weapons to the floor. Sereth kicked the blades and bows out of reach, and pulled the

130

daggers from their belts. Finally, he frisked them, retrieving three more daggers.

"Now lie down," Lad commanded.

"Do as he says," Hensen insisted.

The guards did as they were told, but not without considerable reluctance.

"We should have brought more rope." Sereth jerked one of the pillowcases free from the bed, and began cutting off strips of the shimmering silk.

"I must say that you surprise me, Lad," Hensen said as Sereth bound his guards. "I didn't think you'd go to war for a traitor. Taking me prisoner won't get Sereth his dear wife back, you know. In fact, it will only get her killed."

The man's nonchalance piqued Lad. "We're not here just for Sereth's wife, Hensen. We're here for Kiesha. Where is she?"

"My assistant?" The bewilderment on Hensen's face looked genuine, but the minute blood vessels around his irises dilated involuntarily. "Why would you—"

Lad's hand shot out, his fingers pressing on the fragile cartilage of the master thief's larynx. "Just answer my questions or I'll start removing pieces of you and nailing them to the wall. Where is Kiesha?"

The muscles of Hensen's throat flexed under Lad's fingers. Fear finally registered in the man's eyes. "I don't know. I didn't see her come in tonight, but she should be in her room."

"Where's her room?"

"Second floor, east wing, end of the hall. But I don't—"

"Come on." Lad released Hensen's throat and propelled him out of the room with an arm twisted behind his back. The time for questions would come later. Right now, they had to find Kiesha before she managed to escape. Sereth followed silently, daggers at the ready and looking like he'd enjoy putting them to use. The master thief chattered on, his casual tone belied by the tension Lad could feel in in his gait.

131

"I don't know what Sereth has told you, Lad, but let me assure you that he would say anything to get his wife back. He's completely beyond reason, you see. He barged in here not long ago and had to be restrained. Kiesha has nothing to do with—"

"Quiet!" Lad emphasized his order with a careful twist of Hensen's wrist. "Kiesha has *everything* to do with this!"

Hensen shut up.

They descended the stairs swiftly and proceeded down the hall. Lad squeezed Hensen's arm in warning, then gestured Sereth toward the designated door. A dagger in one hand, the Master Blade carefully turned the knob, and the door swung open without resistance. The glow of a guttering bedside lamp revealed a small, plain room. The bed was empty and tidily made up, but there was a clothespress big enough to conceal a squad of guards inside. Sereth crept toward it, clasped the handle, and yanked it open. Finding it overflowing with dresses, he shook his head. Dropping to one knee, he glanced under the bed. Again, nothing.

Kiesha wasn't there.

Lad gritted his teeth and propelled Hensen into the room, leaving the door open so he could see down the hall. They hadn't checked all the rooms and he didn't want to be blindsided.

"Search everything." As Sereth began a more thorough search, Lad backed Hensen against the wall. "Where is she?"

"I honestly don't know." The thief rubbed his wrist. "Nor do I know why you're interested in my assistant."

Lad pinned him against the wall by the throat. "I'm interested because Kiesha killed my wife!" He tightened his grasp until the man's eyes bulged. "And *you* ordered it!"

"I...didn't!"

"Master!"

He turned to see Sereth standing beside the bed. "She hasn't been here. The sheets are cool. And if you kill him, we'll never find her or Jinny."

132

Sereth was right, of course. Lad released Hensen's throat and caught up the front of his robe. "You're going to start talking right this moment, Hensen. Explain to me why my wife was murdered, and you might die easily."

Hensen coughed, cleared his throat, and took a deep breath. "Kiesha was only trying to protect you."

His last shadow of a doubt vanished with the thief's words. Kiesha was not only Wiggen's killer, but also Lad's protector. "Who ordered her to protect me? You?"

"Well, yes, I assigned her that task. I received a contract to protect both you and Mya. The death of your wife was an unfortunate accident. Kiesha thought another assassin—"

"Bullshit!" Lad pinned Hensen to the wall again, pressing hard on his chest. He felt the ribs sag under the pressure. "The fight was over when she killed Wiggen! *Nobody* could have mistaken her for an assassin! Tell me the truth! Who ordered Kiesha to kill my wife?"

"I..." Hensen struggled to breathe, and Lad eased the pressure, allowing him to talk. "I did *not*, and Kiesha wouldn't—"

"Master."

Sereth held a long, flat mahogany box, the lid tilted open. Inside, a blowgun of matte black metal and dark ebony nestled in the soft velvet lining, beside it a row of familiar black darts. A flat brown glass bottle and dropper sat in a separate recess. Even without opening it, Lad knew it contained white scorpion venom. Without a doubt, this was the weapon that killed Wiggen.

"Master, something doesn't make sense." Sereth gestured at the overflowing drawers and clothespress. "If she left, she went without taking many of her clothes. And if she was covering her tracks, leaving the blowgun and darts behind was stupid. And Kiesha *isn't* stupid."

No, things weren't making sense, and it frustrated Lad to no end. He turned back to Hensen. "I'm going to ask you one more time. Why did Kiesha kill Wiggen?"

"I don't know."

"Where is she?"

"I don't know. You must believe me!"

"He's lying," Sereth said with a sneer.

Only one way to find out...

"Sereth, I'm leaving, and Hensen's coming with me. Call in your people and search this place thoroughly. Be careful. I don't want any of his staff harmed, but I want them secured."

"Master, let me go with you!" Sereth cast a malignant glance at Hensen. "I can help question—"

Lad held up a hand. "Sereth! I need you here. Kiesha may be hiding in the house, and only you can identify her. Once you're done, come to my home to report your findings."

"But Jinny—"

"Don't worry. We're going to ask Master Hensen a few questions, then you and I will go get your wife."

Sereth heaved a sigh, but nodded and backed down. "Very good, Master."

"You're assuming that I'm going to tell you where she's being kept," Hensen said indignantly. "I see no reason to give up my only bargaining chip."

"I assume *nothing*, and I can think of twenty-one reasons—" Lad looked the master thief up and down. "Make that twenty-*three* reasons why you'll tell me where she is. But we need to go someplace where no one will hear your screams before I start removing those reasons."

"Before you *what*?"

Lad knew many ways to render someone unconscious. He picked the one least likely to break the thief's neck, and caught the falling body on his shoulder. Lifting the weight easily, he looked to Sereth. "Fetch the carriage."

"Yes, Master."

Chapter 8

Lad breathed in the earthy aroma of oak and stone that permeated the wine cellar beneath his house. The smell of fear soured the pleasanter scents, and the coppery odor of blood would soon join the mix.

Amidst the racks of bottles and neat rows of casks, Master Hensen sat bound to one of Lad's ornate dining room chairs. A pained squeak escaped his gag as Lad tightened the last knot. The thief stared wide-eyed into Lad's blank expression, then looked away. By the sweat on his upper lip, the pulse pounding at his throat, and the reek of fear, Lad could tell that the man knew what was coming.

I have to do this. There's no other way.

The idea of torture sickened him, but he saw no alternative. He would do anything to discover who was responsible for Wiggen's death. Even this.

Lad walked behind the chair, reached out for Hensen's neck. The thief tensed in expectation of the violence he knew would soon come, then relaxed when Lad untied the gag. Hensen spat out the wad of cloth that had ensured his silence during the short carriage ride. His first words were predictable.

"You're making a mistake."

Before Lad could answer, a metallic clatter from the stairs drew their attention. Dee came down bearing the same silver tray he used to serve Lad's breakfast, now heaped with kitchen implements. He put the tray down on a small folding table beside Hensen's chair. The thief's eyes widened at the pile of

135

knives, forks, spoons, garlic presses, corkscrews, and other assorted culinary tools.

"Sorry, sir, this is all I could find. I could call for an Inquisitor if you wish." Dee's calm voice contradicted the clenched jaw and stiff posture. Dee apparently didn't care for the gruesome task his master was about to perform.

"These are fine, Dee." Lad picked a nutcracker out of the tangle of metal. The thought of applying it to Hensen's fingers, the pending crunch of bone beneath the serrated jaws, nauseated him. *I have to do this.* "I can make do. Go upstairs and wait for Sereth."

"Very good, sir." He nodded and left, closing the cellar door behind him.

"Don't *do* this!" Hensen's voice was raw with desperation.

Lad examined the cluttered tray of steel and remembered all the horrible devices he'd seen in the Grandfather's subterranean torture chamber. He remembered how he had hated that place. Swallowing bile, he looked around at his benign surroundings. Had the Grandfather's torture chamber once been a cellar with casks of wine and ale? Had Saliez once tied a captive to a chair and reluctantly applied crude tools to elicit information? In doing so, had he developed his taste for torture? Would Lad?

I have to do this. There's no other way.

He told himself it was for Wiggen, but in his heart he knew that was a lie. The vengeance was for him. But even more than vengeance, he needed to know *why*.

"You don't need to do this, Lad!"

"Don't I?" He examined the nutcracker in his hand, imagining too easily the places it could be applied, and dropped it back onto the silver tray. "Then you better start telling me the truth, Master Hensen."

"I've *told* you the truth." He swallowed hard, sweat breaking out anew on his forehead. "We can discuss this like civilized men."

Lad scrutinized Hensen, watching for signs of deception. The man might be able to maintain a stony façade, but few could control their involuntary responses, and after five years with Mya, Lad was a master at reading them. "Let's discuss, then. You said you didn't order Kiesha to murder my wife."

"That's correct. We had a contract to protect you and Mya for one month."

"Who contracted you to protect us?"

"Baron Patino, a local noble."

Patino... A noble... Lad didn't recognize the name, and he didn't know any nobles. "Why did Patino want us protected?"

"He didn't give a reason, just paid half our fee in advance to keep you and Mya alive for a month. We looked into his background, but found no connections to the Assassins Guild or any other illegal organization. We knew from Sereth that there was trouble brewing within your guild, and we knew from a spy at the *Golden Cockerel* that Mya had received orders from the Grandmaster of Assassins to craft a new guildmaster's ring and assume the position."

"Moirin was yours?"

"Yes, but she vanished without a trace." Hensen frowned. "We assumed she'd been discovered and you disposed of her."

"She was discovered, but took poison before we could take her."

"A pity." Hensen sounded about as upset as if he'd just broken a favored teacup.

"Pity?" Hensen's blasé attitude ignited Lad's temper once again. His lip curled back in an involuntary sneer. "You better pity your assistant, Master Hensen. She *murdered* my wife! I'm going to find her and kill her for it. And if you don't want me to remove your fingernails with a paring knife and pliers, you're going to help me! Is that clear?"

Hensen's features hardened. "Perfectly clear, but if you kill me, Sereth's wife perishes. Kill me, and I'll be unable to answer any more of your questions. Kill me, and the Thieves Guild will

137

wage open war on the Assassins Guild. Every building you own, every business you run will burn, and the streets and alleys of Twailin will flow with blood. Kiesha told me that your wife's death was an accident! She had no reason to lie."

The cellar door thumped, and Sereth came down the stairs. "Master, we searched the house from rafters to cellar, but didn't find Kiesha." The Blade's eyes roved over Hensen. "We secured the household staff, and I left a squad of Blades to watch over them. We probably have until sunrise before someone comes calling."

"Which is when my guild will learn that you've taken me captive, and horrible things will start to happen." Hensen looked to Lad, his eyes imploring. "Things that don't *need* to happen."

"Don't believe a word he says, sir." Sereth radiated loathing for the man like heat from a kiln. "He'll say anything to save his own skin."

And yet he's not just telling me what I want to hear. It didn't make sense that Hensen stuck with his story of an accident. His concern for his guards hadn't shown such devotion, so why wouldn't he just give up his assistant? Why risk torture to convince Lad that Wiggen's death was a mistake? Frustration stoked Lad's rage.

"Kiesha murdered my wife, and it *wasn't* an accident. The fight was over. Nobody could have mistaken Wiggen for an assassin."

Hensen shook his head stubbornly. "Kiesha had no motivation to kill her. Our only orders were to protect you."

"Your orders..." Lad's mind shifted gears. Even if Hensen wouldn't answer his questions, he had given him another place to look. "Patino..."

"Patino?" Sereth stepped forward, his brow furrowed. "*Baron* Patino?"

"What do you know about Patino?" Lad asked.

"Kiesha met with him yesterday at the Westmarket bazaar."

"Ridiculous!" Hensen's outburst seemed too spontaneous to be faked, but he'd already proven himself a smooth liar. "She doesn't know him. She must have been merely spying on him. Gathering more information to—"

"No." Sereth was adamant. "They had a conversation, strolling arm and arm like old chums."

Lad snatched up a corkscrew and held it in front of his captive's eye, seething. "What did I say about telling me the truth?"

Hensen didn't respond, just kept shaking his head. "Why would she lie to me?"

"Hensen!" Lad longed to jam the spiral of steel into the man's hand to get his attention, but held back. Even if the thief was playing him for a fool, once Lad crossed that line, there was no going back. He would become just like Saliez, the man who had made him a killer. "You said you investigated Baron Patino. Tell me what you found out, *everything* you found out."

"Nothing." Hensen shifted minutely in his seat. Lad noted the movement; was it discomfort or a tell? Was Hensen lying? "We looked into his family, his associations, even his mistresses. He's nothing but a low-ranking noble, albeit a wealthy one."

"And who conducted this investigation?"

Hensen seemed to wither in his seat. "Kiesha."

"So, you still think Kiesha had no reason to lie to you? That her killing of Wiggen was an *accident*? Because either Kiesha lied to you, or you're lying to me right now." Lad's grinding teeth chirped like distant crickets in the ensuing silence. He longed to lash out, to take that step that would make him that much closer to Saliez.

Wiggen…

"I'm *not* lying. If it truly wasn't an accident, as you insist, then someone else must have ordered the kill."

"And that someone might be Patino." Lad turned to shout up the stairs, "Dee!"

139

Dee trundled down. His eyes scanned the scene, and the corner of his mouth twitched. "Yes, sir."

"Send runners to Bemrin and Mya with instructions to investigate one Baron Patino. They're to pull in all the resources they need. I want to know what he eats, who he sleeps with, where he is every hour of the day, and I want it now!"

"Yes, sir."

"We have the name of Wiggen's killer. Kiesha. Have Mya's start the hunt for her. Sereth will give a detailed description and all her disguises later, and we'll have an artist make sketches. For now, she's slim, blonde, pretty, and works as Master Hensen's assistant. And Dee, make sure Mya knows that she's dangerous, and that I want her alive."

"Yes, sir." Dee hurried out.

Lad paced the confines of the cellar, feeling like a wild animal in a cage. He tried to organize his thoughts, but nothing made sense. What role did Patino play in all this? Lad's only interactions with Twailin's nobility occurred five years ago, when he murdered nobles on Saliez's orders. Could one have been a relation of Patino's, and Wiggen's death the baron's revenge? He shook his head. The possibility seemed remote. Then Lad remembered Mya's supposition about who might be protecting him. A connection between the Grandmaster and a minor noble seemed even less likely.

"That's it!" Hensen's eyes widened again, but this time they shone with the light of discovery instead of fear. And they were focused on Lad, or more precisely, Lad's left hand. "The guildmaster's ring. Your wife wore it."

"How did you..." What other presumably secret information did Hensen know? It didn't matter; he needed answers. "Yes."

"And she could never take it off, isn't that correct?"

"Yes."

"And Mya received orders to have a new ring forged and declare herself guildmaster."

140

Lad stiffened. He knew where this line of reasoning was headed, and it wouldn't do to have Hensen blurting out information that Lad would rather keep quiet. Sereth didn't know about Mya's theory that the Grandmaster might have sent someone to protect him, or Lad's notion of the Grandmaster's potential involvement in Wiggen's death.

And it's going to stay that way.

"Implicating one of my own people isn't going to get you out of that chair!"

"I wasn't implying that. I was just pointing out—"

"He's *playing* you, Master!" Sereth brandished a dagger. "He'll spin any tale he can think of to get out of this. Give me ten minutes with him, and I'll find out where they're keeping Jinny."

"Jinny?" Lad's mind stumbled over the name.

"My *wife*, sir."

"Yes." Lad had been so caught up in the puzzle of Patino and Kiesha, he'd forgotten about Jinny. Once Hensen's abduction was discovered, Sereth's wife would suffer. Lad's gut twisted. He was making progress in his interrogation of Hensen, but... He looked at Sereth. The Master Blade regarded him respectfully, but desperation haunted his eyes.

Wiggen is dead, and Jinny is still alive...for now. Lad turned his attention back to Hensen. "Sereth's wife."

"She's quite safe," said Hensen.

"But she won't stay that way for long. You said—"

"I *lied*, dear boy!" Hensen's bark of laughter hedged toward hysteria. "She's fine until I give the word otherwise. If I should die, however..."

"He's still lying." Sereth step forward menacingly. "Let me question him."

"As I said," Hensen began, looking nervously at the blade in Sereth's hand, "Sereth's wife is my only remaining bargaining chip." His eyes flicked back to Lad. "So let's bargain."

"Jinny is *not* a bargaining chip!" Sereth's dagger moved, but Lad's hand closed on his wrist before the tip pierced the back of Hansen's hand.

"No, Sereth!" His reaction had been visceral, the decision made without thought. Lad could neither stand by while a bound man was tortured, nor do the job himself. He would not become another Saliez. He drew a deep, cleansing breath, and the revulsion at what he had almost done ebbed away. "If we hurt him, we start a war. If we kill him, your wife suffers." He released his grip on Sereth's wrist and looked at the master thief. "But I'm not going to release you in exchange for Sereth's wife."

"No, I didn't think you'd agree to that." Hensen twisted his lips wistfully. "And frankly, you need my help to discover who was truly responsible for your wife's murder."

"Your *help*?" Now it was Lad's turn to look skeptical. "Now you want to help?"

"I've been helpful from the very start! And trust me, dear boy, I want to know who's behind this as much as you do. More, perhaps."

"Why?"

"I've been betrayed by one of my closest people, and you ask me that? Someone used Kiesha to set up the Thieves Guild to take the blame for your wife's murder. Whoever it is might even be trying to start a war between our guilds. I want to find out who that is, and you want to find out who ordered Kiesha to kill your wife. We're looking for the same person!"

Who ordered Kiesha... If she was acting under orders, did she really deserve Lad's vengeance? He, too, had killed on orders. *Only because I couldn't disobey.* To find out the truth, they had to find Kiesha. Maybe Hensen was right. Lad needed all the help he could get.

"What do you want in exchange for this help?"

Hensen lifted his chin and took a deep breath. There was relief there, surely, but something else, too. Resolve, perhaps?

"I would like an agreement from you, Lad, that you won't kill Kiesha for what she's done."

"You *what*?"

"I've told you the truth about what she said to me. Since she had no motivation of her own to kill your wife, and I didn't tell her to do it, she must have been following someone else's orders." Hensen looked up imploringly. "She was nothing but a weapon, Lad. Surely you can understand that."

Lad understood that better than Hensen knew, but he still didn't trust the master thief. "Why do you care so much about Kiesha? You weren't so concerned about your guards, or Moirin, or even your bed partner for that matter."

Hensen opened his mouth, paused, glanced at Sereth, and said, "I care about her because I created her."

"*Created* her? You mean you trained her?"

"I saw to her training, yes, but I mean created." Hensen sighed and closed his eyes. His face seemed to age in that instant, sagging with defeat. "She's my daughter."

"That's ridiculous! You undressed her right in front of me!" Sereth looked to Lad. "He's lying through his teeth!"

"I'm *not* lying. Not about this." Hensen looked up at the Blade with reinforced resolve in his eyes. "I went to great lengths to hide her identity, Sereth. If anyone knew, they would have used her to get to me."

"Just as the other masters used Lissa to manipulate me," Lad said.

"And just as you're using Jinny," Sereth hissed through clenched teeth.

"Exactly." Hensen smirked at the Blade. "We're thieves and murderers, Sereth, not saints."

A chill invaded Lad's bones. Could he believe Hensen? If Kiesha was indeed his daughter, then he couldn't blame the man for trying to protect her. But if Lad agreed not to kill her, and it turned out that Kiesha had been acting on her own initiative... His vengeance was being thwarted at every turn.

"Tell us where Sereth's wife is being held, and I'll agree not to kill your daughter, but *only* if she tells me who gave her the order to kill Wiggen."

"Very well."

"And you'll help me find her."

"I'll do everything I can in that regard. You have my word."

"Don't trust him, Master." Hatred honed Sereth's words.

"I don't," Lad assured the Blade. "That's why Master Hensen will be staying with us for a while. At least until we find Kiesha. And I'm going to bring Enola in to help. I'm sure she's got some kind of potion to make sure he's not lying to us."

Sereth frowned, but nodded. "Yes, Master."

"If I'm to stay here, I hope you can provide better accommodations than this." Hensen's cool exterior was back, like a film of ice over a raging river. Lad longed to shatter that façade, but didn't dare risk their fragile agreement. Inconceivably, he needed Hensen.

"I'll arrange something more comfortable *after* we free Sereth's wife. Where is she?"

"There is a tailor's shop on the corner of East Dunley Street and Bellhaven Avenue. The proprietor's name is Rolf Emurry. Two of my people are watching over her in the loft above the shop. Tell them my package is to be delivered today, and you're to take charge of it. They'll ask you to pay in advance, and you'll give them a single silver penny. Only then will they release Sereth's dear Jinny into your hands."

"If you're lying—"

"I would have to be *monumentally* stupid to lie to you," Hensen said with an indignant look. "You'd give me to Sereth, and he'd start cutting off pieces of my very cherished anatomy."

"That you can count on, Master Hensen. Dee!"

"Yes sir?" His assistant was through the door and down the stairs in an instant. "I've sent runners to Mya and Bemrin. Did you need something else?"

"Yes. Send a runner to Jingles. Have him send two Enforcers to watch over our guest. Send another to Enola. I need her to tell me if someone's lying. Keep Hensen company until we get back. Sereth, let's go get your wife."

"Yes, *sir!*" Sereth sheathed his dagger and, for the first time since Lad had known the Blade, he smiled.

"What a *lovely* neighborhood." Bemrin squeezed Mya's arm as they passed yet another well-heeled passerby. They'd been walking for fifteen minutes, and the blithe smile had not left his face. "Right at the corner and halfway up the block, my dear."

"I'm not 'your dear', Bemrin." Mya maintained her mien of insipid contentment. "Just because I put on a dress doesn't mean I can't break you in half."

"I don't doubt that for an instant, my dear." He gave her a wink.

Mya gritted her teeth and kept smiling. Bemrin's obvious enjoyment of the situation annoyed her even more than the ridiculous frippery she'd donned for this excursion. Dressing to walk Barleycorn Heights was one thing, passing herself off as Hightown gentry was another.

She knew that her fretting about her clothes and Bemrin's pomposity resulted from a deeper distress. A pre-dawn surprise mission from the guildmaster was bad enough. Scouring the city for Kiesha had put her on edge, and the deeper implications of Dee's note were unsettling.

Sereth... With every Inquisitor and Hunter in the guild searching for Wiggen's killer, how had a Blade stumbled upon her? What did a minor noble have to do with anything, and how did the Thieves Guild fit in? And would taking the head of the rival guild as a prisoner precipitate a war? *Because that's all we need...*

But it was the language of the note that had made Mya's skin crawl. She knew Dee, and when he used terms like *"extracted information"* there was no doubt in her mind what he meant. She remembered Hensen from years ago, when she enlisted his help in the search for Lad, and knew the Master Thief wouldn't give up information without payment...or inducement.

Lad won't go there! her conscience insisted. Then she thought about his murder of Yance, and the devil's advocate at the back of her mind whispered, *This isn't the Lad you loved.* If he had crossed the line into torture, he was truly lost.

Mya tried to distract herself by admiring the scenery. Baron Patino lived in one of the richest sections of Hightown. Marble façades and polished brass carriage lamps shone in the mid-morning sun, just as the people they passed glowed in their silk and satin finery.

Bemrin leaned close. "You really should see a proper tailor about your gown, by the way. That's more than three years out of style and doesn't quite fit."

"That's because its five years old, and I haven't worn it in that long." It was also the only one she owned with a high neck and long sleeves to cover her tattoos. In fact, the last time she'd worn this gown, she'd been casing nobles for Lad to murder. She had been a different person then, terrified in the shadow of the Grandfather.

And now I'm terrified in the shadow of Lad.

"You've been Master Hunter for five *years*, and you haven't bought a new gown?" Bemrin sounded incredulous.

"I've had no reason to. I have others to do my spying for me."

"Where's the fun in that?" He squeezed her arm again and beamed. "Just relax, and do try to remember that we're on the same side."

"Right. I keep *forgetting* that part."

Truth be told, if the Inquisitor didn't annoy her so much, she would have congratulated him on the speed with which his people had unearthed the location of Baron Patino's townhouse, as well as details about his estates, title, money, and social life. His Inquisitors were still out canvassing the city, digging up information on Patino, while her Hunters tracked down Kiesha. The two masters had reserved Baron Patino for themselves. Posing as a moneyed couple out strolling among their rich neighbors, they intended to scout the neighborhood, listen to the gossip, give Patino's home a careful look, and perhaps pick up his trail. If the baron himself came strolling out today, Mya would stick to him like a tick on a dog. Who knows: he might even lead her to Kiesha. Lad hadn't given orders to snatch Patino, but then, a missing noble would precipitate a man-hunt by the Royal Guard, not so a missing thief.

Rounding the corner, Mya stopped short. Two Royal Guard carriages were parked in front of the baron's townhouse. Across the street, a small crowd of well-bred spectators stared at the spectacle and talked amongst themselves.

"Don't stop!" Bemrin hissed, tugging her into motion. "And wipe that 'I'm guilty' look off your face."

"I do *not* look guilty!" She followed his lead, and they resumed their staid pace. Her face burned with embarrassment at her gaff. Master Hunter, and she had gaped like a virgin in a brothel. *Damn, I'm out of practice!*

"My dear, if you looked any guiltier, you'd have a noose around your neck. Let's try for mildly curious, shall we?" The Inquisitor patted her hand. "And do try to walk a little more like a lady instead of a stalking panther, won't you?"

"Fine." Mya cursed him for it, but he was right. Smiling again, she adjusted her gait, shortening her step and swaying her hips.

Bemrin squeezed her arm again. "And please, let me ask the questions. Finesse is my forte, after all. When we need to break someone in half, I'll leave it all to you."

"Pompous twit," she murmured just loud enough for him to hear. Damned if he wasn't right about that, too. Hunters excelled at finding people, tracking them down and bringing them back dead or alive. Inquisitors weren't just interrogators, they were the guild's spies, invisible and everywhere.

"Why of *course* I'm a pompous twit, my dear." Bemrin laughed easily and smiled at her, then lowered his voice. "And we're walking through a *sea* of like-minded people, so I should fit right in, no?"

Mya focused on the low conversations as they approached the crowd. Her stomach soured at the tidbits she overheard: "tragedy…" "terrible…" "so young."

"Pardon me." Bemrin nodded politely to a passing woman. Richly dressed, she dabbed her nose with an embroidered handkerchief. "What seems to have drawn the attention of the Royal Guard to this quiet neighborhood?"

The woman looked at him with tearful eyes. "It's the good Baron Patino. He's passed away. Such a lovely man, too, and so young."

Mya struggled to maintain her composure. *Dead?*

Thankfully, Bemrin's expression showed only appropriately feigned sadness. He tsked and shook his head. "Passed away, you say. Was he ill?"

"Not that I noticed, and I saw him just yesterday at the market. I've lived next to him for three years now, and never met a kinder man."

"But what could it have been? His heart?"

Yeah, with a poisoned dart in it! Mya had harbored doubts about the involvement of a noble in Wiggen's death when she first read Dee's note, but for Patino to die the very same day they received orders to investigate him pretty much cinched it. Mya didn't believe in coincidence.

"They don't know the cause," the woman said. "His valet found him this morning lying in his study, and sent one of the kitchen boys to fetch the guard. The baron's maid spoke with my maid, who told my butler, who told… Well, you know how word gets around." She lowered her voice to a whisper. "Some are suggesting poison..."

"Who would *dare* such a thing?"

"Well..." the woman bent closer, a glint of scandal shining through her distress, "...he *did* have lady friends, but Lady Patino *knew* he kept other company. Such an odd relationship..."

"The Nine Hells have no wrath like a woman scorned, it's true." Bemrin shook his head sagely. "Such a shame." He squeezed Mya's arm. "Shall we continue our stroll, my dear?"

"Of course." She had to admit, Bemrin was smooth.

As they walked on, Mya's mind raced far, far ahead. When they were a block away, she gauged that they were sufficiently alone to speak. "Lad will want details, and fast."

"How to get them is the question." Bemrin actually sounded worried. "I have no eyes in the Royal Guard, and this is out of the City Guard's jurisdiction. But perhaps..." The Master Inquisitor cocked his head in thought, then nodded. "...I'll send in a distraught young lady. Tears and a low-cut gown often yield results. If Patino was known as a lady's man, one more attractive mourner asking for details shouldn't invite undue attention."

"Not a bad idea." Mya gazed at Bemrin with budding respect. He might be a pompous ass, but one did not rise to the position of Master Inquisitor without knowing how to get information.

"Right then! I'll delve the Royal Guard for details, and you go tell the guildmaster that Patino's dead."

"Thanks a lot!" Lad would be furious at the news. She swallowed her fear and resolved to think positively. Their last conversation had ended well. Why worry? *Just because he may have tortured Hensen to get information, only to find out that the object of his interest is dead? Oh, yeah, he'll take that well.*

Bemrin raised a hand to hail a passing hackney, and the coach jerked to a halt. "Tell our master that I'll report as soon as I can. And do be careful."

"Thanks." Mya didn't believe his false concern for a second. She allowed him to hand her up into the carriage and managed to keep from smacking him as he bent to kiss her gloved hand. Backing off with a smile, Bemrin closed the door and called up to the driver, "Greensleeves Way. And hurry."

"As you wish, milord!"

Mya fought for a deep breath as the whip cracked and the coach rumbled off toward Lad. She felt stifled by the encumbering dress, the enclosed carriage, and the mission Bemrin had coerced her into. Biting her lip, she dreaded what she might find at her destination.

"Not a mark, you say?" Norwood crouched beside the body.

Aside from his grayish pallor, Baron Patino looked asleep. *But a dead noble without an obvious cause of death warrants a visit from the Royal Guard.* Norwood sighed—*All part of the job*—and resigned himself to a boring investigation that would undoubtedly reveal some malady or hidden illness. Strange as it might seem, sometimes young men died. At least the captain hadn't had to travel far; his office was only ten blocks away.

"Nothing, sir." The corporal in charge of the investigation shrugged. "No bruises, no look of pain on his face like you see when a man's had a heart attack, no vomit or sign of intoxication, and no blood."

"And he's not been ill, and didn't go out for dinner, by the word of his valet," another guardsman added. "His man went to bed around ten last night, and the baron was reading here in the study." He gestured to a book beside a comfortable chair.

Norwood stood and went to the lamp beside the chair. He laid a hand on the glass chimney; it was cool. "Any lamps on when you got here, corporal?"

"Just that one beside the door." He pointed.

The lamp was out now, since there was enough light streaming through the high windows to illuminate the room. Norwood went to it and felt the chimney, detecting slight warmth. The other lamp had been put out long before this one.

"So, he got up from his reading, put out his reading lamp, took two steps and dropped dead without making a sound." That sounded strange to Norwood, but there were no signs of violence or foul play. "And the valet said the exterior doors were locked when he got up this morning?"

"Tight as a drum, sir. The wife's hysterical."

"I want to talk to her." Hysteria could be faked, and she wouldn't be the first noble wife to kill a husband. If the house hadn't been broken into, and this did turn out to be a wrongful death, the list of suspects narrowed considerably.

The familiarity of the situation pricked his memory. *A locked home and a dead body...*

"Check all the windows and the attic for signs of forced entry, and send a carriage for Master Woefler. Ask him to check all the baron's decanters for poison, and the baron himself while he's at it. Oh, and ask the baroness and servants if anything has gone missing, even something seemingly unimportant."

"Already checked for signs of a break-in, sir. Not so much as a scratch on a casement. The butler and valet reported that nothing's missing."

Nothing missing, and no sign that anyone broke in... Norwood considered again the similarities to something he'd seen. *Something recent...something...Woefler...magic...* He snapped his fingers when finally he remembered. *Vonlith!* Similar circumstances, except for the dagger wound in the brain.

Norwood looked down at the dead baron again. Patino was a score of years younger than the guard captain and looked to be in good health. "Damned strange..." Norwood didn't like it when nobles dropped dead in his city, and liked it even less when there was no apparent explanation why they were dead.

Maybe I'm just getting paranoid. He swept his eyes around the room one more time. *Not a single thing out of place. Not a dropped glass, not a book off the shelf, not a single sign that anyone came or went.* He felt a chill down his spine.

Captain Norwood turned to the corporal in charge. "Once we take the body, send a messenger to the Royal Physicker. I want a reason why this man's dead, even if we have to cut him open to find it."

The corporal swallowed and jotted down a note. "Yes sir."

CHAPTER XI

Waiting...

Lad paced back and forth across the polished wood floor of his dining room. A lifetime of self-reliance had ill-prepared him for the guildmaster's position. He issued orders, then had to wait while other people carried them out, wait for information, wait on results... *Wait for someone else to find Wiggen's killer.*

In contrast, Hensen sat comfortably at the table, sipping tea and nibbling scones, seeming to revel in his status as guest, rather than prisoner. Convincing the Thieves Guild that their master was here voluntarily hadn't been easy, but they'd done so. Neither of them wanted a guild war. The two Enforcers looming at the thief's shoulders belied his guest status, but Hensen ignored them. Not being tied to a chair and threatened with torture had done wonders for the man's calm.

Lad's, however, was in tatters.

The recovery of Sereth's wife had gone as easily as Hensen said it would. Lad had been afraid that the Master Blade might retaliate against those who held her, but he'd just gathered the confused woman into his arms and walked out. They were together now in the next room, getting reacquainted while Sereth worked with an artist to produce accurate sketches of Kiesha. He could hear their whispers through the closed door, though he tried not to listen. They had two years of catching up to do, and didn't need anyone eavesdropping.

"You really should learn to relax and enjoy your position, Lad." Hensen chased the last bite of his scone with the dregs of his third cup of tea.

Lad shot him a smoldering look. "Your daughter murdered my wife, and I'm still not convinced you didn't have a part in it. I'll *relax* when I know who ordered Kiesha to kill Wiggen."

"I have just as much at stake in this as you do, yet I'm relaxed and calm, while you pace and fret." Hensen sipped his tea and sighed. "Worrying only transforms minutes to hours, and gives you indigestion. You must learn to be like a swan: serene and calm on the surface, paddling like hell under the water, and always on the lookout for alligators."

"I'm not interested in your philosophy, Hensen, I'm interested in—"

Dee pushed through the door from the kitchen carrying a tray with fresh pots of blackbrew and tea, and another plate of scones. Lad eyed the blackbrew, but decided against another cup. His nerves were already jangling. Waiting was killing him, and nothing he tried helped. Concentration, meditation, even his daily exercises had gone by the wayside, all useless to ease his pain or order his thoughts. He'd thought that a lead would make him feel better, but he didn't. He felt like a rat in a trap, gnawing at his own foot to escape.

"Master."

Dee's voice brought Lad's eyes up, and he followed his assistant's gaze out the front windows. A well-dressed lady had just disembarked from a hackney outside his house. Only when she turned toward his front door did Lad realize it was Mya. He barely recognized her in the get-up. The frills and lace made her look incongruously...female.

"Finally!"

Her arrival, however, set him teetering between relief and anxiety. Lad needed her keen mind to help him with the puzzle, but—he glanced at Hensen—he couldn't let her in the same room with the master thief. Hensen might blurt out something

154

about the contract to protect them. From there, she would make the connection to the Grandmaster's potential involvement in Wiggen's death. Lad had to keep her and the other masters in the dark on that score, or risk rebellion.

"I'll talk to her in the parlor, Dee. Keep our guest company."

"Yes, Master."

Lad strode into the entry hall and opened the door before Mya could knock. She opened her mouth to speak, but he held up a hand. "Not in front of Hensen." He kept his voice low and conspiratorial. "In the parlor."

As Mya stepped inside, her gaze flicked curiously toward the dining room and Hensen sitting there eating scones. Her eyes widened in surprise, then the corner of her mouth twitched.

Lad reached past her and slid closed the door to the dining room. "In the parlor. Now!"

"Yes, I'm just…" She nodded and bit her lip. "Yes, Master."

He followed her into the parlor and closed that door, too. "What have you found out?"

Mya clenched her hands in front of her and took a deep breath. "Patino's dead."

"Dead?" Lad's head pounded, his pulse suddenly racing. He stepped up to Mya, straining to keep from grabbing and shaking the details out of her. "Patino was our only lead! How?"

"We don't know yet." She swallowed hard, her face pale, but she stood her ground. "Two Royal Guard coaches were parked outside his house. We couldn't get any details other than that his valet found him this morning, dead in his study. A neighbor said that Patino had affairs with other women, so Bemrin's sending someone to the Royal Guard to pose as a bereaved mistress, hoping to get more details."

"Kiesha!" Lad glared at the closed door. "She killed Patino to cover her tracks."

Mya nodded. "It's a cinch he didn't just *coincidentally* drop dead."

"Yes." His mind spun. Kiesha was the key to everything. Only she could confirm who was truly behind Wiggen's murder. "I need you back on the street, Mya. I want Hunters at every gate in and out of the city, anywhere someone might slip through. If Kiesha's running, she may leave Twailin."

"What about Hensen? He might know where she would hide."

"I'm working on that. He's cooperating."

"Why?"

"We made a deal." Lad struggled with himself, and made a decision. Mya needed to know this much, anyway. He needed her mind on the job as much as he needed her on the street. "He told us that Kiesha's his daughter."

"His *what*?" Her jaw dropped. "You think that's the truth?"

"I..." Lad recalled the look on Hensen's face and nodded. "I do. He insisted that Kiesha had no motive to kill Wiggen, which makes sense. Someone ordered the hit. I agreed not to kill her if she told me who gave her the order. Since then, he's been...helpful. I'll send information to you at the *Cockerel* as soon as I get it. The sketches of Kiesha should be done soon."

She glanced in the direction of the dining room. "You want me to talk to him?"

"No, Mya. He trusts me, and Sereth scares him. Between the two of us, it's working."

"How did *Sereth* find all this out?"

Was that jealousy or just curiosity? "It's a long story. Dumb luck. He was tailing Kiesha for another reason, and found the crafter she'd murdered. Then he searched and found the darts. But that doesn't matter. I need you to do *your* job, Mya."

Tightening her lips, she nodded. "Yes, Master."

Lad could see her mind at work, processing the information he had given her. He would have to be very careful around Mya, but then, he'd always known that. She never stopped looking out for herself.

He showed her out, thinking as he watched her trundle down the steps and made her way up the street. She looked back over her shoulder, then away when she saw his eyes still on her.

Back to work.

Lad strode through the dining room and opened the door to the adjoining sitting room. By the window, the artist was finishing up a sketch of Kiesha. Sheets of parchment strewn across the low table showed a dozen different likeness: Kiesha as a well-bred lady, Kiesha as a maid, Kiesha as a trollop.

On the other side of the room, Sereth and Jinny huddled close on a divan. Jinny was so petite that she seemed fragile beside Sereth. The adoration in her face as she gazed up at her husband took Lad aback. Suddenly it was Wiggen gazing up at him with love in her eyes.

Wiggen...

"Master?"

Lad snapped out of his trance. Sereth and Jinny stood before him, barely a step away, and he hadn't even noticed them move. *Not again! Not now!*

"We've got news. I need you in here." He was about to tell Jinny to stay put when he saw how tightly they clutched each other's hands. Separating them seemed...wrong. She already knew so much about guild business that excluding her now would accomplish nothing. He nodded them both through, and motioned the artist to continue her work.

As they passed, Jinny tugged her husband to a stop, and looked up to Lad. "Sir. With all that's happened, I never got to thank you properly."

"You don't have to thank me."

"But I'd like to." Jinny released Sereth's hand and reached out tentatively, laying her slim fingers on his shoulder. "Sereth told me about your wife. After such a loss, for you to bring us back together... Well, I thank you, and I'm sorry for your pain."

"I..." What was he supposed to say? Freeing Jinny had been part of his agreement with Sereth. Lad hadn't done it out of sentimentality. But seeing her freed, seeing the two of them together, did something to him; for just a moment, he felt good. He had done something right. Finally. "Thank you."

"You're welcome." Her hand left his shoulder and reclaimed her husband's. The couple entered the dining room and took seats as far from Hensen as they could.

Hensen cast a dismissive glance at them before addressing Lad. "And what news did your Master Hunter bring?"

"Patino's dead." Lad fixed the master thief with a hard stare. "And it doesn't take much imagination to figure out who killed him."

"Kiesha." Sereth nodded knowingly. "Covering her tracks."

"Possibly." Hensen didn't sound convinced. "She *is* thorough. How did he die?"

"We don't know yet. Bemrin's looking into it."

Hensen brightened. "Well, then, let's think about this. If she was going to kill him, she'd use her favored method, yet her weapon is at the house."

"She slit the gnome toymaker's throat," Sereth pointed out.

"Maybe she's changing her method," Lad suggested. "If she knows we're hunting her, she might have deliberately left the darts at the house and used a different weapon to make it less likely to connect her to the killing."

"But if she's gone to all that trouble, why not get rid of her weapon and the darts? That would be the easiest way to hide her association to the killings." Hensen frowned and shook his head in denial. "Kiesha may have played me false, but she is intelligent and thorough. She would *not* have gone to the trouble to kill the gnome, yet neglect to dispose of her blowgun and darts."

Lad had to admit that Hensen's logic seemed solid. "We need to know how Patino died."

"Even if the baron's throat was slit, it *still* doesn't mean Kiesha did it. I admit, it seems likely, but…"

"It's *more* than likely," Sereth growled.

"We're looking into Patino's associations, too. There has to be a connection either to me or the guild."

"As I said before, it must have something to do with the guildmaster's ring." Hensen nodded to the band of obsidian and gold on Lad's finger. "Wiggen wore it."

"But nobody knew she wore it until the fight in the courtyard," Lad countered.

"The other masters thought Mya wore the ring. One of them might have recruited Kiesha before they took Lad's daughter." Sereth shrugged. It didn't seem likely, but it was possible. "Maybe they contracted Kiesha to kill the wearer, thinking it was Mya, and Kiesha fulfilled the letter of the agreement by killing Wiggen."

"But the masters were already dead when she killed Wiggen." Lad shook his head.

"And we were contracted by Patino to *protect* Mya!" Hensen endured Sereth's glare without flinching. "And she did! Her report was precise. She arrived just as the fight started, and killed five assassins that night."

"That's true." Lad wasn't about to tell them where he learned that. "We've got too many questions and not enough answers. I need to know more about Patino. He's known to have mistresses, so Bemrin's sending an Inquisitor posing as one to Royal Guard headquarters to see what she can find out."

"You should tell him to be careful," Hensen warned. "Our investigations found that Patino had two mistresses, and his wife knew about them. If she should see yours, there'll be questions."

Lad nodded to Dee. "Send a runner to Bemrin with that. Tell him that I want his report before sunset tonight."

"Yes, Master." He ducked out of the room.

159

Lad sighed. It was back to waiting again. "Sereth, take Jinny home. If you think of *anything* else that might help us find Kiesha, report to me immediately."

"There was one thing, sir. She often met me dressed like a prostitute, so you might check the brothels. And..." Sereth looked nervously to his wife, then to Hensen. "Twice, she tried to seduce me. It was probably on his orders, just another way to manipulate me, but—"

"I did *not* order Kiesha to seduce you," Hensen blustered. "I considered having someone do so, but it wouldn't have been Kiesha."

"Then why would she?" Sereth countered.

"She was lonely." Jinny's slight voice drew every eye in the room. "We spoke some. I told her how much I missed you, Sereth, trying to talk her into letting me go. It didn't work, of course, but she told me to count myself lucky that I'd had you in the first place. She said..." Her gaze slid over to Hensen, then down. "She said she had never had anyone to love."

Hensen's face flushed. "Ridiculous!" He lifted his cup of tea and sipped.

Lad saw a ripple atop the dark liquid in the cup. Was love— or the lack of it—motivation enough for Kiesha to double cross her own father?

"Murder? You're sure?" Norwood gaped at the duke's wizard as if the man had just told him his pension had been canceled. For once, he wished his intuition had been wrong. The murder of a noble commanded precedence over all other investigations. He looked to the intricate diagram on his wall. The Fiveway Fountain killings would take a back seat to finding Patino's killer.

"Without a doubt, Captain." Woefler's boyish enthusiasm remained undaunted. "And it was lucky that you called on me immediately. There was very little residual magic left when I arrived. Undoubtedly, it's completely gone now."

"Magic? I called you there to look for poison."

"And I did. Finding none, I indulged my curiosity, poked about for magic, and found it!" The wizard grinned in triumph.

"Damn!"

This didn't bode well at all. Assassination was bad enough. Magical assassination was exceedingly rare, and usually meant sophistication, money, influence, and power. In most cases, this would rule out a simple matter of marital strife turned lethal. Jealous wives rarely hired magical assassins to murder their husbands when a drop of deadly nightshade in his brandy would do. Baroness Patino, however, certainly had the financial means, so he would have to consider the possibility.

"And there wasn't a mark on him. What magic can kill like that?"

Woefler wagged a long finger. "I asked myself that very question, Captain."

"And?"

"Well..." Woefler's face lit up with pleasure, and Norwood stifled a sigh of despair. The wizard enjoyed nothing more than explaining his craft. "...there are a number of spells that disrupt the human body. Different spells leave different signatures. Very few leave none."

"Signatures?"

"Visible evidence. Things like burns, frostbite, or necrotized tissue. There are less-destructive spells. For example..." Woefler plucked what looked like a desiccated chicken foot from the depths of his robe and muttered a few arcane syllables. A phantasmal clawed hand detached from the foot and wafted over Norwood's desk. It closed around the lamp and lifted it several inches. "I could use this spell to reach into your chest and grasp your heart, which would undoubtedly kill you."

"So?" Norwood eyed the phantasmal claw and refused to be terrified.

161

"So, Captain, while the spell would leave no marks on your body, it would cause you considerable pain. You would probably die clutching your chest, your face contorted."

"Neither of which we saw on Baron Patino."

"Precisely." The ghostly hand lowered the lamp to the table and vanished. Woefler tucked the dried chicken foot away with a satisfied smile. "The magic that killed Baron Patino did so without external injury or causing him any apparent pain. I only know of one spell that can kill painlessly. I believe his soul was harvested."

Norwood stared at the wizard. "*Harvested*? What does that mean?"

"Simply put, it's the act of separating the soul from the body. The technique was first discovered eons ago, when necromancy was still in its infancy." Woefler shifted uncomfortably. "Of course, necromancers harvested souls for use in their magic…or to extend their own lives. That's been outlawed here in the Empire, but other disciplines have mimicked the effect as a form of painless execution."

"Execution? I've never heard of any such method of—"

"Captain, please let me explain. You wouldn't have heard of this, because it's under the purview of wizards. The Wizards Guild polices itself. We have our own laws, and our own executioners. When needed, they use a soul-harvesting spell."

"You're suggesting that Patino was murdered by such magic?"

"Exactly." Woefler smiled. "No other spell could have killed him without leaving some type of signature."

"And who might be capable of casting such a spell?"

"Oh, I could perform it with a bit of research, and a few of my more proficient guild brethren might be able to do the same, but the aura I detected in Baron Patino had an odd…flavor."

"Aura?"

162

"Magic leaves trace auras. Any wizard can sense them. *This* aura, however, originated not from an arcane spell, but a divine one."

"A *divine*...you mean a priest?" Norwood flopped back in his chair, utterly flummoxed.

"Or priestess, yes." Woefler grinned. "You find that surprising, Captain?"

"I find that astounding! In thirty years of investigating violent crime, I don't think I've seen a single murder committed by a member of the clergy."

"I don't mean to offend, Captain, but how would you know if you had?" One of the wizard's eyebrows lifted. "You said yourself that Baron Patino's death appeared to be completely natural. Any number of people could have been likewise murdered, with no one the wiser."

Woefler had a point. The captain had always considered members of the clergy to be healers of body and soul, not assassins. "Can you tell me which god this priest or priestess worships? It would narrow the search."

"I'm afraid not, Captain. There was just enough aura remaining for me to distinguish it as divine magic, nothing more."

"Well, it could explain why we didn't find any sign of forced entry to Patino's house. If the assassin could kill with a wave of his hand, he could have murdered Patino from across the street."

"Um...no, Captain. Soul harvesting, whether arcane or divine in origin, requires a touch. The murderer was in that room."

"All right..." Norwood tried not be upset that Woefler had transformed a simple case of a dead baron into a nightmare murder investigation. He had asked for the wizard's help, and Woefler had provided valuable information. Where to go with that information was the problem. Norwood was accustomed to dealing with criminal organizations, not churches. This case would take some thinking.

"Thank you, Master Woefler. I appreciate your help."

"Happy to oblige, Captain." The wizard stood and straightened his robes. "I'm going back to the palace. Do you wish me to inform Duke Mir?"

"No, no. I'll do that." Another thought came to him. "Oh, and please keep this quiet for now. I don't need rumors of murder flying around Hightown, especially if a homicidal priest might be listening. As far as anyone else is concerned, Baron Patino died of heart failure."

"Oh, which reminds me; since I discovered the cause of death, I rescinded your order for an autopsy. I didn't think the baron's family would appreciate him being cut open without reason."

"Oh, yes! Thank you!"

"And you needn't worry about rumors, Captain. My lips are sealed!" Woefler's eyes twinkled with mischief as he nodded farewell and opened the office door.

A cacophony of raised voices from the outer office shook the room, some screeching obscenities, others wailing in angst, and several more pleading for calm.

The wizard looked back with a pained expression. "Unfortunately, not *all* lips are sealed."

"What in the name of..." Norwood rounded his desk, stalked to the door, and gaped at the scene.

His guardsmen were attempting to restrain four raving young ladies and a fuming baroness with only marginal success. All five were casting everything from poisonous glares, to harsh words, to the contents of their handbags at one another. Baron Patino's widow, clad in appropriate mourning, flapped and fluttered like a great black vulture, trying to get past the two guardsmen who had bravely interposed themselves between her and the others. Royal Guards were trained in dealing with squabbles between nobles, and though they dare not lay hands on the baroness, they formed a wall between her and her foes. The other four, dressed in various shades and degrees of finery,

164

enjoyed no such immunity, and struggled in the grasp of guardsmen, fighting to get at each other's throats.

"I think I'll leave through another exit, Captain."

"There are no other—" Norwood shut his mouth as Woefler murmured an arcane phrase, stepped through a dark fissure in the air, and vanished.

"Coward," he muttered, turning back to the screaming match. He took three strides into the fracas and bellowed, "Quiet this instant!"

Silence fell.

The captain took a moment to assess the quiet but still-hostile women. Two of the young ladies, obviously well-to-do, given their stylish gowns and tasteful jewelry, merely glowered at one another. The baroness ignored them, instead glaring daggers at the other two. One, a delicate young lady wearing a low-cut saffron gown, dabbed her tear-sodden eyes, and clutched a broken parasol. The fourth took Norwood's breath away. Her form-fitting crimson dress made her seem a rose among daisies. Stunningly beautiful, she stood with the poise of a queen, head high in defiance, hair like waves of molten chocolate tumbling over creamy shoulders and daring décolletage.

Norwood cleared his throat. "Now, what in the Nine Hells is going on here?"

It was obviously the wrong question. All five women immediately started screeching at him and one another. The two ladies of standing railed at one another like sailors, while the young lady in saffron simply wailed, tears streaming down her cheeks. The rose struggled to free a hand, her painted nails resembling bloody thorns.

"Please…be…civil!" Silence fell again, and Norwood nodded to the baroness. "Lady Patino, what's this all about?"

"I came here to clear up a simple misunderstanding," the baroness seethed, "and I find that my late husband has been consorting with common whores!"

Saffron Gown wailed at an even higher-pitch, while Crimson Rose countered with a poisonous glare and taunted, "Oh, come now, Baroness, you can't tell me you didn't know your dear husband was diddling half the women in Twailin!"

"Why you lascivious tramp! I should have you arrested!"

"On what charge?" Crimson Rose countered. "Last I heard there's no law against cuckolding a shrew!"

"I'll have your head!" The baroness lunged past the two intervening guards, reaching for the other woman's throat.

Crimson Rose broke the guardsman's hold on her arms with a quick jerk, and dodged like a prize fighter, still taunting. "And I had your husband's, so get over it, Baroness!"

"You vile piece of filth!" Baroness Patino lunged again, but Norwood stepped between the two.

"No wonder your husband went philandering if he had you to come home to!"

The captain grabbed Crimson Rose around the waist while addressing the baroness. "Lady Patino, I must insist that you calm down this—"

The baroness took no heed. The roundhouse swing she cast at the woman in red had real force behind it. Crimson Rose saw the blow coming and ducked. Lady Patino's fist met squarely with Norwood's chin, and set his ears ringing.

A burly private relieved Norwood of the crimson-clad woman, and the captain rounded on the baroness. "Lady Patino, that is *enough*!"

She took a step back, stopped short by the volume and tone of his order. He couldn't arrest her for accidentally striking him— nobles enjoyed immunity from such petty crimes—but he'd be damned if he would let this row continue.

"Corporal! Separate them all. Put them each in a different room under guard."

"Aye, captain!"

Saffron Gown wailed anew. "Why am I to be arrested? I've done nothing wrong. I just came to find out what happened to poor Euey!"

"No one's being arrested. We're just separating everyone for your own safety until we can get things settled." Norwood turned back to the baroness. "Lady Patino, you said you came here to clear up a misunderstanding. I would very much like you to do so."

"In private, Captain." She flashed a glare at the other women as they were being taken away. "I'll not have rumors about this spreading throughout the city."

"Very well." He waved her into his office and closed the door firmly behind him.

"Please have a seat, Baroness." Norwood rubbed his jaw as he took his own chair. His ears had stopped ringing, but the baroness packed quite a punch. He felt better with his desk between them. "I must admit that I'm surprised at your behavior, milady. When we spoke at your home this morning, you mentioned that you knew your husband spent time with other ladies, and didn't have a problem with his conduct."

"Yes, well…" She pressed her lips together in a hard line and looked away. "I'm afraid I wasn't completely truthful with you this morning, Captain. I knew of two of his…acquaintances. They're both ladies of high standing, and the affairs were discreet. Or at least, I thought they were."

"I'm afraid I still don't understand."

"Then *listen*, Captain, and I will endeavor to *help* you understand." Her eyes flashed back to his, and she spoke with the authority of one long used to being obeyed.

He spread his hands in a gesture of surrender and leaned back in his chair. "I'm listening."

"The two ladies I refer to, Jondelee Oaks and Vurita Miles, are from good families, but not noble blood. I knew of their associations with my husband because I approved them in the first place as a means to overcome…family difficulties."

"Please elaborate on these difficulties." The captain couldn't question the baroness outright about her husband's death without revealing to her that it was murder. Perhaps learning more about these difficulties would shed light on the crime.

"The baron, as you know, has no heirs and, despite our best efforts, we have been unable to conceive a child." She took a deep breath and sighed. "It was necessary to...contract the services of a surrogate."

"I see." It was not unheard of for royalty to have surrogate mothers produce heirs, and Norwood instantly understood why the baroness would want to keep the issue confidential.

"Miss Oaks and Miss Miles were candidates for that service, but neither knew of the other, or that we were interviewing more than one young lady. They both arrived at our home late this morning asking about Eusteus' death, and instantly fell to blows when each realized why the other was there. Your guards restrained them, and insisted they be brought here to clear up the mess. I insisted on coming along." She fixed him with another significant look. "I won't have them spouting rumors about me. I've warned them, but in their current states, I had to come to make sure."

"Perfectly understandable."

"Well, I arrived and found two more...women here asking about Eusteus. One of them, the one in red, is little more than a common tramp. I'm afraid I lost my temper." She looked away, withdrew a silk handkerchief from her handbag and dabbed it to her eyes. "I've just discovered that my late husband was a whoremonger, Captain. If this gets out, I'll be a laughingstock."

Norwood didn't dare tell her that he suspected it was already all over the city. He watched her closely, wondering if her tears were genuine. She had already lied to him once today, by her own admission.

"How do you propose we resolve this situation, milady? No laws have been broken, and I can't very well imprison any of these ladies just to keep them from spreading rumors."

"Jondelee and Vurita will keep their mouths shut. They know I'll ruin them both if they start telling stories. No contracts have been signed, so they have no claim to any compensation. The other young lady, the one in that *ghastly* yellow dress, seems to have been honestly duped by my husband. Though I'm not pleased with her, I bear her no ill will. If she agrees to keep her affair with Eusteus a secret, I have nothing else to say. As for that *whore* in red..." Her face flushed, and she pressed the handkerchief to her lips. "I would see her publicly flogged if I had my way, but as you say, no law has been broken. I would blame my philandering *husband* if he were alive to..." She turned away, and a muffled sob escaped the handkerchief.

Norwood wasn't sure what to do to console her, so he merely waited until she pulled herself together. "We'll issue them all warnings in the interest of preserving your reputation, milady, but nothing more can be done."

"I understand, Captain."

"Very well, then." Rounding his desk, he extended a hand to her. "You have my most sincere condolences on your loss. I'll do everything in my power to preserve your good name."

She took his hand and stood. "Thank you, Captain."

Norwood ushered the grieving widow out of his office and closed the door. "Well, now I've got five suspects instead of one." The women had seemed quite willing to kill one another. Might one of them have turned their fury on the baron? As he returned to his desk, absently rubbing his jaw, he wondered if any of the late baron's pugnacious paramours were associated with any of the local ecclesiastical orders.

Chapter XII

Norwood followed the footman across the lush palace lawn, squinting at the blazing midday sun gleaming off of the white garden wall. Precisely at the center of the lawn, a colorful blue-and-white-striped awning shaded an elegant luncheon. The Duke and Duchess of Twailin sat on silk-upholstered chairs at a small table, sipping wine and enjoying the dazzling beauty of a bright and cloudless day. The captain of the Royal Guard felt a twinge of guild that he was about to ruin that day.

"Milord Duke." Norwood stopped ten feet from the table and bowed. "Milady."

"Ah, Captain Norwood." Duke Mir regarded him with a thin smile, dropped his napkin onto his empty plate, and rose. "Punctual as always. You're familiar with the captain, aren't you Aerieanna?"

"Of course." Lady Mir shaded her eyes from the glare and smiled up at Norwood. "It's good to see you in health, Captain. You'll forgive me if I don't linger to listen to matters pertaining to the Royal Guard. Such dreary topics give me a headache."

"I don't blame Your Ladyship." The captain bowed as she rose. "They often give me headaches as well."

An amused smile graced the duchess' lips. Nodding to her husband, she strolled toward the palace. A footman paced in her wake, a shading parasol held high above her coif.

"So, Norwood, what warrants an appointment on such short notice?" The duke gestured toward the rose beds that lined the wall, and Norwood fell in beside him.

"Unfortunately, milord, murder."

Mir stopped mid-stride. "Murder? Who?"

"Baron Patino, milord."

"You're positive? I heard that he passed of natural causes."

Norwood wasn't surprised that was what the duke had heard. He'd spread that news himself. "That's the official explanation, milord, but Master Woefler discovered the remnants of the magic that killed him."

"Magic? That's unusual, isn't it?"

"Quite, milord, which is why I'm approaching this cautiously. I'm spreading the news that it was natural causes to give the impression that we don't know it was murder." They resumed strolling.

"You hope to put the culprit at ease and draw him out?"

"Him or her, milord. It's an even more unusual case than you might think. The magic, it seems, was wielded by a priest or priestess."

"You jest!"

"No, milord." Norwood shrugged helplessly. "I trust Master Woefler's judgment when it comes to such things."

"Yes, as well you should." The duke walked in silence for a while, then sighed deeply. "Damn it, I thought this violence was at an end!"

"Violence, milord?" Norwood knew what the duke meant, and felt he needed to nip this notion in the bud. People were beginning to feel safe for the first time in more than a year, and he would try to hold back the river with a mop and bucket before he'd let that feeling be tainted. "By all accounts, the violence *is* at an end. There hasn't been a single killing south of the river since the Fiveway Fountain incident, except for an occasional derelict in The Sprawls, and there's no reason to link simple gang violence to the death of a baron. I believe this is an isolated incident."

"I suppose so." Mir pursed his lips. "So how do you plan to proceed?"

"Discreetly, milord."

"Yes. Yes of course, but a *noble* has been murdered, Captain. We must direct our resources appropriately. As you just said, that other matter seems to have burned itself out. Let the City Guard take over the investigation of the Fiveway Fountain incident."

Norwood bit his lip to hold back an acerbic retort. It rankled him that the life of a single baron outweighed those of nearly thirty commoners, but he had been expecting just such an order.

"I'll do so if you command, milord, but I think it dangerous. Shifting Royal Guard efforts may start rumors. To maintain secrecy, I planned to personally conduct the murder investigation with the help of a few select guardsmen. That's why I came to speak with you, milord. I need your help looking into Baron Patino's background."

"What kind of help?" Suspicion creased Mir's brow.

"I'd like to access the Royal Archives to obtain the official version of the baron's life: financial details, the line of succession for his title and properties, religious affiliations, that kind of information. But to do so, I'll need a writ of permission from you."

Norwood had already received much of this information from Lady Patino, but he didn't know if he could trust her. By imperial law, the baron's title, properties, and most of his wealth would go to his heir. The baroness would retain her title and receive a stipend, but only until she remarried. Unless she married another noble, any subsequent children would be commoners, since the baroness had held no title prior to her marriage. The captain had to admit that this soured her motive for killing her husband, but jealousy was still a huge motivator, and Baroness Patino topped his list of suspects.

"The Royal Archives are in Tsing, Norwood. I'm not about to have you away from Twailin for a month!"

"No, milord, but I can ask questions by correspondence. A fast messenger takes little more than a week one way." *Which*

172

will give me time to finish with the Fiveway Fountain investigation.

"But to wait weeks for the information you need will give the killer time to flee."

"Which is another reason I want to keep this investigation as small and secret as possible, milord. If we don't shout from the rooftops that this was murder, why should the killer flee?"

Mir chewed his lip for a moment, and then shook his head. "No. No we must pursue this with all alacrity. I'll send an immediate appeal for the information you need. You should have an answer tomorrow."

"Tomorrow?" Norwood stopped short, staring at his liege in puzzlement. "How..."

"After that...difficulty a few years back, I asked Master Woefler to devise a means of magically corresponding with Tsing." Mir looked sternly at Norwood. "This is a *secret* means of communication, mind you. *No one* is to know of it."

"Or course, milord!" Norwood could see the advantages to such a boon, not the least of which was military.

"Good. Give a list of the information you need to Master Woefler, but don't ask for the man's entire life history. I can make the request high priority, but the more you want, the longer it will take."

"I'll have a list to Master Woefler this afternoon, milord! Thank you." This would speed up his investigation immeasurably.

"Find whoever killed Baron Patino, Norwood. That will be thanks enough."

"I'll do my best, milord."

Lad drew the black silk scarf up to secure it just below his eyes as he watched the coach lurched away from the curb in front of the Royal Guard headquarters. *If you want something done right, do it yourself*, he thought.

Bemrin's report had been worse than dismal. The Master Inquisitor had deployed his operative before he received Lad's warning that Patino's widow knew about his mistresses. Consequently, not only had his spy obtained no information about the baron's death beyond "natural causes", but she had planted herself smack in the Royal Guard's sights. Captain Norwood had questioned her himself. Fortunately, the talented young Inquisitor's cover story, along with copious tears, seemed to have satisfied him. Unfortunately, the Royal Guard would be checking up on her to ensure that she kept her alleged affair with the baron a secret. She was effectively out of commission until they lost interest, just when Lad needed all the operatives he had combing the streets.

Lad didn't believe Patino died of natural causes, but how could Kiesha have killed him to make it look natural? Her previous methods had not been particularly subtle. She did favor poison, however, so perhaps an envenomed needle. An inconspicuous wound might be overlooked by a hasty investigator.

But not Norwood. The captain was known for his diligence. And there was only one way to find out exactly what the captain of the Royal Guard knew.

"So here I am…"

Lad had first gone to Norwood's townhouse, but discovered some changes since his previous visit. All the windows were now barred, and instead of one huge mastiff on the back porch, there were two, both in the captain's bedroom. Neither precaution posed an impervious barrier to Lad, but he balked at killing the man's dogs just to ask a few questions.

Instead, he'd come to the Royal Guard headquarters. Peering into the captain's office window from a nearby rooftop, Lad devised a better plan to get him alone for a chat. It was no great distance between Norwood's work and home, and a Royal

Guard carriage always transported the captain to and fro. Lad would simply share the ride.

The coachman's whip cracked and the carriage accelerated. Lad tensed as it approached the line of shadow where he waited, gauging the rocking of the carriage as it rumbled over the cobblestones.

Noise and motion mask your movements. Use them to your advantage. Remember! The moment the vehicle passed into the gloom, Lad moved.

Three steps and a perfectly timed leap put his foot on the carriage step and his hand on the door handle without any jostle to alert the driver. The latch turned easily—*Vehicles rarely have locks. Remember!*—and he was inside, a flicker of shadow in the darkness. Norwood only had time to draw a breath before Lad's hand clapped over his mouth, pressing his head back hard against the cushioned seat. The captain reached for the dagger, but Lad plucked it from the sheath before he could touch it.

"Quiet, Captain!" Lad pitched his voice low to prevent the driver from hearing. The hissed command, or perhaps the dagger he held up before the captain's face, ceased Norwood's struggles. "I have questions for you about Baron Patino's murder. As before, I'll provide what information I can in return. If you call out, I'll vanish, and you'll get nothing. Nod if you understand."

The fear and anger in Norwood's eyes evolved into recognition and frustration. But there was curiosity there, too, and after a moment, he nodded.

"Good." Lad released his hold on the captain's mouth and, as proof of his sincerity, returned the dagger hilt first. "Please put that away."

"Don't you *ever* use a godsdamned front door?" Norwood snatched the dagger and jammed it into its sheath, his eyes flinty before widening with realization of what Lad had said. "Wait! How did you know Patino was murdered? I've kept that a secret!"

Lad sat down across from the captain. Already he'd learned two important details: the baron's death was, in fact, murder, and Norwood knew it. "I knew he was murdered because I know what he was involved in that got him murdered. What I need to know is how he was killed."

"If I tell you how he died, you tell me what he was involved in."

Lad considered for a moment, then said, "Very well."

"Patino was killed with magic."

That caught Lad off guard, but the darkness and the cloth over his face hid his surprise. Kiesha might be a thief and an assassin, but by all accounts, she was no mage. "Why do you think it was magic?"

"The duke's wizard told me. Apparently, Patino's soul was harvested...by a priest."

Lad thought about it. He wasn't religious, but living in a city with temples dedicated to nearly a dozen gods, one was accustomed to seeing their devotees everywhere. They had access to places laymen didn't. It would be a good cover for an assassin. But that didn't answer the Kiesha question. "He's sure it was a priest?"

"Or priestess, yes. He was sure it was divine magic, not arcane. Death was painless and instant, so it looked natural." Norwood's eyes narrowed. "So what was Patino involved in to get him murdered?"

"He contracted some people to interfere in the recent war between the Assassins Guild factions. One of those people killed...someone very important to me. The assassin's vanished, but we discovered a link to Patino. It seems likely that the baron ordered the killing."

"Son of a..." Norwood's jaw clamped down hard on the curse. "What motive would he have to get involved in your guild war?"

"I have no idea. Do you know if Patino was connected to any organizations that might have an interest in the Assassins

176

Guild?" If he was killed by a priest, maybe he was involved with a cult. *Bemrin probably has spies in half a dozen temples. Maybe he can unearth something.*

"I'm working on getting information about the baron's associations, but it'll take time."

"How much time?"

"I don't know. The inquiry has to travel to Tsing and back." Norwood shrugged and glanced out the window.

Was that an evasion? Lad clenched his teeth. "That could take weeks. I don't *have* weeks, Captain."

"Then look for yourself!" Anger flared in Norwood's eyes. "I don't work for you!"

Lad gauged Norwood carefully. The man could only be pushed so far before he clammed up completely. "I'll make you a deal, Captain. If you agree to share whatever you learn about Patino with me, I'll respond in kind."

Norwood glared for a few moments, seeming to fight an inner battle, then finally relented. "Fine."

"Very well. The black darts that were used in the Fiveway Fountain killings were also used to kill my...friend. The person who fired those darts worked with Patino. We discovered the dart maker, but he's dead and the murderer has vanished. Now Patino's dead. I thought she might be covering her tracks by killing Patino, but magic is not her method." *At least not that we know of. What other secrets might Kiesha have been hiding from her father? An association with a mysterious cult?*

"Her? The assassin is a woman?"

Damn! Lad had not intended to give up that bit of information. "Yes."

"Her name?"

"I'm sorry, Captain, but I can't tell you that." If he provided Kiesha's name and Norwood found her first, Lad might be cheated of his vengeance.

"You said Patino contracted someone to interfere in your guild war. Who did he contract?"

Lad wasn't about to give him Hensen's name either, but he had to give the captain something. "As strange as it sounds, the Thieves Guild."

"You're telling me Baron Patino transacted with the Thieves Guild?" Norwood frowned. "I need a name to confirm this."

"I can't give you a name. It would…complicate things." *But if I ever have to eliminate Master Hensen, I now have a means.*

"You're not giving me much to go on."

"And you've given me even less, Captain."

The carriage lurched as it rounded a corner, and a glance confirmed that this was Norwood's street. They didn't have much longer.

"So now both of us have more questions than answers." Norwood cursed under his breath. "Marvelous!"

"We both have one more thing than we had before." Lad hunkered back into the shadows as the carriage slowed. "You know Patino had some link to organized crime, and I know how he died, which changes my theory on who killed him. It also suggests that there might be a third party involved in this." *If Kiesha hadn't killed Patino, then why was he murdered? Did this negate the connection between Wiggen's death and Patino, or just make it more convoluted? Lad had a lot of thinking to do.*

"All right." Norwood begrudged him a nod. "If I find out anything out about Patino, I'll…hang a white handkerchief from my bedroom window, and you can get in touch with me. Just try not to scare the shit out of me next time."

"Fine. Goodnight, Captain."

Lad watched as Norwood exited the carriage, called out, "Regular time tomorrow, Sergeant!" to the driver, and stomped up the walk to his townhouse.

But can I trust him? How much of what Norwood told him was true? He had no way to tell. He'd gotten good information from him in the past, and in the end, Lad had no choice but to trust the captain.

Lad settled against the carriage door, one hand on the handle, intending to hop out at the first shadowed corner. He watched Norwood unlock the townhouse door as the carriage lurched into motion. The captain stepped inside, highlighted by a lamp in the front hall. Then, as he turned to close the door, a dark cloud formed behind him, coalescing into a robed figure with one luminous hand outstretched.

No! As the townhouse door swung shut, Lad moved.

"Cocky son of a bitch thinks he can pop in whenever he wants…" The irony of actually working with the Assassins Guild to try to solve a murder didn't escape Norwood, but he felt that the ends justified breaking the rules in this case. He'd obtained invaluable information. Knowing that Patino was involved with organized crime changed the whole focus of his investigation.

Despite the success of the encounter, Norwood's hands trembled as he worked the key in the lock. The speed and strength of his visitor had shaken him badly. Had he grown so slow in his years behind a desk that an assassin could disarm and subdue him so easily?

The latch clicked, and he stepped inside, cringing at the aroma of boiled meat and cabbage filling the air. It was the cook's night off, and his wife had made dinner. Contemplating another tasteless meal followed by a night of indigestion, he swung the door closed. As he threw the heavy deadbolt, the light of the hall lamp wavered, and the scuff of a boot on the carpet behind him caught his ear.

A visitor? Nobody ever greeted him at the front door when he arrived, not even those two flea-bitten dogs. Curious, Norwood turned, and the keys fell from his grasp.

A crimson-robed figure strode forward, face hidden within a deep cowl. His glowing outstretched hand, like a grim harbinger of death, shocked Norwood into action. The dagger he'd tried to draw in the carriage leapt into his hand, and he slashed. The blade sliced across the outstretched palm, and the hand snapped back. A curse escaped the dark recess of the hood.

Norwood tried to step back, but in turning, his feet crossed. He tripped and fell against the door, the heavy brass hinge gouging him between his shoulder blades. The cloaked figure resumed its advance, the pearly glow that engulfed the outstretched hand now tinged red with blood.

Magic! Norwood recalled Woefler's phantasmal hand and dire words—*I could use this spell to reach into your chest and grasp your heart*. He reached for his sword, but the long blade was caught between his backside and the door. He couldn't free it without moving dangerously close to that deadly spell.

The door slammed open without warning, flinging Norwood aside like a rag doll. The ensorcelled hand missed him by a hair's breadth. He hit the wall hard, but managed to keep both his dagger and his feet, despite being rattled by the impact.

A figure burst through the shower of splintered wood, a blur of black in the lamplight. Impossibly fast, a foot lashed out to strike Norwood's assailant precisely at the elbow. The joint snapped with a sickening crunch, the impact spinning the crimson-clad attacker around. Another curse, or perhaps some dark invocation, hissed from beneath the hood. Shattered arm pressed to his abdomen, Norwood's assailant backed away.

"Who are you?"

The assassin from the coach advanced, his voice edged like a razor. Norwood would have asked the same question had his mouth not been as dry as a desert. He settled for drawing his sword.

"The right hand of death!" The words seemed more of a threat than an answer. With one unintelligible word, darkness writhed about the assailant's uninjured hand, spreading swiftly to engulf him.

180

The captain's savior struck again, so fast that Norwood could barely follow the movement. His foot lashed through the swirling darkness, scattering tendrils like blown smoke, but struck nothing. There was nothing left to hit.

"Damn!" The assassin turned to Norwood, the light of the hall lamp striking him fully in the face. Though the dark cloth concealed most of the man's features, a curious pair of mica-hued eyes reflected the light. "Did he touch you?"

"No." Norwood shook his head and regained his composure. "No, I managed to keep him off me until you...arrived." He looked at his dagger. The tip bore a tiny streak of blood. *Not so slow after all,* he thought with satisfaction. "We both marked him." He wiped his dagger clean on his jacket and sheathed his weapons.

"I believe we've just met Patino's killer, Captain."

"You *think?*" A harsh, nervous laugh escaped his throat. "And now I know how he got into the baron's home. This hall was empty when I opened the door. He must have popped in just like he popped out." He remembered Woefler's little trick in his office. Evidently priests could do it, too.

"And he obviously wants you dead. The question is, why?"

"Dear, is that you?"

The feminine voice from the back of the house spun the assassin around, and he started for the door. "Be careful, Captain. You've drawn the attention of some very deadly people."

"Wait!" Norwood felt the need to say...something. After all, the man had saved his life. "I...um... Well...thank you."

"Thank me by staying alive, Captain. Someone knows you're looking into Patino's murder and doesn't like it."

"Right." Norwood blinked, startled by the suddenly empty doorway. The man was there, then he wasn't.

Other thoughts quickly distracted him. That someone wanted him dead was troubling enough, but that someone knew of the murder investigation was even more disconcerting.

Besides himself, only Master Woefler and Duke Mir knew that the death had been murder. Where had the leak occurred? Then he realized that at least one more person knew: the man who had just saved his life.

"What in the names of all the Gods of Light... What happened to the door?"

Norwood turned to find his wife standing in the hall, her hands clutching a sodden dishcloth, her face livid. Turning, he examined the shattered casement. The two-inch deadbolt had been knocked from the frame, leaving a sizable divot in the oak beam and scattering splinters down the hallway. The door itself, also solid oak, was split its full length. He stared for a moment, trying to reconcile the force it would have taken to do such damage.

Who the hell is this assassin?

"I...It was an accident, my dear."

"An accident? The door is *ruined!*"

"Just some ruffians trying to break in, but I ran them off," he assured his wife. "Don't worry. I'll have the door fixed tomorrow." He swung it closed, but it didn't fit well. He settled for hooking the security chain. "I'll nail a board across it for tonight."

"Ruffians? In this neighborhood?" His wife's face paled. "What's this city coming to?"

"I ask that question every day, my dear." Norwood shook off his dire thoughts and turned to her. "Now what is that luscious aroma coming from the kitchen? Did you have dinner catered by a master chef again?"

"Did I..." She blinked at him, taken aback by the change in subject. "Oh, stop it! Come eat before it gets cold."

"Of course, my dear." Norwood hurried to comply. The only thing more daunting than being attacked by one assassin and rescued by another was his wife's potato-cabbage stew gone cold.

182

Chapter XIII

With all the comings and goings lately, the neighbors will think Lad's quite the socialite.

Mya mounted the steps to his house, diligently practicing her lady-like stride and feeling silly in her new dress. She planned a foray into Hightown after the meeting, and wasn't about to go all the way back to the *Cockerel* to change. The dress was more comfortable than her old one, thanks to Bemrin's tailor, but the light blue color clashed with her red hair. *Never trust a journeyman Hunter to pick out a dress for you.*

"Miss Mya." Dee met her at the door. He didn't comment on the color of her dress, which was very politic of him, not to mention healthy. "The others are already in the study."

"Thank you, Dee." She lowered her voice. "I know Lad didn't take the news about Patino well. How is he doing?"

Dee's look of startlement took her aback. Then she remembered how closely he had kept her confidences when he was her assistant. His loyalty was to Lad now.

"Never mind. It's not my business." She started past him. "Forget I asked."

Dee held out a hand to forestall her passage and lowered his voice to a bare whisper. "Please, Miss Mya, I know you're worried. He...didn't sleep at all last night, and he didn't want breakfast this morning. Something's really got him worked up."

"Thank you." The look on Dee's face told her that she wasn't the only one who cared about Lad. Mya followed him down the hall, deep in thought. She hoped one of the other

183

masters had good news. Her Hunters had made no progress tracking Kiesha.

Dee opened the door to the study, and she found herself in the company of the other masters and Lad. Thankfully, Hensen wasn't here. She's been surprised to see the master thief sipping tea at Lad's table the previous morning, and felt no small amount of relief that he hadn't been tortured. *But why was only Sereth in on the interrogation?* Maybe she'd just have to ask Sereth.

"Mya, sit down." Lad paced like a caged wolf, his bloodshot eyes darting around the room at every turn. "We've got a lot to discuss."

"Yes, Master." She settled onto the divan and said casually, "Oh, Dee, would you bring in something to eat? I missed breakfast putting on this ridiculous outfit."

Dee raised his eyebrows at her request, then his eyes lit in understanding, and he nodded. "Of course, Miss Mya." He ducked out of the room.

"You need a lady's maid, Mya." Bemrin brushed his silk brocade jacket with a practiced gesture. "I find my valet indispensable."

"The *last* thing I need is a—"

"Talk about your servants some other time," Lad ordered, his eyes raking over them all. "I met the man who killed Baron Patino last night."

That brought them all up short.

"The *man?*" Mya gaped at Lad in surprise. How had he discovered the killer when all her Hunters and Bemrin's Inquisitors couldn't? "I thought Kiesha killed him."

"We were wrong about that." Lad resumed pacing.

"So, he really *was* murdered?" Bemrin's brows arched skeptically. "All my people were able to get from the Royal Guard was that Patino died of natural causes."

"I have my own informant, and if he says that Patino was murdered, then he was murdered."

He went to Norwood again! Mya wasn't really surprised.

Chris A. Jackson

"How did you find him?" Jingles asked. "And more to the point, where is he now?"

"I didn't find him. He tried to kill my informant, and I had to intervene."

That's not good, Mya thought. If an assassin was desperate enough to try to take out the captain of the Royal Guard, things had just stepped up a notch.

Lad stopped pacing and faced them. "That was right after my informant told me that Patino was killed with magic, by a priest."

"A *priest*?" Sereth asked with a furrowed brow.

"Yes. And the attacker last night certainly wielded magic." Lad paused as the door opened.

Dee entered in a cloud of heavenly aromas, and placed a huge tray of pastries and blackbrew on the table.

Lad's eyes lingered a moment on the repast before he began pacing again. "Evidently, this man can kill with a touch. Patino died without a mark on him. As to where he is now; before I could take him, he vanished in a puff of...something like smoke."

As the masters muttered oaths of surprise and consternation, Mya poured herself a cup of blackbrew, generously buttered a scone, and began to eat. Bemrin also served himself. The others evidently weren't hungry. Mya wasn't hungry either, but she did her best to look as if she was enjoying every bite.

"Smoke, Master?" Enola worried her lip and shook her head. "Did it smell of brimstone?"

"It didn't smell of anything, come to think of it, and it dissipated as soon as he vanished. Why?"

"Creatures of the Nine Hells generally leave behind bad smells or burns. A powerful priest might summon such a creature do his killing for him, though I think they tend toward violence, and would certainly leave marks on the corpse, if they even *left* the corpse." She wagged a wrinkled finger. "On the

185

other hand, a specter or ethereal devourer can kill with a touch, but they're incorporeal."

"He didn't leave any trace behind, and seemed corporeal enough when I broke his arm," Lad said.

"So, Kiesha did *not* kill Baron Patino. This...man did." Bemrin's lips pursed.

Hensen must have loved that, someone to take the blame off Kiesha. Mya washed the last bite of scone down with blackbrew, and took another pastry. "Dee, these are absolutely delicious!" she stage-whispered.

Lad glared at the interruption, stared a moment at the cheese pastry in her hand, then continued. "It fits the facts. What doesn't fit is who in the Nine Hells this assassin is, and what happened to Kiesha."

"Maybe he killed her, too." If pity had been butter, Sereth's comment wouldn't have dampened a single slice of toast.

"We've found no body, but..." Bemrin shrugged.

"Bodies can be made to disappear." Jingles twitched his wrist, his silver bracelet chiming. "Ask any catfish or alligator downriver."

"He wasn't concerned about disposing of Patino's body." Mya glanced at the others. "And I've had Hunters watching the docks day and night. No bodies have been dumped in the river."

"There's a big difference between slipping a dagger between a thief's ribs and pushing her into the river, and hauling a baron's corpse out of a house in Hightown." Jingles grabbed a muffin and took a huge bite.

"Did you get a good look at him, Master?" Bemrin nibbled his pastry and sipped blackbrew.

"No." Lad strode to the table and snatched up a scone almost as if the delicacy had offended him. Mya cheered inwardly as he took a bite. Her ploy had worked; she'd tricked him into eating something. "He wore a cloak with a deep hood. I saw his hands and caught a glimpse of his chin."

"But he looked human."

186

"Yes." Lad took another bite and nodded, considering Enola's question. "Yes, he seemed human. And his voice sounded perfectly normal."

"He spoke?" Bemrin's eyebrows arched again. "What did he say?"

"I asked him who he was, and he said, 'The right hand of death.'" Lad swept the masters with his gaze. "Does that mean anything to anyone?"

It didn't to Mya, and she shook her head with the others.

"Sounds like he was just trying to scare you, Master." Sereth shrugged.

"That's what I thought."

"I can certainly research that phrase, Master." Bemrin put his cup down and finished his pastry. "It might be a title of some sort."

"Do that. And ask around the temples about death cults or priestly assassins." Lad wolfed down the last of his pastry and resumed pacing. "Any more ideas?"

"If this man can pop in and out like a fart on the breeze and kill with a touch, I think we need to beef up security." Jingles looked concerned. "Especially around you, Master. He could pop in while you're sleeping and…well, off you."

"The thought *had* crossed my mind." Lad folded his arms and glowered. "Increased security's not a bad idea. The same goes for the rest of you as well. Everyone should have bodyguards watching day and night, even when we're sleeping. If this man tried to kill my informant just because he was asking questions about Patino, he might decide to take us all out for the same reason."

Mya cringed at the thought of having someone standing in her bedroom while she slept. In fact, she didn't want anyone in her apartment at all. She looked to Enola. "You think this man can just pop in anywhere?"

"Magic can accomplish amazing things," Enola admitted. "I'm no expert on transposition spells, but I can ask some questions."

"Do that, but be careful." Lad snatched up another scone, and Mya stifled a smile. "Also, Enola, since you're the only one among us who has any real experience with magic, find out what kind of spell might have killed Patino."

"Necromancy, maybe." Enola chewed her lip. "I'll check on it."

"Jingles, assign four of your best Enforcers to each of the masters, and myself as well. Two will be awake and guarding us every hour of every day." His eyes pinned them each in turn. "Is that clear?"

While the others simply nodded and agreed, Mya looked at Lad skeptically. "*Every* hour?"

He stared at her for a moment, and understanding dawned in his eyes. No one else knew of Mya's tattoos, and she wanted to keep it that way. "Barring bathing and such, of course, but someone needs to watch the room while you sleep."

"I guess I won't be *sleeping* much, then."

Bemrin and Jingles chuckled.

"If the assassin can travel with magic, he could be anywhere. Locks and doors won't keep anyone safe." Lad finished the last of his scone. "What I want most is to find Kiesha, preferably alive. Hensen has given us some more ideas about where she might hide, and I want them all checked. Dee has a list. I also want everyone to start thinking about who would benefit by Patino's death, who would order Keisha to murder my wife, and why."

"Yes, Master," they all said.

Mya jerked her head toward Bemrin as she said, "We're still looking into Patino's associations. I don't trust Hensen's report, since Kiesha was in charge of the investigation."

"She's absolutely right." Bemrin nodded in agreement. "I don't think we should trust *anything* Hensen told us."

188

"Then get out there and gather the facts yourself. Add any affiliations with cults or churches to your search of Patino's associations. If he was killed by a priest, maybe there's some connection. I've got someone looking into his past, but it'll take time." Lad looked to Bemrin. "Try not to bring the Royal Guard down on us this time."

"I'll be more discreet in my inquiries, Master." Bemrin bowed his head in subservience. Maybe he was learning a little humility.

"Do that." Lad swept the room with his gaze once again. "If there's nothing else, get to work."

Mya lingered to let the other masters leave first, finishing her pastry before following. Lad had already begun pacing again, but there was another pastry missing from the tray. She smiled. *Well, at least I got him to eat something.*

Captain Norwood stepped down from his carriage onto the courtyard of the duke's palace, brushing at the gooey white slobber on the leg of his trousers. The source of the noisome stain hopped down after him: four hundred pounds of canine. The two mastiffs observed their new surroundings attentively. Their hand-sized tongues lolled as they panted and drooled onto the manicured gravel drive.

"Excuse me, Captain." A palace guard stepped forward, one hand raised in a gentle forestalling gesture. The other held a halberd, its foot-long head gleaming in the mid-morning sun. "You can't bring those…um…pets into the palace."

"They're not pets, they're guard dogs, and they're staying at my side." In fact, the two mastiffs were the only reason Norwood had gotten any sleep last night after the attempt on his life. The dogs had drawn stares and questions when he stopped by his office that morning, but he couldn't have cared less. If that murderous priest popped in, Tango and Brutus would take him apart before he could get near Norwood. "I need to see Master Woefler, and then the duke. You can admit me through the servant's entrance so the dogs don't startle anyone."

"They don't look safe to me, Captain. I've the security of the duke's family and guests to consider."

"Oh, come on, man! They're well trained. They're not going to eat anyone unless I tell them to." He patted Tango and Brutus affectionately on their massive heads. "Hells, they won't even crap on the duke's silk rugs!"

"Well, I didn't mean—"

"They'll be no trouble. You have my word on it, Sergeant, and I'll take full responsibility if they so much as piss on a potted petunia." The attempt on his life had put him in no mood to deal with nonsense. "Now call me an escort and stand aside, or call Duke Mir, and I'll discuss it with him." He turned and strode for the servant's entrance, Tango and Brutus padding along at his heels.

"But, sir!"

Norwood ignored the guard's protestations. A footman intercepted him at the door, having watched the exchange from the main entrance. Thankfully, it was Thomsen, an old hand who knew the Norwood well.

"Don't mind the sergeant, Captain." The footman winked and lowered his voice. "He's a bit of a tight arse, if you know what I mean. Now, sir, does the duke's mage know you're coming?"

Norwood stifled a snort of laughter. "Yes, but I've never been to his chambers, so I'll need a guide. I'll be attending the duke afterward."

"Of course, Captain." Thomsen raised a white-gloved hand, and a page appeared before he could even extend a finger. "Merciel, conduct Captain Norwood to Master Woefler's quarters, then wait and take him to the duke in the gardens afterward. I'll inform his lordship that you'll see him at his leisure, Captain."

"That'll be fine."

The page bowed to Norwood, his eyes widening at the sight of the two mastiffs. "This way, sir."

Norwood let his mind wander as he followed the page. Despite hundreds of previous visits, it never ceased to astound him how vast the duke's palace truly was. It had been a fully fortified king's castle once, but the expanding Tsing Empire had swallowed the Kingdom of Twailin two centuries ago. The usurped king's son—after watching his father's head roll through the dirt of the outer courtyard—had readily agreed to be named duke of the new province. Since then, the duke's palace had served as a bastion of the Noble House of Tsing in the hinterlands of Twailin.

As he walked, he contemplated his tentative plan. Just how it would work depended on what Woefler had to tell him, but more importantly, on whether the wizard would go along. If Norwood could find the leak of information, he could find the assassin. He dismissed the Assassins Guild; not only had his visitor last night not known that Norwood was conducting an investigation, but he had saved his life. That narrowed his scope. If his plan worked, and he caught the killer alive, he might even find out how this was all connected to the Fiveway Fountain massacre.

And that, he thought, *would be a double feather in my cap*!

Lost in thought, the captain followed the page down a flight of stairs, nearly bowling into the young man when he stopped abruptly in front of an unmarked door. The page rapped the brass clapper thrice and said loudly, "Captain Norwood to see you, Master Woefler."

The latch clicked, and the door opened of its own accord. "Show him in."

Norwood squinted at the brilliant light that flooded out the door, and entered the vast chamber. Three steps in, however, he stopped, his hand drifting to the hilt of his sword. Tango and Brutus growled and bristled at his heels.

Woefler turned from his seat across the room, wide eyes fixed on the dogs, his face pale. He looked more upset than Norwood had ever seen him. "What in the name of the lost books of Azrael are *those* things?"

"I might ask you the same thing," the captain countered, pointing past the wizard to the figure lounging on a low divan. "Is she really on *fire*?"

The wizard sat upon a stool in front of an easel, his arms folded over his chest while four tiny paint brushes levitated before a startlingly lifelike painting. The model of the painting, and the subject of Norwood's concern, was a ruddy-skinned woman no larger than a child, with hair of living flame. Her eyes gleamed red, and a gown clung to her like a second skin, as if molten gold had been poured over her curvaceous shape. Arching a fiery eyebrow at him, she plucked a glowing coal from a nearby brazier and popped it into her mouth like a tasty tidbit.

Woefler glanced over his shoulder, and then looked back to Norwood. "Yes, she is. Now please explain why you've brought those two monstrous dogs into my chambers."

"These are my new bodyguards, Tango and Brutus."

"Well, they can't come in here. You'll have to leave them outside."

"Why?"

Woefler waved a hand, and his brushes descended to their paint pots. "First of all, you have no need of bodyguards in my quarters. Secondly, dogs don't particularly care for magic. It's said that it smells *wrong* to them. They tend to bite things they don't like, so mages, as a general rule, do *not* care for dogs."

The news couldn't have pleased Norwood more. He patted the slobbering beasts affectionately. "Well, I like them quite a lot, but I suppose they can wait outside." He turned to the page. "You don't mind watching them for me, do you, Merciel?"

"Um...no, sir." The youth eyed the two canines dubiously. "As long as they don't...um...dislike pages, too."

192

"They're gentle as lambs." Norwood nudged Tango and Brutus out of their threatening postures. "Come on, boys. Heel." The dogs whined, seemingly reluctant to turn their backs on the wizard's chambers, but followed. Outside, Norwood bade them to sit and stay, which they did without complaint. The page stood by nervously, still uneasy. "Don't worry, they won't move until I come back."

"Yes, sir."

Norwood went back into the room, and the door closed behind him of its own accord.

"Why in the names of all the Gods of Light do you need two dogs the size of ponies to guard your person, Captain?" Woefler seemed to have relaxed, now that the dogs were gone, but his voice still carried a burr of annoyance.

"I find them comforting." Norwood looked around the room. Whatever he had expected of a wizard's chambers, it was not this.

He'd imagined a small, cluttered cubby smelling of sulfur and smoke, rife with tattered books, stacks of parchment, oddments and doodads. This was more of a lavishly appointed suite than a laboratory or workshop. The chamber seemed to have been freshly cleaned by an army of obsessive maids, organized by an equally detail-oriented archivist, and decorated by someone with impeccable, if somewhat eclectic, taste. There were bookshelves, to be sure, but the volumes were neither dusty nor disorganized. Glass-fronted cabinets stood between the shelves, their contents displayed in tidy rows. These curios, however, would never be seen on a staid dowager's mantle. Figurines of ivory, precious metals, crystal, and ebony danced, moved, and writhed on their little bases. Even the rug appeared to be animated, the threads and patterns changing and shifting as he stared. Norwood felt nauseous with all the movement as made his way to the center of the room, where comfortable divans surrounded a low table. An array of decanters, blackbrew and tea pots, jars and glass-domed serving dishes brimming with hors d'oeuvres were laid out as if for a pending party.

Lowering himself to a seat, he spoke once again. "After someone tried to kill me last night, I felt the need for additional security."

"What?" Incredulity replaced annoyance on Woefler's face.

"I said, someone tried to kill me last night." He peered at the miniature woman. "Um, is that a…"

"Tweorijle's from Hades, but you needn't worry." The wizard smiled in a dismissive manner. "She's constrained by the circle of runes there on the floor."

"Must you ceaselessly torment me with that word?" The tiny devil's voice sounded like bones being ground to dust between a pair of granite blocks. Turning her blazing eyes back to Norwood, she looked him up and down. "Your visitor looks positively delicious. May I eat him?" She popped another ember into her mouth and smiled with black, burning teeth.

"No, you may not." Woefler sighed and transferred his brushes to a pot of solvent. "Forgive me, Captain, but Tweorijle is miffed that I discovered her true name and bound her to my service."

"I am not bound yet, Wizard." The devil's sensuous smile curled into a feral grin. "Not yet."

Norwood peered closer and realized that, as the devil moved, so did her image in the painting. He wasn't sure he wanted to know what Woefler was doing, and didn't ask.

"But you will be bound, my dear, you will be." Woefler drew a silk cover over the painting. "That's enough for now, I think. You may go home." He waved a hand, and the burning woman vanished in a puff of noxious smoke. "She's sort of a work in progress."

"I understand." Norwood didn't actually, but felt safer simply agreeing rather than having Woefler elaborate to the point of petrification. *Best to get right to the point.* "You received the report from Tsing?"

194

"I did, but what's this about an attempt on your life?" Woefler sat on one of the plush divans and poured himself a goblet of amber-hued wine. Lifting the glass cover from a platter, he asked, "Won't you have something?"

"I'm not hungry, thank you." The captain wondered about the array of food and drink. Had Woefler ordered all this just for him? It seemed extravagant. "I'll explain about the attack in a minute, but I'd like to read the report from Tsing first, if you don't mind."

"Of course." Woefler plucked a pastry from the platter and replaced the cover.

Norwood blinked. Beneath the glass dome, the plate was full again. *More magic...* The captain shifted uneasily. Magic was rare and dangerous. To use such power for simple convenience didn't seem right.

Oblivious to his guest's discomfort, Woefler popped the morsel into his mouth and waved a hand. A thick roll of parchment floated over from a shelf as he chewed, swallowed, and chased the bite with a sip of wine.

"I'm afraid it's rather dry reading. Maybe you'll get more from it than I did." Taking the parchment out of the air, he handed it over.

Norwood untied the string that bound the roll and opened the report. "You read it?"

"I had to transcribe it from the messaging scroll, Captain." The wizard pointed to an ornate golden stand on a nearby table. A scroll stretched across the flat surface, rolled into a pair of spindles at top and bottom. Beside it, a long-feathered quill pen stood in an inkpot. "Just as the emperor's archmage had to transcribe the report onto an identical messaging scroll in his laboratory. I hope the information was worth our time."

"So do I."

While Norwood read the report, Woefler continued munching and sipping wine. The wizard was right; it was dry reading and offered little insight. Nothing even remotely illegal or suggesting a connection to the Thieves Guild or Assassins Guild. *There has to be one somewhere.* Norwood had already thrown off any thought of the baron being killed for his money, or something as trite as jealousy. This murder was not so mundane. Rerolling the scroll, he lost himself in thought. Perhaps, there was something here that he could work into his plan to identify the information leak.

"Satisfied, Captain?"

"Not really." He regarded Woefler. Could the amiable wizard be involved in some murderous conspiracy? *No.* If he was, Norwood would already be dead. That didn't mean, however, that he hadn't inadvertently leaked information.

"To get back to your original question, Master Woefler. Someone tried to kill me in my home last evening." Norwood gave an accurate account of the attack, and the assassin's vaporous escape, only leaving out the part about his savior assassin. If anyone found out he'd been exchanging information with the Assassin's Guild, there would be all Nine Hells to pay. The last thing Norwood wanted was a manhunt to scare off his informant or, worse yet, make him angry.

"Really?" The wizard's eyes fairly glowed with intrigue. "A coincidence is quite improbable, Captain. That was surely Baron Patino's killer."

"Yes, that's what I thought, too, but it raises a disturbing question: How did he know I was investigating Patino's death? I told no one but you and the duke."

"Yes, that is disturbing, but before we go there, Captain, let me ask you *how* this man vanished. What exactly happened? What did you see, hear, smell, or even taste? Did your skin tingle? Was there a temperature change? If so, was it hot or cold? Any details at all would help."

Norwood thought back. His memories of that moment were quite vivid, right down to his own pounding heart and the blood on the tip of his dagger. "I cut him, and he pulled back. I asked who he was. He said, 'the right hand of death', and then some

196

black mist or vapor bloomed from somewhere near his hand, and it...consumed him. There was no sound, no smell that I remember, and I didn't feel anything like heat, cold, or static."

"Consumed him..." Woefler put down his wine glass and leaned forward. "Describe that, please."

"The dark vapor came up fast, like...streamers of black smoke, and as it swirled and spread over his body, there was nothing left. His hands and feet were the last to vanish, but his body was already gone. When I put a blade through it, the stuff just swirled away like mist on the breeze. It happened fast."

"That is *very* interesting, Captain." Woefler nodded. "Yes, I think this was most definitely an interplanar shift, not a transposition spell like mine."

"What's an...interplanar shift?"

"A means to step from our plane of existence to another. My spell, the one I performed in your office, opens a kind of passage between two points in our world. I simply step through, as I would an open door." He smiled, pleased by his explanation, and reached for the wine decanter. "Are you sure you won't have a glass of this remarkable sherry, Captain? You look as if you could use a drink."

"Well, it's not even noon yet, but..."

"Nonsense." Woefler poured both of their glasses full. "A sailor friend of mine once told me that the sun is *always* over the yardarm *somewhere*."

"Very well. Thank you." He took the glass, sipped, and had to agree; the sherry was remarkable. The warm glow trickled into his stomach, but didn't do much to relax him.

"Now, you were hypothesizing about how this assassin learned you were investigating Patino's death. Let me assure you that no one learned it from me."

"But you copied down my inquiries to the Royal Archives here in your chambers. Could someone spy on you here?"

"No, Captain." The wizard looked affronted by the suggestion. "The entire palace is protected from magical intrusion. And I always have protection, so no one could have heard our discussion in your office, either."

"Well, what about someone sneaking in and reading the message you while you were out?" He nodded to the scroll on the golden stand.

"Even if someone *could* get in here without being reduced to ashes, the message I sent is not here. It's in Tsing."

"But you said you had to write it down there, on the scroll."

"Yes, I did. Let me explain how this magic works." Woefler sipped his sherry and plucked another dainty from the tray. "When I write on that scroll, the words appear on an identical scroll in Tsing, not the scroll here. I destroyed your note with your inquiries as soon as I transcribed them, so there was no trace for anyone to find here in my quarters. The scroll in your hand is the only copy of the return message, and I only received that this morning, *after* your assassination attempt."

"That narrows the potential leak points considerably. Duke Mir's the only other person here who knows of the investigation..."

Woefler was already shaking his head. "If you haven't noticed, Duke Mir can be rather paranoid about security. He would not pass information that you gave him on to anyone else, not even the duchess. Your leak is not in Twailin."

"So, the leak is a thousand miles away..."

"It seems so, Captain, but this magical messaging system is as secret there as it is here. Few would see your inquiry."

"Who might have?"

"The emperor's archmage, definitely. I doubt he took your request to the emperor himself for approval, so at least one imperial page to deliver it. Then there's the royal archivist, of course, and probably one or two assistants." He shrugged. "No more than six people, and none who would care about your inquiries."

198

"Someone apparently does. And somehow they got a message to this priest in Twailin, thinking that if they killed me, they'd stop the investigation."

"Captain, I think you are misunderstanding the magic involved here. If this assassin does indeed travel by interplanar shift, then distance means nothing. He could transport himself from Tsing to your home in the blink of an eye."

"Marvelous." Norwood downed his sherry and sighed. His plan wasn't quite working out how he thought it would, but with a wizard on his side... "Master Woefler, I'd like to set a little trap for our killer, but I need your help."

"I'd be *delighted* to help." Woefler grinned like he'd been offered a title. "What do you need?"

"A map of the empire that shows the baron's estates, to start with. He has three; two are relatively close to Twailin."

Curiosity glinted in the wizard's eye. "Are you planning pay a visit to further your investigation?"

"I am." Norwood could see the wheels working behind Woefler's eyes. *At least he's on my side.*

"And since that is outside of your jurisdiction, you'll need permission from the Duke."

"Yes, but I'll tell Duke Mir I'm going to one estate, while I'll really be going to another. That way, if someone shows up to kill me, it'll confirm that the duke wasn't the leak."

"And you'll have me send a query to the emperor about this estate you really plan to visit, so if someone comes to kill you, it will be confirm that the leak is in Tsing."

"Yes. And you'll include some language to make it clear that I have found irregularities with the baron's death. Don't call it murder, but say that I'm investigating."

"Of course."

"And I need you to make sure the message says exactly where I'm visiting and when I'll be there."

"You plan to use yourself as bait..." Woefler's intrigue faded with concern. "The duke won't like that, Captain."

199

"The duke doesn't need to know." He narrowed his eyes at the wizard. "Does he?"

Woefler's smile broadened, and he reached for the wine decanter. "Hunting murderers is such thirsty work, Captain Norwood."

The corners of Norwood's mouth twitched. "Only one more, Master Woefler. Just while we look at the map. I have to speak to the duke straightaway."

Chapter XIV

Lad jerked out of his trance-like state and whirled, batting away the hand that had touched his shoulder. Dee's yelp of pain stopped the killing blow that would have followed.

"Don't do that!" Lad relaxed from his fighting stance and glared at his assistant. "Don't *ever* touch me without my being aware of you! I could have killed you!"

"Yes, sir." Dee rubbed his wrist where Lad had struck. "I called, but you didn't respond. I'm sorry, sir."

"You'd be sorrier if I broke your fool neck by accident." Lad cursed inwardly, blinked, and took in his surroundings. It was dark. He'd come up to his room to change clothes, stopping just for a moment to watch the sunset from the balcony. That must have been a half-hour ago. Once again, he'd been lost in thoughts of Wiggen and Lissa, the first time he held his daughter in his arms... *Gods I miss them both so much...* He blinked again and focused on Dee. "Next time just stomp your foot or throw something at me."

"Yes, sir. Your guards are downstairs. They were worried."

"I just came up to change. I didn't think I needed an escort."

Dee frowned in disapproval, but just nodded toward the door. "Dinner's ready, sir. Hensen's waiting in the dining room."

"Let him wait." Lad strode to his wardrobe and flung open the door, suddenly irritated by Dee's oppressively protective attitude. He knew he should eat, but the thought of food clenched his stomach. He picked out a dark shirt and trousers.

"On second thought, go ahead and feed him. I'm not eating. I'm going out."

"Sir, please. Do you think going out is wise?"

"You're my assistant, not my keeper!" Lad stripped off his fashionable silk shirt and donned the dark linen one.

"Yes, sir, but I believe keeping you alive falls under my purview." Dee picked up the fallen shirt and folded it. "You said yourself that someone might be out to kill you, someone who can magically appear anywhere he wants. If I had been that person just now, you'd be dead."

Lad stopped and glared. Once Dee finally realized that the guildmaster wasn't going to kill him for speaking his mind, he seemed to grow bolder with each passing day. But what irritated Lad was not so much Dee's mothering interference, but that he was right. He had been thoughtless to leave his guards downstairs, and to consider going out alone. He flung the dark trousers back into the wardrobe and started pacing. "I *can't* just sit here waiting, Dee! It's driving me crazy! I've got to *do* something!"

"Well, if you don't mind my asking, sir, what are you waiting for?" Dee placed the silk shirt on a shelf, then picked up the trousers and started to fold them.

"What?" The question snapped through Lad's dark mood. "What do you mean?"

"I mean, why don't you do something? You said you're waiting on information about Patino from your informant. How long will that take?"

"*Weeks*, apparently. The inquiry has to go to Tsing and back."

"And so do you." Dee tucked the trousers away and closed the wardrobe door. "You and Miss Mya, that is."

"I can't just leave, Dee! We haven't found Kiesha yet."

"Master, we both worked for the Hunters long enough to know that, if you don't find someone within the first couple of days, the search is apt to drag out for weeks." He shrugged.

"And if she's found in your absence, she'll be kept safely locked up until you return."

Lad grudgingly conceded that point, but persisted with another. "And if my informant needs to contact me with news about Patino while I'm gone?"

"The news will also be here when you return. But there's also the opportunity for you and Miss Mya to conduct your own investigation while you're in Tsing. Someone there will have known the baron. He may even have relatives living in the city. Posing as gentry, you might be able to pick up information through social channels."

Lad peered at Dee. His assistant seemed to have all the answers.

"But sitting in a *carriage* for weeks?" The prospect of so long in a rolling coffin grated like sand between his teeth.

"Or sit here for the same weeks waiting for word on Patino or for someone to find Kiesha, and *then* have to go to Tsing."

"The Grandmaster isn't expecting me for another month."

Dee shrugged again. "His instructions said *within* two months, sir. You can go earlier. I'll send a fast courier ahead to inform him of your pending arrival. I've got your clothes ready for a final fitting, and I can charter a carriage in a day. Besides, if you're traveling, an assassin won't know where to find you."

Lad could think of no more arguments. Dee was right. Once he got this meeting with the Grandmaster out of the way, his time would be his own. The trip needn't be a waste of effort. They could investigate Patino in Tsing, and Lad might be able to determine if the Grandmaster was behind Patino's contract to protect Lad and Mya.

What if there's a link to Kiesha...to Wiggen's death? The ring on Lad's finger seemed to constrict, a garrote around his soul. Even if the Grandmaster admitted to orchestrating the killing, there was nothing he could do about it. Lad shook his head to clear his thoughts. He was getting ahead of himself. *I need facts, not supposition.* Only then would he have a focus for his vengeance.

"Fine. Set it up." He doffed the dark shirt and pulled out the one Dee had just put away. "Send runners to Mya and Sereth. Tell Mya that we're leaving day after tomorrow, whether she's ready or not. Inform Sereth that he'll be in charge of the guild in my absence."

"Sereth, sir?"

"Yes." Sereth owed him, not only for Jinny's life, but for his own as well. The Master Blade understood that debt, and would repay it with loyalty.

"Very well, sir, but you may want to send Hensen home, and give Sereth explicit orders not to kill him while you're gone." Dee folded the discarded shirt and put it away. "You may have noticed the...um...friction between them."

"*Friction?* That's putting it mildly, but you're right." Lad strode to the door. "I'll tell Hensen he's going home, and you draft the messages. I'll sign them after dinner."

"Very good sir."

Lad ignored the satisfied smile on Dee's face. Let him enjoy his little victory. At least this gave Lad something to do.

The knock on the front door sent Sereth's hand to the hilt of his sword. His two bodyguards reacted by moving to interpose themselves between him and the door.

Don't be stupid, Sereth! Assassins rarely knocked, especially ones who could pop in and out magically. *But it might serve as a distraction...*

"Jinny?" he called up the stairs. She had been in their bedroom unpacking clothes she hadn't worn in years. Sereth had ordered all their belongings moved to his new house, and the two of them had been unpacking all afternoon. The place was starting to feel like a home, but his nerves were on edge, and he hadn't heard her in a while. "Jinny!"

"I'm here, Sereth." She stepped onto the landing, a bundle of clothes draped over one arm and a dagger in her free hand. She held the blade as he'd taught her. She was no assassin, but she could defend herself well enough.

That's my Jinny.

"I heard the knock. Who is it?"

"Probably just business." The smile he flashed her fell as he turned back to the door. Few outside the guild knew where he lived, and he intended to keep it that way. He nodded to one of his bodyguards. "Open it."

The Enforcer complied, revealing a breathless young woman in a sweat-stained jerkin. "Message for Master Sereth." She held out a sealed scroll tube.

The Enforcer reached for it, but Sereth's paranoia flared. "Don't touch it!"

Both bodyguard and messenger froze.

Sereth stepped forward. "Who is it from?"

"Your master, sir."

That boded well; a guild messenger would never blurt out Lad's name. "Come in."

The messenger stepped through the door without hesitation, and showed no trace of anxiety when the Enforcer closed it behind her.

"Now, hold out the scroll." She did so, again without hesitation or any sign of nervousness. Reaching out his hand, the tingle from Sereth's ring assured him that the scroll case wasn't dangerous. He took the tube. "Wait. I might have a reply."

He popped the waxed seal, unrolled the scroll, and read. He blinked and read it again, wondering if this was some mistake. Swallowing hard, he read it a third time to make sure he understood. Convinced that he wasn't hallucinating, he turned back to the messenger. "Inform my master that I received his message, and that I'll follow his orders to the letter."

"Very good, sir." The young woman bowed and left. The door thumped closed, and the two Enforcers relaxed.

"Stay here," Sereth ordered his bodyguards. "I want a private word with Jinny."

"Yes, sir." They folded their arms to wait. They knew he wasn't going to go traipsing off alone.

At the top of the stairs, Jinny met him with worry in her eyes. "What is it?"

"Lad's leaving Twailin." Sereth took a deep breath and let it out slowly, trying to calm his whirling thoughts. "He's going to Tsing to meet the Grandmaster. Leaving in two days."

"That's a long trip."

"Yes. Two weeks each way."

Jinny gripped his arm. "Sereth, what's wrong?"

"Nothing's wrong, Jin." He smiled at her and almost laughed at the irony. "He's leaving me in charge of the guild while he's gone."

"He's...*what*?"

Sereth unrolled the note again and read aloud. "You will act as interim guildmaster in my absence. Upon my return, you will resume your duties as Master Blade."

Jinny's grip tightened. "Sereth! That's..." She faltered, then said, "That's good, isn't it?"

"Yeah! Yeah, it's good." He smiled weakly and patted her hand. "I...I just didn't expect it."

"Why not? You're a master. That means that you're good at your job."

"Yes, but think about it, Jin. This shows that he *trusts* me." Sereth shook his head. Lad had already trusted him to keep the secret of Hensen's contract with Patino. Though he was curious about why Lad wanted to keep it from the other masters, he wasn't about to violate that trust. Sereth owed Lad more than he could ever repay.

"Well, then he's smarter than I thought he was."

Sereth stared at Jinny in surprise. "What do you mean?"

"Oh, I know we owe him our lives, Sereth, but he just seems a little...I don't know. Odd, I guess."

"He's been through a lot, Jin." He squeezed her hand, impulsively pulled it up to his lips and kissed her fingers. *More than I ever want to go through.*

"Day after tomorrow? He's got to be *kidding!*" Mya reread Lad's note and cursed beneath her breath.

"Problem, Miss Mya?" asked her new assistant, Geltin. He was no Dee, but he was learning.

"Hells yes, there's a problem." She dropped the letter and leaned back in her chair, her dinner suddenly unappetizing. "I'm leaving for Tsing in thirty-six hours."

"That's...a problem all right." Geltin's eyebrows arched. "Want me to call in your senior journeymen?"

"Yes. I'll have to put Pictor in charge until I get back."

"That'll make his day." Geltin chuckled and scratched notes in his book.

"Well, Sereth is going to be acting guildmaster while Lad and I are gone, so that'll un-make it." For some reason, Pictor didn't like Sereth. Mya mused on Lad's decision. It didn't really surprise her; of all the masters, Sereth seemed to be the most forthright and stable. After Sereth found out about Kiesha, Lad had been relying on him a lot. She felt a stab of anxiety.

Leaving in two days... Two weeks alone in a carriage with Lad.

Pushing away from the table, she stood and stared into the cold hearth, forcing her mind back to the task at hand. She had a lot to do before they left. *Why the sudden rush?* Not that she had a choice, of course. She had to go. She was a slave, after all.

"Send a reply to the guildmaster. I'll be ready. That's all for tonight, Geltin. We'll finish the rest in the morning."

"Yes, Miss Mya." Geltin picked up his things and left without another word. At least he'd learned her moods well enough to know when not to argue. Her two bodyguards moved to follow as she keyed the hidden latch that opened the door to her subterranean abode. Her safe place.

Hardly safe anymore since the whole damned guild knows about it. It had been a thin deception anyway, and there had been no way to flout Lad's orders about keeping the Enforcers at her side.

"Come on." They followed her through the portal, glow crystals brightening their way as they descended into the apartment. The place was clean and quiet, as always. Paxal saw to the former, and Mya saw to the latter. One Enforcer stood beside the stairs in the main room, while the other followed her wherever she went. The only time she had any privacy was when she bathed and dressed. She wasn't about to let them see her tattoos. There were enough rumors about her already.

Mya went to her bedroom and opened the expansive clothespress, picking out the things she would pack. Traveling dresses, shoes, pajamas…

Nearly a month alone with Lad…

As the Grandmaster stipulated in his letter, they'd be posing as a couple to minimize suspicion. That meant sharing a room. A warm sensation trickled down her spine and centered in her stomach, igniting a sweet fantasy in her mind's eye. She'd once crouched in the rain and watched through a fogged window as Lad and Wiggen made love. She imagined herself there, feeling his touch, taking away his pain, being with him…

Maybe…maybe it could happen…

Oh, stop it! She threw a few more outfits onto the bed. Everything was ready except for her formal dress and a corset she was having altered. Bemrin's tailor had promised them soon.

I'll be damned if I'll leave before they're done!

Mya sighed and looked at the pile of dresses, wishing she could travel in pants and shirt. *I'm going to need two trunks to carry all this!* Not only would she be uncomfortably clothed, but they'd be sitting in a coach all day with nothing to do but watch the scenery go by. She'd have to bring something along to keep her mind busy, keep her from dwelling on the fact that she was alone with Lad. *Maybe some books...* She had shelves full that she never had time to read.

Striding out into the main room, still trailed by her bodyguard, she began selecting books from the shelf, piling them on the spare chair. When she'd picked out a score, she reviewed her selections, putting some back and picking others. Finally satisfied, she stepped back, frowning at the stack resting on the chair's plush cushion.

For the first time, Mya wondered what had possessed her to furnish this place so elaborately. She hardly ever used the divan, and no one had ever sat in the spare chair. She'd created a private sanctum, and furnished it like she was expecting company.

Wishful thinking? The thought recurred to her: *Two weeks alone with Lad...* Mya bit her lip, closed her eyes and remembered that night in the rain again.

It could be me. It should be me...

Her fantasy died a premature death as she recalled Lad's words... *There will never be anything between us but business...* They plagued her night and day, a constant reminder of her utter folly.

Don't be stupid, Mya. She went to her desk and sat, intending to immerse herself in work. She had plenty to do if she was leaving in two days. *Two weeks...alone with Lad.*

Love is a weakness.

Chapter XV

"Driver!" Norwood thumped the roof of the carriage. "Left at the crossroads!"

"What?" Tamir snapped out of his doze and blinked. His bleary eyes were drawn out the window to the passing crossroad signs. "Why are we turning? Mountainview's to the right."

"I know." It was time to spring the surprise on Tamir. They were more than a day out of Twailin, and there was no chance of a careless word being overheard and spread. "We're not going to Mountainview. We're going to Farthane."

"Captain, I don't…" Tamir nudged Tango aside to better see out the window as the carriage made the turn. The wind caught a thick streamer of white spittle dribbling from the mastiff's drooping jowl and splatted it onto Tamir's shoulder. "Godsdamned slobbering hound!"

Tango just stared at him and panted, enjoying the breeze on his face.

Tamir leaned out again and looked back as the carriage behind them, also emblazoned with the crest of the Twailin Royal Guard, stayed on course to the right. "Where are they going then?"

"Mountainview. Corporal Donnely has his own orders."

"Orders?" Tamir looked perturbed. "Pardon my askin', sir, but what the hell's going on?"

"We're going to Farthane to catch an assassin, Tam."

The sergeant's eyebrows shot up. "What assassin is that?"

210

"The one who murdered Baron Patino, then tried to kill me three nights ago."

Tamir scowled, then looked at Tango and Brutus taking up more than their fair share of the seats, and realization dawned on his face. "Thought there was somethin' strange about you suddenly bringing a couple of dogs with you everywhere. Why'd you keep it quiet?"

"It's a long story, Tam, and now that we're out of Twailin, I can fill you in." Norwood related the whole story, from Woefler's discovery of the murder to the decision to keep it quiet and set a trap for the killer. It was a relief to finally get it off his chest. He didn't like keeping secrets from Tam. To his credit, Tamir didn't take his exclusion personally. "So, we're setting up a trap, and you're going to be a big part of it."

"Okay." Tam looked at the two dogs again. "Why the canine cadre?"

"Because dogs don't like magic, and the assassin we're after reeks of it."

"So, you're going to sic these two on him when he pops in? That ought to startle him, but how do you plan to catch someone who can disappear in a puff of smoke?"

"With this." Norwood reached into his pocket and withdrew a thin golden chain. He wrapped one end around his hand. The other end dropped to the floor of the carriage, twitching like a snake. The two mastiffs growled at it. "Woefler loaned it to me."

"Magic, huh?" Tamir looked at the length of chain skeptically. "What's it do?"

"It keeps our assassin from disappearing in a puff of smoke."

"That's all?" Tamir's face scrunched in a scowl. "It doesn't keep him from killing you, too?"

"No. I'm hoping Tango and Brutus will distract him long enough for me to get this thing around an arm or leg. That's all it takes to keep him from escaping. It sticks when it's flicked against something living. I've practiced with it. It's not hard to use."

"And how *do* you plan to keep him from killing you?"

"The usual." Norwood patted the sword at his side. "If he can't escape, I can put a blade to his throat. That ought to persuade him to come quietly."

"And if he *doesn't* come quietly?"

"Then I put a blade *through* his throat." Norwood coiled the chain and put it in his pocket. "I want him alive, but I'll settle for dead. The important thing is, if he shows up, we'll know there's a spy in the Imperial Palace."

The sergeant's eyes widened. "The Imperial Palace! A little out of our jurisdiction, ain't it?"

"We're the Royal Guard, Tam. If the Imperial Palace isn't royal, then I don't know what is."

"Okay." Tamir scratched his jaw and frowned. "So, tell me about this trap we're settin' up."

"We'll need to enlist the help of the estate manager, but it's important to keep things quiet. This is what I want you to do…"

Lad worked a finger under his cravat and tugged to loosen it slightly. He'd only had the thing on for ten minutes, but it already felt as if it was choking him. Or maybe it was the course of action he had chosen that felt like hands tightening around his throat.

Leave Twailin…

The notion of wasting an entire month traveling to Tsing—before he found Kiesha, before he knew who was truly responsible for Wiggen's murder, before he had answers—infuriated him. Unfortunately, Kiesha was the one with the answers, and she had vanished.

Lad gripped the balcony rail and gazed out at Twailin, his city. He'd spent a quarter of his life here. He knew every street, alley, shop, and warehouse, but even with the entire Assassins Guild and a good portion of the Thieves Guild searching for the Hensen's daughter, he'd been unable to find her. No blood, no body, no trace...no answers.

Who wanted Wiggen dead? He twisted the ring on his finger. *This has to be the part of the answer...* He'd been over it a thousand times, and it always came back to the ring.

I put it on her finger. He clenched his fist on the ring until his knuckles ached and his hand trembled. *I wanted to protect her, and I killed her.*

"Careful with that!" Mya's acerbic tone drifted up from the street below. She was in a foul mood, probably irritated at the short notice for their trip.

Well, she'll just have to get over it.

A knock interrupted his thoughts, and Dee entered the room.

"Miss Mya's here, Master."

"I heard. I'm coming." Lad looked out over the city once again, scanning the tumbled conglomeration of rooftops lit by the morning sun. Five blocks west of the Eastmarket wall, he picked out the distinctive roof of the *Tap and Kettle*. Smoke wafted out of the chimney, and he could almost smell the fresh-baked bread, feel the bustle of the inn coming to life, hear the sweet gurgles of a baby waking. *Lissa...* The clean smell of her hair, the soft clenching of her tiny hand around his finger... *Gods!* He swallowed a lump in his throat. He longed so deeply to see her, touch her, that his chest ached.

I will *see her again...* He might never be able to be her father, but he vowed to watch her grow up, if only from afar. He couldn't risk putting her in danger, but he could catch glimpses of her. *It's better this way.* He tried to reconcile himself to that unbearable thought. Forbish and Josie would raise her well. Tika and Ponce would watch over her as protective uncles. They'd love her as she deserved to be loved. As he couldn't...

Lad turned away before he lost himself in thought, and followed Dee from the room. His two bodyguards thumped

213

down the stairs behind them, incongruously loud compared to their master's silent tread.

"Master..." Dee overcame his hesitance after a moment. "May I suggest that during your trip you...be more clumsy, or at least less light on your feet? You don't want to draw unwanted attention."

Lad wasn't used to using a disguise. He chalked the advice up as one more thing he had to do to make his alternate identity realistic, and adjusted his steps to make more noise. It felt strange, just like the clothes, the shoes, the house... At the front door, Dee held out a walking stick—a tapered length of beautiful dark wood topped with a gilded handle shaped like a bird's head—and a top hat.

"No."

"Sir, please." Dee looked determined.

"No, Dee. I absolutely refuse to wear the hat." The jacket, waistcoat, tie, trousers, and hard-soled shoes were oppressive enough. Why gentry thought it necessary to dress in such finery just to sit in a carriage all day mystified him. "It's stupid! I'll wear the rest, but I draw the line at the hat." He snatched the cane and refreshed his gentlemanly persona in his mind.

He'd been trained for stealth, not deception, but he had been taught to observe, to pick out minute details, look for anomalies in behavior, speech, and manner that might indicate a hidden threat. Now he used all he had learned from watching the moneyed gentry of Twailin. Casual steps, head high, loose stride, easy manner, tap-tap of the cane on the steps; a perfect gentleman.

His trunk was already secured aboard the carriage, a huge conveyance built for comfort. A matched team of four horses stood patiently in the traces, hooves clacking on the cobblestone street. Mya's two Enforcers were finishing with a pair of larger trunks from her hackney, securing the last in the carriage's covered boot under her scrutiny. They'd only be taking three Enforcers with them: one as driver, two posing as their servants.

214

Mya turned at his approach, and Lad was struck again by how strange she looked dressed as a gentlewoman, rather than in her usual trousers and shirt. Today she wore a russet-colored traveling dress, nothing fancy, but still incongruously feminine. The corset gave her a much more pronounced figure, pinching her slim, athletic shape into an hourglass.

That can't be comfortable.

She stopped, noting his scrutiny. A small hat topped her short red hair, and she peered at him from behind a lacy veil. "What?" She walked over with a sway to her hips and a bounce to her gait that she hadn't possessed before.

"Nothing." A pair of ladies strolled toward them, curious eyes drawn to the activity. Lad tried to appear casual, wondering what a gentleman would say to a lady in an instance like this. He had no idea. "You look...very nice this morning."

Mya opened her mouth to say something, but then caught sight of the passersby. "Thank you." She raised a hand to adjust his cravat. "So do you."

Lad stifled the urge to bat her hand away, and forced a smile of his own. "Ready?" He held out an arm as he'd seen gentlemen do, and gestured to the carriage door.

"Yes." She took a breath and let it out slowly. "Yes, I am."

The hand she put on his forearm trembled. Was she nervous or frightened? Why? The passing ladies were obviously no threat. Maybe she was just as reluctant as he to board the conveyance.

They nodded to the inquisitive ladies as they passed, and Lad opened the door to allow Mya to climb in first. He knew Dee had already checked it for hidden dangers, but his long habit of caution chafed at his forced calm. *Two weeks in this travelling coffin...*

"Be *careful*, sir."

Lad turned, surprised by the note of concern in Dee's voice. How strange that this unassuming man appeared to truly care for him. Previously, when they both worked for Mya, Dee had barely acknowledged Lad, much less shown any indication that he liked him. And yet, since becoming his assistant, Dee had helped him immeasurably, and Lad had repaid him with a short temper and sharp words. It seemed unfair now.

"Don't worry, Dee." Lad gave him a smile. "Thank you for...everything. I'll see you in a month or so."

"Very good, sir." Dee smiled, bowed, and stepped back, the very image of propriety.

Lad boarded the carriage and settled into the thickly cushioned seat across from Mya. Despite the spacious cabin and the breeze wafting in the open windows, the walls seemed to close in around him, the air heavy. He tugged at his cravat and swallowed, his breath coming short. The carriage lurched into motion, the noise of hooves and iron-rimmed wheels on the cobbles masking the sounds of the city. *Blind, deaf, and confined to a box...* Lad's knuckles whitened on the head of his cane.

"Are you all right?" Mya asked.

"I'm fine," he lied. He forced himself to relax, leaning back against the soft upholstery and stretching his legs out comfortably. Still, Mya stared at him. "I don't like carriages."

"Neither do I." A smile flickered across her mouth. "You taught me that."

Lad looked out the carriage window, watching the familiar scenery pass them by. *Leave Twailin... Leave Lissa...* He forced a deep breath and closed his eyes, trying to ease his mind into the light meditation he'd used for years. As always of late, his thoughts turned to Wiggen, bittersweet remembrances of the scent of her hair on her pillow as she slept, the touch of her hand on his face, the brush of her lips on his neck...

Gone. She's gone.

A rustle of cloth and the creak of leather opened his eyes. Mya held a small book in her hands.

"What are you reading?" The question was out of his mouth before he thought about it. Anything to distract his mind.

216

"Just a novel." She shrugged and met his eyes. "A made-up story."

"I know what a novel is."

"Sorry."

He looked back out the window. They were coming to Eastgate. Lad hadn't been outside the city in five years. The last time he had passed this portal, he'd been a different person, less than human, bereft of emotion, and ignorant of what he was. Sometimes he longed for that blissful ignorance again.

Wiggen...

"Didn't you bring anything to do during the trip?"

"No." Lad glanced at her with a flash of irritation. "I suppose I should have brought a novel along."

Ignoring his sarcasm, Mya opened her handbag and withdrew another book. This one was larger, with a leather binding and colorful paint on the edge. She handed it over. "Here. This will pass the time, and might even be helpful."

"The City of Tsing, Heart of the Empire Past and Present," he read aloud. It had never occurred to him to read about Tsing before arriving. Though long familiar with reconnaissance, he generally learned through experience, firsthand observation, and exploration. The notion of reading a published tour guide to learn about their destination beforehand now seemed ludicrously obvious. *Why didn't I think of this?*

"It's pretty dry reading, but there's a lot of information, and even some maps." Mya sat back again and opened her book. "It's a big city. I thought it would help to at least know our way around."

Though seemingly relaxed, she sat stiffly, and Lad took a moment to surreptitiously examine her more closely. Her foot jiggled under the folds of her dress, and her finger tapped on the spine of her book, uncomfortable or nervous. *Why?* Maybe it was the carriage.

"Yes. It should be useful." He flipped open the cover and read the foreword, then thumbed ahead until he found a map.

Streets crisscrossed the page, buildings jammed together in long blocks. It *was* a big city. Then he flipped the page and found another completely different map, and another, and another. "There are maps of several cities here."

"Those are just Tsing's districts." Mya looked up with a hint of amusement in her eyes. "There are six of them, and the Imperial Palace besides."

He counted the number of blocks across a single district. "But each one of these is as big as Twailin!"

"Yes, and most are much more heavily populated." She went back to her book. "I told you it was a big city."

"Yes, you did." He'd known that, but he'd had no real sense of how big. In all his years living in Twailin, he'd never seen a map of the entire city. He'd learned its streets, alleys and rooftops by walking them, not by reading about them. It had taken him weeks to fully explore it, and months to learn all its nooks and crannies. Tsing would take *years* to learn. "Have you been there?"

"No." Mya didn't even glance up, but her foot tapped faster.

Of course. She's nervous about being summoned by the Grandmaster. Lad had been so focused on his own problems that he'd forgotten her predicament. Masters were rarely summoned thus, and when they were, it generally wasn't good. He had no idea how he might ease her fears, or if he should even try. "This *will* be helpful. Thank you."

"You're welcome." Her eyes continued their back and forth migration across the pages.

Lad flipped through the maps, piecing together the districts of Tsing in his mind, marveling over the vastness of the city. What would it look like? What the people would be like? Turning to the table of contents, he perused the chapter titles: A Millennium of History, Biographies of Fifty-eight Emperors and Empresses, Economics and Trade, The Military, The Rise of Nobility, Laws Past and Present, and a final section on Entertainment and Leisure. This would be helpful indeed.

He glanced back to Mya. *She's always thinking ahead, planning and plotting, looking for every advantage. I just stumble through, reacting to whatever comes my way…* She was right; he didn't think like an assassin. She, however, most certainly did.

I should have given Mya the guildmaster's ring.

The thought was futile, of course. She hadn't wanted it in the first place, and it was pointless to consider how things might have been different. The decision was made the moment he put it on. He was guildmaster. He could do nothing but be guildmaster. But he could not run the guild alone. He needed people like Mya, Dee, and Sereth, those who seemed to truly want to help him. He needed to learn how to better *let* them help him. Unfortunately, the only thing he'd learned was that managing people was a lot harder than killing them.

The carriage rumbled beneath Eastgate's high arch. Twailin was now behind them, and the city of Tsing ahead. Lad flipped to the first page of the book and began to read.

Chapter XVI

Norwood looked out the window as the carriage pulled up to the Farthane way-inn. Backlit by the twilit sky, the building cast a long shadow across the village commons. *Perfect timing.* He had hoped to arrive after dusk, when traffic would be sparser—not that a village this size had much in the way of bustling crowds to hide an assassin—but not too late for dinner.

"Stay, Tango." The captain reinforced his command with a hand signal. The dog regarded his master with intelligent eyes, silent and obedient. Norwood glanced at Tamir, who sat back in the shadows. He knew his job, though he'd groused some about it.

Norwood opened the door. "Brutus, guard."

The mastiff hopped down from the carriage and froze, scanning the surroundings. This was where things could get dangerous. If Norwood's theory was correct, and his ploy worked, the assassin could strike at any time. The instant he left the carriage might be that time. Norwood tried to look casual as he stepped down and closed the door behind him.

No assassin. Norwood wasn't sure if he was glad to still be alive, or disappointed that his plan might not work.

A stableman stepped out of the barn door and hobbled across the courtyard toward him. Before he could approach close enough to see Tam inside, the captain banged on the side of the carriage and called up to the driver, "Bring the estate manager back as soon as you can. Don't take no for an answer!"

"Yes, sir!" The coachman cracked his whip, and the carriage clattered off into the deepening darkness.

The stableman neared, halting when Brutus growled. "Help you, milord?"

"Yes." Norwood scratched Brutus' massive head to calm him. "I'll be staying the night, and need stabling for my team when they return."

"Of course, sir. Talk to the missus about rooms." The man nodded toward the inn door, then peered nervously at the mastiff. "No dogs allowed in the inn, and I don't want him in the barn. The horses won't like it."

"He stays with me." Without waiting for an argument, Norwood strode toward the inn, Brutus at his heel. He wasn't about to sleep without the mastiff in the room, not tonight. A tall woman stopped him at the door.

"No dogs in the house, sir. He'll have to be kept outside."

"This isn't a dog. This is my second in command, Sergeant Brutus. He likes meat, and lots of it. I'm Captain Norwood of the Twailin Royal Guard." Norwood fished a gold crown from his pocket and held it up. It was more than the price of a room, board and stabling for two days.

"Don't care if you're Duke Mir himself. No dogs in the house." She crossed her arms, ignoring the coin.

"Your charter to operate this inn as an official way-station on the Imperial Highway is sanctioned by Duke Mir, ruler of this province. It'd be a shame if I had to advise the duke to *revoke* your charter due to your refusal to accommodate members of the Royal Guard." He still held out the coin.

She frowned, but took the coin and bit it. Looking down at the dented gold, she stuffed it into her apron pocket, stepped aside, and jerked her head toward the common room. "Late for supper. Stew and bread. Plenty of cold mutton for your *sergeant*."

"That'll be fine. I'd like a private room for dinner, if there is one. I have business to discuss with the Farthane Estate manager."

"Down the hall in the back. It'll be a silver crown."

"Dinner for two in the back room, then. My driver's bringing the estate manager. See that he's shown back, will you?"

"She, you mean?" The woman looked dubiously at him.

"Yes, she." He hadn't known the manager was a woman. He probably should have, but it didn't matter.

"I'll have it served when she arrives."

"Very good. Heel, Brutus."

Norwood walked through the room, ignoring the few patrons. Brutus would growl if anyone made a move. The private room had a table, cold fireplace, one window, and four simple chairs. He took the seat facing the door and window and told Brutus to sit.

The mastiff's growl snapped Norwood out of a doze. His hand was on his dagger when the door opened to admit an irate woman in well-tailored workman's clothes.

"Captain Norwood, I presume?" She didn't sound happy. "I'm Emi Jeico, manager of Farthane."

"Yes." He stood and extended his hand. Her powerful grip surprised him. "Thank you for coming." Norwood ushered her to a seat, and told the maid who had escorted her back, "Knock before you come in. I don't want to be disturbed except by the staff bringing dinner."

"Yes, sir." The maid closed the door.

"I hope you haven't eaten. I ordered dinner for two."

"As a matter of fact, Captain, I *have* eaten, and this *summons* has disturbed my digestion." Jeico took a seat, her eyes narrow and suspicious. "Your sergeant wouldn't give me any details. What's this about?"

"First, let me offer my condolences. Baron Patino is dead."

"What?" Her eyes widened. "When?"

"Ten days ago. As for why I'm here, that's a sensitive issue." He lowered his voice. "You see, few know this yet, not even his wife, but Baron Patino was murdered."

"Murdered?" Her eyes widened further, her belligerence stifled by shock.

"Yes, ma'am, and I'm here to ask your help in apprehending his killer."

Mya lay in bed, staring at the ceiling and listening, determined to stay awake despite her weariness. The first three days on the road had left her frustrated beyond reason, and she intended to do something about it.

The first long day had established a maddeningly silent routine. Aside from an occasional comment about the book Lad was reading, there was no conversation, no discussion, not even any arguments. They dined in silence, and that was the last Mya saw of Lad until the next morning. The following day and the next had been the same: board the carriage after a silent breakfast, ride in silence, eat dinner in silence. Lad would slip into the room after she was abed, and was gone before she awoke the next morning. The only reason she knew he'd been there at all was the rumpled pillow and blanket on the floor.

Mya took a deep breath, trying to control her frustration. This was so different from the easy banter they used to engage in as they walked the streets of Twailin, sharing ideas, observations, and theories. Then, she had felt safe under Lad's vigilance. Now, she was fearful of him, afraid to open her mouth. She didn't know what to make of his mood. The few times he had spoken, he asked her a question about the book, then seemed irritated when she tried to strike up a conversation. Every moment felt like a trial of patience, a silent torture designed to drive her mad.

Tonight, she vowed, *that's going to change.*

Mya shifted in the bed, her blousy pajamas tangling about her legs. She'd never worn anything to bed until she'd been assigned her Enforcer bodyguards. Now she slipped them on over her wrappings every night.

Where is he? It was late, and she was getting drowsy.

Her silly fantasies had been crushed, of course, when he insisted on sleeping on the floor. Mya no longer harbored any fantasies, but this ridiculous silence was going to end.

The door latch clicked quietly, and Mya froze, shutting her eyes and slowing her breathing as if asleep. She listened to the faint rustle of cloth as Lad entered and began to undress in the dark. Mya dared to open her eyes a slit. Starlight through the gap in the drapes provided enough light for her rune-enhanced eyes to see the play of muscles under his skin as he draped his shirt over the back of a chair. A fine tracery of scars wove around his body where some of his magical tattoos had burned away. Unlike Mya's, Lad's original tattoos were invisible. Only the new ones—the runes etched into his skin by Vonlith—could be seen, a line of black spiders on his chest. As he stepped out of his trousers to pull on the loose silk pants he slept in, warmth spread through Mya that her enchanted wrappings would not abate, a visceral heat that she knew she could never quench.

Lad stretched out on the floor, flat on his back, and pulled the blanket up. For some time, Mya listened to him breathe, long inhalations and exhalations, steady and unchanging. Peering closer, she saw that his eyes were open, their luminosity winking in and out as he blinked.

Enough, she thought, stifling her fear. *He thanked me for the book. Maybe he'll let me help.*

She sat up in the bed and leaned back against the headboard. "You don't sleep, do you?"

Lad jerked, turned to look at her, then away. "No."

"Would you like to talk?"

"No."

"It might help."

"Nothing will help, Mya." He flashed her an unreadable look, and rolled over. "I've tried everything. Nothing helps."

With a reckless impulse, she swallowed her fear and asked, "Have you tried holding a carrot between your toes?"

He was on his feet in one instantaneous, fluid motion to glare at her. "Mocking me *certainly* won't help!"

"You're sure?" Mya repressed the pointless urge to fight or flee, refusing to let him intimidate her. If he held everything in, he would eventually crack. Mya knew all about cracking; she had cracked once. "You seem to be focusing on being angry with me right now instead of obsessing, so it might."

Lad whirled away, wrenching open the window drapes to stare outside. Starlight illumed his torso, muscles tense beneath his skin, pulse pounding at his neck.

Silence...

"We could talk about something else."

Silence...

"You think Hensen's telling the truth about Kiesha, or is he just trying to protect her?"

"He's telling the truth." Lad drew in a deep breath and let it out slowly, his body relaxing just a bit with the exhalation. Mya knew the technique; she used it herself.

He's trying, at least.

Not knowing what else to do, she pressed on. "And he said he didn't know why she killed Wiggen."

"Yes."

"And you believed him on that, too."

"I...don't know. He said she told him it was an accident."

"An *accident*? How could she kill anyone by accident?" A lot of things about this just didn't make sense. Maybe talking it through would give her better insight. Anything to keep Lad talking. "What I don't get is what Kiesha was doing at Fiveway Fountain anyway! Why would the Thieves Guild give a damn if we all killed each other? And if she was just spying, why would she kill anyone, much less Wiggen?"

Lad tensed, and his breath came a bit quicker, but he remained silent.

What's going on? The hairs rose up on the back of Mya's neck. "Lad?"

A long moment passed, then Lad sighed and turned around, his face a blank mask. "I didn't tell you everything. There was something I didn't want the masters to know, but...now..."

"Okay." This didn't sound like Lad. Why would he withhold information? "What didn't you want us to know?"

"Kiesha was there to protect us, you and me."

"What?"

"Hensen was contracted by Patino to keep us alive. She killed five other assassins during that fight. She was also the one who killed the assassin who tried to murder me in that Eastmarket alley. She saved my life."

"But...we assumed that the *Grandmaster* was behind that. So if Kiesha was protecting us, why would she kill Wig—" The puzzle pieces clicked together in Mya's mind, and fear squeezed her heart in a vice. "The ring! Gods of Light, you don't think..."

"What I *think* doesn't matter, Mya. I don't *know* what to think. I need to find Kiesha to find out where her orders came from. I don't think it was Hensen. It could have been Patino. And...it might have been the Grandmaster..."

"But...we're going to *meet* him!" She got up and began to pace, her steps halting. She had to think. Something didn't fit. *Think!*

"Yes. Maybe I'll discover the truth."

"But how could he know? Nobody knew Wiggen wore the ring but you and me!"

"Until the fight started."

She shook her head. "No. He couldn't have known there even *was* a ring! He ordered me to have one forged, remember?"

226

"Yes. It doesn't make sense." He sighed and lifted his hand to stare at the band of gold and obsidian. "I just wanted to protect her."

So that's it! *Guilt...* Mya knew about that, too.

"We'll get to the bottom of this, Lad, but blaming yourself for Wiggen's death isn't going to help."

His glare stopped her pacing. "How can I *not* blame myself? The only thing that makes sense is that Kiesha killed Wiggen because she wore the ring. I put the ring on her finger. I told her it would keep her safe."

"And it *did*!" She met his ire, forcing her voice to calm. "She saved Lissa with it! If she hadn't been wearing the ring, she would have been killed by Horice."

"If she hadn't been wearing the ring, she wouldn't have been there in the first place."

"Okay. Maybe, but you can't keep blaming yourself. It'll kill you, Lad!"

"You're wrong. I *can* blame myself, and I do." He looked out the window. "I killed her."

"Fine. Blame yourself!" He snapped around, eyes hard, but Mya refused to relent, determined that he would listen to the truth, even if it meant her death. "But if you think killing Kiesha, or whoever was running her, is going to make you feel better about Wiggen, you're being stupid."

"I don't *care* about feeling better, Mya!" Two steps brought him to her, his luminous eyes blazing. "I'm going to find out who did this, and I'm going to kill them!"

Mya bit back her terror and held her ground, determined to help him despite himself. "For five years you told me you weren't a killer, and now all you want to do is murder someone. You told me you were *more* than just an assassin."

"I *was* more!" Lad trembled, seething with rage. "I was a father and a husband, but all that's gone!"

"Gone?" She clenched her jaw against a sharp retort. "You still have a family, Lad. You still have Lissa! If you kill for vengeance, could you ever face her again? Could you face Forbish and the rest of them? If you become a murderer, you'll be alone forever." *Like me...*

"I *should* be alone!" The pain in Lad's voice cut her like a razor. "I put my whole family in danger just by being what I am, Mya. They're better off without me."

She knew it was true, but coming from him it sounded wrong.

"No, they're not, and *you're* not better off without *them*." Mya knew what it was to be alone. She couldn't let him do that to himself. "You told me they make you stronger, make you human. Now, for fear of putting them in danger, you want to become nothing but a murderer?"

"I can't be guildmaster *and* have a family, Mya. It's not safe for them!"

"Then I'll take it." Mya bit her tongue in surprise. *Where in the Nine Hells did that come from?* Where, she didn't know, but she knew it was the right thing to do.

"What?"

"I'll take the ring." She might not be able to help him the way she wanted to, but she could help him in this. "We'll tell the Grandmaster that you put the ring on by mistake."

"But..." Lad stared at her, speechless for a moment. He looked down at the ring on his finger, then back to her. "But you didn't want it."

"That doesn't matter. I'm an assassin, Lad. That's all I'll ever be. You're...more than that."

His countenance softened, and Mya felt as if those luminous eyes stared into her soul. "Why would you do that?"

Love is a weakness...

"Because I was wrong to be afraid of it." She brushed her hair back behind her ear. "If the Grandmaster doesn't kill me outright for burning his letter, I'll tell him I'll take his offer. He wanted me to be Twailin guildmaster in the first place. We can convince him you're not very good at it, that you're better as my personal bodyguard." Her mind spun ahead, warming to the possibilities. *This just might work.* "If he agrees, I'll help you find whoever is behind Wiggen's death, and we'll see an end to it. After that, you can be a father again. You can leave; take your family and go. You never signed a blood contract, so the guild can't track you down. You're the only assassin in the guild who can escape. Nobody will dare touch you as long as I'm Twailin's guildmaster." She would be a slave forever, but that would change nothing, and maybe, just maybe, she could give Lad his life back. He could be a father again.

Lad stared at her so long that Mya fidgeted under his scrutiny.

"And if he refuses?"

Mya shrugged. "Then we're back where we started. We won't know unless we try."

"What if he's behind Wiggen's murder?"

Panic screamed through Mya's mind. *He's going to get you killed!*

She forced the fear down. She was ready to die for him a moment ago. Nothing had changed, but she might be able to convince him to exercise some restraint. "Then bide your time. Kowtow and kiss his feet, if that's what he wants, but don't do anything stupid. Neither of us can touch him. If we find out he's responsible, then we back out and make a plan. Maybe you can have someone cut the ring off and go back."

"I could have someone cut it off now."

"No." Mya shook her head, her mind in full assassin mode now, thinking of the potential problems, all the pitfalls that could get them killed. "He'll never see you if you're not wearing the ring. Besides, you said yourself that it's a long shot that he had anything to do with this. We'll meet with him, get the facts, and plan from there. Kiesha's the key. If we don't learn anything in Tsing about Patino or the Grandmaster, we'll find Kiesha on our own, and discover the truth."

He stared at her, his face unreadable. "You're...brilliant, Mya. I didn't think..." He shook his head. "I didn't think I could ever escape."

The flicker of hope in Lad's eyes sent a surge of warmth through Mya that she'd never experienced before. *I did that. I gave him that.* "Now, how do we get you to sleep? Have you tried meditating?"

"Yes. It doesn't work. I can't concentrate."

"Well, you could try alcohol, but you don't want a hangover tomorrow."

"Alcohol makes it worse." He shrugged and turned back to the window. "And it gives me nightmares."

Mya knew about nightmares, too. She still had them.

"Okay, then." The obvious solution flashed into her mind, but she knew that if she suggested sex, the fragile trust she'd forged would be shattered. "How about exercise? I know sitting in a carriage all day has my muscles in knots. Have you been doing your dance? Your perfect fighting style?" She knew he hadn't since they left Twailin.

"No. Not for...some time. I can't focus."

"You need to. Come on." She pushed a chair out of the way, and kicked Lad's blanket and pillow into the corner. "I'll help. We can do it together."

"There's not enough space in here."

She grinned and nodded to the window. "I'm sure we can find someplace secluded outside."

"But..." Doubt flashed across his eyes, reluctance.

"You have to *want* to do this, Lad." She saw his resistance stiffen. *Wrong approach.* "Do you want to sleep or not?"

"Yes, but..." He took another deep breath and closed his eyes. "Forcing myself...to get over this...seems...wrong."

Guilt... She knew that poison, and how to draw it out.

"Getting a decent night's sleep doesn't mean forgetting about Wiggen." His eyes flicked open, filled with pain, but less anger. *That's it!* Now she knew the lever she could use to get

230

him past this guilt. "Would she *want* you to drive yourself crazy like this?"

"No."

"Then let's go out and get some exercise."

He hesitated as if he might pose yet another excuse, then relented. "All right." He retrieved a dark shirt from his trunk and slipped it on while she opened the window.

Mya slipped out of her pajamas. Her wrappings were comfortable, and she didn't want to give Lad time to change his mind by changing into her work clothes. A quick glance out the window confirmed that no one was about. "Ready?"

"Of course."

"Then follow me."

Mya took two steps back, then a running dive through the window. Cool night air and starlight engulfed her. She flipped as she fell the three stories, landing in the courtyard silently and all but invisible. Lad landed like a feather beside her, taking the shock of the drop on the balls of his feet.

"This way." She took off at a dead run, sparing only a quick glance back. He was there, right on her heels, his footfalls no louder than her pounding heart.

They dashed through the courtyard gate, across the road, over a low stone wall, and up the sloping hill of a fallow field beyond. At the crest of the rise she stopped, and he beside her. The short run had neither of them breathing hard, but her muscles were loose and warm. They stood on a low knoll, a quarter mile from anything or anyone, alone under the starlit sky.

"Secluded enough?"

"Yes."

"Then let's begin." Side by side, they both clenched fist to palm in front of their chests, and bowed.

They commenced in perfect unison.

Step, sweep, spin, punch...

Two shadows in the darkness, invisible save to one another.

Block, step, turn, strike...

231

Mya felt Lad moving with her as she increased the cadence, perfect in their synchronicity.

Lunge, step, kick, spin...

Faster, yet still their motions were as one, a single deadly creature spinning through the night.

Mya's heart pounded, not with exertion, but elation. She recalled the battle in the courtyard near Fiveway Fountain, their deadly dance together through the blood and rain, the flashing blades and gore. Now, as then, they were bound by a synergy that transcended anything physical, much less carnal.

This... Mya increased the pace to a blinding cadence, her feet churning the loamy soil as she spun. *This is all I'll ever have with him. It's enough...*

The sequence ended with them poised in the final bow. A light sweat dampened Mya's brow, but she was hardly tired.

"Again!" She slipped into the opening stance.

"Yes." He followed, every move as fluid as water on glass.

They began again, two killers seeking solace in physical perfection, fighting their inner demons the only way they could, if only for the hope of a dreamless night's sleep.

If only...

Chapter XVII

Lad bolted up off the floor, kicking away his tangled blanket to land on the balls of his feet, poised to kill.

Another knock sounded at the door, and a maid called out, "Sir. Ma'am. Breakfast."

"We'll be down shortly." Mya smiled at him from the bed. "You slept."

"Yes, I...I *did* sleep." Still groggy, Lad rubbed his face.

Gods, how I slept... And for the first time in weeks, his dreams had been silent. They'd returned to their room very late, exhausted and drenched in sweat. While Mya padded out to the bathing room, Lad had quickly washed with a damp cloth, and lay down in his makeshift bed. He hadn't even heard her return.

"I'm glad." Mya's gaze flicked down from his eyes, then back up. Only when he followed that gaze did he remember that he'd doffed his sweat-damp silks before bathing the night before. He stood before her mother naked and, while his mind wasn't quite awake yet, the rest of his body certainly was.

He snatched up the blanket and wrapped it around his waist. "Sorry."

"Don't be. I've seen you naked before. It doesn't bother me." Mya brushed her hair back as she looked away.

Not like this you haven't. Wiggen had taught Lad modesty, informing him laughingly that he couldn't go taking his clothes off in front of just anyone...only her. His chest tightened with the remembrance, and he turned his back as Mya got out of bed. He heard her doff her pajamas, then the slither of her wrappings

233

as she pulled them off the clothes tree where she'd hung them to dry overnight.

As he reached for his trousers, motion drew his eye to the mirror beside the dresser, and he stopped short. Mya stood with one foot on the dressing chair, her back toward him as she wound her wrappings around her leg. A lattice of tattoos covered her like black lace, shimmering on her smooth skin, rippling as she moved, dark and liquid.

Lad looked away, angry at the instinctive tug of lust. He knew his reaction was natural, purely physical and impossible to suppress, but that didn't stop the guilt. It made him feel unfaithful to the only woman he had ever loved. Grabbing his trousers, Lad pulled them on and struggled to button them.

Despite the embarrassment, he felt remarkably better, able to think clearly for the first time in days. *Exercise and sleep...* They'd repeated the dance a dozen times, improvising as they progressed, modifying the sequence to complement one another. It had felt good to move, to concentrate, to immerse himself in the sequence, to stretch both body and mind.

"Thank you for coaxing me into exercising. I feel much better."

The sound of Mya's wrapping halted for a moment. "I'm glad I could help," she said hesitantly, then resumed.

Lad stole another glance as he donned his shirt. Covered from the waist down, she continued wrapping with quick, deft motions, the magically enhanced material writhing to cover every bit of tattooed skin as she wound it around and around.

So wrapped in secrecy...

Mya glanced over her shoulder, caught his gaze in the mirror, and stopped again, the bundle of black cloth poised at her waist.

Lad looked away first, snatching up his waistcoat and pulling it on. They finished dressing in silence, the only words a muttered curse from Mya as she cinched the laces of her corset. The silk and metal contraption creaked, squeezing her figure into an hourglass shape. Wiggen had never worn a corset. Such affectations seemed as silly as the cravat he was struggling to tie, and the hard-soled shoes that tortured his feet.

Lad packed their few items in their trunks as Mya pulled her voluminous dress over her head. Finally, he was free to turn around.

"There!" She finished tightening the laces and smoothed the skirt. "Presentable once again."

Lad shrugged into his jacket and tugged it straight. "Ridiculous, isn't it?"

"A little." Her eyes roved over him from head to toe. "Your tie's crooked. Here, let me fix it."

As she stepped close and reached up to adjust the bothersome thing, Lad suppressed the urge to step back. Mya's proximity had always set him on edge, and her touch made him grit his teeth. *But not last night*, he realized. They'd spent half the night working themselves to exhaustion, always close, often touching, and he'd felt no reticence. *So why now?* He held still while she adjusted the cloth and pin, tugged the lapels of his jacket, and patted the wrinkles out. Her hands lingered for a scant moment longer than necessary before she stepped back.

"There. Perfect." She bit her lip.

Another tell. Lad wondered at her nervous mannerism. Since her outburst last night, Mya had not shown her usual fear of him. *But these tells...* She was clearly hiding something. His thoughts turned to her offer to take the guildmaster position. *Was she sincere?* Mya never did anything that didn't further her own ends, and when he'd asked her why, she'd brushed her hair back, yet another sign of evasion. *What's her motive?* Did she have some scheme brewing? Would she denounce him as a usurper to gain the Grandmaster's favor? He didn't like to think it, but she'd betrayed him in the past. Then, last night, she'd helped him. *Why?*

"Let's go." Lad flipped the trunk lid closed. When he turned around, she was already fidgeting at the door, her nails ticking together as she flicked her finger and thumb, yet another tell. *What's bothering her?* "Are you all right?"

"I'm fine." She opened the door and hurried through. "Just hungry. I can smell the bacon from here, can't you?"

"Yes." Lad followed, his mind awhirl. Was she regretting her offer to help him, or was there something else she was keeping from him? He would find out sooner or later. At least now he could think straight.

Nice place, Norwood thought as he looked out the window at Baron Patino's estate. Pea gravel crunched under his boots as he stepped down from the carriage. Brutus growled at the workers bustling about the outbuildings; there were too many people about for the dog's liking. For now, Norwood was fine with the crowd. An assassin wasn't likely to strike with a dozen folks looking on. He patted the dog's head.

Norwood looked around, scrutinizing the estate. The gravel drive circled a granite sculpture of the Patino coat of arms taller than the captain. The house itself, a pillared edifice in the plantation style, stood two stories high, with arched walkways and white-stone balustrades on the second-floor balconies. Beside the drive and beyond the house, stables, barns, sheds and workers' quarters were set amidst vegetable gardens and corrals, everything spotlessly clean.

"Have them stable the carriage. I'll be a while."

"Yes, sir." The driver and single guardsman lounged back in their seats, blissfully ignorant of the danger their captain might be walking into. Tamir was the only one Norwood had told, and he was nowhere in sight. Playing this so close to the vest was dangerous, but his plan would only work if the assassin thought Norwood was here without protection.

A burly man with sleeves rolled up over well-muscled forearms approached, two bright-eyed sheepdogs following at his heels. Brutus growled at the long-haired animals, and they cowered behind their master.

"Easy, boy."

"And can I be helpin' you, sir?" The man's voice had a thick back-country brogue.

"Yes. I'm Captain Norwood of the Royal Guard. I'm here to see Mistress Jieco."

"Mistress said someone would be comin' by, Captain." The man looked him up and down. "I'm Sinthas, the foreman. The mistress should be—"

"Right here." The estate manager stepped out the front door onto the porch. She was dressed in trousers and boots, a riding crop in her hand, her hair bound in a tight braid, and a broad-brimmed hat flopping against her back from a strap around her neck. Her sharp eyes said plainly that she wasn't happy with this. She hadn't been happy last night either, when he told her his plan, but in the interest of capturing Baron Patino's killer, she'd agreed to help. "I hope this doesn't take long. I've work to do."

"I'm afraid it may take a while, ma'am." Norwood nodded politely. "But I don't want to keep you from your work. I just need to see the account books, so if you show me where they're kept, you can get about your business."

"Fine." She turned to the foreman. "Saddle my horse, Sinthas. I'll be ten minutes."

Norwood mounted the steps to the porch, but Jieco stood in front of the open door, preventing his entrance.

"You'll have to leave your dog outside, Captain. We don't allow animals in the house under *any* circumstances." She gestured, and a boy ran forward. "Yeshi here will see to him."

"No need." Norwood held his hand out, palm facing the dog, and Brutus sat. "Brutus, stay."

The mastiff sat and looked up at him, a thick strand of drool dripping from his pendulous jowl.

"He'll stay there?" Jieco looked skeptical.

"Until all Nine Hells freeze over or I call him." *Not the complete truth, but enough.* Norwood gestured to the house. "Shall we?"

"This way, Captain."

He followed her into the manor house, leaving the door ajar behind him. If the assassin struck, he wanted to be able to call on Brutus, and despite the mastiff's brawn, a latched door would easily thwart him.

So far, so good.

Their boot heels clicked on polished white marble as they crossed the impressive entrance hall. The Patino crest in burnished brass hung upon one wall. Jieco turned left and led him down a short hallway with four doors along the sides, and a fifth at the end. Norwood tried to maintain a casual posture, wondering if a killer lurked behind one of the doors. Tam and Tango were here somewhere, he just hoped they were close.

Jieco unlocked the door at the end of the corridor and gestured him inside. The study was bright and cozy at the same time. High windows on two walls let in ample light, and plush chairs in front of the cold hearth looked perfect for relaxing and reading. Unfortunately, Norwood wasn't here to relax. Just as well, for he could never relax under the eyes of generations of Patinos who stared down at him from their portraits upon the dark-paneled walls.

Emi Jieco waved toward a bookshelf crowded with ledgers. "There are the books, Captain. I hope you know what you're looking for."

"I do. Thank you for your help." He nodded toward the corridor. "I don't want to keep you from your work any longer."

"Very well. Please try to put things back where you found them."

"I'll try not to disturb anything, ma'am."

"Thank you." Looking sternly at him, as if afraid that he would wreak havoc on her neatly organized ledgers, she finally left, closing the door behind her.

Norwood checked his watch. *Perfect.* Picking a ledger from the shelf at random, he brought it to the huge desk that dominated one corner, facing the center of the room. Two ornate lamps stood atop it for nighttime work, their bases of burnished malachite and gold gleaming in the sunlight. Norwood slid into the comfortable chair and opened the ledger. Something warm and wet nudged his knee from beneath the desk.

"Good boy," he whispered, patting the mastiff's huge head. *Close indeed!* "Stay. Quiet."

Tango settled back down. That he had remained perfectly still beneath the desk was a testament to his superb training. All was ready. The trap was set. Now he had nothing to do but wait.

The plan was simple. Norwood was the bait, seemingly alone and vulnerable. He wanted to take the assassin alive for questioning, and with the two mastiffs and Tamir close by, he had a chance. He just had to keep the man from using magic to escape. The captain dipped his fingers into his jacket pocket and withdrew the fine golden chain that Woefler had given him. It felt cool and reassuring. He wrapped one end around his hand to keep a good hold on it.

The hard part would be waiting.

And not letting him touch me...

Norwood had no idea what other magic the assassin could wield. He was betting his life that the killer wanted the captain's death to appear natural, as he had Patino's. In that case, he'd have to get close enough to touch him. Of course, if he blinked in with a dozen men wielding poisoned blades, Norwood wouldn't have a chance.

No, he'll try the same way he tried before. He'll use magic. In Norwood's experience, killers didn't generally change their methods unless forced to. He knew the man was mortal, as vulnerable as anyone to a dagger or sword. If it came down to life or death, the captain would have no qualms about putting a blade through the assassin's heart.

Norwood pretended to skim over the neat columns of numbers, notations, expenditures, and names. It was all a sham, but the killer couldn't know that. He flipped a page, ears straining for the scuff of a boot on the hardwood floor, an indrawn breath, a rustle of cloth.

Waiting...

Norwood strived to stay alert, to listen. He thought to call for blackbrew, but rejected the idea. The assassin could pop in at any moment, and the captain didn't want a servant in the room when it happened.

He's going to come for me. Any moment...

His eyes blurred over the meaningless numbers and notations, expenditures for supplies, equipment, wages, and a thousand other details that kept the estate running.

Waiting...

The sun crept across the carpet as the morning wore on. It was getting difficult to keep his eyes open, and his mind kept drifting off to errant thoughts. *If I don't pay attention, I'll end up asleep on the desk.* He flipped another page.

A light puff of breeze touched the hairs on the back of his neck, and he reached back to scratch.

Breeze?

The windows were closed.

A flicker of motion reflected in the gleaming chimney of one of the desk lamps; a flutter of crimson.

Tango growled.

Norwood lunged up and kicked the chair backward, gratified by the dull thud and the hiss of pain that followed. "Tam!" he bellowed as he twisted around to face his attacker. Too close—a hand blurred by inches from his face, a pearly glow trailing vaporous wisps. Norwood whipped the golden chain at the assassin's arm, but it merely flicked off the man's shoulder.

Damn!

The assassin kicked the chair aside and lunged, his outstretched hand still glowing. Norwood's backside bumped up

240

against the desk. Drawing his dagger, he realized with a sinking heart that the short blade couldn't keep that deadly hand from touching him. He heard Tamir's yell from the hallway, and knew his sergeant would arrive too late.

Tango smashed into the back of Norwood's legs, toppling the captain backward over the desk. The mastiff leapt up from his hiding place, slobbery jaws wide enough to grasp the assassin's entire head and strong enough to crush it.

As Norwood landed amidst the shards of the shattered lamps, an inarticulate cry escaped the assassin's throat. The captain rolled to his feet to see Tango's massive jaws gripping the cowl of the man's robe. Cloth tore as they tumbled backward, Tango landing firmly atop. Dagger in one hand and the golden chain in the other, Norwood vaulted over the desk. Behind him, the door burst open, but he couldn't look back. He had to get the chain around the assassin before he vanished, but there was a huge dog in the way.

"Tango! Off!"

Too late... A pearly glow flashed around the enraged canine, and Tango went limp.

The assassin heaved the dog off and rolled to his feet, the tattered hood of his cloak pulled away to reveal swarthy features and dark, close-cropped hair streaked with gray. He spoke a word that shivered the air, and dark tendrils of magic flowed outward from his hand.

"Not this time, you bastard!" Norwood flung the chain at the man's arm. The gold links wrapped around his assailant's wrist twice, sticking like glue. The dark tendrils faded, and he there he stood. "Now, you son of a—" Norwood dropped his dagger and drew his sword; he needed a longer weapon to keep the lethal magic at bay.

The assassin jerked his arm, but the enchanted links held fast. The end that Norwood gripped cut into his hand, but he refused to let go. As the tip of Norwood's sword cleared the scabbard, the assassin spoke again, a single meaningless word.

241

Darkness flashed through the room like a sheet of black lightning. Norwood's heart skipped a beat, and the sword drooped in his nerveless grasp. Ice water filled his veins, despair unlike anything he'd ever felt gripping him. Every dark moment of his life revisited him in the span of a heartbeat: every failure, every heartbreak, every defeat. His knees quaked and his muscles slacked. He heard Tamir cry out, but he was too deafened by his own anguish to understand.

The assassin jerked his arm away, and the golden chain cut across the back of the Norwood's hand, wrenched free of his slack grasp. Backing away, the man peeled the chain from his forearm and cast it aside. Once again, vaporous black tendrils formed in his hand and began to spread.

"No!" Norwood wrenched his mind free from the pit of despair and raised his sword. Behind him, a deep growl sounded.

Brutus bowled him aside as he launched himself from the top of the desk, jaws wide. The dog plunged right through the swirling darkness, scattering the vaporous magic like smoke on the wind, then crashed into an ornate coatrack in the corner. When the mists cleared, the assassin was gone.

"Damn it to the Nine Hells!" Norwood turned a wary circle, lest the assassin pop right back in behind him, but the only other person in the room was Tamir. The sergeant looked more like he'd seen a ghost than a killer. With another curse, the captain snapped his sword back into his scabbard.

"What in the hell *was* that, sir?" Tamir's free hand clutched his chest. "That...flash of darkness. It felt like someone grabbed my heart right out of my chest."

"I don't know, Sergeant." Norwood grimaced at the shattered glass, scratched desk, and the ledger soaked in lamp oil. So much for his promise not to make a mess. "I did, however, get a good look at him."

A whine brought him around. Brutus stood, head down, mournfully nosing the still form of Tango.

"Damn it to hell." The captain knelt and pressed his fingers into the dog's warm flesh, but detected no pulse, no breath. Tango had saved his life, without a doubt, but had paid the ultimate price for his loyalty. Brutus whined again and nosed the corpse, then sat down and looked up into Norwood's face as if asking for him to fix things. The captain scratched the mastiff's massive head. "I'm sorry, boy."

"What now, sir?" Tamir asked.

Norwood clenched his jaw and tried to think past the lingering despair of the assassin's magic. Though Tango lay dead, and they had failed to capture the assassin, his trap had actually worked in one respect.

"This case just got much bigger, Tam." Norwood bent to retrieve the golden chain, and noticed the blood on the back of his hand where the links had sliced into him. "Our assassin knew exactly where and when to find me. We know one thing for sure now: there's a spy in the Imperial Palace." He took a deep breath and let it out slowly. "We're going to Tsing."

"You're *sure*, sir?" Tamir worried his lower lip and furrowed his brow.

"Yes, Sergeant. I'm oath-bound to protect the Noble House of Tsing. That includes the Emperor himself. If there's a spy in the Imperial Palace controlling that assassin, there's an threat to His Majesty's safety. I've got to go." Brutus nosed his hand, and he scratched him behind the ears, trying to offer the poor beast some solace. "Besides, the son of a bitch killed my dog. I'm going to put a sword through him for that, if nothing else."

"We're coming into Farthane," Lad said as they passed the sign post. "You wanted to stop?"

Mya looked up from her book. She'd been quiet, which wasn't unusual, but her nervousness from this morning seemed to have subsided. "Yes. Farthane's one of Patino's estates. I sent Hunters to Willamshire and Mountainview, but when you decided to go to Tsing early, I figured we might as well stop on the way and ask some questions."

He looked at her with furrowed brow. "It's just a plantation. Are they likely to know anything?"

"Maybe not, but there's no harm in asking around." She gave him an exasperated look that he'd learned to read long ago. "You *did* tell me to look everywhere. If Kiesha got out of Twailin, she might have come here."

"Good point." Lad peered out the carriage window as they topped a low hill. "It's evidently a fair-sized village." Ahead in the vale were a number of small buildings, homes, a granary, and a mill, aside from the way-inn. The manor house stood upon a nearby hill, large and white, with expansive green swards, planted fields, and stone-fenced pastures dotted with white flecks of sheep.

"Good." She put down her book. "The more people, the less likely we are to draw attention."

Lad rapped the roof of the carriage with the handle of his walking stick. "Stop at the inn for lunch."

"Aye, sir!" the driver called down.

As the carriage rolled into Farthane village, Lad was reminded of the first village he'd ever seen, the hamlet of Thistledown. He cast his mind back, remembering how ignorant he had been of the vagaries of human interactions. He hadn't even known what money was, let alone the need of it to pay for things like food. It was shortly after that first disastrous encounter with civilization that he met Mya. She had ridden up on a tall gelding and offered him a ride to Twailin, but his trained suspicion had told him to refuse.

The image of her on her horse came to mind as if it had been yesterday. Her sweat-damped shirt had been half open, exposing the swell of her high breasts as she leaned down to talk to him. At the time he hadn't understood, but now it seemed obvious what she'd been trying to do. Even then, she'd been using enticement to get what she wanted.

Is she still trying to do that? He recalled her tattoo-clad back and legs as she wound them in black cloth. She could have waited until he was out of the room to dress, but hadn't. Had she done that on purpose? Was she trying to seduce him? If so, why? A flutter in the pit of his stomach betrayed his body's undeniable response to the memory, but he ignored it.

The way-inn hove into view as the carriage passed the mill. The high, tiled roof fairly glowed in the midday sun. In the courtyard, figures bustled about tending horses and wagons, and trying to hitch a team of recalcitrant mules to a huge wain mounded with cargo.

Their driver slowed to allow a coach approaching from the opposite direction to pull into the drive. As the coach turned, Lad saw a familiar coat of arms emblazoned on the door. The coach stopped, and a massive dog hopped out, followed by a broad-shouldered man in uniform. Recognition hit Lad like a hammer blow.

Norwood!

"Drive on!" He didn't think Norwood could identify him, but he wasn't about to take the risk. Lad thumped the roof of the carriage with his cane, and shouted again. "Drive on! They're too busy. We'll stop at the next village."

"Aye, sir!" The whip cracked, and the carriage surged forward.

"Lad, what—"

"Look at the coach!" He leaned back in the seat, wary of curious eyes. "Familiar?"

Mya glanced out. "Shit!" She, too, leaned back out of view. There was no point in taking chances; Mya was well known in certain areas of Twailin. "He must be investigating Patino."

That made sense. The captain had weeks to wait for an answer from Tsing, just like Lad did, so he was out asking questions, looking for motives, doing his job.

"Rotten luck that he's right where we wanted to stop." He glanced back. "Maybe he knows something we don't."

"I can't imagine he tells you everything."

"What?"

"Norwood *is* your informant, isn't he?" The corner of her mouth twitched. He'd seen that enough to know she was suppressing amusement. Lad was not amused.

"Yes, he is. When did you figure that out?"

She shrugged. "When I had people watching Norwood's house, one of them noticed the open attic vent. They hadn't seen a thing, and I don't know anyone else who could have done that, so I assumed you visited him. When you told us about Patino's murder, I assumed you had visited him again. It's quite a risk."

"Not really." It piqued Lad that she had figured him out, and he wasn't about to justify his actions to her. "Have you told any of the other masters?"

"Of course not!"

Lad watched her for tells, and saw none. The carriage rumbled on for a few long minutes before Mya spoke again.

"You really should tell the other masters that Norwood was the assassin's target. It changes things."

"Not that much. I don't want anyone to know. Just like Hensen's contract to protect us. If they make the connection, they might think it...treasonous."

"As long as you're not selling out the guild, I don't see why they would." She cocked an eyebrow. "You're not, are you?"

He glared at her. "No."

"Good." Mya opened her book. "So, Norwood's hunting Patino's killer, too. That could complicate things."

"Yes." Lad gazed out the window, wondering what he would do if Norwood found Kiesha before he did. "Yes, it could."

Chapter XVIII

The carriage rumbled up yet another hill, and Lad sighed. Thoroughly sick of traveling, he wanted nothing more than to arrive in Tsing.

Until recently, the ever-changing scenery had helped to capture his attention. The rolling pastures around Farthane had given way to the sweeping hills of lake country, then a deep forest of old-growth oaks so draped with moss that they looked like hoary gray giants. Then they'd climbed the torturously steep Forendell Pass, through craggy mountains and hidden vales, where the way-inns were high-walled and fortified against marauding bands of ogres. Though none could say when the last attack had occurred, right now, Lad would have welcomed such a distraction.

For the last two days they had traversed long valleys between rolling hills, each the same as the next, a seemingly endless progression of cultivated land. The farther west they progressed, the more the countryside seemed...wrong, almost industrial. All the land was either cultivated or pastured, the few wooded areas nothing but unnatural rows of planted trees.

The carriage leveled out as they crested the hill. They were supposed to arrive in Tsing today, but thus far, Lad had seen no evidence of the city. He glanced out the window, and the vista ahead struck his mind like a bolt of lightning.

"Stop!" Lad banged the roof with the head of his walking stick. "Stop the carriage!"

"What?" Mya jerked up from a half slumber as they lurched to a halt.

Lad ignored her. He flung open the door and stepped out, wide eyed and slack jawed at what lay before him.

"Finally," Mya said as she stepped up beside him. "The sea."

In the distance, the ocean stretched to infinity, sparkling blue and never ending, fading into a distance so misty that he couldn't tell where the water stopped and the sky began. But it wasn't the sea that struck Lad so profoundly.

"Tsing..." Lad whispered, trying to take it all in. "Impossible..."

"I guess the book really doesn't do it justice."

Mya's voice seemed flat. Lad couldn't conceive how she could be so blasé. It was as if all the maps from the book had been laid out before him, and life breathed into them. The jumbled spires and lofty edifices of Temple Hill, built of multi-hued stone and gilded with precious metals, gleamed like gemstones. Farther west, the Heights District shone like a hill of white marble above middle-class Midtown and the poorer Dreggars Quarter. The brown smudge to the south must be the confusion of dilapidated warehouses, tenements and shanties, that made up the Downwinds District. Most beautiful of all, the Imperial Palace thrust up from atop the high bluff like a glistening white mountain. The afternoon sun reflected from the gleaming walls and towers like a beacon. This ivory icon of the empire alone occupied more space than any single Twailin district. The entire city was girded by a high, crenellated wall embellished with lofty towers, the whole bristling with siege weaponry. And the bay beyond sprouted a forest of masts, ships from all corners of the world come to trade in this grandest of ports.

Lad simply couldn't wrap his mind around a city so vast.

"Bit of a shock, isn't it, Master?" the Enforcer holding the reins asked.

"Yes." Lad tried to imagine learning such a city. "It would take years…"

"What would take years?"

He looked at Mya and only then realized he'd spoken aloud. "To know this place." He shook his head, wondering if anyone could ever truly know this city as he knew Twailin.

"Why would you *want* to?"

Her derision took him aback. Was she serious or being sarcastic? Since they had started exercising together, Mya's unease around Lad had subsided, and she'd slipped back into her familiar cynicism. Her words now were sharper, and he realized that she had been grimly silent all morning. He supposed she was nervous about their meeting with the Grandmaster, but how could she look at such a wonder with a jaded eye? Lad longed to explore the city, learn about the people, immerse himself in the essence of this immense metropolis.

"It's just a city. A big, dirty, dangerous city."

"No…" Lad didn't know how to explain the city's appeal. "It's a living, breathing creature. Now that I see it, I wish we had more time to experience it."

"I don't." Without another glance, Mya reboarded the carriage.

"Best move on, Master," the driver called down. "Don't want to be late for supper."

"Right." Lad climbed back aboard, and they jostled into motion, descending the long incline to the city of Tsing, heart and soul of the empire.

Lad pored over maps again, tracing the route to their inn. They would enter through the River Gate, one of fourteen that pierced the wall. The carriage slowed, and he looked out to find a steady stream of carts, wagons, coaches, and people afoot and ahorse slowing their progress. Thankfully, at this time of day, most of the traffic was going the other way.

The gate itself was wide enough to accommodate four wagons abreast. Their carriage lined up behind others like it, while the heavily laden wagons and carts queued to their right. Each vehicle was being stopped and inspected by constables. Lad remembered from the book that all goods brought into the city were valued and taxed.

Finally, they arrived at the gate, and a dour-faced guardsman with the imperial crest on his iron cap knocked on the carriage door. Lad, wearing the bored expression of the well-to-do that he'd long practiced, leaned forward into the vehicle's open window.

"Yes?"

"Names please?"

"Laurance and Mya Addington. We're from Twailin."

"No title?"

"No."

"Your purpose for visiting Tsing, sir?"

"Business."

"What type of business?"

"Various imports. I have contracts with several guilds to be signed and ratified by a magistrate."

"Not bringing in any goods now, are you?" The guardsman looked into the carriage, his eyes lingering on Mya much longer than they had on Lad.

"No."

"And how long will you be staying?"

"No more than a few days, I should think."

A cry rose up from the wagon parked beside their coach, and several guards moved in to surround it. From a hidden nook beneath the wagon, a constable dragged a skinny girl with a heavy iron collar around her neck. A burly man jumped down from the wagon seat, but three swords were drawn and in his face before he could intervene. The constable speaking with Lad glanced over, but the matter was already under control. In moments they had the wagon driver in manacles, the girl in custody, and the wagon pulled out of the way. Constables began systematically dismantling it, bundle by bundle.

"Smuggling slaves?" Lad's eyes were drawn to the poor wretches the constables were dragging from the additional hidden nooks within the cargo. He knew slavery was legal, but that didn't mean he had to like it.

"Not your business, sir." The constable scowled and continued in a bored monotone. "By city ordinance, only constables, military, and nobility may wear blades longer than three hands in public. All others must be stowed away until you leave the city. It's also illegal to carry readied bows or crossbows. They must be unstrung or dismantled and stowed. Do you or your men carry any prohibited weapons?"

"No, sir. I read about the laws, and we already have them packed away." The ordinance seemed strange, but meant nothing to Lad, since he never carried a weapon anyway. His Enforcers weren't happy about it, but could manage with daggers and fists if there was trouble.

The constable nodded to the cane in Lad's hand. "That's not a sword, is it?"

"No. Just a walking stick."

"Let's have a look." Lad handed over the stick without hesitation and, after prodding and twisting the brass head to no avail, the constable handed it back.

"You have lodgings arranged?"

"Yes."

"And you're familiar with the city?"

"No, but my driver is."

"Fine." The constable stepped back and pitched his voice up to the driver. "I'd advise you to get north of the river and stay there, you hear?"

"Aye, constable."

"Very well, then. Move on."

The carriage clattered forward.

"They're certainly efficient." Mya's tone sounded less than appreciative, if not quite cynical.

"Yes, they are." Lad watched out the window. "And numerous."

At the first major intersection beyond the gate, two more constables directed traffic, and as they turned right onto a broad bridge over the river that divided the city, Lad saw four more posted at each end.

North of the river, constables patrolled the streets in squads of four. The people's reaction to them was far from easy. Citizens went out of their way to avoid the squads, passing with quick steps and downcast eyes. Even so, Lad noted more than one instance of constables stopping passersby for questioning, and the worry and fear in the eyes of those being questioned.

A squad of six horsemen clattered past, fully armed and armored, the imperial crest gleaming on barding and tabards. The rider in the fore wore plate armor and a rippling cape of blue and gold. *A knight?* Commoners fairly fled from their path, their haunted gazes following the riders until they were out of sight, and even then they hurried on with worried glances over their shoulders.

"Something's different here." Lad glanced at Mya, then back out the window. "They're all afraid."

"They're commoners." Mya said the term like it explained everything. When Lad just stared at her, she sighed and elaborated. "They're *always* afraid."

"Not like this." He knew what she meant. He'd worked for the Assassins Guild long enough to know the common folks' fear of those against whom they couldn't defend, but this was different. "Look at them."

She did, and after a while she shrugged. "I suppose it is different. In Twailin they're afraid of *us*. Here they seem to be afraid of constables."

"Yes, but it's a lot worse." Even Twailin at the height of the recent guild war and the Royal Guard crackdown hadn't felt this oppressive. "This isn't like Twailin at all. Just look at their eyes."

Mya looked, and just shrugged again. "They just look like commoners to me."

Perhaps Mya had been at the top of that food chain for too long to notice, but Lad had been around his family, had seen the suppressed fear they lived with every day of their lives. This was worse. Lad lapsed into silence, but continued watching as they progressed deeper into Midtown.

The air became close, thick with the odors of a quarter-million people living in close proximity. The few times they glimpsed the river, he saw that the further west they progressed, the thicker it ran with filth. At times the stench of tanneries or abattoirs wafted in from across the river to the south, where the air hung low and yellow-gray with smoke. It grew warmer, and the breeze lessened. Lad began to sweat. He loosened his collar and glanced at Mya. Despite her thick layers of feminine finery, she appeared to be fresh and unaffected.

"Don't you *ever* sweat?"

Mya gaped at him for a moment, then laughed shortly. "That's *not* something you ask a lady, Lad. And, no." She pulled up the cuff of her sleeve to show him the edge of her black wrappings. "I'm perfectly comfortable. Remember?"

"Right." He recalled that her enchanted wrappings kept her cool or warm regardless of temperature. She'd suggested he purchase something similar, but Lad wasn't used to such luxuries.

Looking out the window again, he reflected on how alike and different he and Mya were. *Like Twailin and Tsing*, he thought. She was more worldly, wilier, and cynical. And like Tsing, she was steeped in fear.

The coach jerked to a stop. Up ahead, a well-dressed couple crossed the street, flanked fore and aft by bodyguards who parted the throngs of commoners with piercing glares. The man wore an ornate rapier in a gilded scabbard proudly at his hip. *A noble.* Lad watched the crowd, their furtive glances and downcast eyes. Men touched their caps and ducked, their shoulders slumped like beaten curs skirting a pack of wolves. The women curtsied and turned their faces away.

"Fear..." Curiosity roiled his gut. "Why are they all so afraid?"

"I don't know," Mya replied, staring through narrowed eyes at the spectacle, "but you're right. Everyone's terrified."

"They're afraid of the constables, the military, and the nobles. Why would they be?"

"I don't know." She cocked one eyebrow. "We could find out."

Excitement welled up in him. *To go exploring in such a vast city...* Then the ring seemed to tighten on his finger and he frowned. "We aren't here to poke into local problems. We're here to meet the Grandmaster and look into Patino's associations."

"Of course." She looked away.

Still, Lad's curiosity nudged him. Why would commoners here, in the heart of the empire, be afraid of the very people— constables, nobles, and knights—who were their sworn defenders? Commoners in Twailin didn't fear the City Guard, or even the Royal Guard, unless they were doing something illegal. And why fear nobles? He'd seen plenty of resentment between the classes in Twailin, but fear?

Even from the outside, Mya could tell that the *Drake and Lion* was the finest inn they'd seen in two weeks. In fact, it might be the finest she'd ever seen. The thought of staying in such luxury lightened her dark mood another bit. The pending meeting with the Grandmaster still had her worried, but the strangeness of the city and the curious behavior of the locals distracted her from her fears.

Deep in the Heights District, the inn stood in the company of upscale shops and multi-story townhouses. It reminded Mya of the finest neighborhoods of Hightown in Twailin, except that this was nowhere near the height of luxury in Tsing. Uphill, the townhouses evolved into palatial homes, and the shops to exclusive clubs and eateries. Downhill from the inn, the neighborhoods were as nice as Barleycorn Heights. Below that, Midtown spread out in a jumble of tile and slate roofs, reminding her of West Crescent, though immensely more vast.

So many people... She wondered how the Assassins Guild operated here. How were they organized? What kind of scams and rackets did they run? Did they even operate in the rarified air of the Heights District?

The carriage door opened and an attendant extended a white-gloved hand to assist her. Smiling at him, she accepted his help in stepping out of the carriage. "Thank you."

The fellow's eyes flicked up to hers for an instant, surprise plain in his face before he looked down. "Milady." He released her hand, bowed to Lad as he stepped from the carriage, and gestured to the foyer. "Milord. I'll see to your baggage immediately."

Did I say something wrong? Mya wondered, thinking about the look he'd given her. All she had said was thank you. She'd spent enough time in Hightown practicing her fine-lady persona to know that even nobles generally thanked people for their services. It was a matter of decorum. Had he not expected to be thanked? Maybe not, considering what they'd seen between the commoners and nobles. *Strange...*

Lad stood staring out over the city, apparently mesmerized by the sight.

"Are you ready, dear?" she asked.

He didn't move, didn't even acknowledge her question. Mya chilled with dread. Lad had done this several times during their trip to Tsing, losing himself so deeply in thought that he was nearly insensible.

Casually, she sidled up to him, careful not to touch him. She had made that mistake only once, barely dodging his lightning-fast strike. They couldn't risk that happening in public.

"Come along, dearest! You can look at the scenery from our room."

Lad looked at her as if she'd appeared from nowhere. "Right. Sorry, I must be tired from the trip." He extended his arm, and she put her hand on it.

"A bath and a nap will perk you right up." She breathed easier, disaster averted.

They strolled up the inn steps while the attendant ordered a team of porters to collect their baggage. A uniformed doorman swept open the wide door—teak and brass that looked newly polished—and bowed from the waist as he greeted them.

"Welcome to the *Drake and Lion*, milord and lady."

The lobby was resplendent with more gleaming wood, bright brass, marble columns, crystal chandeliers, and brilliant red carpeting. On the wall behind the front desk, a serpentine drake battled a roaring lion—the elaborate golden crest of the inn. Elegant men and women moved gracefully across the floor, as much in their element as fish in the sea. One woman wearing a brilliant yellow gown with matching purse air-kissed a companion, then abruptly turned into the path of a passing servant. The collision was slight, but the woman's purse fell, the contents scattering across the carpet.

To Mya's astonishment, the woman's face contorted into a mask of rage. Her discordant shriek shattered the lobby's soothing ambiance as she lashed out her frilled parasol with rabid ferocity.

"How *dare* you! I'll see you in the stocks for this and whipped as you deserve! I've never seen such incompetence!" The parasol cracked against the man's head as he scrabbled to collect the fallen bits and bobs. "Fifty lashes, I swear by the Gods of Light! You're utterly useless!"

Chris A. Jackson

The servant fumbled the contents back into the purse, muttering apologies. A particularly vicious blow sent the purse flying from his grasp, scattering the contents a second time. Mya expected a manager or inn employee to step in and stop the violence, but no one else seemed to be paying the scene the least bit of attention. No, that wasn't quite right. Elegant guests walked past with smug expressions, while other employees hurried by, averting their eyes. Lad stopped cold, but Mya tugged on his arm, urging him into motion. The last thing they wanted was to look out of place.

"Come on," she whispered so quietly that only Lad would hear. "Ignore it."

She felt his tension as they walked past the dreadful scene to the broad front desk. A woman gowned in black and white greeted them with a broad smile, acting as if she didn't hear the woman's screeching voice reverberating off the marble walls.

"Welcome to the *Drake and Lion*, milord and lady. I trust you have a room reserved?" She looked expectantly at Lad as she opened a thick leather-bound book.

"Yes, we have. Laurance Addington," Lad said.

The shrill shrieks finally abating, Mya stole a surreptitious glance. The woman in yellow had stopped flailing her parasol, but the improvised weapon had done damage. The man was trying to staunch blood flowing from a cut on his forehead as he gathered the scattered items. Still no one paid the slightest notice.

"Does this," Mya inclined her head toward the fracas, "happen often here?"

"Of course not, Mrs. Addingdon." The receptionist looked aghast. "The *Drake and Lion* prides itself on the efficacy of its attendants. Rest assured, that one will be duly punished for his clumsiness."

Mya opened her mouth to say that she meant the beating, not the inadvertent bump that sent the lady's handbag to the floor, then thought better of it.

257

"Ah, here we are! Addington. A suite for two, lodgings for your servants and coachman, and stabling. If you would sign here, sir." The receptionist presented a piece of embossed parchment and a pen, and Lad signed without a word.

"Excellent!" The receptionist beckoned a porter. "Jamis, show the Addingtons to their suite, and have their servants quartered."

"Yes, ma'am." Jamis bowed to them and gestured. "This way, please."

The Enforcers with their own small bags were led toward the back of the lobby, while Jamis escorted Lad and Mya up the grand staircase, trailed by several porters hefting their trunks. As they rounded the first landing, Mya stole a glance back. The yellow-clad woman clutched the hapless, bleeding servant by the collar, dragging him to the front desk.

"I demand this oaf be punished. Fifty lashes and a day in the stocks! He's utterly useless!"

"Of course, Lady Clovis. I'll see to it personally. Let me assign another servant to your..."

Mya reminded herself to take a closer look at the chapter on local laws in her Tsing book as the voices from the lobby faded. In Twailin, deliberately striking a noble was punishable by imprisonment at the least and hanging at the worst, depending on the severity of injury. Nobles enjoyed immunity from petty offenses, but could not assault commoners with impunity. How could things be so different here? She exchanged a glance with Lad and saw the same question in his eyes.

Jamis turned off at the third landing and lead them to their suite. Escorting them inside, he directed the porters to stow the luggage, and presented Lad with keys.

Oh, my! The room was lovely beyond Mya's expectations. The outer room was furnished as a living area, with silk-upholstered chairs and divans grouped for cozy conversation. There was a large, ornate table for dining in front of one window, and a lower one better suited to sipping tea beside the divan. The walls sported stylish paintings, but none could compare with the view out the three large windows. Mya pulled aside the beautifully sheer drapes and gazed out across the city all the way to the bay.

Finished with the luggage, the porters tipped their caps and bowed out of the suite. Jamis backed away with a sweeping bow. "If there is nothing else, sir..."

"Actually, Jamis, could you stay for a moment? I'm unfamiliar with the city and have some questions."

Mya cringed. *What's he doing?*

"Of course, sir." Jamis looked uncomfortable as the door closed behind the last porter.

Mya shot Lad a warning glance, but too late.

"That...occurrence in the lobby. How does it come about that a guest can assault one of the inn's employees without consequence?"

Jamis' eyes widened and he stammered, "Lady Clovis is noble-born, sir," as if that explained everything.

"And that gives her the right to beat a free man with impunity?"

"She may do as she wishes, milord, as any noble-born may." Jamis looked confused.

"I...see." Lad looked stunned.

"You'll forgive our questions, Jamis," Mya cut in with an easy smile. "We're from Twailin, you see. Our customs are different there."

"Of course, ma'am." He bowed.

"We've had a very long trip, and we're tired." She pulled a silver crown from her purse. "For your trouble."

Jamis stared at the coin as if it would bite him. "Ma'am, please. I'm paid by the inn. I mustn't take anything additional. If they found out, I'd be dismissed."

"Pardon my misunderstanding." Mya smiled disarmingly to hide her astonishment, and put the coin away. *Fired for accepting a tip? What the...* "Once again, my provincial roots are showing. We Twailins often give a little something extra for exemplary service."

"I...I see," he stammered. "Please, ma'am. I meant no offense."

"None was taken." She opened the door and let Jamis escape. "Please arrange for a bath for the two of us. We're a little road dusty, I'm afraid."

"At once, ma'am."

Mya closed the door behind him and leaned against it, shaking her head. "That was..." She fell silent, at an utter loss for words.

"Bizarre," Lad finished for her. He took off his jacket and began to pace. "Did you hear what he said about the noble-born? They can abuse anyone they wish with no provocation or consequence! No *wonder* everyone's afraid."

"But to fear being punished for accepting a *tip*?"

"How could anyone live like that? Why don't they just leave?"

"No money, no means, and no place to go, I suppose." Mya shrugged. Having escaped from her own torturous childhood and making a life for herself from her own wits and skill, she found it hard to sympathize. "I'd heard that the laws here are harsh and enforced without mercy, but this is beyond heavy-handed. It's *ridiculous*."

"It's also dangerous." Lad went to the window and looked out at the city. "People can only be brutalized so much before they rebel."

"No wonder they won't let anyone carry a sword. Commoners with daggers and cudgels wouldn't stand a chance against constables in mail and armored knights. They're beaten into submission, and have nothing to fight back with."

"I want to go out tonight."

Lad's statement caught Mya off guard. "Where?"

"I don't know yet, but I want to have a look around. Maybe south of the river."

"We were warned not to go there."

"Exactly." Lad glanced at her, his eyes hard. "That's why I want to go. Are you going to sit here and read a book all night, or come with me?"

"Are you kidding?" Mya's heart skipped a beat with excitement. Her greatest pleasure these last two weeks had been their nightly exercise. She wasn't about to miss a chance to go out with him, regardless of where they went or what they did. "Just try to go without me."

A knock on the door interrupted their conversation. It was Jamis, along with a team of servants carrying the biggest copper tub she'd ever seen. Several more servants carried steaming buckets of water.

"Your bath, ma'am."

"Oh. Come in."

They set the tub in front of one of the windows, where the afternoon sun made the copper gleam. Jamis unfolded a little brass table and arrayed on it thick, cotton towels, several types of brushes, and soaps in various colors and scents. Bucket after bucket of hot water splashed into the tub, the clouds of rising steam smelling of rose petals.

"That's the biggest tub I've ever seen," Mya said with an involuntary grin.

Jamis looked horrified. "You said for two, ma'am. If you'd prefer, we can bring a smaller one."

"Oh, no! This is fine. A tub for two is just what I asked for." The last thing Mya wanted was to get him in trouble for mistaking her remark. Besides, the startled look on Lad's face was priceless.

"Would you like bath attendants?" Jamis asked.

"No, thank you. We can manage."

"Will you be dining in the dining room, or would you prefer dinner to be brought up?"

"Here would be nice. We're a bit tired from our trip."

"As you wish. I'll bring up a menu presently."

"Oh, just pick out something nice for us, Jamis. We trust your judgment, and we're not picky. Give us an hour."

His flash of surprise this time was followed by a tentative smile. "Very good, ma'am. Dinner in an hour."

"Thank you."

Jamis shooed the other servants from the room, bowed once again, and closed the door behind him.

Lad stared at the tub, an anxious look on his face. Mya would have laughed, his thoughts were so readable, but she dared not for fear of shattering their fragile trust. For her part, she gazed at the great, steaming basin with regret; sharing it with Lad would have to remain a fantasy.

"You first." She sighed as she headed for the bedroom. "I'll unpack."

"All right." Lad started untying his neck cloth. "I'll hurry so the water doesn't cool."

"Take your time," she said as she closed the bedroom door.

Mya smiled at the sound of splashing from beyond the door. Opening her trunk, she drew out her dresses and hung them to air. At the bottom lay a pair of dark trousers, soft boots, a shirt of deep crimson, and her four best daggers. These she arranged on the bed for later. The night might turn out to be interesting after all.

Chapter XIX

Lad froze, invisible in the shadowed alley, Mya a half step behind. The clatter of metal from just ahead told them another squad of constables was near.

At least they're noisy. Lad edged deeper into shadow, cocking his head to pinpoint the squad's location. *Ahead and to the left, crossing our path.* He motioned to Mya that they would wait, rather than skirt around the patrol as they had others.

They weren't doing anything truly illegal, but they didn't want an encounter with the law. Though it was near midnight, the patrols hadn't let up. Few commoners walked the streets so late, and those who did were apt to be stopped and questioned. They had seen several exchanges, and not all had ended peacefully.

Lad had considered using the rooftops for prowling, but he didn't know this city. Plunging through a rotten roof would end their night quickly. The streets were safer, despite the patrols. They'd evaded several since leaving the *Drake and Lion*. This one was right between them and their goal: the Imperial Plaza.

They'd perused Mya's Tsing book during dinner, deciding where to explore. Over the centuries, the Imperial Plaza had served as an open market, a jousting arena, a venue for traveling fairs, and even a zoo. Its present incarnation, a public arena for punishment, drew Lad's interest like a moth to a flame.

The squad of constables clattered past without spotting them. Motioning Mya forward, he hurried on. The maps in the book were deceptive; Tsing on the ground proved to be much larger than Tsing on paper. What he'd thought would be a quick jaunt had already taken an hour.

Finally, the street opened into a broad open space. At its center, three banners fluttered atop tall poles: the blue and gold flag of the empire, a deeper blue banner sporting the crest of the Imperial House of Tsing, and a long, black pennant set with a pair of silver scales denoting the Royal Magistracy, the judiciary arm of the government. Beneath the flags, the plaza was crowded with wooden structures: gallows, stocks, and tall posts sporting manacles.

More than half were occupied.

"What in the Nine Hells..."

Though Mya's whisper barely rose over the rustle of the fluttering flags, Lad gripped her arm and nodded toward the squads of guards patrolling the perimeter of the plaza. She fell silent, and they eased back into the shadows.

While they waited for the nearest patrol to pass, Lad counted. Corpses dangled from six of the ten gallows. Offenders were restrained in more than half of the score of pillories. In the small forest of whipping posts—there were at least fifty—wretched forms sagged in their manacles, their backs stripped and bleeding from the lash.

"Justice." Lad spat the word like a curse.

"What?" Mya whispered, glancing nervously at the patrol.

"I said *justice*." The display made him sick. "I'll wager that fellow from the inn's here somewhere. Fifty lashes for dropping Lady Clovis' handbag."

Mya's eyes flicked over the forlorn shapes. "Why haven't we ever heard anything about this?"

"Fear." Lad nodded to the gallows. "Maybe those are the dissidents. I don't know. Twailin's a long way from here. Maybe the truth is lost in the miles."

The patrol neared, the guards talking amongst themselves. Though they paid no attention to the unfortunates inside the plaza, they cast sharp glances outward.

Lad gauged the squads, their pace and position. This was going to be dangerous, but Lad had to have a closer look. Grasping Mya's arm, he nodded toward the close patrol, and whispered for her ears only. "Wait for them to pass. Be ready."

"Ready."

The constables strolled by an easy stone's throw away, their eyes passing over the shadows that concealed the assassins. Lad squeezed Mya's arm. "Come on."

They edged out of the shadows into the dappled light of the street lamps and dashed across the wide avenue that bordered the plaza. Lad kept one eye on the patrol, but none looked back.

Crouching low, they ducked amongst the pillories. Only when they had crept far enough in that they were no longer visible from the avenue did they slow and stop. Next to them, a man sagged heavily from the wooden stocks. Lad quietly read the parchment tacked to the face board.

"Forin Masterson, for insolence to a Noble-Born, five days in the pillory and seventy-five lashes." He touched the cool flesh of the man's flayed back, but he didn't respond. He was dead.

"Good Gods of Light." Mya sounded sick.

They moved on to another.

"Juliana Tailor, for cheating a Noble-Born with poor craftsmanship, one day of pillory and ten lashes." The woman's dress was torn down the back, her pale skin scarred by ten red, weeping wounds. She stirred as they passed, her swollen eyes blinking in the dark.

"Please...water..."

They had no water, and there was no well nearby. They crept on until they reached the first of the gallows.

"Fiona Lorent, for thievery from a Noble-Born, death by hanging, public display of the body, and indenture of descendants for one generation so all shall know her crime."

"She stole food."

Lad froze, and Mya drew a dagger. Neither had noticed the old man huddled in the darkness beneath the gallows.

"What?"

"She was a cook's assistant in one of the noble houses." The man's wheezing voice sounded like the rustle of dried rushes. "She took food they was gonna throw away. For that, they called her a thief and hung her. She took it for me, and they killed her for it. I killed her. My own daughter."

"You didn't kill her." The vehemence in Mya's voice surprised Lad. There was no cynicism or sarcasm, just anger. She nodded toward the three fluttering flags. "*They* killed her."

"Aye, because of me." The man's head drooped, and his shoulders shook with quiet sobs.

Lad touched Mya's arm. "Come on. I've seen enough here. I need to find someone who can tell us what's going on."

"Good luck," she said. "They're all too afraid."

"I know."

They waited among the pillories for the next patrol to go by, then raced across the avenue back into the concealing gloom of a side street.

"You still want to go south of the river?" Mya asked.

"Of course."

"How did I know you were going to say that?" Her sarcasm was back.

"Because you know me, Mya. You know I need an answer."

"Some answers can get you killed, you know."

"I know." Lad picked up his pace to a slow, silent jog. "Now let's figure out how to get over one of the bridges without being spotted."

Mya stared up at the massive structure spanning the river and swallowed hard. "You've got to be kidding me."

"Of course not," Lad said absently as he examined the immense stone tower that jutted up at the river's edge.

A hundred feet wide and twice as tall, the tower and its twin anchored a bridge that spanned mouth of the river. The span between them wasn't built for traffic. There were plenty of bridges upriver for that, broad, flat structures, well lit and well guarded.

This bridge was built for defense. As part of the city wall, the battlements bristled with siege engines, and could shield legions of archers. The crowning glory was a portcullis of a size Mya had never dreamed possible. It extended the entire width of the river, poised like the fangs of a great dragon's maw, ready to plunge into the river below.

Lad looked at Mya. "There's cover here. We can get across without being seen. You can do this, Mya. You sent me into more difficult spots than this in Twailin."

"I know I *can* do it, but…" She swallowed again and forced a smile. "I'd just rather bluff, lie, cajole, or bribe my way through."

"That won't work here." He nodded to the patrol that had just passed. "They're gone. Come on."

Lad dashed across the wide avenue that bordered the river before she could protest, vanishing into the shadow of the great tower. Mya followed, listening for a call of alarm.

Silence.

"Good," Lad whispered. "Don't worry. Just follow me."

Don't worry, he says… She gritted her teeth. "I'm right behind you."

They crept around the tower to a narrow walkway bordering the river's edge. Mya wrinkled her nose against the stench of the river. She did *not* want to fall into that water. Beneath the bridge, they found the track through which the portcullis rose and fell. A foot wide, the iron-edged groove ran up the tower's side and into the shadows of the overhead span.

"Up," Lad whispered, wedging his hands and feet in the track. "Careful, the iron is rusty."

267

"Right." She watched him ascend like a spider climbing a thread. Mya knew that her runes would allow her to match Lad's feat, but she'd never applied her strength this way. She mimicked his stance, her hands and feet braced, and started up. Progress was slow, but not as strenuous as she thought it would be. She reached the raised portcullis, and allowed herself a grin of accomplishment. The grin faded when she glanced back over her shoulder to see Lad already a third of the way across the river, scrabbling along like a monkey.

You can do this... Mya grasped the portcullis. The iron bar was as big around as her arm and covered in rust, making her grip difficult, but she tightened her grip and followed Lad.

Pausing for a moment mid-span, she made the mistake of looking down. Black water flowed sluggishly past, ready to swallow her should she fall. *Don't think about it!* She forced her fears aside and refocused on her task.

Hand over hand, foot over foot, she pulled herself across. When she finally reached the far side, she not only felt better, she felt good, giddy with her success. She descended and dropped lightly beside Lad, barely breathing hard.

"Well, that was fun!" Mya couldn't suppress a grin.

"Yes." Lad looked at her and flashed a thin smile. "Don't grin. Someone might see your teeth in the dark."

"Right." She closed her mouth, silently chastising herself. She knew better. "Go ahead. I'll follow."

Lad waited for yet another patrol to pass around a corner and out of sight. "Come on."

Mya followed him into the Dreggars Quarter, immediately noting the difference from the north side of the river. Though Midtown's modest homes and shops had been a big step down from the Heights in class and quality, this was a plummet into a whole new world. Rusty iron barred shop windows, paint peeled on cracked tenement doors, and, in a gutter, a dead cat swarmed with flies and maggots. Mya had seen worse in The Sprawls district of Twailin, but not much worse, and the Downwind

268

Quarter was reputed to be even shoddier. She hoped they didn't go that far.

"Ssst!" Lad's hiss brought her up short. From around the corner came the clatter of another guard patrol, this one larger and moving faster than those north of the river. She tugged on Lad's sleeve, and they vanished into the shadows of an alley. A moment later, six heavily armed constables strode by.

"Mean streets," she whispered when they'd passed. "Even the guard doesn't linger."

"Let's find a pub or inn where we can talk to someone. It's late, but there's got to be someplace open."

"All right." Mya's nerves still tingled with the exhilaration of crossing the bridge, but doubt clouded her thoughts. *What does he expect to learn?*

They recognized a pub only by the lamplight shining through cracked shutters, the sound of muted laughter, and a thick-shouldered bouncer lounging at the door. Lad stepped off the curb to cross the street, but Mya grabbed his sleeve.

"You sure you want to go in there? People in neighborhoods like this don't usually talk to strangers."

Lad paused, obviously considering her concern. He was listening to her. *Good.*

"It can't hurt to try." He patted the pouch on his belt. It didn't jingle, since he'd stuffed a handkerchief into it to keep the coins silent, but she got the point. "Maybe we can make some friends."

"Don't draw too much attention." Mya hoped he didn't take offence at her suggestions. Lad was the most deadly assassin she'd ever known, but his interpersonal skills lacked subtlety. "Let me do the talking. Like I said, bluffing, lying, cajoling, and bribery are my game."

"Fine. You talk, I'll pay." He stepped into the light of the guttering streetlamp.

"And be careful. If you flash too much coin, we'll get mugged." She received a scowl for her advice.

The bouncer eyed them, but made no comment as they approached the pub. Mya flashed a smile, but his face remained grim. *Nothing like a warm welcome*, she thought as they passed inside.

Twenty minutes later they left the pub, a few coins poorer and no richer in knowledge. Their offer of drinks had been turned down, and Mya's casual questions received only suspicious stares.

"I told you so," she said.

"You did, but they can't all be like this, and we're not in a hurry. Let's find another."

"Fine."

They crept through the streets, evading the sparse patrols and a few skulking types. They tried two more pubs and got the same blank stares and suspicious looks.

"This isn't working, Lad."

"One more." They rounded another corner and spied a likely pub. The windows were barred, of course, but the shutters were open and a cheery yellow glow spilled through the reasonably clean windows. From the voices, it sounded as if there was quite a crowd. "That one looks better."

Mya stopped to consider their location. "How many blocks from the waterfront do you think we are?"

"Two." Lad pointed down the street. "Steepway Stair is right over there, the shipyards just down the bluff."

Mya cocked an eyebrow at him. She had always taken it for granted that he knew his way around Twailin, but even here, after only studying maps, Lad seemed right at home. *That makes one of us.* She nodded toward the pub. "That explains the crowd. The shipyards work 'round the clock. One shift must have recently come off work."

"Good. Maybe they're thirsty. Come on."

The place was surprisingly homey. The long wooden bar was clean and bright, if not fancy. Fully half of the booths and tables were occupied. The patrons had the look of shipyard workers, with thick, tar-stained hands, and smelling of wood shavings and creosote. The more pleasant aromas of ale, wine, and well-cooked food advertised the pub's wares better than any menu. Two servers bustled about, smiling good naturedly at their customers.

Nobody smiled at Lad and Mya, however.

The looks they received weren't friendly, but they weren't as suspicious as those at their previous stops. Still, every eye she caught quickly looked away. They chose a table in the middle of the room.

"Can I get something for you?" The barmaid brushed her skirts impatiently.

"Highland Summerbrew, if you have it."

"Aye, we've a barrel tapped." Her eyes darted to Mya. "And you?"

"Some mulled wine, thank you."

"Very good." The woman hurried away.

"See, I told you this looked like a friendly little place." Smiling at Lad, Mya slouched back in her chair.

Lad never slouched. Nudging his toe under the table and cocking an eyebrow seemed to get her point across. He smiled back and sloped his shoulders a trifle. "You did. How can you drink hot wine in the summer?"

At least he's trying. Mya wondered if Lad could ever truly relax in a crowd. She pitched her voice just louder than normal, but not by much. "I like the spices, and the heat never bothers me. You always order Highland Summerbrew?"

"It's only really good this time of year. Forbish always had it in season. It's my favorite."

"Paxal always made mulled wine for me. We're creatures of habit, I guess."

The barmaid returned with their drinks. Foam brimmed Lad's tankard, and clove-scented steam wafted from Mya's. "Sixpenny, if you please."

Lad fished a silver half-crown from his pouch—twice the cost of the drinks—and handed it to the barmaid. "I wonder if you could do me a favor. I'm interested in doing business in this part of town, but we're new here, and don't know the...ins and outs of things. Would you let your patrons know that I'd be happy to stand a round to anyone who'll give a little advice?"

His delivery had improved with practice and a little coaching from Mya.

"I'll ask," she agreed grudgingly, tucking the coin into her pocket without offering change. Apparently, when no noble-born were about, tips weren't proscribed.

Lad smiled at her. "Thank you."

Mya kept a furtive eye on the woman as she circulated from table to table, chatting with her customers. Despite the hum of voices, Mya could easily pick out the barmaid's words. She delivered Lad's message without embellishment, seemingly disinterested in whether anyone took him up on his offer or not. Sipping her wine, Mya avoided meeting the glances that flicked toward them in the barmaid's wake.

A chair screeched on the floor, and a big man lurched up.

"Don't, Tori." The man's table companion grabbed his arm. "You don't know them."

"Don't care." The big man jerked his arm free and stumbled a step, obviously drunk. "Not scared of nobody no more."

His companion scowled and looked away as Tori snatched up his tankard and drained it, slamming it back down too hard. His crooked path to their table drew stares from a few other patrons, and a lingering glare from the barkeep. Oblivious to the attention he'd drawn, the man stopped at their table and looked down first at Lad, then at Mya.

"Name's Tori," he said.

Mya pushed out a chair with her foot and said, "I'm Maci and this is Lem. Have a seat, Tori. What are you drinking?"

Tori looked down at the chair, then back at his own table, where his companion steadfastly ignored him. Sniffing, he wiped his nose with the back of his hand and sat down. "Mardie knows what I drink."

Mya motioned to the barmaid, then looked Tori over. He appeared to be a laborer of some kind—longshoremen or shipwright perhaps—with broad shoulders and thick, calloused hands. The knife at his belt was made to cut rope or wood, not flesh. "Do you work in the shipyards?"

"Yep. Fifteen years now, and not a pot to piss in for my labor. You interested in business, you best take it across the river."

"Why?" Mya gestured around the homey pub. "This place seems to be doing well."

"Jemly's been runnin' this place long as I can remember, and he ain't gettin' rich doin' it."

The barmaid arrived and smacked a mug of ale down on the table in front of Tori. "Twopence." She snatched up the silver half-crown Lad held out, then shifted her glare to Tori. "You be careful, Tori."

"I don't need to be careful." Tori lifted his tankard and took a long pull as she bustled off. "Got nothin' to lose, so nothin' to be careful about." The last he said loud enough for everyone to hear.

"Why wouldn't she want you to talk to us, Tori?" Mya sipped her wine, keeping her tone easy. "It's not like we're constables or nobles. We're just trying to make a living."

"Livin's harder than you might think south of the river." Tori sipped ale, his eyes narrow over the top of his tankard. "And we don't worry too much about the caps or nobles down here. There's other worries, though." He lowered his voice. "You ask Jemly where half his profits go every month."

"Oh?" Mya raised an eyebrow and shared a look with Lad. That sounded suspiciously like a protection racket, though there was no way to know what organization was running it. She doubted whether the barkeep even knew who he was paying. From the corner of her eye, she noticed a man slinking out the pub door, glancing back at them over his shoulder. She ignored him and turned back to Tori. "So, businesses north of the river don't have that problem?"

"Don't know." Tori drank and frowned. "They got other problems. Up there, you got the nobles up your ass every turn, and the caps bustin' your head if you so much as look at one of 'em wrong. Ain't *no* good place to earn a livin' here."

"Why stay, then?" Lad asked.

"Where the hell would I go?" Tori shrugged massive shoulders and stared into his ale. "Been here my whole life. Born here, lived here, and I'll die here."

"Seems like Tsing's a hard place to do business."

"Anyplace else easier?" Tori looked at Mya dubiously. "None I heard of are. If it's not nobles and constables, it's thugs. Same everywhere."

"That's enough, Tori." The barkeep rounded the end of the bar, his face a mask of hard lines, and put a hand on the man's shoulder. "You've said enough."

"Oh le'me alone, Jemly. I'm not hurtin' nobody." Tori lifted his tankard, but Jemly took it from his grasp with surprising ease.

"And you've drunk too much. Your mouth's gonna get you in trouble."

"We're just talking. What's the harm in talking?" Lad protested.

Jemly turned his glare on Lad and Mya, but fear lurked beneath his hard mien. "I don't know you. You dress like cutthroats and ask too many questions. I want you outta my place *now*."

"We're not causing any trouble, and I don't see why—"

Lad's hand closed on Mya's arm, cutting off her protest with a hard squeeze. "We didn't mean to cause any trouble. We'll leave." Lad stood, and Mya reluctantly pushed back her chair.

Hard gazes followed them out, the friendly pub atmosphere stifled by a few simple questions. Crossing the street, they stopped to talk.

Mya let out a gusty breath. "Well, that explains some things. It sounds like the nobles have a stranglehold on everything north of the river, and the guilds and gangs have the same south of the river. No wonder everyone's afraid."

"Yes, but why does the emperor tolerate it? Something still doesn't make sense." Lad shook his head, his brow furrowed. "The guild probably pays off the constables to keep their noses out of guild business, but they can't pay off the military. Why doesn't the emperor use soldiers to clean up the Dreggars Quarter and Downwinds?"

"Why hasn't Mir cleaned up The Sprawls?" Mya shrugged. "Probably not worth it. The wealthy use the poor as cheap labor to make money. The poor need somewhere cheap to live. Clean up the neighborhood and rent goes up. Labor costs go up, profits go down, and with them tax revenues. The wealthy lose money, and the empire loses money, so where's the incentive? It's simple economics." Mya looked around uneasily as the hairs on the back of her neck stood up. "I think we should go."

"We might ask some more questions if—" Lad stopped and cocked his head. "There's someone—"

"I think you've asked enough questions." A man stepped out from the shadowed alley in front of them.

Shit! Mya had only been listening for the obvious racket of constables, not the subtle noises of lurkers in hiding. Behind them, a boot scuffed stone, then another. Whoever these people were, they were trained in stealth. That became even more obvious as three more figures stepped out of the shadows ahead.

"What's the harm in asking questions?" Lad's query drew a dry chuckle from the speaker's throat.

"Last person to ask me *that* question stopped breathing all of the sudden." His hand fingered the hilt of a dagger at his belt. "Horrible tragedy."

"Who are you?" Mya asked, gauging the figures emerging from the shadows.

"Another unwelcome question," said a man behind them. Steel wisped against leather as a dagger left its sheath. "Curiosity killed the cat, they say."

"Good thing we're not cats." She immediately regretted the reflexive quip. This could go wrong too easily.

"You got a smart mouth." The leader shifted his attention to Lad. "You need to shut her up."

"If you figure out how to do that, let me know." Lad shot Mya a wry look, and she gaped at him.

A joke from Lad? A frisson tingled up Mya's spine. Lad wasn't afraid, and these thugs were used to being feared. *All right then. If that's how he wants to play this...* "Three behind and four in front? You think you need so many to shut me up?"

"I know *exactly* how to shut you up." The leader drew the dagger he'd been fondling. "And I know exactly how to keep you from asking any more questions."

"We don't want trouble." Lad eased into a ready stance.

"We don't?" Mya flashed a dangerous grin and turned her back to Lad, her shoulder blades brushing his. "Can't we have a *little* trouble?"

"No trouble. Now, who do you work for and what's your territory?"

"You've already found trouble." The leader of the thugs snapped his fingers, and his people fanned out, circling the pair of assassins. "The only question now is how much pain you need to shut you up."

"You don't want to try that, friend." Lad shifted. She could feel his heightened readiness like a high-pitched vibration up her spine. Long nights of practice had attuned her to his every move. She shifted to accommodate his stance. "Who do you work for?"

"I'm not your *friend*. Your questions aren't welcome here, and neither are you."

"Our first night in Tsing, and we've already worn out our welcome." Mya tsked as she gauged the three people facing her: one man with a staff, and a man and a woman holding daggers. Mya licked her lips, and decided which would be the first to die. *Staff man. He's got reach, and he'll use it.*

"Don't kill anyone, Mya."

Lad's order caught her off guard. He sounded serious.

"Why not?" She rose onto the balls of her feet, the energy of her runes humming beneath her skin.

"Because they can't answer our questions if they're dead." Lad shifted left, and she moved with him. This brought one more foe into Mya's range, a woman with a chain locked to her wrist, a spiked ball dangling from the end.

Her first, then… "We're still asking questions?" This fight would be a lot harder without killing. Her opponents stopped, shifted positions, and advanced again, chain woman now between the dagger wielders.

"Please, Mya."

"Fine." Chain woman began spinning her weapon in a figure eight. "Ruin my fun."

The attacks came in a flurry of steel and wood.

The thugs were good, well trained and used to fighting together, but they had never faced anything like Lad or Mya. Staff and chain came at Mya simultaneously, hardwood whirling down at her head and steel lashing up at her groin. She caught the end of the staff in one hand, and used its momentum to flip sideways so the spiked ball missed her hip by an inch. Snatching the chain, she jerked hard, at the same time snapping the staff in half with her foot. Staff man stumbled back, and chain woman was pulled forward. Mya cracked the broken end of the staff across the bridge of chain woman's nose. When Mya's feet touched back down, chain woman landed flat on her back, out cold, her face a mass of blood.

One down.

277

A concussion from behind Mya shivered her spine with its force. Only Lad hit that hard. Mya wasn't surprised to hear a body fall to the ground. Lad's leg brushed hers, and she moved to guard his flank as he moved to guard hers.

Perfect...

The pair wielding daggers lunged, one high, one low. Mya dropped into a ground-sweeping spin, her foot tripping both assailants. Pushing herself up off the ground with her hands, she continued her spin, and caught a glimpse of Lad. He spun also, deflecting attacks with his feet. Their eyes met, and he flung out a hand to her.

Yes!

Clasping wrists, they combined their rotation, spinning around their clenched hands. Mya leveled a roundhouse kick to the temple of one of Lad's opponents, pulling her blow to keep from breaking his neck. He went down hard.

No killing...

Bone crunched as Lad struck down one of Mya's foes. Something flicked her hair. She heard the slap of a hand against metal near her ear, and a dagger spun into the darkness. Lad had just saved her life.

Their spin continued, then Lad released his grasp, and Mya reluctantly let go. They were back to their original opponents. Dagger woman was down, clutching her chest. Dagger man rolled aside, and flipped to his feet in a remarkable display of agility, though he didn't attack. Mya stopped her spin and centered herself, reflexively aligning her stance with Lad's.

So perfect...

Staff man lunged at her, now wielding two daggers. Mya grabbed his wrists, wrenched his arms in opposite directions to pull him in, and smashed her forehead into his nose. He fell like a steer in a slaughterhouse, and Mya snatched his blades. Behind her, a wet pop heralded a hoarse cry. A shoulder or hip had been wrenched out of joint. Lad had probably just immobilized his last foe.

Mya's last opponent backed away, flipped his blade, and threw. The dagger tumbled end-over-end in the lamplight, as slow as a falling feather to her accelerated senses. *Never throw a knife at a monster...* She threw both of her stolen blades, and caught the oncoming dagger by the hilt an inch before it pierced her chest. *...you'll just piss her off.*

Dagger man went down with both blades lodged hilt deep in his shoulders.

Silence...save for labored breathing, moans of pain, and nine distinct heartbeats.

No killing.

Mya turned to find Lad holding the leader's dislocated arm behind his back, and the man's own dagger at his throat. She grinned. "We're having all *kinds* of fun tonight!"

"*Fun?*"

She couldn't interpret the look on Lad's face. *Anger? Disgust?* He shook his head and cast the man's dagger away.

"Now about those questions..."

"You're both dead for this!" the man spat between gasps of pain. "The guild will have your heads!"

"*Which* guild?" Mya approached the man, brandishing the dagger, her lips pulling back from her teeth in a snarl. "If you like your eyes, you'll tell us."

"Which guild do you think?"

"Well, you don't look like a teamster or longshoreman to me."

Of course he was reluctant to tell them; admitting that you were in the Assassins Guild was usually a death sentence. But the way these thugs had fought, it couldn't be anything else.

Mya held her hand up before the man's face, the obsidian master's ring glinting on her finger. "Maybe you should have answered our questions *before* you attacked us, idiot."

The man's eyes widened and his clenched jaw dropped open. "You... You're *guild?*"

"Yes. See how easy it is to ask questions and get answers?" Lad released his hold on the man's wrist and stepped to Mya's side. "Now, who are you? Which guild and faction do you belong to? And who ordered you to attack us?"

The man's eyes flicked to Lad's hand and widened even further when he saw the gold and obsidian on his finger. "I'm Borlic, journeyman Enforcer in the Tsing Assassins Guild. Nobody *ordered* me to attack you. I've standing orders to handle anyone who asks too many questions in my area." He swallowed and winced as he tried to move his arm. The shoulder was still out of joint. "Who *are* you?"

"I'm the Twailin Guildmaster, and this is my Master Hunter. We're here to meet with the Grandmaster."

"Twailin?" The man's eyes widened. "Twailin doesn't *have* a guildmaster."

"He's new." Mya tossed the dagger away and turned to Lad. "Maybe we *should* kill him. He doesn't seem too quick on the uptake."

"No, I have more questions." Lad fixed the man with a curious look. "Do you pay the constables not to bother you?"

"Yes, but only south of the river."

"Why not north of the river?"

"No need." The man shrugged, wincing in pain at the motion. "We don't run rackets north of the river."

"Why not?"

"I don't *know*. I'm just a journeyman. They don't tell me how or why, they just tell me what to do."

"Fair enough." Lad bit his lower lip and looked around at the groaning and unconscious assassins. "Sorry about the mess. Maybe next time you'll answer a few simple questions before you start a fight."

"Yeah, maybe." Borlic's glare told them that he'd no more follow their advice than he would sprout wings and fly away.

Idiot...

"Let me take care of that arm."

"Wait! I—"

Lad grabbed the man's wrist and planted a foot in his armpit. One hard jerk popped the bone back into the socket and elicited an anguished cry from between the assassin's clenched teeth. When Lad released his grip, Borlic crumpled to his knees, cradling his arm.

"Come on." Lad stepped over a fallen assassin and walked away.

Mya hopped over the body and fell in beside him, her steps bouncing with the lingering exhilaration of the fight. A giddy ebullience bubbled up from her stomach, and she couldn't keep a smile off her face. "That was very nice of you, tending his arm like that."

"It was the least I could do."

"I still think we should have killed him. They started it, after all."

"No, you don't."

"I don't?" She stared at him, suspicious of some joke, but he was dead serious.

"You told me so just the other night. Killing someone doesn't make you feel any better."

Mya thought for a moment, the pleasant feeling ebbing. "Yes... Yes, I did say that." She hated it when he used her own words against her.

Chapter XX

Norwood's carriage plunged into darkness, swallowed by the tunnel that passed from the Imperial Palace's outer court to the inner. The first heavy iron portcullis rumbled down behind them, and the second rose only high enough to admit several more palace guards. The carriage jerked to a halt, and a heavyset sergeant rapped on the carriage door. Norwood sighed. They'd already been checked over twice, but they were apparently going to be checked yet again. At least now Norwood knew what they would ask of him.

"I'm Captain Norwood of the Twailin Royal Guard. I'm here with vital news for the emperor." He held out his signet ring. "This should verify who I am readily enough."

The sergeant took the ring and looked up at him dubiously. "Be just a moment." He walked away, under the portcullis, undoubtedly to verify Norwood's claim.

"Tight-arsed lot, aren't they?"

Norwood scowled at Tamir's comment. "That's enough, Sergeant. They're charged with keeping the emperor safe. They have to be thorough."

"Yes, sir."

They waited. The guard sergeant was back in only a few minutes with the ring and a scrap of parchment. "Here you are, sir. Present this to the commander of the inner court."

"Thank you, Sergeant."

"Best of luck to you, sir." The sergeant saluted and signaled the men managing the portcullis. The heavy grating rumbled up its track, and the carriage clattered forward into the inner court.

"Son of a..." Tamir clamped his jaw down on his exclamation, but Norwood wouldn't have faulted him. This was his first sight of the Imperial Palace inner court, too, and his breath caught in his throat.

"It's something, isn't it?"

"That's putting it lightly, sir."

The carriage circled the expansive parade ground. Perhaps a hundred imperial guards stood or marched about in rigid formations, their tabards, helmets, and weapons glittering like gems in the sun. The palace itself loomed before them, a massive stone structure sporting hundreds of gilded embrasures, lofty windows of stained glass, and towering spires of polished white stone and gold.

"At least now I know where my tax money goes."

"One more comment like that, Sergeant, and I'll leave you in the carriage with Brutus!"

"Yes, sir."

The carriage rolled to a stop, and Brutus heaved his bulk up from his spot on the floor, his stubby tail twitching.

"Not this time, Brutus." Norwood held out a hand, palm toward the dog's nose. "Stay!"

Brutus eyed him dubiously and whined.

"Sorry, boy." The captain followed Tamir out of the carriage, unfolding his legs gingerly. His backside was numb from the long ride. They'd pushed hard since Farthane, but a broken wheel had delayed them half a day. They'd left the last way-inn well before sunrise this morning to arrive in Tsing early. Norwood was exhausted, but he vowed not to rest until he delivered his message to the emperor.

Spies in the palace. Who would believe it? The answer was easy: no one. That was why Norwood had no intention of mentioning spies until he was in the imperial presence. He hoped that an urgent message that concerned the safety of the emperor would get him inside the palace, but he'd never attempted anything like this before. He shuddered to consider what could happen if his message arrived too late, if the "right hand of death" somehow gained access to the emperor.

A dozen imperial guards approached in tight formation, a grim-faced commander at the fore.

"They certainly have this place buttoned up tight." Tamir stood at parade rest beside his captain, looking worried.

"They do indeed."

Norwood knew the sociopolitical situation in Tsing, his position affording him news that others rarely heard. Tynean Tsing II had not exactly ingratiated himself with the general populace, and the iron-clad security surrounding the palace was a direct result. Thankfully, Duke Mir despised the heavy-handed practices employed in the central empire, and fought tooth and nail to maintain his own less strict system.

The commander, dressed in breastplate, greaves, steel gauntlets, and gleaming helm, saluted Norwood's rank insignia, and Norwood saluted back. This was where he would have to pull out all the stops. Not being in the same chain of command, the captain could not order the guardsman to let him see the emperor. However, the insignia on his collar did command respect, and he hoped that the man would recognize that they were, in truth, brothers in arms, with the empire's best interests at heart.

"I'm Commander Ithross. May I help you, Captain?"

"Yes, you may. I'm Captain Norwood of the Twailin Royal Guard." He handed over the note from the gate guard.

Ithross scanned the note, and an eyebrow rose skeptically.

Norwood tried not to interpret the reaction too suspiciously. He had to walk a fine line between discretion and urgency. Not just anyone could be the spy he sought. It had to be someone highly placed, or with special access, an imperial page or secretary, maybe. The chance of an Imperial Guard commander being involved was miniscule, but he had tipped his hand just by riding through the gate. The spy knew who Norwood was, and might already know that he was here.

Norwood forged ahead. "I've critical news for the emperor's ear alone. We've ridden halfway across the empire to deliver it. It may concern His Majesty's safety."

The commander looked up from the note. "*May* concern?"

Norwood was bristled at the man's tone. "That's right. Isn't it your job to ensure the emperor's safety?"

The commander's face hardened. "Yes it is, Captain, but let me tell you for your own good that you had better be damned *sure* this concerns His Majesty's safety before I submit your name for an unscheduled audience. Emperor Tynean is not a temperate man."

Norwood nodded, taking the advice in the spirit in which it was given. "Your advice is well received, commander. Rest assured, His Majesty will want to hear what I have to say."

"You'd be better off writing your message down and letting me deliver it to the emperor's secretary." He gestured to the lathered team in the traces of Norwood's coach. "Looks like you've traveled hard. I can put you up in comfortable quarters while you wait for the reply."

"Thank you for the offer, but no, Commander." Norwood's resolve firmed, despite the temptation. "I must speak to His Majesty personally, and as soon as possible."

"It's your head." The commander pointed to Norwood's sword. "You may as well leave your weapons in your carriage, sir. Not so much as a paring knife is allowed in the imperial presence, and it'll save me the trouble of storing them away."

"All right." He unbuckled his sword belt and handed it to Tamir. The sergeant stowed it in the carriage along with his own sword, five daggers, a pair of brass knuckles, a garrote, and a set of throwing stars that he had secreted behind his belt buckle.

At Norwood's incredulous stare, he shrugged. "Just a few personal items, sir."

"You must feel a stone lighter."

"Yes, sir." Tamir's face remained blank.

He knows I'll order him to stay behind if he mouths off. Tamir had argued long and hard to accompany his commander into the Imperial Palace, and the captain had finally agreed. Having another pair of eyes when there was a spy about could save the emperor's life.

Norwood turned to Commander Ithross and waved toward the looming doors of the palace. "Lead on, Commander."

The commander signaled his troop, and four guardsmen fell in around them. "This way, sir."

Norwood wasn't surprised when Ithross led them to a postern door in the corner of the courtyard. He knew that only nobles rated an entry through the front doors, but he was disappointed nonetheless. The main entry hall was said to be beautiful beyond compare. Instead, they were ushered through passages no more grandiose than the interior of the Twailin Royal Guard headquarters. Tamir muttered something under his breath about scullery maids and chimney sweeps, but a glance from Norwood silenced him. After a long walk through a veritable labyrinth, the commander opened a door and led them into a small sitting room.

"I'll warn you, Captain," he said, "the emperor's schedule is set weeks in advance. He may not even see you today. All I can do is send a message that you're here."

"I understand, Commander, but please impress upon His Majesty the fact that I bear news that could influence his safety and *certainly* concerns the security of the empire." Norwood's tone brooked no argument.

"I'll use your exact words, but you'll still have to wait."

"I understand that."

"Good." The commander gestured to the ornate chairs. "Make yourselves comfortable."

At the commander's signal, the four guards took station at the room's two exits, standing at parade rest, hands on their swords. Tamir looked around and opened his mouth, but a glare from Norwood shut him up.

"Have a seat, Sergeant. We've got some waiting to do."

"Yes, sir."

They sat down to wait. Unfortunately for their already sore backsides, the chairs were made for elegance, not comfort.

A sliver of sunlight crept across Lad's face, and he stirred from a deep, dream-laden sleep.

Wiggen...

He refused to open his eyes, instead compelling the memory of her...hair draped across her scarred cheek, lips curled in a smile, eyes gleaming with love...

Oh, Wiggen...

By sheer force of will, Lad rolled up from the divan. A glance at the wall clock told him it was midmorning. They'd not gotten back to their room until the small hours of the morning, and the stress of the night's events sent him into a deep and uninterrupted sleep rich with dreams of Wiggen.

Striding to the window, he flipped the latch and opened it wide, taking a deep breath...and instantly regretting it. The morning sea breeze wafted the stench of rotting fish and open sewage into the room. With a grimace of disgust, Lad slammed the window closed.

Doesn't the wind ever blow the stink away? Granted, Twailin often stank, especially during the dry season when the river no longer ran full enough to wash away all the detritus of the city, but nothing like this.

The bedroom door opened. Mya stood there in her pajamas, her hair sticking up at all angles. "We overslept."

"We don't have to catch a carriage today, so what does it matter?" He pulled the bell rope beside the door. "Hungry?"

"Ravenous." She retreated back to the bedroom.

Lad tidied up his sleeping area, fluffing the pillows and putting away the blanket. The divan was more comfortable than sleeping on the floor, at least. A knock sounded at the door, and Lad answered it.

A servant in the inn's livery stood there expectantly. "Yes, sir?"

"Breakfast for two, please.   Eggs, toast, blackbrew, sausages…whatever's available."

"Very good, sir. Be ready in half a glass."

"That's fine." He closed the door.

Lad changed into trousers and a light shirt, but didn't bother to button the top button and didn't even touch the hated neck cloth. If they went out later he would have to dress in the full rig, but not for breakfast in his own room. He stared at his shoes for a moment, and decided to wear his more comfortable pair, even though there was a bit of blood on one from last night's fight.

He'd relived the encounter in his mind a half-dozen times on their way back to the inn last night, recalling the strangely comfortable synchronicity he experienced fighting alongside Mya. He'd enjoyed exercising with her, honing their skills in tandem, and now it felt…natural to have Mya at his back. Her exuberance after the fight, however, her casual bloodlust, disgusted him.

At least nobody died.

A knock at the door interrupted his thoughts. He answered it and admitted two white-clad servants with heavy trays. Scents of food and blackbrew swirled after the man and woman as they entered.

"At table, sir, or in the bedroom?"

"The table, please."

The bedroom door opened and Mya emerged, her dress loosely laced, her hair damp and slicked down. "That smells wonderful!"

Chris A. Jackson

While the man arranged a white linen tablecloth and arrayed napkins, utensils, and a tiny crystal vase with two yellow roses, the woman stood aside, eyes fixed upon the floor, her arm trembling beneath the heavily laden tray.

"Can I take that for you?" Lad asked.

She gaped at him in terror. "No! Please, sir. We could never allow a guest to help us. It would be an unforgivable breech of etiquette." She swallowed and looked down again. "I mean no offense, sir, but we're forbidden."

"No offense was taken." Lad backed away, exchanging a glance with Mya as the waiter unloaded the tray.

Mya just shrugged and waited patiently as the waiter poured fresh juice and blackbrew, removed the domed silver covers from their plates, and positioned the cream, sugar, and marmalade just so.

Finished, the waiter bowed. "Anything else, sir?"

"No. Thank you."

"My pleasure, sir." He turned to Mya and bowed again. "Ma'am."

When the door closed behind the servants, Mya said, "I don't think I'll ever get used to that stiff propriety." She took her seat and quaffed a third of her cup of steaming blackbrew, sighing in bliss.

"It's the fear that bothers me." Lad sat and sipped the piping hot brew more carefully. Mya's magical runes evidently also blocked the pain of a burned tongue. "I've almost gotten used to Dee waiting on me, but...being guildmaster... I don't like people to fear me. It makes me feel..."

"Like a monster?" Mya put her cup down too hard, the fine porcelain rattling in the saucer.

"A little, I guess." He'd never thought of himself as a monster. A murderer, yes, but not really a monster. "At least Dee doesn't seem to fear me anymore. He knows I need his help, and tells me what I need to hear."

289

"Dee's surprised me. He seems to be very good at whatever he does, except killing." Mya cut a piece of egg and perched it on a slice of toast. "But if we can convince the Grandmaster to give me your ring, you won't have to deal with Dee or being guildmaster anymore."

"No, *you* will." Lad ate a piece of sausage, thinking about their pending meeting with the Grandmaster. Could they really convince him that Lad had taken the ring by mistake? Could he be free of the Assassins Guild? His stomach flipped at the thought—to be with Lissa...to be a father again... But if the Grandmaster ever found out that Mya had freed Lad, there would undoubtedly be repercussions. Nobody ever left the Assassins Guild. "And you'll probably have to deal with—"

The knock on the door startled them both. There was enough foot traffic up and down the halls that neither of them paid much attention to it. They hadn't summoned another servant, and an interruption by the inn's staff seemed unlikely. Lad looked questioningly at Mya.

"The only person we're expecting..." The color drained from Mya's face, and she swallowed hard.

Lad knew perfectly well who they were expecting: the Grandmaster's representative. He also knew that Mya dreaded the encounter, but he wasn't sure why. The Grandmaster would be a fool to kill Mya for something as trivial as burning his letter, and one did not rise to the head of the Assassins Guild by being foolish.

Lad downed his blackbrew, and stood. "I'll get it."

When Lad opened the door, he found himself staring at a fine lady. Middle-aged, yet still handsome, she was clothed in high fashion, her jet-black hair arranged in a complex coif topped with a lace-veiled hat. Calm eyes scrutinized him from beneath the veil. Decades of training, however, revealed to Lad the truth: she was no fine lady. Tiny scars on her hands bespoke years wielding a blade. The dress fit well, but Lad detected an imbalance in the voluminous folds that denoted heavier objects hidden within. Then he recognized one of the rings on her fingers. It matched his perfectly.

Lad stepped back. "Come in please."

Her eyes assessed him as he had assessed her, and she smiled. "You must be Laurance Addington." She swept into the room with an easy, relaxed air. "And you're Mya Addington."

Mya stood and smoothed her dress. "Yes."

Lad closed the door. "And you are?"

"Lady Tara Monjhi." She nodded and smiled pleasantly. "You may call me Lady T. Everyone does. I'm your Tsing counterpart, Lad. The Grandmaster sent me to welcome you to the city. But I've been informed that you've already been exploring, including the Dreggars Quarter."

Lad walked to Mya's side, considering how to reply. It wasn't surprising that word of their conflict with the Enforcers reached the local guildmaster.

"I was curious." Gesturing to their quickly cooling breakfasts, he asked, "Can I offer you something? Blackbrew, a scone? The mango juice is delicious."

"No, thank you." She strolled around the room, casually swinging the parasol that dangled from her wrist. It reminded Lad of Jingles' cane, and he wondered if there was a blade in it. "I wish you wouldn't have gone out on your own. I could have arranged a tour to satisfy your curiosity."

"My apologies for injuring your people." Lad poured blackbrew into his cup and lightened it with cream. Mya, he noted, still stood like a statue, her pulse pounding at her throat. "They wouldn't take no for an answer."

"Oh, that's no matter." She waved a hand in dismissal. "They learned a valuable lesson."

"Then I'm happy we could educate them for you." He picked up a scone and took a small bite. "I'm interested in how you do business here. Your Enforcer said you pay off the constables to do business south of the river, but not north. How does that work?"

"It works quite well." Her eyes narrowed. "My business practices are not up for discussion. I don't think they would be of use to you in Twailin anyway."

"Just curious." Lad shrugged. She certainly wasn't as forthcoming as he'd hoped. "So, you're really a noble? You have a title?"

"Yes, I *really* have a title." Her cheeks flushed, betraying either embarrassment or ire. "Purchased by the guild, of course. It opens many doors here in Tsing."

"I imagine it does." He washed the bite down with blackbrew. "Tsing is very different than Twailin. I'm sure you understand my curiosity."

"Of course I do." She regarded him again, and Lad had difficulty reading her expression. Disdain? Smug superiority, maybe? "Aside from a warm welcome, I'm here to inform you about your appointment to meet the Grandmaster." She turned away, staring out the window at the distant bay. "I will arrive here precisely at six tonight and personally escort you to your meeting."

"Of course you will." She glanced at him, irritation plain on her face. Lad maintained a neutral mien. If this was Lady T's idea of a warm welcome, she needed a lesson in manners. Mya's heartbeat increased its cadence. "Only guildmasters and," Lad indicated Mya with a tip of his cup, "people of special interest know the Grandmaster's identity. He wasn't likely to send a journeyman to escort us."

"Quite right." Lady T's ingratiating smile didn't reach her eyes. She strolled to the door, her steps and carriage as smooth as the lines of her elegant dress. Resting a hand on the doorknob, she turned to them and said, "Six o'clock sharp, and don't wear any weapons."

"Why not?" It seemed an odd request. "It's not like either of us could hurt the Grandmaster."

"Because I said no weapons." Lady T's gaze swept them from hair to toes, and her upper lip curled to show perfect teeth. "And try not to dress like...commoners."

"We'll try to measure up to your exemplary standards, Lady T." Lad's smile was no more genuine than his visitor's.

Her short laugh sounded like the bark of a small dog. "Good luck with that." Lad listened to her footsteps recede down the hall.

"Were you *trying* to make her angry?" Mya's whisper barely rose above her heartbeat, the terror in her eyes shining like twin points of ice.

"No. I was treating her exactly as she treated me." He went back to his breakfast. "I'm not her servant, and I'm not afraid of her."

"No, but you can bet that she's the Grandmaster's favorite guildmaster." Mya crossed her arms as if hugging herself, her shoulders hunched with tension. "Pissing her off is just asking for trouble! If you want to have any hope of convincing the Grandmaster to give me your ring, you've got to play up to him."

"Him, yes. Her, no." Lad ate a sausage. "What do you think about her title?"

"Knowing what we do about how Tsing works, I'd be surprised if the guild *hadn't* bought her a title." Mya paced, ignoring her breakfast. "They're not hard to come by. There are enough penniless nobles, and you can't *eat* a title. Hell, *you* could buy one if you wanted."

"I don't." The thought of money buying nobility nauseated him.

Lad felt strangely calm. The time of their meeting was set, and they had a plan. Soon he could get back to his investigation, find Kiesha, and maybe even get his old life back. He glanced up at Mya. She had begun biting her nails.

"Mya. Are you all right?"

"No." She glanced at him, her eyes flinty. "No, I'm *not* all right. Masters don't meet the Grandmaster unless it's serious,

Lad. He could…he probably called me here to execute me for disobeying him. To make an example of me."

"No." Lad stood and faced her. The affable, wise-cracking Mya of the past couple of weeks was nowhere to be found here, and Lad felt sorry for her fear. She'd helped him, and he owed her. Lad had been a wreck, but she had persisted despite his rebuffs, and helped him sleep, given him focus, even hope. He had to try to help her overcome her fear. "He won't kill you, Mya. You're too valuable. He wanted you to be guildmaster. He won't throw you away just to make a point."

"The Grandfather threw people away all the time!"

"Have you heard anything to make you think the Grandmaster is like Saliez?"

"No." She let her breath out slowly, and the tension in her shoulders eased a trifle. "Ruthless and cunning is all I've ever heard."

"Then don't worry so much. We have a plan. Sit down and eat something."

"I'm not hungry." Mya went into the bedroom, not quite slamming the door.

Lad sat, but his food had lost its appeal. From behind the door, he could hear Mya pacing, back and forth, back and forth across the bedroom. He hadn't helped her very much.

Norwood's drooping eyes shot wide when the door finally opened and Commander Ithross clattered back into the room. The surprise on the guardsman's face brought Norwood to his feet, his back stabbing him from so long in the uncomfortable chair.

The commander was accompanied by a slim fellow wearing dress doublet, breeches and hose, and carrying a ledger under his arm. Behind them came a tall, broad-shouldered man dressed like a cross between a high lord and a court jester. His clothes were beyond flamboyant—yellow tunic, lavender hose, bright red shoes, even a peacock feather tucked behind one ear. The riot of color strangely complemented his ebony skin.

"Captain Norwood," said Ithross, gesturing to his companions, "this is Master Tennison, the emperor's secretary, and Master Keyfur, of the Imperial Retinue of Wizards."

Norwood nodded politely, wondering if he had just been introduced to the spy. Both the secretary and the mage would be well placed to intercept messages, and likely possessed the means to contract a magical assassin to do his dirty work.

The little ferret of a secretary looked at him dubiously and said, "For some unfathomable reason, His Majesty has granted you a brief audience. The emperor's schedule is very full, but there is a gap in approximately ten minutes, assuming his current appointment doesn't run overtime."

"Excellent!" Norwood tugged his wrinkled jacket straight, eager to complete his mission. "Let's go."

"Not quite yet, Captain. Before I escort you into the imperial presence, you must submit to a simple security measure."

"Very well. What measure is that, Master Tennison?"

"A magical measure." Tennison gestured to the wizard. "Master Keyfur, would you please tell the captain what's involved?"

"Certainly." The wizard's voice rumbled low, as melodious as an opera singer's. Plucking the feather from behind his ear, he waved it in a lazy circle. "A simple spell, really, to ensure that you are who you say you are, and that you're not here under false pretenses."

"A truth spell?" Norwood tried to remain calm. He would rather pet a crocodile than allow Keyfur to cast a spell on him.

"Yes. Are you familiar with them?"

"Yes. I've seen Duke Mir's mage, Master Woefler, use them." There were two types that Norwood knew of, one that compelled the person to speak the truth, and the other that simply informed the wizard if the person was lying. "I can't allow a compulsion spell to be cast upon me. The news I have is for the emperor's ears only."

"Not to worry, Captain. This spell will be of the less-invasive variety." Keyfur waved the feather in an elaborate pattern. "I simply cast the spell and ask a few questions. If you lie, I'll know."

"Fine. Cast it." There was no alternative. He had to submit or he would never see the emperor.

"I already have, Captain." Keyfur grinned.

Norwood swallowed uneasily. He hadn't felt a thing. "Then ask your questions."

"Have you told the truth about the reason you seek an audience with the emperor?"

"Yes."

"Do you plan any violence or subterfuge here in the palace?"

"No."

"Are you in any way armed?"

"I have no weapons, if that's what you're asking."

"Very good." Keyfur turned to Tamir. "And you, Sergeant, do you plan any violence or subterfuge here in the Palace."

"Not unless someone tries to harm my captain, sir."

Keyfur smiled. "A fair answer, and true enough. Do you bear any weapons?"

"Well, I got this here contraption that has a corkscrew, a pair of scissors, a toothpick, a nail file, a fish scaler, and a little thingy that'll trim your nose hairs. But it ain't got no blade, so it's not rightly a weapon. If you don't count this, then no, I've got nothing but my fists."

Norwood nearly burst out laughing at the tiny folding tool that Tamir had picked up in his search for the maker of the black darts, but his sergeant looked serious, as did the guard commander.

"Let's see that," Commander Ithross ordered, and Tamir handed the little device over. After a brief examination, the commander snorted a laugh and handed it back. "It's nothing."

Keyfur smiled, tucked the feather back behind his ear, and turned to Tennison. "They speak the truth."

"Good." Tennison nodded to Norwood. "You and your sergeant will come with me, Captain."

"Very good." Norwood's stomach clenched; it wasn't every day that one met the emperor face to face. "Lead on."

To the captain's surprise, no guards followed as he and Tamir trailed the secretary through another labyrinth of hallways. He wondered about the lack of security until they turned a corner. This corridor, much wider and higher than any they'd seen, was hung with crystal chandeliers and papered resplendently in blue and gold. Coats of arms hung at regular intervals on both walls, and beneath each stood an imperial guard, rigidly at attention, eyes fixed straight ahead. There must have been fifty of them. Certainly such an expenditure of manpower could ensure the safety of one man. Was Norwood being ridiculous to assume a spy could get anywhere near the emperor?

No, he realized with a jolt. *The spy must be someone above suspicion. Someone who could walk right past these guards.*

The secretary's shoes clicked on the polished marble as he led them down the corridor…right past the guards.

Norwood glanced at Tennison. *Maybe…*

Tamir tugged at his captain's sleeve, darted his eyes toward the secretary, and raised an eyebrow. Norwood shrugged, reassured that they both had the same suspicion.

The emperor's secretary stopped before a pair of heavy double doors. Turning to Norwood and Tamir, he instructed, "You will remain at least five strides from His Majesty. You will bow from the waist and remain bowed until called upon to speak. You will not speak out of turn. When so ordered, you will answer questions succinctly, and not deviate or expound."

His nose rose in the air, and his lips thinned. "These few minutes of the emperor's time are more valuable than the both of you, so you will keep your answers *short*! Is that clear?"

"Perfectly clear." Norwood stared into Tennison's eyes, searching for some hint of treason, but saw only pompous indignation and duty.

"Wait here." The secretary twisted the door's golden handle and slipped through the gap with the stealth of a burglar.

Voices rose from behind the closed door, but Norwood couldn't make out any words. He tucked his hands behind his back and tried to calm his nerves.

"You think it's him, sir?" Tamir whispered.

"I…don't think so," he whispered back, wary of the guards only twenty feet to each side. "Keep your wits sharp, Sergeant. While I say speak with the emperor, I want you watching for reactions from his retainers. If something strikes you as suspicious, sing out."

"Yes, sir."

They didn't have long to wait. The door opened, and Master Tennison beckoned them in.

Norwood was surprised at the austerity of the room's décor. Walls of muted hues of blue and gold were broken only by two doors in the room's back corners. Overhead, a simple chandelier supported bright-burning lamps. Upon a low dais rested a simple upholstered armchair, the imperial sovereign upon its cushioned seat.

Tynean Tsing II bore little resemblance to the portrait that hung in Duke Mir's audience chamber, or the silhouette stamped on every gold crown in the realm. He looked older than those images, older even than his purported sixty-two years. The burdens of the empire had, it seemed, left their mark on the emperor. The crown rested upon a head of immaculately groomed silver hair. Deep lines radiated from his eyes and mouth, clearly showing that this was not a face accustomed to smiling. But he sat straight, his narrow shoulders squared, his wizened hands gripping the arms of the chair with strength. His eyes were keen and ruthless.

Imperial bodyguards flanked the emperor's seat, two at each side. Another stood at the foot of the dais, his hand on the hilt of the curved blade at his hip. They all looked enough alike to be brothers: close-cropped hair, weathered skin, steely eyes, garbed in identical surcoats and gleaming mail. Norwood knew the badges on the shoulders their uniforms: blademasters of Koss Godslayer, protectors of the emperors of Tsing for the last five hundred years. They were rumored to feel no pain and know no fear, gifts from their deity for in exchange for pledging their very souls. The rigors of their life-long training shone in the deep scars on their hands and faces, decades of discipline etched in blood. Most horrifically, blademasters had their tongues cut out at an early age. Reading and writing were also banned. There would be no careless words to betray the secrets of either their training or their sovereign.

To the emperor's right stood a man identifiable by the circlet of gold adorning his brow. Crown Prince Arbuckle, the emperor's sole heir. He looked perhaps ten years younger than Norwood, fit and hale, his dark hair barely flecked with white. His lips were pinched tight in what the captain interpreted as irritation. The prince was flanked by his own two bodyguards, as grim, scarred, and expressionless as the emperor's. The only other person stood with a thick tome balanced open on his hip, a long quill pen poised above the page, undoubtedly the imperial record keeper.

"Captain Norwood of the Twailin Royal Guard, Your Majesty." Tennison stepped aside and bowed low.

"Your Majesty." Norwood bowed from the waist, and Tamir followed suit.

"You may rise. We've been told that you bear a message for Our ear alone, Captain." The emperor's voice, belied his age, resonating with the power of one who knew his words commanded an empire.

"Yes, Your Majesty." Norwood straightened. "It is of the highest importance that—"

The emperor's raised hand silenced him.

"We know. A matter of Our own personal safety, and the security of the empire." His lip curled in a derisive smirk. "Well, We suppose We should hear it, and grant your request for privacy." The emperor turned to the crown prince. "Leave Us, Arbuckle, and take Our secretary and record keeper with you. Wait in the east audience chamber. We will arrive shortly and take Our next appointment there."

"Yes, Your Majesty." The three men bowed low before departing through the east door, the prince's bodyguards following at his flanks.

Norwood felt like a bug under a magnifying lens beneath the gaze of the emperor. For a long moment the sovereign said nothing, but simply stared at the two, resting one elbow on the arm of his simple throne and tapping his chin with a long, slim finger. Norwood fixed his eyes on the emperor's feet, his hands clasped tight behind his back, his spine ramrod straight. The silence dragged on for what seemed like an hour, but probably spanned less than a minute.

"So, what exactly have you discovered that is a threat to Our safety, Captain?"

Norwood's heart leapt. This was exactly the opening he needed. With no ears besides the emperor's, he need not fear that the spy would overhear. "Your Majesty, I've learned that there is a spy within the palace. A spy with ties to organized crime in Twailin. I fear the spy might—"

The emperor cut him off with a raised hand.

"Hold your fears, Captain. We're quite safe at the moment. Tell Us how you came about this discovery."

"I was investigating the murder of a noble in Twailin, Your Majesty. Baron Eusteus Patino was killed approximately three weeks ago, and I—" Another raised hand. Norwood froze.

300

What was the sense in all these interruptions? Why couldn't the man just listen?

"You're sure it was murder?" The emperor leaned forward, suddenly attentive, eyes gleaming. "We were informed by Duke Mir that it was a natural death."

"I know, Your Majesty. It was necessary to send a misleading message. I needed an opportunity to investigate Baron Patino without causing a panic. But I'm sure it was murder."

"How do you know?"

"Duke Mir's mage identified the magic used to kill the baron."

"Magic?" The emperor leaned back, his eyes wide. "He found magic?"

"Yes, Your Majesty, a trace left by the murderer. I trust Master Woefler's judgment in these things without question. He said the murderer was a priest, and that—"

"A priest? He could tell you that specifically?"

"Yes, Your Majesty. He was sure of it."

"That's amazing. We had no *idea* Woefler was so adept!"

The emperor's mocking tone sent a chill up Norwood's spine. Did the emperor not believe him, or did he doubt Woefler? Did he think this was some kind of fabrication? It was time to set things straight.

"Your Majesty, he is *quite* adept. And I know that he was correct. The very day I started my investigation, an assassin tried to murder me, also using magic. I could only assume that this was the same man, so I set a trap. That's how I know there's a spy in the palace, Your Majesty! I gave Master Woefler a false message to send to Tsing, detailing when and where I would be conducting my investigation. I left myself open for attack, and the assassin took the bait! I got a good look at him, too. If we find the assassin, we can identify the spy."

"How unfortunate." The emperor sounded disappointed.

Unfortunate? What the hells…

"And how does this spy in the palace pertain to Our personal safety, Captain? This assassin attempted to take *your* life, not Ours, and those attempts occurred in Twailin and Farthane, not here!"

Norwood fought to remain calm. "The assassin can transport himself with magic, Your Majesty. He escaped me using it."

"Captain! Something—"

Tamir's urgent whisper was cut off by the emperor's harsh laugh.

"And you think that this assassin might pop in here and assassinate Us? Rest assured, Captain, the Imperial Palace is quite secure."

Norwood couldn't believe what he was hearing.

"Your Majesty, the message was intercepted *here*! The spy must be someone within your inner cadre, someone close, beyond suspicion. An imperial page, or one of the retinue of wizards. Someone close to you is a traitor! Your safety and the security of the empire are at risk!"

"The security of this empire is *not* at risk, Captain!" Tynean Tsing's tone cut like a razor, as if Norwood's claim had been a personal affront. "And neither is my safety."

"But Your Majesty, the evidence suggests—"

"Let me tell you what this *evidence* you think you have suggests, Captain Norwood!" The emperor thrust himself up from his seat and stepped down from his dais, his eyes blazing, his lip curling in a sneer of contempt. His bodyguards moved as he did, keeping him within their protective circle. "It *suggests* that someone in this palace orchestrated the murder of Baron Patino, as well as the attempts on your life. Your assumption that I am somehow in danger is nothing but conjecture."

"But Your Majesty! If someone in the palace—"

"Captain!" Tamir's hand closed hard on Norwood's elbow, his hissed whisper edged with panic. "It was *him*! He had Patino killed!"

302

Chris A. Jackson

"Tam! What—"

"You never mentioned Farthane, but he *knew*!"

"You should listen to your sergeant, Captain." The emperor sneered. "He sees clearly, where you are blinded by duty and loyalty."

Norwood tried to make the last piece of the puzzle fit. "I was told that that Patino was killed because of his involvement with the Assassins Guild. Your Majesty must have...thwarted an infiltration of the nobility by the Assassins Guild?"

Tynean Tsing laughed. "Wrong again, Captain. I *am* the Assassins Guild."

"Good Gods of Light..." Norwood's knees nearly buckled. Of all the possible explanations to the questions whirling through his mind, that was one that he simply could not fathom. "Your Majesty, *why?*"

"You dare to question *me?*" The emperor's sallow features flushed with anger. "Guards!"

The imperial bodyguards closed in, swords hissing from their scabbards.

This is impossible! Norwood stumbled back as Tamir pushed him aside.

Tamir pulled his ridiculous little contraption from his pocket, flipped the corkscrew out and gripped the body of the tool in his fist with the tiny spiral of steel protruding between his fingers.

The emperor of Tsing raised one finger and pointed at Tamir. "Kill him."

"Tam!"

Before Norwood could even attempt to intervene, two of the blademasters struck. Steel parted flesh and bone effortlessly. One cleaved Tamir's wrist, the other cut a furrow from collarbone to crotch. Sergeant Tamir fell back clutching the horrible wound.

"No!" Norwood dropped to his knees, trying to stem the torrent of blood that poured from his friend's gaping chest.

303

Tamir's expression registered only surprise. His mouth tried to form a word, but it was drowned by a gout of bloody froth.

Tam!" Norwood clutched Tamir's remaining hand, but there was no strength in the man's grip. Tamir's eyes lost focus, the flow of his life's blood ebbing.

Laughter crackled like shattering glass, harsh and discordant. Norwood lifted his gaze from his friend's dead eyes. The emperor's smile turned his stomach, and the captain reached automatically for the hilt that was no longer at his hip. Two swords hovered inches from his face, waiting for a word from the emperor. Norwood had no hope of avenging his friend, even if he'd had a sword, but that didn't stop him from wanting to kill Tynean Tsing, the very man he had come here to protect.

"We must admit, Captain, you found your quarry." The emperor folded his bony hands across his chest, and the lamplight glinted off a gold and obsidian ring on his finger. "You'll need to answer a few more questions before you die for…let's say…a treasonous attempt on Our life."

"Treason?" Norwood's bloody hands clenched into fists. "It's *you* who've committed treason here, not me! You've betrayed your oath to this empire! You're nothing but a—"

The emperor raised a finger, and a blade descended to Norwood's throat.

"Take care, Captain. You must be able to speak in order to tell Us who else is privy to your little discovery. We can't afford any loose ends. But We do *not* need you…undamaged." Tynean Tsing turned toward the room's other door and called, "Hoseph!"

Norwood's would-be assassin entered in a swirl of crimson robes, and the captain knew just how deeply he had been betrayed.

"Show Captain Norwood Our hospitality, Hoseph. We will be down later to speak with him." The emperor of Tsing whirled away, followed so closely by three of his bodyguards that they seemed controlled by his thoughts.

Norwood knelt in Tamir's blood as the harbinger of his death approached. Weaponless, with two swords at his throat, he had no chance of escape. Hoseph reached out a hand, and black tendrils swirled forth, icy vapors that chilled his skin and froze his soul. The last thing he heard before the world faded around him was the condescending voice of Tynean Tsing II.

"Thank you for your diligence in the pursuit of Baron Patino's murderer, Captain. If you hadn't come all this way, We would have had to go to no end of trouble to kill you."

Chapter XXI

I'd like to find the sadistic, woman-hating bastard who designed this and make *him* wear one for a month!" Mya drew the corset laces tighter, and cloth and metal creaked. She tied the knot and took a half-breath, all the restrictive garment would allow, and glanced in the full-length mirror.

The corset squeezed her meager bust and slim hips into a caricature of femininity. Wearing only the corset, stockings, and ankle-high shoes, she looked like a one of the painted doxies on Red Street, back in Twailin—except for her wrappings, of course.

With a huff of resignation, Mya pulled her gown from the airing rack. The latest formal fashion was for daringly low décolletage, which Mya's runic tattoos forbade. Instead, her dress had a flesh-hued backing covered in black lace to give the effect of a low cut without revealing her wrappings. She'd considered going without them, but didn't want to sweat.

"Like I need one more thing to make me nervous." The pending meeting already had her stomach in knots.

She donned the pettiskirts, then slipped the frothy gown over her head. The side laces tucked cunningly away under her arms, but the garment felt more cumbersome than her comfortable traveling dresses. She tugged the padded bustle into place, and checked herself in the mirror. What she saw took her aback.

"Damn! Who the hell is that?" Vastly different than her traveling dresses, or even the fancier ones she wore on forays into Twailin's Hightown district, the gown clung enticingly to her corset-enhanced figure, the skirt draping elegantly to just above the toes of her shoes. The deep-crimson hue accented her hair perfectly. Bemrin's tailor had done a beautiful job.

Perching the crowning touch of a ridiculous little hat atop her head, she tried to affix it with the attached ribbons, but her hair was so short, they kept slipping free. With a disgusted sigh, she gave up and sought help.

In the suite's main room, Lad stood before a mirror trying to arrange his lacey cravat. If the frown on his face was any indication, his preparations were as trying as hers.

"Having trouble?

"Yes. This lace is frustrating. I can't seem to..." He glanced back at her in the mirror, blinked, and shook his head. "I know more than a hundred knots for climbing ropes and restraining or capturing people, but I can't...manage...this."

"I'll make you a deal." She held out the silly hat. "You help me put this thing on properly, and I'll help you with your tie." Mya knew no more about tying a cravat than he did, but it would be easier with the knot in front of her, rather than using a mirror and working backwards.

"Deal." His expression changed from frustration to curiosity as he turned to look at her more closely. "That dress is...very different. I hardly recognize you."

"Neither do I." Mya strode forward and dropped the hat on the divan. "Here. Let me do that."

Lad stood perfectly still as she tied the cravat, fixing it in place with a topaz pin that matched his eyes perfectly. *Good choice, Dee.* A few tugs and it was done. Even without his jacket, and his unruly hair still askew, he was beautiful. Mya caught herself staring and turned away, reaching for his jacket.

"Here." She held it for him as he slipped his arms into the lace-cuffed sleeves. With a quick jerk, it fell into place. Custom tailored to his shape, it fitted him like a glove. Mya smiled and smoothed the wide velvet lapels. "You look perfect."

"I feel stupid." He picked up her hat and looked at it dubiously. "How does this fit on your head?"

"It doesn't. It just sits on top. The veil goes in front, and you tie these ribbons into my hair to hold it on."

"Oh. Right."

Mya turned around and stood still, secretly relishing the sensation of Lad's fingers in her hair. He cinched the ribbons tight enough to resist a hurricane, and she thanked her runes for blocking the pain. When he was done, she looked in the mirror.

"I look like I'm going to a funeral." The distraction of dressing slipped away, and a ball of dread coalesced in Mya's stomach. Depending on how the Grandmaster reacted, this could very well be her funeral.

"Don't worry, Mya."

"What?" She caught Lad's eye in the mirror. He looked concerned and...something else, something she couldn't identify. "I'm not worried." She brushed her hair back around her ears and rubbed her nose.

"Yes, you are. I've known you long enough to tell when you're worried."

Mya froze. *He's reading me! Gods, all these years he's been reading my tells?* She'd been the one to teach him how to spot people's inadvertent twitches and habits, and he'd been using it to analyze her. Wishing she knew just what Lad had cued in on, Mya stiffened, hoping to stifle her nervous habits.

"I told you before: the Grandmaster's not stupid. He won't hurt you. You're too valuable to him."

"Let's hope so. Otherwise our plan's worthless. But if we play this just right, you'll be free of the ring and can be a father again." Mya turned to face him, hoping that he would heed her.

Lad stepped back, a darkness the like of which she hadn't seen in days flashing across his face. "Tell me the truth, Mya. Why are you offering to do this for me?"

308

Of course, she couldn't tell him the truth. Instead, she looked him square in the eye and sidestepped the question. "You want a *list* of all the reasons I owe you my life?"

Turning her back on him, she stalked to the window. The evening sun blazed across the city as it settled toward the watery horizon, the sky the hue of blood. "Besides, when you consider all the things that led up to it, Wiggen's death was my fault."

"What?"

"You said so yourself. If the other masters hadn't tried to use you against me, they wouldn't have taken Lissa, and if they hadn't taken her, Wiggen wouldn't have died." She turned away from the view and regarded him solemnly. "So I owe you. I took part of your family away, the least I can do is give the rest of it back."

"You're wrong, Mya." Lad shook his head, but his eyes never left hers.

"How so?"

"No matter what you did, Wiggen wore the ring. That was the reason she was killed. The moment I put the ring on her finger, I signed a contract on her life."

"You couldn't have known."

"*You* would have." The pain in his voice felt like a knife slipping between her ribs. "You think like an assassin. I don't."

"Then go through with our plan. You have a chance at freedom! It's more than anyone else in the guild will ever get."

"I'll stick to our plan. Don't worry."

"Good." She tried to take a deep breath, failed, and glanced at the wall clock. "It's time to go."

Lady T awaited them in the lobby of the *Drake and Lion*, tapping her frilled parasol on the marble floor. She looked nervous. *About me or seeing the Grandmaster?* Lad wondered.

At their approach, she turned, and her face shifted from nervous to contemptuous in the flick of an eye. *Not about me, then.*

Her dark eyes took them in from head to toe, and she nodded in grudging approval. "I trust your cane isn't a sword. I said no weapons."

"No weapons, but I see that you're wearing four."

"Six actually." Smiling slyly, she gestured to the door. "Shall we?"

"Yes." Lad held out his arm, and Mya put her hand on it. They'd fallen into this routine so thoroughly over the past two weeks that it almost felt natural, her fingers resting there.

The inn's doorman did his duty, and they followed Lady T onto the street. Her carriage made the one that Dee had chartered look like a tinker's wagon in comparison. The wood and brass gleamed, and ornate filigree glittered in the evening sun. A pair of golden lion heads roared on the forward corner posts, and the coat of arms of the Noble House of Monjhi adorned the carriage doors. Four perfectly matched geldings stood in the traces like marble statues topped with feathery headdresses. Two liveried footmen held the door and handed the ladies up into the carriage. Lad followed, swallowing his apprehension. Lad and Mya sat side by side, facing their guide. He held his cane between his knees, his hands clenched on the brass bird head.

"You look nervous." Lady T smiled as if she had a secret.

Is she goading me? Lad tried for a serene smile in returned. "I don't like carriages. They're nothing but coffins with wheels." He twirled his finger as they lurched into motion. "Restricted movement, too much noise, confinement, and motion. I've killed in them before."

"And you, Mya? Why are you afraid?" Lady T's expression as she looked at Mya told Lad for certain that she was baiting.

Mya smiled. "I'm a Master Hunter being summoned to meet the Grandmaster, milady. I'd be a fool not to be worried."

"Yes. Yes, you would be."

They fell into uneasy silence as the team labored up the steep cobbled streets. The clatter of hooves and iron-rimmed wheels on stone echoed off the buildings. Lad fixed his gaze out the window and tried not to obsess about the pending meeting. When that didn't work, he resorted to his long-practiced discipline for easing tension, clenching and relaxing each muscle in his body one by one. By the time he'd progressed through the sequence twice, the carriage had reached its destination, and he felt somewhat calmer.

"Here we are." Lady T opened the door and stepped out.

Lad followed, and found that they'd stopped where a wide avenue dead-ended at the bottom of the steep bluff. High atop the limestone cliffs towered the sheer stone walls of the Imperial Palace. Before them stood the largest wine shop Lad had ever seen. A bas relief of twining vines and bulging grapes decorated huge arched wooden doors, the name on the sign covered in gold leaf.

"Vin' ju' Tsing. I've read of this place," Mya said in a conversational tone. "They're famous. The oldest winery in the empire. The caverns where they age the wine are delved far back into the bluff."

"You're quite learned." Lady T tapped her parasol against the cobbles—*A nervous habit?*—and led them to the front door. Two doormen swung the doors wide, and they entered the shop's cool interior.

"Lady T! You honor our humble establishment once again." A man in a dress coat, the winery crest embossed on the breast pocket, approached and bowed deeply. A ring of heavy brass keys dangled from his belt. "Your usual accommodations?"

"Please, Joffie. I'm entertaining my friends, the Addingtons, and I thought I'd showcase a few of your fine vintages." She gestured to Lad and Mya as if they were long-lost cousins.

"Of course. This way, please."

They followed him through the racks of bottles to a thick, iron-bound door at the back of the shop. Joffie worked a brass key in a door, and ushered them inside. The temperature dropped as they entered a long tunnel. Joffie plucked a lantern from a peg and struck it with one of his keys. A glow crystal flared to life within, and he handed the light to Lady T.

"I trust you know your way, milady." He bowed low.

"I do. Thank you, Joffie." She ushered them forward, and the door closed behind them.

"The shop's a front?" The cavern had been hewn from the living stone, the walls polished smooth. Rows of barrels, each wider than Lad was tall, stretched into the darkness, and the air smelled of oak and wine.

"Not at all." Lady T gestured to the barrels. "The guild bought the winery decades ago. It brings in quite a good income, but even Joffie doesn't know who *really* owns it."

"I see," Lad said. It made sense, considering the secrecy around the Grandmaster's identity. "Will the Grandmaster meet us here?"

"Hardly." Lady T stopped at the eighteenth barrel on the left, and bent to press her ring into a seemingly undistinguished spot on the support block of the massive tun. The wedge of stone receded into the floor, and the huge barrel rolled two feet to the right, revealing a dark passage. She handed the lamp to Lad. "Please proceed and wait on the other side. I have to secure the door."

Lad didn't need the lantern, of course, but complied. He and Mya stepped through a short, narrow passage and into a featureless square room. A loud click and rumble signified the wine barrel rolling back into place.

Lady T arrived. "Cozy, isn't it?" Despite her smile and casual manner, her voice trembled with anxiety, and her hand quivered slightly as she raised it and pressed her guildmaster's ring into a tiny niche where two of the walls met. A seam opened in the middle of the north wall, so fine a joining that even Lad had not noticed it. The thick slabs of stone moved aside without a sound. Beyond, a smooth passage stretched into darkness.

"Of course," Mya said, nodding to the wall. "Only guildmasters meet with the Grandmaster, so the passage is keyed to their rings."

"The stonework..." Lad ran a finger down the edge of the block that had moved. As smooth as glass and not a hint of wear. He'd been trained to recognize such workmanship...and the traps they concealed. "Dwarven?"

"You're both observant." Lady T put her lantern on the floor and gestured into the passage. "If you would step inside, I'll close the door."

Mya flinched as cool white light—sourceless and casting no shadows—lit the passage. *Magic.* It seemed to Lad an extravagance when a simple torch or glow crystal would do.

"This way." Lady T strode past them without looking back, the strange illumination brightening before her as she went.

"Not that there's any other way to go," Mya whispered so quietly that only the two of them could hear.

"Come on," he whispered back, and they proceeded side by side. The strange illumination brightened before them and faded behind, so that they seemed to walk but never get anywhere.

After several minutes, Lad looked around curiously. He had assumed that the passage would turn east into the hill of the Heights District, perhaps emerging in one of the lavish estates. And yet, his unerring sense of direction told him that the path continued north, angling upward at a precise angle into the bluff.

Where the hell are we going?

On and on they walked. No one spoke, each lost in their own thoughts. For Lad's part, he wondered about Mya, her evasions, her promise to help him. Was it real, or was she plotting something to her own advantage? What would her fear motivate her to do? Could he trust her?

At last they reached a switchback in the tunnel, and Lad's suspicions were confirmed. The maps from Mya's book clear in his head, he stopped and looked up.

Mya stopped as well, looking back at him askance. "What?"

Lady T halted and turned, her mien impatient. "Is there a problem?"

"We're under the palace."

The Tsing guildmaster's features twitched with surprise, quickly lapsing back to irritation. "Yes, we are. Now follow me. We mustn't keep the Grandmaster waiting." She strode on without another glance back.

Lad's mind whirled. The Grandmaster resided in the palace? It struck him as the ultimate audacity, or the pinnacle of foolishness. Why? Who was he? A royal adviser, guard, servant, or chamberlain? Lad could no longer contain his curiosity.

"Who is he?"

Lady T didn't even look back. "Patience. You'll find out soon enough."

"Why not just tell us?"

"Because it's not my information to give." Her clipped tone edged toward anger.

"But—"

Mya put a hand on Lad's arm and shot him a warning glance. The fearful plea in her eyes silenced him. She was right; they would learn the Grandmaster's identity soon enough, and badgering Lady T for information would only buy them trouble.

They followed in silence.

Another switchback, and the echo of their footsteps changed. They were coming to the end of the tunnel. Lad gauged that they'd ascended some two-hundred feet from the wine shop. The passage ended as it had begun, with a featureless wall. This time, Lad spotted the niche that would accommodate the guildmaster's ring before Lady T raised her hand and pressed it home. Two massive stone slabs moved aside in utter silence.

When the doors stopped moving, the light of the passage behind them extinguished.

Ahead gaped another wide, stone corridor, but this one wasn't dwarf-wrought. Imperfections betrayed the less-skilled stonework of men. The light here was the soft, warm flicker of wall-mounted lamps.

"Come." Lady T strode forward.

Three swordsmen stepped from the shadows beyond the light.

Lad tensed, and he heard Mya draw a sharp breath, but the swordsmen showed no signs of aggression. All were tall and lithe, with broad shoulders and hard eyes. They wore the livery of imperial guards, with an insignia on the left shoulder: a golden circle surrounding a blue and silver sword. Lad knew the device from his training: they were blademasters of Koss Godslayer. Trained from birth and imbued with their god's gifts, they represented the apex of fighting prowess.

"Blademasters? You're *kidding* me."

Lad turned at the incredulity in Mya's tone. She had evidently recognized them, too.

"I have never *kidded* anyone in my life." Lady T nodded to the blademasters. "Now these men will search you for weapons. I truly hope you followed my advice."

Two of the blademasters approached. The third stood back, his sharp eyes inspecting Lad and Mya as if he saw right through them. The search was professionally inquisitive and thorough. Lad wasn't bothered in the slightest, even though they took his cane away, but he wondered how Mya would endure the search. She tolerated little more than a handshake from her closest associates. Though she stood completely still, the muscles of her neck tensed as the guard probed the folds of her dress, even forcing her legs apart to explore between. He inspected her shoes, her hat, and finally her unyielding corset. He rapped the hard stays with his knuckles and frowned.

"They're called *stays*." Mya's voice sounded stoic, but Lad knew her. The pounding pulse at her temple, the flush of her skin, and the imperceptible tremble of her chin gave her away. She was terrified. But in typical Mya fashion, she bluffed her way through. "I'll take it off, if you like, but I don't think the Grandmaster would appreciate meeting me if I was disrobed to the waist." Her gaze slid over to Lady T. "Or maybe he *would*."

"Enough." Lady T waved the blademasters back with a flicker of something akin to sympathy in her eyes. She had undoubtedly felt those probing fingers often enough. "A corset's not a weapon, and neither of them can harm your master anyway. Take them to him; he's waiting."

Their master? Lad's mind raced. *They're imperial bodyguards!* Since the empress had died decades ago, and there was only one heir, that narrowed possibilities down to two. *Impossible...*

Lady T turned to Lad with a thin smile. "Good luck."

"Thank you," he said, more out of habit than true gratitude.

The Tsing guildmaster's tense shoulders relaxed as she stepped into the passage leading back to the wine shop and the door closed silently behind her. Lad wondered why she had been so nervous.

The lead blademaster gestured and turned. Lad and Mya fell in line behind him, and the other two flanked them as they started down the corridor.

Lad tried to relax and focus. *Think like an assassin. Remember the plan. Patience... The truth is coming.*

CHAPTER XXII

I*t can't be*, Mya insisted to herself. She took as deep a breath as the thrice-cursed corset would allow, and let it out slowly, but still her heart hammered. The Grandmaster couldn't be some low-level courtier or advisor. Lady T had mentioned the blademasters' master. That meant either the person they'd been assigned to protect, or the head of their order. The notion of a mute, illiterate Grandmaster was ludicrous, and imperial guards were only assigned to the imperial family.

The crown prince? But they were in the dungeon; the faint odor of human confinement confirmed it beyond doubt. What would a prince be doing in the dungeon?

Gradually, the odor of confinement faded, and more enticing aromas filled the air. Meat, bread, spices; despite her fear, Mya's mouth began to water. Her stomach had been too roiled to attempt lunch, and breakfast had been many hours ago.

The blademaster led them to a pair of heavy double doors and knocked in a complex staccato. A latch clicked and the door opened. Yet another blademaster peered out, his hard eyes inspecting them.

Four? Four blademasters? Mya's head swam. *It can't be…*

The man stepped aside, pulling open the door and gesturing them inside. Mya's breath came short, but she didn't know if it was from the constricting corset or her fear of finally meeting the Grandmaster. *Just don't faint…* She moved inexorably forward as if drawn by an invisible shackle and chain.

The sight that met her eyes was unexpected, to say the least.

A table stretched before them, the white linen cloth arrayed with porcelain plates, silver utensils, and crystal goblets. Four servants in simple white smocks stood before a sideboard heavy with silver-domed platters. To the left stood a man in crimson robes, the cowl pulled back to reveal a stern mien and dark eyes. Another blademaster—*Five!*—stood behind the high-backed chair at the end of the table. And in the chair sat an elderly man in blue and gold robes. Atop his silver hair rested a circlet of gold set with blood-red rubies.

It can't be...

"Welcome." Without rising, the silver-haired man gestured to the two other chairs at the table. "Guildmaster Lad, Master Hunter Mya, please join me. I am, as you may have already guessed, the master of our illustrious guild."

Mya stood stunned. She knew that face. How could she not? She saw it whenever she pulled a coin from her pocket. *Emperor...and Grandmaster*, she confirmed as she spied the gold and obsidian ring on his finger.

She dropped into a deep curtsy, her eyes cast down. "Your Majesty."

Beside her, Lad stood like a statue, unbending. She dare not look up, though she longed to shake him out of his paralysis. This was much worse than she could have imagined. How could they conceive of manipulating the man who ruled the entire empire!

"Well, I see that at least *one* of you recognizes me, and knows the proper deference to show an emperor."

"Emperor?" Lad sounded puzzled. "Your pardon, Grandmaster, but I don't understand how...how you can be emperor *and* Grandmaster?"

"*How?*" Annoyance edged the word. "Suffice to say that I *am* both emperor and Grandmaster. As such, your life is mine to *spend*, Guildmaster Lad. It would be wise to show proper respect."

318

"Of course." Lad bowed briefly. "But...should I call you Your Majesty, or Grandmaster?

Gods, he's overdoing it! Their plan was for Lad to act naïve, not clueless. He ought to be good at it by now. He'd done it for five years as her bodyguard: simple, literal, and socially inept. It had led her to underestimate him. That was what they needed now, not blatant idiocy.

"Ha!" The Grandmaster's humorless bark of laughter startled Mya. "I was told that you had expanded your faculties beyond that of a simple weapon, but I daresay those tales were exaggerated!"

"I meant no offense, Grandmaster."

"No, I don't suppose you did." Several heartbeats of silence. "No matter. We're here to discuss guild business, so you'll both address me as Grandmaster. In the unlikely event that you *ever* encounter me in public, however, you will address me as is befitting an emperor. Is that clear?"

"Perfectly clear, Grandmaster."

"Good. Now, Lad, Mya, join me at table, and we'll discuss a few things."

"Yes, Grandmaster." Mya rose from her curtsy, but kept her eyes averted from the old man's face, hoping that Lad's poor first impression Lad wouldn't doom her, too.

The servants directed Mya to the seat to the Grandmaster's left, and Lad to his right. The five blademasters stationed themselves behind and to each side of their master, and one each behind Lad and Mya. Without a word, the servants began to pour wine from crystal carafes into their goblets and plate out generous portions of food.

"First, let me introduce my intermediary, Hoseph." The Grandmaster indicated the crimson-robed man who hadn't been invited to sit. Hoseph didn't seem to regard the omission as a slight, but bowed in recognition. "As a high priest of Demia, he holds no rank within the guild, but his skills are indispensable. He will be your primary contact. Questions or requests for me will go through him. His voice is my voice, his commands are my commands. He is, you might say, my right hand."

"The right hand of death."

Lad's words startled Mya as she recalled the phrase he had attributed to Norwood's would-be assassin. Lad cocked his head inquisitively, inspecting the priest, and she followed his gaze. Though Hoseph's expression remained mild, his eyes regarded Lad with cold calculation.

Lad continued, "You killed Baron Patino."

"Actually, *I* killed Baron Patino," the Grandmaster corrected, sipping his wine with a contemplative air. "Hoseph simply delivered the sentence. And I would have killed that bothersome Captain Norwood as well, if you hadn't intervened. Which begs the question: why *did* you intervene?"

From the undertone of menace, the Grandmaster did not appreciate being thwarted.

"I was using Captain Norwood as a source of information, Grandmaster. Had I known the attempt on his life was arranged by you, I would have acted differently." Lad looked back to Hoseph. "How's your arm?"

"Quite well, thank you."

As a servant placed a luscious filet of beef on Mya's plate, she noted the ghastly thin wrists below his sleeves. All the servants were just as thin, even skeletal, their eyes deeply sunken in their sockets. Their simple clothing also was not at all what she imagined palace servants would wear. They couldn't help but overhear guild business, and they certainly knew the Grandmaster's identity. *But why starve them?*

"I can see that you're concerned about the servants, Mya."

Her eyes snapped to his for an instant, then back to her plate. "Yes, Grandmaster."

"Don't be. These are men who have, for one reason or another, incurred my wrath. I've spared their lives in exchange for their service. Unlike my blademasters, they still have their tongues, but you needn't worry about them telling stories. They never leave this area, and never will. They're already dead to the world, you see. They just haven't stopped breathing yet." The Grandmaster raised his wine glass. "But enough of that! I propose a toast to new beginnings, a welcome to my newest guildmaster. And you, too, Master Hunter Mya, of course."

Lad and Mya raised their glasses. Mya sipped, though she longed to down the entire glass to steady her nerves. The exquisite vintage cleared her dry mouth with a heady rush of flavors. The food was just as wonderful, but it may as well have been chalk for all that she enjoyed it.

The emperor ate with relish, the servants attentive to his every move. He spoke between bites and sips of wine. "You have both proven yourselves capable of command, but now you must try to see the larger picture. The Assassins Guild has far-reaching goals, and its leaders must be farsighted. The guild was once like many others; a powerful but simple criminal organization focused on profit. My predecessor envisioned something greater, and recruited a young crown prince into her fold. I was groomed to assume command, to change the guild into something never previously contemplated. And her ploy worked. With my father's untimely death…"

The corner of Tynean Tsing's mouth twitched, leaving Mya no doubt about who had arranged that death. *We have something in common.* The thought both terrified and intrigued her.

"…I became the most powerful human in history."

"You play both sides of the same coin." The words tumbled from Mya's lips of their own volition, but she found herself unable to stop. It was just too perfect. "Law and crime, succor and fear, life and death… You win every toss. It's…brilliant."

"Precisely, Mya." The Grandmaster raised his glass to her, one silver eyebrow arched in pleased admiration. "You grasp the perfection of our arrangement."

To Mya's surprise, she found herself flushing with pleasure at the recognition, and raised her own glass. As they sipped, their eyes locked, and she realized that her fear had ebbed. She was still nervous, but the terror was gone. *This might actually work out.*

"I don't understand." Lad's eyes flicked from Mya to the Grandmaster and back.

"No, I see that you don't." The emperor placed his goblet delicately on the table and steepled his fingers, his mouth set in an aggravated moue. "Understand this, if you can. I've created the perfect system of governance. History tells us that empires rise and fall at the whim of the people; when oppressed, they rebel, if given too much freedom, they want more. I have discovered a way to break that cycle. Empowering my nobility with immunity from prosecution devotes them to my cause. They flock to my court, willing to do anything to maintain their status. If that includes paying higher taxes or instituting my edicts in their provinces, so be it. Of course, such free rein for the nobility induces resentment in the lower classes. That's where the Assassins Guild comes in. They keep the general populace under control, ferreting out and crushing the seeds of rebellion before they sprout. I hold the reins to both the empire *and* the guild; absolute power and utter control." He sat back with a self-satisfied smile.

"I...see." Lad took a bite of his meal, washed it down with a sip of wine, then looked back at the Grandmaster. "So, you rule by fear. The commoners fear for their lives, and the nobles fear for their privileges."

The Grandmaster cocked an eyebrow. "I'm impressed, Lad. You *do* understand."

"But it's not a permanent arrangement. Fear is a poor motivator, and you won't live forever."

He's going too far. Mya shot Lad a warning glance, but he wasn't looking at her.

"Fear is an *excellent* motivator!" the Grandmaster insisted, his eyes flinty at Lad's evident disapproval. "And I will live...long enough. My son has proven inadequate to inherit either of my offices. Once he has produced an heir, he'll be eliminated, and I'll take my grandson or granddaughter under my wing and teach them what true power is. The line of Imperial Grandmasters will continue."

Mya felt suddenly sick, and Lad voiced the question that she dare not ask. "You would kill your own *son*?"

Tyrean Tsing dropped his fork noisily onto his plate, his displeasure clear. "I can see why you think fear is a poor motivator, for you obviously have an impaired sense of what *should* be feared. I know this isn't your fault, but a result of the manner of your creation. Saliez wanted a weapon without fear, and he got one."

Lad's face remained neutral, emotionless. "As you say, Grandmaster, I was created with particular restrictions, but I...freed myself to a certain degree. I do feel fear, though not, perhaps, as most people do."

"Which is why you weren't my first choice for guildmaster." He turned to Mya. "Your Master Hunter understands fear. Don't you, Mya?"

"Perfectly, Grandmaster." She nodded respectfully, keeping her gaze averted.

His eyes flicked back to Lad. "Which brings up the question of *why*, exactly, you wear the guildmaster's ring."

"At the time, it seemed the prudent thing to do, Grandmaster." Lad looked down at his plate, his countenance clouding over. "My...wife had just been murdered, and in my state of mind, I thought only that if I wielded the Twailin guild, I could find her killer."

"And how is that going for you?"

Mya snapped her eyes to the Grandmaster's, but he was staring at Lad. His tone suggested derision or amusement rather than true concern. *He knows something*, she realized, and her blood ran cold.

"Not well." Lad nonchalantly picked up his wine and sipped, raising his head to stare into the Grandmaster's eyes.

Don't! Mya willed Lad to hear her silent plea. *Don't go there, Lad! Please!*

"I know who the killer is, a thief named Kiesha, but I can't find her. She was somehow connected with Baron Patino, whom, correct me if I'm wrong, you contracted to secure Mya's and my safety until she could assume the guildmaster position."

The Grandmaster stared right back at Lad. "That is correct."

"So, you killed Patino to break the connection between the emperor and the guild."

"Also correct."

"Did you order Kiesha to assassinate my wife?"

"I did not."

That's enough! Mya downed her wine in one gulp. *Time to stop this before it goes too far.*

Lad's shoulders slumped, his trembling hand rippling the wine in his goblet. The Grandmaster's words hung in the air: simple, straightforward, and devastating. Another dead end. Lad put his goblet down so he wouldn't spill the wine, and raised his eyes once again to the Grandmaster's face.

Was he telling the truth? The man's expression gave away nothing, but Lad didn't expect it to. Tynean Tsing had lived with secret dual identities most of his life. He could probably lie without the slightest outward sign.

Mya cleared her throat and spoke up. "If I may, Grandmaster, I'd like to propose a solution to our apparent dilemma."

"Our dilemma?" The Grandmaster looked at her curiously. "Please, enlighten me as to what dilemma you think we have."

"At the risk of incurring the displeasure of my guildmaster," she glanced at Lad, "I must say, and I think you'll agree, that Lad's not well suited to his new position."

Lad glared at Mya, secretly impressed with her calm delivery. Her voice held a tremor of fear, which would placate the Grandmaster, and her tone was clear and precise. Best of all, her body language remained mute: no brushing her hair behind her ear, no rubbing her nose or clicking her fingernails.

He shook off his disappointment, and resolved to continue their plan. "For not being well *suited*, I've increased guild profits in less than a month!"

"Yes, by instituting practices that I perfected over the last five years." Mya turned to present her case to Tynean Tsing. "Grandmaster, while Lad makes a mediocre guildmaster, he remains a superb weapon. His skills in combat are unmatched and, as you can see, he looks harmless. While he certainly kills like an assassin, he doesn't necessarily *think* like one."

"That is clear." The Grandmaster's eyes snapped back and forth between them. "State your proposal, Mya."

"Your original intention was to make me Twailin's guildmaster. You have the ability to grant your own wish. Take Lad's ring and give it to me. He can return to his position as my bodyguard and personal weapon, to be employed as he was designed for the best interests of the guild," she paused and shifted her eyes to Lad's, "instead of his own."

Mya's cool, confident gaze startled Lad. *She's just following the plan. She's not really intending to enslave me. She wouldn't.* But doubt remained. He was so used to reading her tells, and now there were none.

"Interesting…" The Grandmaster's slow smile sent a shiver up Lad's spine. "I'll consider this proposal under two conditions, Mya."

"It's not my place to barter, Grandmaster." Mya looked mildly horrified. "My life is yours to spend. You can command me as you wish."

"I'm glad you see it that way." The smile broadened, and Lad's worry with it. "First, you will reinstitute standard guild practices with regard to protection racketeering, extortion, and intimidation in Twailin."

Horror gripped Lad's stomach like a vise. *Would she actually do that?* The devil's advocate in the back of his mind whispered, *Of course she would. How could she not do as he commands?*

Mya tilted her head quizzically. "Of course, Grandmaster, if you command it, but may I ask why? Profits are up significantly, and our competition is foundering. The new system is more productive."

"We'll get to *why* in a moment." The Grandmaster's eyes shifted to Lad. "The next condition is that you, Lad, sign a blood contract. Saliez was remiss in not insisting on that from the start. Without the guildmaster's ring, you're too dangerous to be without some kind of control."

Lad stifled his impulsive response. There was only one answer he could possibly give, considering the five blademasters in the room. "If you so command, Grandmaster." He bowed his head in deference, worried that his eyes would reveal his defiance. He had absolutely no intention of signing a blood contract. If he did, he would be nothing more than a slave again. He would never be a father, never have a family.

"Good." The Grandmaster dropped his napkin onto his plate and stood. "Come with me."

Lad stood, and Mya followed suit. Though she briefly met his glance as they rounded the table, she remained unreadable, immediately averting her eyes. Was she betraying him? Had her plan been a deception from the start? Lad hadn't thought of the blood contract, but Mya certainly would have.

They filed out of the room, the emperor and three of his blademasters at the fore, then Lad and Mya followed by two more, and lastly, Hoseph. The hairs prickled on the back of Lad's neck with the priestly assassin behind him. Hoseph seemed an enigma: more than just an intermediary, and certainly

326

more than just a killer. But Lad couldn't worry about him right now. He had to concentrate on the Grandmaster...and Mya.

Lad glanced sidelong at her, wishing he could read her mind. She kept her eyes steadfastly ahead, her hands relaxed at her sides. No tells, no evasions, and no clue about her motives.

The Grandmaster spoke as they walked. "The primary flaw in your new practices, Mya, is that you fail to understand the true mission of the Assassins Guild. I consider that partially my fault for letting the Twailin guild go so long without a guildmaster. As a mere master, you had no comprehension of our mission, so your error is forgivable."

"Thank you for understanding, Grandmaster."

Lad chilled to realize that he seemed to be suddenly out of the loop of communication. He might still wear the guildmaster's ring, but he had essentially been dismissed.

The Grandmaster stopped at a large double door and worked a key in the lock. Fetid air wafted out as two of the blademasters pulled open the doors. The lighting here was poorer, oil lamps guttering low, but Lad didn't need it to make out the barred cells that lined the corridor. Urine-soaked straw, stale sweat, and overflowing chamber pots explained the stench.

"The true mission of the Assassins Guild is control." The Grandmaster gestured to the cells as they passed. "Much as the empire controls the populace with laws, the Assassins Guild controls it with fear."

Sallow faces met Lad's gaze from within the cells. He wondered why the Grandmaster spoke so freely about the guild in front of the prisoners, until he realized, *Their lives are already spent.* None of these people would ever leave this place. But unlike the servants, these had no apparent use. *Why keep them alive at all?*

The Grandmaster's voice droned on. "I'm sure that *you*, Mya, can understand how the interplay of the guild and the empire enhance the efficacy of both."

327

"I understand perfectly, Grandmaster." Mya did look at Lad then, and her eyes regarded him without a hint of the emotion or sincerity she'd previously shown. "It's an elegant system."

"Thank you."

"But what about profits, Grandmaster? They'll fall if we revert to the old system."

"Profits are secondary to control, Mya. The Assassins Guild is not a public service enterprise. It is my weapon, much as Lad was Saliez's weapon." Another pair of even larger double doors came into view, these with an intricate dual locking system. The Grandmaster produced two keys and gestured. "Hoseph, if you please."

"Yes, Grandmaster." The priest strode forward and took the proffered key. He and the Grandmaster turned the keys in the two locks, and a heavy mechanism clicked.

With neither the Grandmaster nor Mya granting him a glance, Lad wondered if he might just walk away. Of course, the blademasters wouldn't allow him to retreat until permission had been granted by their master, and he wouldn't do that until Lad signed a blood contract. He was trapped.

The Grandmaster slipped the keys back into his pocket and looked earnestly at the Mya. "Money is nothing but another form of control, Mya. Guild profits are necessary to provide incentive to our members. To me, they are insignificant. Imperial taxes bring in more revenue in a single month than the Assassins Guild does in ten years. The guild's sole purpose is control: control through fear. Do you understand?"

"I understand," Mya said.

"You *think* you do." The Grandmaster's thin smile held all the warmth of a glacier. "Very soon, you will."

Chapter XXIII

Tynean Tsing gestured two blademasters forward while continuing his speech.

"Control is achieved through discipline. When you give an order or make an offer for *advancement…*" The Grandmaster's eyes flashed to hers, and Mya's heart froze for a moment. "…you must make sure you are obeyed."

"Yes, Grandmaster." Despite her apprehension, Mya marveled at the elegance of the scheme. Controlling the empire both legally and illegally was an unsurpassed coup. She had spent her entire life seeking power as a way to escape fear. Now the Grandmaster was declaring that fear was a *means* to power. It made a perverted kind of sense. *And you'd better get used to it. This is your future, Mya. Your only future…*

"And when you are not obeyed…"

The blademasters grasped the great bronze rings that hung from the doors and pulled. As the heavy doors swung smoothly outward, the already rank air was defiled by a thick metallic tang so strong that Mya gagged. Lad's shocked gasp breached her disgust, and she looked into the room.

Oh, dear gods.

"…you must deliver punishment." The Grandmaster strode forward, and they followed into the wide, low-ceilinged room. "Here is where you will learn the true meaning of control."

A massive stone pillar centered the circular chamber. To the left and right, lining the curved outer wall, stood various devices with no use other than to deliver agony. *A circle of pain…* Mya recognized many of the devices from those in the Grandfather's basement. Over here lay a rack, the gears gleaming and the great wheel well polished. Over there stood a set of stocks, similar to those in the Imperial Plaza, except that the inner edges of the neck and wrist restraints were studded with nails. Right next to her, a solid wooden chair was firmly fastened to the floor, the stout arms tipped with vices that could crush fingers.

Mya swallowed bile as she recalled Saliez's delighted recital of the many ways one could inflict pain without quite killing.

Like a professor lecturing a favored student, the Grandmaster continued to speak as he strolled around the inner pillar. "In my early years of training, I discovered a talent for inquisition. Although my imperial duties keep me busier than I want, I make time to come down here and practice my skills. Training in inquisition will be useful to you, Mya. I cast no aspersions on your expertise as a Hunter, but inquisition is your means of punishment, your control, and control is key."

Mya struggled to maintain her composure, clenching her hands in an effort to control her body language. She couldn't afford to let the Grandfather discern her true reaction to this ghastly place.

"Norwood!"

Lad's exclamation froze Mya in her tracks. His face shone pale, the muscles of his jaw bunched. She followed his gaze, and wished she hadn't.

The captain of the Twailin Royal Guard hung in an iron cage, his wrists manacled over his head. Sharpened screws threaded through the bars had pierced his body at hips, knees, and feet. Norwood's skull was pinned in place by four iron rods, also sharpened and screwed down tight. Blood seeped from the wounds and puddled on the floor beneath the cage. His eyes were closed, but Mya could still detect the shallow rise and fall of his chest. He was unconscious, but alive.

The Grandmaster looked mildly amused. "Needless to say, Lad, Captain Norwood will no longer function as your informant. I hope, however, that he will provide me with information on his investigation into Baron Patino's death." The Grandmaster shot a sour look at Hoseph, then turned his attention to Mya. "I'm sure he could also provide insight into the Twailin Royal Guard, which would undoubtedly benefit your future operations, Mya. Perhaps you'd like to aid in the inquisition."

"I..." Mya's stomach clenched on the few sips of wine and bites of food she'd taken, and she looked away. The view in the other direction, however, was no better. "Dear Gods of Light..."

Hidden until now behind the massive pillar, six waist-high stone slabs stood like the spokes of a huge wheel. Each was grooved and canted to drain into a central iron grating in the floor. Atop one Mya saw...herself, bleeding and torn as the Grandfather had once displayed her, strapped down, skin flayed from flesh. Mya clenched her eyes and choked back vomit. *Not me... Not real...* When she opened them again, she realized that she was both wrong and right. It wasn't her, but it was all too real, and worse than she could ever have imagined.

The Grandmaster chuckled. "Let me assure you, Mya, the Gods had nothing to do with what you see here." He strolled over to the slab. "I had originally intended this to be a gift to my newest guildmaster, but, since I intend to accept Mya's proposal, think of it as a last concession before you relinquish your position, Lad."

Tynean Tsing plucked a glistening steel hook from a tray beside the slab and gestured them over, waiting until they stood beside the wreckage of what had once been a human being. "Let it also be a reminder that this is the consequence of insubordination. I have spies everywhere, both within and outside the guild. *This* is control."

Positioning the hook in muscle, the Grandmaster pulled his victim's bleeding face toward him. To Mya's horror, bloody lips gasped for breath, a thin mew of agony issuing from a ravaged throat. The mutilation had been very carefully performed to keep the victim alive. Mya wondered if this poor soul was still sane...and thought not. She could almost feel the Grandfather's knives once more parting her own flesh.

Never again!

"Who...is she?"

Lad's voice, so contorted by disgust, snapped Mya from her morbid musing. *She*? Now she noted the spare patches of blond hair, the delicate hands twisted and broken, the small, dainty feet scorched by live coals. It was indeed a woman.

"Why, Kiesha, of course! The woman who killed your dear Wiggen."

He tortured her for...what? *Punishment, information, entertainment*? Suddenly Mya's mind leapt ahead. If Kiesha had killed Wiggen at the Fiveway Fountains battle, had watched Lad and Mya fight, how much had she seen of Mya's abilities, her magic, her secrets. *And how much did she tell the Grandmaster*? Did he know Mya was a monster?

Lad stepped forward and stood beside the slab, gazing down at the mutilated woman. "Why would you *do* this?"

The utter revulsion in Lad's voice drew every eye in the room.

"As an example." The Grandmaster's lips curled back in contempt. "When Kiesha learned that your wife wore the guildmaster's ring, she should have brought the information to me. Instead, she took the initiative and murdered your wife. There were other solutions that could have been employed without earning your enmity. She then went to Baron Patino, risking exposure of my dual identity. She cost me much, and she has paid the price. Perhaps you should heed the lesson."

"You think this will make me fear you." Lad's words weren't a question, but an accusation. "You think this will make me *obey* you."

Mya gaped at him. *He's mad*! *The Grandmaster will kill him for that. He'll strap Lad down and flay him alive, and I'll have to stand here and watch it.* She opened her mouth to explain, to intervene, but another glance at Kiesha kicked in her innate sense of self-preservation. *I can't save him. If I try, I'll die here, too...or worse.* She edged back, feeling exposed in the wide-open area between the slabs and the central pillar. Thankfully, the blademasters paid her no mind, assuming defensive positions around their master.

"I hoped it might, but I see you still don't understand." The Grandmaster ran a fingernail down an exposed nerve in Kiesha's ravaged arm. The woman's raw, inarticulate wail of agony shivered up Mya's spine. "*This* is the path to control."

"Stop it!" Lad's shout echoed off the walls. He stumbled back from the slab, horror and disgust twisting his features.

The Grandmaster turned with murder in his narrowed eyes. "That *almost* sounded like a command. I see that you're in need of this lesson if you're going to be of any use to me at all. Take care that you don't displease me as Kiesha did." His eyes flicked to Mya, and his lips thinned in a razor-slash smile. "Mya understands, don't you?"

"I understand, Grandmaster." Mya curtsied deeply. It sickened her, but there was no way she could tell the man who owned her life that he was a sadistic pig. Her eyes flicked up to Lad's. She willed him to follow her lead, to kowtow and escape, to sign anything, *do* anything, to survive. *Think, Lad! Think like an assassin!*

"Yes, I believe you do. You were greatly prized by Saliez for both your mind and your obedience. That, along with your recent successes as Master Hunter, are why I offered you the Twailin guildmaster position." Tynean Tsing gestured, and his blademasters flanked Lad. "Saliez understood my methods. He was using them to send Duke Mir running into my arms for help. With my magistrates and soldiers to institute my edicts, the city would have been fully incorporated into my system of control." The razor smile returned. "That was the reason you were created, Lad; to be used as a weapon, to grant me control through fear. That is your *only* function."

The tendons in Lad's neck tensed, and Mya cringed.

"All those murders…" Lad's voice quivered with rage. "It wasn't *about* trade restrictions or pressuring the Thieves Guild out of drug trafficking at all…"

"Of course not! It was, and always will be about control, *my* control." The Grandmaster snapped his fingers. "Hoseph! The contract."

The priest drew a rolled piece of vellum from beneath his robes. Mya recognized it immediately. She'd signed one herself. The vellum was cured human skin, the script embossed on its surface imbued with rune magic. Once signed in blood, the spell would bind the signatory to the guild for life, rendering escape and rebellion impossible. Things had come full circle. If Lad signed, he would become nothing but a weapon once again.

"This is the only way you'll walk out of this room, Lad." The Grandmaster drew a gleaming kris from his embroidered robes and held the tip under Lad's nose. "Prick your finger and sign."

Lad looked down at the document, then at the blademasters surrounding him.

Sign it! Mya thought. He had no hope of besting them, not five. And even if he did, he still couldn't touch the Grandmaster. There was no way out.

"Bide," she whispered for his ears only. His eyes flicked toward her, then back to the Grandmaster. "Lissa," she whispered. "Think of Lissa."

That hit him hard.

Clenching his jaw so tightly she thought his teeth might shatter, Lad looked toward Mya, and she quailed. Madness lurked behind those twin chips of mica. He would die before he became a slave again.

I can't let him die.

"Sign it!" Mya stepped forward, closer, but still outside the ring of blademasters. "It won't change a thing, Lad. I'll be your master as I was before."

334

"Listen to her, boy. I'll make her guildmaster, and she'll wield you. I need your expertise in Twailin if I'm ever going to get Mir to capitulate." The Grandmaster thrust the kris forward, almost pricking Lad's nose with the tip. "Sign it or die!"

Lad took a deep breath, closed his eyes for a moment, then opened them and looked right into Mya's soul.

He's mad...

"I'm sorry, Mya." He shook his head and pushed aside the blood contract. "No. I won't sign it."

They'll kill him! A pit opened in Mya's soul, a swirling void that swallowed her fear. She couldn't let them kill Lad, but she knew better than to think that they could win. They couldn't kill the Grandmaster. They might escape, but he'd hunt them down. *Think! Think like an assassin.* She needed some advantage, some trick, but if Kiesha had told the Grandmaster Mya's secrets, she had nothing.

Nothing but death.

Everyone dies. Strangely, the thought brought Mya solace. It didn't matter if you were good, bad, pious, or irreverent. In the end, death took everyone.

At least it won't hurt. Her tattoos made sure of that. Mya looked down at her hands, the hands from which she had washed the blood of her mother, and wondered about the afterlife. Would their souls meet? Would she murder her mother again in hell?

Mya stared, helpless as the Grandmaster drew back the dagger, Lad's death glinting in the torchlight.

Yanking loose the laces of her dress, Mya prepared herself to die.

CHAPTER XXIV

The gleaming kris thrust toward Lad's throat, a killing strike that he could not block.

He could, however, move.

To Lad's hyper-accelerated senses, the knife moved like syrup on a cold morning. He twisted just enough to let the serpentine blade pass harmlessly by.

The blademasters surrounding him tensed, but didn't intervene, awaiting their master's commands. Frustration contorted the Grandmaster's face, and he slashed again.

Again, Lad moved.

Without adjusting his stance, he bent away from the stroke. The wavy blade sliced through the air an inch from his eyes, so close that Lad saw his reflection in the fine, layered steel. He straightened and regarded the Grandmaster's flushed face. Tynean Tsing wasn't accustomed to being so easily thwarted. Lad couldn't attack, but perhaps he could provoke a reckless action or even a heart-attack; the emperor was not a young man.

"I was made to kill, Grandmaster." Lad unfastened the buttons of his jacket with provocatively slow ease. "Not to stand like a steer in a slaughterhouse."

"You impudent…" Spittle flecked the Grandmaster's lips and his hand quivered with rage. Five swords hissed quietly from their scabbards as the emperor's blademasters prepared to kill at his word.

"Wait!" Mya lurched forward, hands out and open, her eyes wide with horror. Shouldering her way through the cordon of blademasters, she interposed herself between Lad and the Grandmaster. "Please, Grandmaster. You needn't kill him! I can control him!"

What's she doing? Lad's mind spun. He hadn't expected help from that quarter. Ruled by fear, Mya always put her safety and self-interest first. *What is she plotting?* Lad's eyes narrowed in suspicion. She'd tricked him before. He focused on the vulnerable spot at the base of her skull. *Never again.*

The Grandmaster waved her away. "Not without a contract, Mya. He's too dangerous. Stand aside!"

Motion caught Lad's eye. Glancing down, he saw the laces of Mya's dress hanging loose. She'd untied them. *Why? Mobility?* Was she preparing to fight with him? *She has to know I can't win, and Mya never plays a game she can't win.*

"No!" Mya's tone shifted from pleading to demanding. "Don't be *stupid!*"

Lad gaped. *She's provoking him!* Could she be planning some trick, some bluff? *Can I trust her?*

The Grandmaster's face flushed with rage. "Do you wish to die *with* him, Mya?"

"If you're foolish enough to waste such a perfect weapon, then yes. I'd rather die than be the slave of a sadistic *moron!*"

The dagger thrust came without warning, but still slow to Lad's perceptions. Mya could have dodged the clumsy attack easily...but she didn't.

The kris slammed between the stays of Mya's corset. Her agonized cry echoed through the room, but rang false in Lad's ears. Mya felt no pain. The Grandmaster jerked the blood-drenched knife free and stepped back.

When her knees folded, dread pierced Lad to the core. *Did the blade pierce her heart? Was it poisoned?*

"Mya!" Lad caught her before she struck the floor. Her face was contorted in agony, her hands clutching the wound in her belly. Something wasn't right. *Why would she—*

The soft rip of cloth drew his gaze down. She'd torn her dress open at the bottom of her corset, and her bloody fingers pulled two slim hilts from beneath the hard metal stays.

She's shamming! The Grandmaster didn't know of her runes. Her ruse gave them a slim and transient advantage.

"You're brilliant," he whispered.

Her feigned cry trailed off pitifully, but her eyes were clear as they met his. "Flip me."

Always thinking...lies within feints within subterfuge.

"Yes," he whispered back, gripping her beneath the arms. *Two daggers...two targets. Who*? "Hoseph." The priest's magic was a deadly unknown.

Mya nodded minutely.

The Grandmaster backed away, the tread of his hard shoes loud in Lad's ears. "Kill him."

"Ready?" Lad asked Mya.

"Always."

As the blademasters advanced, Lad flung Mya up in a twisting flip. Her voluminous dress fanned out like a crimson flower opening to the sun, detracting attention from the short, slim blades that flew with unerring accuracy. One struck Hoseph in the upper chest, and the priest staggered back. Another plunged deep into a blademaster's eye. The man's head snapped back, his sword clattering to the floor as he fell dead.

Two more blades flew before Mya landed, but the advantage of surprise had been spent. Steel sang as one blademaster parried the flying metal. Another dodged so that Mya's blade only scored a deep gash in his cheek. Bright red blood pulsed from the wound, but the swordsman seemed not to notice.

Mya landed and drew two more blades, whirling to set her shoulders firmly against Lad's. They assumed the opening position of the dance of death, perfectly mirrored. Her ploy had evened the odds slightly, with one blademaster down and Hoseph struggling to remove the dagger from a splintered rib. But four blademasters remained; a deadly circle of steel.

338

"Kill them!" the Grandmaster shrieked.

With blinding speed and perfect coordination, the blademasters struck.

Mya flung her last two daggers with little hope of a lethal strike. The flashing steel did force her opponents to parry and dodge, however. Mya used the opportunity to crouch and sweep a leg out from under one of the swordsmen.

Lad's foot whipped past her shoulder as he spun high, striking Mya's other opponent in the wrist hard enough to shatter bones. To balance his move, she spun low, tripping one of his opponents. The man turned the trip into a flip and slashed at her, his sword slicing frills from her billowing petticoat.

Gods, they're fast! Faster than any human she'd ever fought. Maybe they weren't human. Maybe they were monsters like her. What gifts might Koss Godslayer bequeath to his warrior monks?

As her spin brought her back around, Mya's first opponent lunged again, not at her, but at Lad's back. Mya parried the strike to Lad's spine with the flat of her hand and lashed out with a foot. The hard heel of her shoe struck the joint of the blademaster's knee with a satisfying crunch. The man went down, splinters of bone protruding from his torn trousers. Before she could finish him, however, his companion slashed.

With a broken wrist? Mya dodged the surprising attack an instant too late, and the tip of the blade snicked through three corset stays. Warm blood flooded down her belly, and for once she blessed the restricting garment; it had saved her life by preventing her viscera from spilling out. Her wrappings slithered together over the wound even before the flesh healed.

Two wounds already, and the fight's just beginning. If she lost too much blood, she would weaken and slow. Against these opponents, that would be deadly.

Wood and metal crashed behind her, and she hoped that Lad fared well. With her would-be eviscerator slashing at her throat, she didn't have time to look. Mya snapped her head back, and the blade passed within a finger's breadth of her nose. Lashing out with a twisting double kick, her first snapped her opponent's elbow like a chicken wing, but her second, intended for his head, missed entirely. The man spun impossibly fast, ignoring his broken arm as he shifted his sword for a reverse thrust.

No pain… Not human…

The blademaster with the broken leg was up—the protruding bone vanishing back into the recently pulped flesh as he slashed.

We're in trouble… Their healing would make disabling strikes useless. *Lethal strikes…*

As two blades came at her, Mya knew that she couldn't block both. Realization struck like lightning as she assessed the angles. If she dodged either one, Lad would take a sword in the back. There was no choice to make.

Steel grated against steel as the reverse-thrust pierced Mya's corset, plunging through her flesh and emerging from her back. *No pain…* Gritting her teeth against the madness of allowing herself to be impaled, Mya clapped one hand over the sword's guard to prevent the blademaster from twisting it and severing her spine. A chop to his wrist with her free hand broke his grip, and a whirling kick deflected the other blade before it could cleave her skull.

As Mya pirouetted, she drew the blade from her viscera, cold steel slipping through her organs. Lad was still unmarked. He slapped aside thrusts and slashes, keeping his two opponents at bay with flashing kicks. His jacket was slashed, but she saw no blood.

Thank the gods.

Mya completed her spin, slashing out with her stolen sword to deflect the predicted attack from the blademaster with the bloody knee. Steel rang, and the stroke passed harmlessly aside. Her other opponent, now swordless, had drawn two daggers, his broken arm also miraculously healed. He raised one dagger to deflect the arc of her slash, while thrusting the other low, inhumanly fast. Fortunately, Mya wasn't merely human. Altering the sweep of her blade, she intersected the man's wrist. Hand and dagger tumbled away in a spray of blood. She deliberately took the dagger thrust, though dangerously close to her heart—*Not used to fighting monsters, are you?*—and sliced her sword back across his neck. With one hand gone and the other trapped by his own thrust, he couldn't parry.

The blademaster's head tumbled away in a crimson fountain.

Heal that! she thought, wrenching the dagger from her chest to deflect yet another sword thrust. *Three to go!* A sudden thought occurred to her; something didn't add up.

Hoseph...

Mya twisted to catch a glimpse of the priest. He was still on his feet. *Maybe he healed...* With his crimson robes, she couldn't see any blood, but something silver glinted in his hand. She flipped her dagger, and cocked back her hand to throw.

Blackness pulsed through the room, dimming Mya's vision and gripping her heart in a vice of despair. Every shred of shame, every regret and horror she'd ever known, vomited forth in a flood of self-loathing. An anguished cry escaped her lips, and she missed a parry. Steel sliced through silk, flesh, and bone, like shears cutting fine linen. Weakness and despair folded her knees as a crimson fountain spouted from her breast.

Mya watched helplessly as the keen edge of a sword descended toward her face.

Without Mya's advantages of healing and immunity to pain, Lad had his hands and feet occupied just keeping steel from his flesh. The blademasters were skilled indeed, and faster than any human. He scored with a kick, smashing a blademaster's nose, only to watch it instantly heal.

Magic!

Lad trapped one thrust between his palms and kicked aside the other's sweeping slash. The sword twisted in his grasp, and Lad flipped with it, tumbling over the blade with two more lashing kicks. The first landed solidly, breaking the man's jaw and sending teeth flying, but the second met only air. The toothless blademaster ducked and pirouetted, passing the blade behind his back, while trying to wrench it from Lad's hands.

As the other sword descended toward his wrists, Lad yanked to bring the two blades together. The two swords met with a clash. Lad delivered a well-placed kick into the chest of the toothless blademaster, snapping ribs and sending the man crashing into a torture rack. The injury would have put a normal opponent out of action, but Lad knew the man would be back up in seconds. He would have to kill the other quickly.

Unfortunately, bloody nose had no intention of letting that happen. The swordsman wove his weapon in a complex series of slashes and thrusts that kept Lad from landing a mortal strike. When toothless rejoined the fight, neither Lad nor his opponent had managed to do more than deflect the other's strikes and mess up their clothing.

Lad cringed at the particular rasp of steel on steel signifying that Mya's corset had been penetrated again. If the blade had pierced her heart, the next would probably kill him. He had to trust her, just as she had to trust him.

Mya's frilled petticoat brushed the back of his legs as she spun—*She's alive, at least*—and he heard the unmistakable clash of one sword deflecting another. As he slapped aside two more thrusts, a warm spray of blood touched the back of his neck, and a disembodied head tumbled past. He felt a peculiar surge of relief that it didn't wear Mya's silly little hat.

A twisting foot sweep tripped both of his opponents, and allowed him a glance toward Mya. One opponent lay headless on the floor, and she held both sword and dagger. *We might just have a—*

342

A flash of blackness took him by surprise.

In that instant, everyone he'd murdered, every guard and noble the Grandfather had forced him to kill, cried for mercy in his mind. Wiggen died in his arms once again, her bewildered face staring up at him in the rain, tearing his heart from his chest. The worst moments of his life... But Lad had long ago come to grips with the killings; Wiggen's love had healed him, absolving him of guilt. And, oddly, her loss was still so fresh, so raw in his memory, that he experienced her death every time he closed his eyes. Even magic couldn't break an already broken heart. He shook off the momentary disorientation.

Lad's opponents seemed unaffected, and lunged in simultaneous attacks. He intercepted both strikes, slapping one blade aside and kicking the other blademaster's wrist away. A gut-wrenching cry of anguish shivered up his spine, followed by the rip of steel parting silk, flesh, and bone.

Mya!

Lads leapt up and back, lashing out to kick his two opponents and propel himself backward. Arching his back, he caught sight of Mya and her opponent. Blood sprayed from Mya's lacerated torso, and an expression of desolation wracked her features. Her hands hung limp, weapons useless, as her opponent's sword arced toward her upturned face.

"No!"

As he flipped over their heads, Lad clapped his palms together on the blademaster's sword, stopping it mere inches from Mya's brow. His momentum jerked the sword back over the blademaster's head. When his feet met the floor again, Lad stood facing the man's back, the curved sword locked above their heads, neither willing to relinquish their grasp.

Lad couldn't see Mya—the blademaster's broad shoulders blocked his view—but the clash of steel on steel told him she lived. But how long, weakened by so much blood loss?

Hoseph's voice drew Lad's gaze. The Grandmaster stood well away from the fight, clutching his bloody dagger, disbelief painting his features. To his right, familiar tendrils of dark mist slithered forth to engulf Hoseph. The priest was fleeing, leaving his master behind.

Coward...

Lad's opponent wrenched his sword, drawing him back to the fight. Lad tried to trip him, to no avail. A waft of chill air touched the back of his neck.

There should be nothing behind me.

A memory: swirling black mists in Norwood's hallway coalescing into a red-robed figure, one hand outstretched and glowing with death magic...

Hoseph!

Lad couldn't release his grip on the sword without giving the blademaster an opening to cut Mya down, but his feet were free. The rustle of robes and scuff of a shoe gave him a target for a backward kick. His foot smashed into something solid, and he felt bone splinter with the impact. A glance over his shoulder showed the priest tumbling backward over one of the stone slabs. He landed with a solid thud, and didn't get up.

The Grandmaster spat a curse and strode forward, the bloody kris held before him.

With Lad's hands locked on the sword above his head, he couldn't dodge. He also couldn't block or strike the Grandmaster. Lad had no defense against that blade. If he released the blademaster's weapon, he would either be cut down or doom Mya to the same fate. He had to kill the blademaster before he could evade the Grandmaster, but he needed one hand free to do that, and grasping a sword one-handed was perilous.

Think like an assassin, Lad...

Shifting his grip, Lad wrapped his left hand around the blade. His opponent sensed the shift and wrenched the sword hard. Lad gritted his teeth as the edge cut to the bone, but held his grip. With his free hand, he retrieved a tiny vial from under his ridiculous cravat.

Thank you, Enola...

344

Lad had brought the toxin for himself—he would never be a slave again—but now he had a better use. Putting the glass vial between his teeth, careful not to bite too hard, he twisted off the cap and stabbed the envenomed needle into the blademaster's neck. As the kris lashed out at him, he spat out the vial and dodged, releasing his grip on the sword. The blademaster jerked hard as he felt his weapon freed. Agony lanced through Lad's hand, and blood rained down as he twisted away from the Grandmaster's dagger.

The blademaster stumbled, his sword falling from nerveless fingers as the stonefish toxin stopped his heart. His mouth gaped silently, a look of utter astonishment on his face as he pitched forward, dead.

Lad clutched his injured hand to his side as he whirled around to confront the Grandmaster.

"How dare you!" The Grandmaster cursed, but then suddenly stopped, his gaze dropping to the floor.

There, in a splatter of blood beside the dead blademaster, lay three of Lad's fingers. On one of them glittered a circle of obsidian and gold.

CHAPTER XXV

Hands clapped onto the sword before Mya's eyes.

Lad…

The pall of despair vanished from Mya's mind as she watched her angel of deliverance arc overhead. Her would-be killer's arms flew up, and the two men stood struggling over the sword that would have ended her life. Blood loss weakened her limbs, but she gripped her stolen blades with cold fury. She could gut the blademaster in an instant.

The thump of a boot from behind changed Mya's strategy. Her blades flashed up in a blind crossing parry behind her back. Instinct served her well. Steel met steel, gifting her one more moment of life. She spun on her knees and parried another stroke with the quillons of her dagger, a diagonal slash that reverberated up her arm.

Weakness… I'm alive…but for how long? Mya no longer had the advantage of greater strength, but she was still faster…*maybe.*

The force of the blow sent her careening aside. She took the impact on her shoulder, and flung her legs around in a flat arc. Her kick swept the legs from under one opponent, but he was already rolling to his feet by the time Mya regained her stance.

She caught a glimpse of swirling black mists—*Hoseph!*— but couldn't look away from the fight. As she parried four lightning-quick attacks, the crunch of breaking bones and the thump of a body crashing to the floor gave her hope. The

346

Grandmaster's curses drew a glance from one of her foes. Mya lunged, but an intervening blade deflected her stroke.

At the clang of a sword hitting the floor behind her, the two blademasters shared a glance. One nodded, and they shifted to each side. Instead of looking at Mya, they looked past her. They were trying to flank her to reach Lad.

Oh, no you don't! Whirling in a desperate attempt to engage both of them, she glimpsed Lad. He stood too far away to cover her back. He'd broken their bond of mutual protection.

The blademasters circled her in opposite directions, forcing her choose. If she attacked one, the other could attack Lad. She couldn't stop them both. Suddenly one lunged, demanding all her skill. The other turned toward Lad, sword raised. Two steps would bring his blade down on Lad's head, yet the Twailin guildmaster paid his attacker no heed. His attention was riveted on the Grandmaster.

What the hell's he doing?

"Lad!" Mya flipped her dagger and threw, but the blade was deflected even as it left her fingers.

Lad turned, and she saw his mangled hand. He wouldn't last long with an injury like that. Lunging desperately, Mya tried to get past her opponent, only to be forced back. It came down to a contest between his swordsmanship and her speed. Her mind scurried frantically for any way to put that advantage to use, but came up blank. She was an assassin, not a swordswoman.

So think like one!

Mya threw her sword at the blademaster's head, and launched herself. He parried the blade easily, but in doing so brought his sword high, opening himself to her sprawling body check. They fell hard, and Mya quickly rolled away. She came up with her back pressed against the slab where Keisha lay. Beside her glittered the tray of implements that had caused the thief so much agony.

Mya snatched up a steel spike used to split finger bones, then flung the rest of the tray into the blademaster's face. It would only delay him for a moment, but a moment was all she needed. Turning, Mya hurled the spike with all her strength at the blademaster facing Lad. It pierced his skull with a crack, and he fell at Lad's feet.

Lad gaped at her, his mouth opening to form a word, but his warning wasn't necessary. Mya knew what the move had cost her. She'd thrown away all her weapons, and with her back against the blood-soaked slab, she couldn't maneuver.

Everybody dies...

Steel flashed down.

Mya jerked away to keep the blade from cleaving her skull, but couldn't evade the stroke entirely. The razor edge clipped an inch from her hair before slashing down through her shoulder...her clavicle...into her chest. Her left arm went numb. Blood sprayed from the gaping wound, blinding her left eye, but she felt no pain, only weakness. Her mind sparked with one more gambit. Grabbing the haft of the sword, she squeezed with all her waning strength, trapping the blademaster's hand. He tried to pull free, but she held fast.

Her wrappings slithered back together, pulling the sagging third of her torso back into position. The wound closed around the sword in her chest, the bones clicking into place as muscles and sinews mended. Her left arm tingled and came to life. Coughing up bloody froth, she grinned at her opponent with a monster's cold triumph.

No fear, no pain, no mercy...

She had him.

The blademaster reached for the dagger at his belt, but Mya was faster. She kicked him in the crotch with every ounce of her flagging strength.

The impact lifted him off the floor to the sound of cracking bones, both her instep and his pelvis. The shock sent the dagger clattering away, and his grip on the sword failed. Mya planted a second kick in his midriff before he touched the floor, and he folded over, gagging as he hit the ground. Before he could recover, she slipped his sword from her chest and sliced the finely honed edge through his neck.

Done...

Mya collapsed to her knees, coughing blood and gasping for breath. She lacked the strength to lift her head, but managed to raise her eyes. Lad stood facing the Grandmaster, the only person they couldn't kill. She coughed again and spat, surveying the death around them, and wondered if it had all been for nothing.

"Lad!"

He whirled at Mya's warning, realizing at once his grave error. The shock of seeing his guildmaster ring lying on the floor had clouded his mind with vengeance. Vengeance for Wiggen, vengeance for his own creation, vengeance for an empire ruled by terror... He'd forgotten one of his first lessons. *Never get distracted during combat. Remember*!

His distraction may have cost them their lives.

Mya fought desperately to rejoin him, to no avail. Her strength was flagging, and her slashed and bloody dress impeded her movement. The blademaster she faced wielded his sword with far greater skill.

Lad focused on his own opponent's attack. His injured hand throbbed, and he couldn't even make a fist due to his missing fingers. He thought desperately for some advantage. Enola's vial of poison lay somewhere in the mire of blood on the floor. If he could find it, maybe...

From the corner of his eye, Lad spied Mya tackle the blademaster. *What's she—* Another slash snapped his attention back to the fight. He cursed himself for glancing away. *Focus*! He lashed out with a kick in an attempt to gain some ground so he could search for the poison vial.

Metal clattered, and Lad caught a glimpse of a gleaming shaft flying through the air. An instant later, it pierced his opponent's skull. As the man fell, Lad stared beyond him...just as steel slashed down toward Mya.

No!

The sword sliced through her shoulder into her chest. Blood sprayed; the wound looked mortal. If it had reached her heart...

Lad gaped, stunned. *Why?* Mya had sacrificed herself for him. *It doesn't make sense, unless...* Sudden memories of her actions, her words, and evasions came to him. *It can't be.*

Then Mya reached up to grasp the haft of the sword, and the horrible wound closed. Her face shone deathly pale, but the blade had not reached her heart. Lad stared in wonder as she dispatched her foe with a masterful combination of kicks, and a final slash of the blade. She collapsed to her knees, coughing blood, but alive.

She's alive... With that relief, calm settled over Lad's mind, and a new imperative took hold.

Vengeance.

Lad turned to face the most powerful man in the world: Emperor, Grandmaster, the instrument of so much terror, the ultimate source of all Lad's anguish... He glanced down at his severed fingers and the ring upon the floor. He was no longer a slave.

"Don't touch me!" Emperor Tynean Tsing II backed away, the bloody kris held out before him. "You can't touch me!"

"I *can* touch you." Lad stepped forward, grimacing at the pain in his hand, but determined to finish this. "I can more than touch you. I can *kill* you."

"I'm *emperor*! You *can't* kill me! I'll..." His eyes darted around like two cornered rats. "I've a thousand loyal guards in the palace! You'll never get out of here alive!"

"It doesn't *matter* if I get out of here alive, Your Majesty. What matters is that you *don't*."

Chris A. Jackson

The Grandmaster's face paled, and his eyes gleamed with fear. This was probably the first time in his life that Tynean Tsing had been truly afraid. Lad tried to imagine him as a child, introduced so young to a world of blood, pain, and murder. It was something they had in common. The difference was, Lad was made not to feel, but Tynean Tsing was made to enjoy it.

"I understand what you are." Lad took another step, forcing the Grandmaster back until he bumped into a heavy wooden rack. "They made you a monster. They made *me* a monster."

"Here, take it!" The emperor thrust out the hand that bore the Grandmaster's ring. "Cut it off and claim it!"

"No." The idea of putting on that ring made Lad want to retch. "As you said, Your *Majesty*, I'm merely a weapon. You can't bargain with me. I understand what you are, but I can't pity you. There's no reprieve for what you've done."

"I can give you *anything*!" The Grandmaster sidestepped, bumping into the cage where Norwood hung unconscious. He looked back and startled at the captain's blood-streaked face, then turned back to Lad. "Anything you want!"

"Can you take away his pain?" Lad pointed to Norwood, then gestured to Kiesha. "Can you send her back to her father, whole and strong and beautiful?" His words caught in his throat. "Can you give *Wiggen* back to me?"

"I didn't kill your gods-damned wife!"

"But you wielded the weapon that did." Lad stepped within striking distance. "You think that keeping people in constant terror is how to rule them. You're wrong."

"What do *you* know?" The emperor spat in Lad's face and lunged.

Lad caught it easily, crushing the Grandmaster's hand on the hilt with his one good hand. "I know enough. I know love is stronger than fear." He squeezed, and the old man's eyes widened in pain. "And now *you* know fear." He brought the dagger up until it stood before the emperor's eyes. "You know

351

the fear of the common man facing an abusive noble or a sadistic assassin, a man who can't...fight...back."

"Don't!" The ruler of an empire of fear gripped the dagger with both hands, struggling to push it away. "Please!"

"How many have lain in this room and uttered those same words to you, Your *Majesty*?"

"I...I don't want to die!"

"Neither did they. Neither did Wiggen." Lad positioned the point of the dagger beneath the Grandmaster's chin, pricking the skin so that a single drop of blood trickled down the serpentine blade. "Goodbye, Your Majesty."

Lad plunged the dagger up to the hilt, ending a fifty-year reign of terror.

Emperor Tynean Tsing II died instantly and painlessly. It was more mercy than he deserved.

Vengeance.

And yet, Lad felt no rush of joy, no relief, just emptiness. Wiggen was still dead. Though he had changed the course of an empire with a single dagger thrust, all it meant to Lad was one more death weighing upon his soul.

The glint of gold and obsidian caught Lad's eye as the emperor crumpled to the floor.

"Lad!" Mya struggled to her feet and staggered to his side, cursing the tattered and bloody dress that dragged at her every step. She stared down at the fallen emperor and felt suddenly as if a huge weight lifted from her shoulders. "You did it!"

"Yes." He turned toward her, his face pinched in pain. Clutching his bleeding hand to his side, he stepped past her. "Just one more thing to do."

"What?" Mya watched as Lad began scanning the floor, flipping over one of the dead blademasters. "What are you—"

"I'm finishing this." He plucked something out of the blood, then strode over to the slab where Kiesha lay. "I *have* to."

Of course... She staggered after him. "Vengeance."

"No. Forgiveness." Leaning down, he spoke softly into the tortured woman's ear. "Kiesha."

The thief's eyelids fluttered, and her ruined lips murmured, "No...no more...please."

"No more pain, Kiesha."

Now Mya saw what Lad had picked off the floor, a tiny vial and cap. He fitted the cap onto the vial, shook it, then removed the cap again. A needle on the bottom of the cap glinted in the light, and she understood. *Poison.*

"I'm here to end your pain." Lad's voice was quiet, soothing. "I don't blame you for Wiggen's death. You were a weapon, just like I once was."

"End...pain...please," Kiesha muttered, peering up at Lad. Her eyes glinted with madness, but also hope. "Please..."

"Yes, Kiesha. Just relax. The pain will be over soon." Lad pressed the needle into an exposed vein in her neck.

A labored breath, one last sigh, and Kiesha's eyes closed.

"Mercy..." Mya could only stare, staggered by Lad's compassion. She wondered if she could have been so merciful.

Lad stood straight and silent for a moment, then tucked away the vial and turned to her. "Now what?"

The question stirred Mya out of her trance. "I..." She glanced at the fallen emperor, and the sight ignited her. *We just killed the godsdamned emperor!* "First we bind up your hand, then we get the hell out of here." She fumbled with the hem of her dress, straining to tear a swath from her pettiskirts. *Gods, I'm so weak...* Picking up a fallen blade, she sawed at the ragged tear until the fabric came free. "Come here. We don't' want to leave a blood trail."

Lad winced while she wrapped his mangled hand, but stood still. Oddly, he just stared at her. Mya found his scrutiny discomforting, and spoke quickly as she worked.

"Make sure we pick up your fingers. If we leave them behind, they can use magic to trace you. I've used that method myself. There's too much blood to worry about, and it's mingled with everyone else's, so—"

"Mya." Lad hissed in pain as she tied the final knot tight, then clutched her hand in both of his. "Stop. Please. I need to tell you...something."

"What?" His hands felt warm on hers. His eyes no longer gleamed with anger and frustration, but looked at her gently, the way she'd always wanted him to look at her. Her heart skipped a beat. "Tell me what?"

"Thank you." He clutched her hand and stared into her soul. "You saved me. You saved me from myself."

"I didn't." Mya swallowed hard.

"You did. During our trip here, you did for me what I couldn't do for myself. You helped me focus. You reminded me of what I am. You reminded me that I have a family. That I have someone to love."

"Lad, I..." Mya choked on the words. In her entire life, she had only said those words to one person, and that person she had murdered. She doubted she could ever say those words again.

"I know, Mya."

"What?" His words hit her like a slap.

"I know how you feel."

"You..." Her knees began to shake with more than just weakness and blood loss. "You do?"

"Yes." Lad smiled through his pain, and her heart swelled to breaking. "Yes, I do."

"Oh, gods..." She entwined the fingers of her free hand in his hair and pulled him to her, seeking his lips. She found them—oh so warm and soft—and kissed him as she'd so often dreamed of doing. *Can it be...* Then she realized that his lips were passive.

Mya felt something slip onto her finger. Pulling away, she saw the regret in Lad's eyes.

"I'm sorry."

"You..." She lurched back and looked at her hand. Obsidian and gold glinted on her finger. *The guildmaster's ring?* But no, Lad's ring still lay on the floor, encircling his severed finger. *What ring...* Sudden realization ignited in her gut.

"You *bastard!*"

Her slap knocked Lad to the floor. Mya staggered, dizzy with sudden weakness. Lad hadn't even tried to block or dodge the blow, and for a moment she was terrified that she'd snapped his neck. Then he spat blood and rose up on his elbows, the imprint of her hand livid on his face.

"You tricked me!" She felt like kicking him for the betrayal. "You let me kiss you to trick me!"

"I'm sorry, Mya, but I'll only ever love one woman, and Wiggen is dead." He rose to his feet, eying her warily. "Will you let me explain?"

"Explain?" Mya seethed with rage, glaring first at Lad, then at the two rings on her fingers. She wrenched off the ring that had made her Master Hunter and flung it at him. He caught it in his good hand. "Explain *what?*"

"That you're the *perfect* Grandmaster." Lad tucked the ring in a pocket. "You think like an assassin, but you have a good heart. You won't abuse the power, not like *he* did." He cast a disgusted look over his shoulder at Tynean Tsing's body.

"But I don't *want* this!" Mya waved her hand before his face, obsidian and gold flickering in the light.

"Why not?" He cocked his head at her. Even in her anger, the endearing gesture plucked at her heart. "You're safe now. No member of the guild can hurt you."

"You think they're going to *thank* me for killing their Grandmaster? I'll have the empire *and* the guild after my head!"

"Then have someone cut it off. Um...the ring, that is, not your head. But you can't run away from the guild, and they'll know we did it." Lad stepped past her and bent to pick up his severed fingers, removing the guildmaster's ring and putting it into a pocket. "We can't discuss this here, Mya. We've got to go. Help me get Norwood out of that cage."

"We should just kill him," she said, still angry.

Lad looked at her with sympathy in his eyes. "No, Mya."

"Why not? Why not just leave him? He hasn't seen us. He can't tell them anything."

"Because killing him would be wrong. If we leave him, they'll question him, and he won't have any answers. He'll end up in prison or dead."

"Better him than us!"

"I'll do it myself, then." He bent to search emperor's body.

Mya seethed. *I should just leave him alone to explain why he's carrying Norwood's naked body through the streets.* A pang of guilt stabbed her, and she knew she couldn't do it.

"Damn you to the Nine Hells..." She cast about for something, anything to open the iron cage. Scanning the room she suddenly froze. "Where's Hoseph?"

"What?" Lad straightened with a ring of keys in his hand. "He's..." His eyes widened. "He was right over there."

"He's *gone!*" Adrenalin surged through her veins, but with little blood to accompany the urgency, she only felt faint. "We've got to get out of here! He'll be back with more guards!"

Lad hurried to the cage and started fitting keys into the lock. "Hurry! Grab some clothing."

There was no time to argue. Mya started pulling a jacket off of one of the fallen blademasters. "Everything's all bloody! We can't just walk into the inn with—"

"Not now, Mya. Just grab some clothes and help me with him." The door to the cage squeaked open, and Lad loosened the spikes that pierced the captain. "It'll be dark when we leave, so the blood will be less noticeable. We'll worry about getting back to the inn *after* we get out of here!"

"Fine." She grabbed two more jackets that weren't overly soiled, donning one of them. "You'll have to carry him. I'm too weak to carry much more than a *conversation.*"

"Good. Maybe you won't carry a grudge." Lad caught Norwood over his shoulder and stood with little difficulty.

"Smart ass." Mya picked up two fallen daggers and tucked them away, grumbling beneath her breath. If she didn't love him so much, she would have stabbed him long ago.

CHAPTER XXVI

Lad laid Norwood on the doorstep of the temple of the Earth Mother, and tucked the stolen blanket around him. Rapping loudly on the door, he waited until he heard footsteps from inside, then sprinted back to the shadows to join Mya. They peered from hiding as the door opened and a willowy woman rushed forth to kneel beside the captain.

"Well, that was easier than I thought it'd be." Mya tugged at his sleeve. "Come on."

They made their way through the streets of Tsing slowly and silently. Mya's weakness slowed their pace, but at least their route was mostly downhill. The wine shop had been closed and empty by the time they made their way back through the strangely illuminated tunnel, and breaking out of a building was easier than breaking in. Finally they spied the sign of the *Drake and Lion* half a block away.

"I don't suppose you can climb?" Lad asked hopefully, only to be rewarded with a sour look.

"Are you crazy?" She looked up at the sheer walls. "I'm barely walking."

After a moment's thought, he said, "Follow me."

The servants' quarters were on the first floor. Lad slipped from one window to the next, peering into the dark rooms until he recognized his three snoring Enforcers. All it took was a tap on the window to rouse them. Within minutes, they met Lad and Mya at the back door with a couple of blankets. The trip up the servant's stairs to the third floor went well. To any prying eyes, they seemed nothing more than faithful servants escorting their drunken employers to bed.

As surprised as the Enforcers were to find Lad at their window, it was nothing next to their shock of seeing Mya's tattered and bloody gown when she dropped her concealing cloak in the privacy of their suite. She forestalled questions with her usual aplomb.

"Stop gaping and get to work! I want a meal here in ten minutes, and the carriage ready to leave in twenty. Keep it quiet!" She hurried into the bedroom, tearing at the laces of her dress.

Lad tried for a gentler approach. "There's been trouble and we have to get out of the city. I'll explain everything later. For now, follow Mya's orders quickly and quietly."

"Yes, Master."

Lad almost told them he was no long guildmaster, but decided to wait. They would learn soon enough. He closed the door behind them and peeled out of his bloody clothes.

Sooner than he would have thought possible, they were ready, dressed in clean clothes, and full from a hasty meal of cheese, bread, and cold roast mutton. Lad kept his newly bandaged hand tucked under his jacket as he watched the Enforcers heft the last of their bags into the boot of the carriage.

"Ready?"

Lad turned at Mya's question. Though pale, she looked remarkably normal in her traveling dress, though he noticed that she wore no corset. She'd eaten like a starved wolf, and downed two tankards of mulled wine. Truth be told, Lad's dinner sat heavy in his stomach, their conversation gnawing at him.

"I'm ready. Are you sure about this?"

She smiled at him, then looked away. "I'm sure."

Lad held out his arm for her, and she rested her fingers there with only a slight hesitation.

As the carriage clattered along, they both stared out the windows, each absorbed in their own thoughts. Lad watched as the elegant architecture of the Heights District gave way to the more staid buildings of Midtown. Twice they were stopped by patrols. Lad feared the worst, but the constables were only making routine checks for illegal activity, and let them pass. Apparently, news of the emperor's assassination had not yet hit the streets. Only when they turned onto the bridge near River Gate did Mya finally break the silence.

"How long have you known?" She looked Lad square in the eye, her jaw clenched. "How I feel about you, I mean."

"Not long. Not until tonight." He shrugged. "I couldn't figure out why you'd risk your life for me when you had the perfect way out."

"You're an idiot." She looked away and brushed the hair back from her ear.

"Don't do that."

"What?" Her eyes flashed again, as sharp as the daggers in her dress.

"Brush your hair back, click your nails, rub your nose, bite your lip… Those are your tells. You'll have to learn to control them if you don't want anyone to read you."

"Like you've been doing, you mean," she said, looking away again. "Thank you."

Lad wanted to say more, but he didn't know what. After all the years he had spent watching Mya's back, he still felt responsible for her.

At the end of the bridge, Mya thumped to alert the driver—"This will do."—and the carriage lurched to a halt. On the corner stood an inn sporting an incongruous placard depicting a porcupine and a cactus in a compromising position beneath the name, *The Prickly Pair*.

Lifting her hand, Mya gazed at the ring on her finger. "You know I'll never forgive you for this."

"Yes, you will."

Mya reached for the door latch, but Lad stopped her, placing his bandaged hand atop hers.

"You could come back to Twailin. You know people there. You could run things from the *Golden Cockerel*. Sereth would support you."

She smiled, but lifted his hand and placed it back in his lap. "No. The Grandmaster belongs in Tsing."

The Enforcers had unloaded Mya's two bags, hefted them into the inn's foyer, and returned to their seats.

After a moment's hesitation, Mya leaned over and kissed Lad. He didn't protest. Her lips were soft, but they weren't Wiggin's.

When they parted, he said, "I'm sorry, Mya."

"So am I." The Grandmaster of Assassins stepped out of the carriage and hurried to the inn without a backward glance.

"Drive on!" Lad thumped the roof with the head of his cane, and the carriage jerked into motion. His hand hurt, and his heart ached, but he was alive. And he was going home.

As the last light of sunset faded, Mya sat on the crest of the tallest inn in the Dreggars Quarter. She had abandoned her dresses for her favorite dark trousers and shirt. Despite the demise of the sun, the sky was still lit by flames from across the river.

That afternoon, she, along with hundreds of other citizens of Tsing, had watched Crown Prince Arbuckle order a phalanx of knights to release all the prisoners in the Imperial Plaza. Arbuckle himself had set the first torch to the bonfire built from the wood of the despicable machines. Only then had the people allowed themselves to believe the rumors: Tynean Tsing II was dead. Tynean Tsing III had yet to be crowned, but a new era was already dawning on the Tsing Empire.

To say that the populace had gone insane at the news was an understatement. The commoners rejoiced in the streets, while the nobles quailed in their guarded estates. The Imperial Plaza still burned, and other fires bloomed like a field of poppies. Mya wondered if everything north of the river would burn.

South of the river, the mood was more celebratory than vindictive. There were no nobles to rebel against, and no gallows or stocks to burn. In fact, she wasn't the only one who had crossed the river seeking shelter from the storm. Many had fled the turmoil consuming the Heights District and Midtown. They couldn't flee the city entirely. Cordons of constables and soldiers barred every exit, searching for the emperor's assassin.

"At least Lad got out."

Mya looked at the ring on her finger and sighed. She tried to be angry with him for saddling her with this responsibility, but for the life of her, she couldn't hold that grudge. It pleased her to think that he had escaped this life. If anyone deserved happiness, Lad did.

The flames across the river blurred, and Mya wiped her eyes. This was no time to bemoan her lot in life. She had a guild to run, and no idea how to do it. Who could she count on? The Twailin guild was her only surety. Sereth was loyal to Lad, and Mya hoped that he would transfer that allegiance to her.

Lady T? Mya wondered if the woman would survive the wrath of the commoners. If any noble survived, it would be the guildmaster of the Tsing Assassins Guild. But would she see Mya as a liberator or usurper?

Hoseph... The priest was Mya's greatest worry. She had slept last night with her back in a corner and daggers in her hands. He was the only one who knew the truth about what happened last night.

The right had of death. She only had two options: recruit him or kill him. The choice would be his, more than hers. *Burn that bridge later if you must*, she thought, watching the flames with a lightening heart. *First things first...*

362

Raised voices from the inn's common room below floated up to Mya, laughter and singing. Breathing in the fetid night air, she thought of Lad's words. Did she really have a good heart? Only time would tell. Right now, she had work to do.

It was time to think like an assassin.

EPILOGUE

Loren!" Tika burst into the kitchen of *Tap and Kettle*, his brow furrowed with worry. He lowered his voice to a whisper, and switched from Lad's pseudonym. "Lad, there's someone here to see you."

"Who?" Lad hitched Lissa up on his hip and continued stirring the huge kettle of soup. Though there were a few things he could no longer do around the inn due to his maimed hand, he could still hold his daughter and stir soup, and that was more than enough for him.

Tika glanced back over his shoulder and lowered his voice. "Norwood, the Royal Guard captain!"

Lad stopped stirring, every muscle in his body suddenly tense. He'd arrived back in Twailin barely a month ago. Sereth had informed him when Norwood returned a week later. Though Lad was pleased that the captain survived, he considered that chapter of his life over. Now it looked as if he had been wrong.

"He asked for me specifically?"

"He asked to see Wiggen's husband."

The pang in Lad's heart still ached, but he had finally come to accept Wiggen's death. She might not be here in the flesh, but her memory was always with him.

And Lissa... Lad laid his cheek against his daughter's head, inhaled the heady fragrance of her hair, the warm milky scent of her breath. He had vowed never to leave her again...and never to kill. But if Norwood was here to arrest him...

364

"Here, Tika." Lad handed his fussy daughter over to her uncle and fumbled with the apron strings. Taking a deep breath, he tried to relax.

"Da!" Lissa reached out her pudgy little arms. She had clung to Lad since his return, reluctant to be parted from her father. At least she had stopped crying for her mother endlessly every night. She was finally healing. They all were healing.

"You think talking to him is wise?" Forbish paused over the vegetables he had been chopping.

Lad shrugged. "I think it would be unwise to refuse to talk to him."

Forbish frowned. "And if he wants to arrest you?"

Lad draped his apron over a stool and tried to keep his voice light. "I don't think he will. We'll see."

The common room wasn't as busy as they would have liked. With rumors of rebellion and even possible civil war, merchants weren't traveling as much as usual, holding their goods close to home until things settled down. It would either sort itself out or not, and Lad had resolved to have nothing to do with it.

Norwood sat by the cold hearth, a tankard of ale in his hand and a plate of cookies beside his chair. He was feeding one to the huge mastiff that sat beside him, its massive head on his knee. The dog turned and looked at Lad, and its ears pricked up. Norwood followed the dog's gaze and stood with some difficulty as Lad approached.

Lad stopped two steps away, wary of the dog's scrutiny. "May I help you, Captain?"

"Don't worry about Brutus; he's well trained," Norwood said as he patted the mastiff's head. His eyes flicked over Lad, lingering on his maimed hand, then fixing upon his face. "You're Loren? Wiggen's husband?"

"Her...widower, yes. Would you like to speak in private? We have a back room." He waved toward the door that led into the small back chamber.

Norwood smiled and sat back down. "No, thank you. Here is fine."

Wary, Lad pulled up another chair. "Well, then, is there a problem?"

"No. No problem." Norwood absently scratched the dog's head, his eyes on Lad. "I just learned of your wife's death. You have my condolences."

"Thank you. It's been several weeks..." Lad endured his scrutiny for a moment. Norwood seemed to be mesmerized by him, staring into his eyes. "Can I ask the reason for your visit?"

"I wanted to meet you." Norwood sighed and rubbed a spot on his leg near the knee. Lad remembered a wound there from one of the iron maiden's screws, and wondered if it pained him. "You remind me of a fellow I met not long ago."

"Really?" Lad tensed. Did Norwood recognize him from his late-night visits, or had he somehow glimpsed Lad's face in Tsing?

Norwood finally tore his gaze away and picked up his tankard, sipping the ale as he stared into the cold hearth. "He saved my life once."

"Oh?"

"Yes. In fact, I think he may have saved my life twice, though I can't be sure about the second time."

"I see." Lad struggled to remain calm. The captain had somehow put the pieces together. But then, Lad knew the man was good at his job.

Norwood's eyes flicked up to his. "Yes. Yes, I think you just might. Too bad I don't know who this fellow is, because I'd like to thank him. I owe him quite a lot." The captain's wide jaw trembled as he spoke. Like Lad, the man's outward calm seemed threatened by some inner storm. "I think the whole Empire of Tsing owes him."

Lad stared. "Why is that, Captain?"

"Because there are things in this world that need killing, and sometimes you have to look through the bad to see the good."

366

Norwood stood and extended his big warrior's hand. "I'm pleased to finally meet you, Loren."

"And I'm pleased to meet you, Captain." Lad took Norwood's hand in his and easily matched the hard grip with his own. "I'm glad you came by."

"Yes, so am I." He released Lad's hand and looked around the common room with a broad smile. "I like the *Tap and Kettle*. I may visit again, just for a pint and a nibble." He snatched up a couple more cookies, fed one to Brutus and ate the other himself.

"You'll always be welcome." Lad was surprised to realize that he meant it. Despite their differences, he liked Norwood very much.

"Thank you." The captain patted his leg, and the big mastiff lurched to its feet, following its master as he headed for the door. After only a couple of steps, however, Norwood stopped and turned back. "Loren, if you'd ever like to visit, late at night, just to talk, you'd be welcome in my home. I think you might know where I live."

"I think I might."

The Captain of the Royal Guard nodded, smiled, and limped out of the *Tap and Kettle*, his huge dog padding along at his heels.

A high-pitched squeal from the kitchen brought a smile to Lad's lips. Lissa was being fussy again. A father's work, it seemed, was never done.

About the Author

From the sea to the stars, Chris A. Jackson's stories take you to the far reaches of the imagination. Raised on the back deck of a fishing boat and trained as a marine biologist, he became sidetracked by a career in biomedical research, but regained his heart and soul in 2009 when he and his wife Anne left the dock aboard the 45-foot sailboat *Mr Mac* to cruise the Caribbean and write fulltime.

With his nautical background, writing sea stories seemed inevitable for Chris. His acclaimed Scimitar Seas nautical fantasies won three consecutive Gold Medals in the *ForeWord Reviews* Book of the Year Awards. *Pirate's Honor*, a Pathfinders Tale from Paizo Publishing, combines high-seas combat and romance set in the award-winning world of the Pathfinder Roleplaying Game. Not to be outdone, Privateer Press released *Blood & Iron*, a swashbuckling novella set in the Iron Kingdoms.

Chris' repertoire also includes the award-winning and Kindle best-selling Weapon of Flesh Trilogy (*Weapon of Flesh* and *Weapon of Blood* currently available; *Weapon of Vengeance* due out July 2014), as well as five additional fantasy novels, the humorous sci fi Cheese Runners trilogy of novellas, and short stories.

Preview Chris' novels, download audiobooks, and read his writing blog at jaxbooks.com. Follow Chris' cruising adventures at www.sailmrmac.blogspot.com.

Novels by Chris A. Jackson

From Jaxbooks
A Soul for Tsing
Deathmask

The Weapon of Flesh Trilogy
Weapon of Flesh
Weapon of Blood
Weapon of Vengeance

The Cornerstones Trilogy (with Anne L. McMillen-Jackson)
Zellohar
Nekdukarr
Jundag

The Cheese Runners Trilogy (novellas)
Cheese Runners
Cheese Rustlers
Cheese Lords

From Dragon Moon Press
Scimitar Moon
Scimitar Sun
Scimitar's Heir
Scimitar War

From Paizo Publishing
Pirate's Honor
Pirate's Promise (December 2014)

From Privateer Press
Blood & Iron (ebook novella)

JAXBOOKS.COM

www.ingramcontent.com/pod-product-compliance
Lightning Source LLC
Chambersburg PA
CBHW071206250626
47159CB00001B/221